A Way Out

A Way Out

Brook J. Gillespie

Library of Congress Number:		00-192914
ISBN #:	Hardcover	0-7388-5018-7
	Softcover	0-7388-5019-5

This book was printed in the United States of America.

To order additional copies of this book, contact:
Xlibris Corporation
1-888-7-XLIBRIS
www.Xlibris.com
Orders@Xlibris.com

Chip,

Have a great read.

All the best,

Bud J. Gillan

52-GILL

Acknowledgements

As with any large endeavor, one never completes it by himself; A WAY OUT is certainly no exception. Anne-Adele Wight's sound editorial guidance proved invaluable. Any errors still contained within our solely mine. Tom Costello's critical thoughts on the ending helped tremendously. I'd also like to thank my parent and sister for their input and guidance. There are dozens of readers to thank — to all of you, thanks. Lastly, I'd like to thank Geoffrey Marchant, my high school English teacher, for showing me the power of the written word.

Prologue

General Nikolai Leonov walked into the plush suite of the Landhas Gurgassl-Huber Hotel, located in the wine-growing suburbs of Vienna. The Russian spy master's heart beat a little faster as he paused to brush a spec from his charcoal-black suit. In that moment he realized the risks were enormous.

Across the room a well-dressed man stood off to one side, his attention focused on something outside the fifth-floor window. He turned and greeted his guest.

"General. Good of you to come," said the man. Leonov nodded as the two men shook hands. "And your trip from Moscow? Uneventful, I hope."

"Da," Leonov replied. As before the general wrestled with the man's heavy southern ascent.

Leonov eyed his host, a man he knew very little about. Since meeting him for the first time only a week ago, Leonov had devoted considerable resources to learning all he could about his host. Everything he had confirmed led to one conclusion: the man was a power broker in the corridors of Washington, DC.

He gestured for the general to take a seat at a finely appointed table. Both men settled into the antique chairs. "Should we start? We have much to discuss." The general nodded.

"May I assume," continued the host, "that your attendance today is a sign that you are committed to the venture we discussed only last week?"

"I have given it a great deal of thought," Leonov replied,

choosing his words carefully. His English was good, but he could not risk any misunderstandings. "I'd like to hear the details again before I give you my word."

His host smiled. "I understand completely."

Leonov watched as the man busied himself, pouring red wine into two full-bodied glasses. After both men had taken a sip, his host began.

"I represent a powerful group whose members come from the highest levels of the US government and the private sector. This group believes the demise of the Soviet Union is a tragedy not only for the Russian people but also for the world. The reasons are many–economic and political–but the net result is clear: the world is a more dangerous place as a result of the Soviet Union's demise.

"Without two superpowers, the world is out of balance. As you know, the balance worked well for fifty years, and so it can for another fifty. We believe you're the key to making it happen."

Leonov had heard that in their previous meeting, but he admitted to himself that he liked hearing half of it again. He knew Russia was not the mighty force it used to be. That reality left a bitter taste in his mouth, much like a drink from the Black Sea. On the other hand the Americans believed in him, respect him above the others.

His host continued. "I have focused considerable thought on the task and have identified three keys, if you will, that I believe are critical for success. First, the current Russian government must be completely discredited. Second, you will need large and continuous sources of hard currency. Third, the President of the United States must be hindered so that his efforts to isolate your new Russian government will come to nothing."

"Interesting," Leonov commented. "It sounds to me like you might already have a plan in mind."

"Very perceptive, General," the man confirmed. "I do. However, in the end it is your decision, your plan. Only you can rule

Russia. Yes, I can lend assistance and make suggestions, but nothing more. You understand, of course."

"Da, I do," Leonov said. "I appreciate your deferring to me. My decision to act will not be for your benefit. I will act to save Mother Russia from the gangsters who ruin her as we speak."

"Yes, certainly. I completely understand."

Leonov nodded, satisfied by what he had heard. "Please continue."

"Of course," agreed his host. "I think the theft and subsequent sale of one or more nuclear weapons to a client in the Middle East would be an excellent catalyst. The world will never forgive the current Russian government and its military, discrediting it completely. Oil prices will rise sky-high overnight, as will the demand for military arms. These last two consequences will generate significant amounts of hard currency for Russia. However, to take advantage of the price of oil, we must get the Russian oil industry operating at peak performance. Some outside help will be critical. Establishing a relationship with a US business conglomerate would make the most sense. Are you familiar with a man named Alex Davenport?"

Leonov studied his host for a moment a little surprised. He certainly did know Alex Davenport. They had conducted business several times over the years. "Is he aware of the people you represent and our discussions?"

"I cannot speak for him personally," replied the other, "but I think he would agree that a strong Russia is good for the world. However, he has no knowledge of our conversation. For obvious security reasons, a task as delicate as this must be kept absolutely quiet. This is why the people I represent have given me the task of approaching a Russian partner to work toward our common goal. No one else will learn of your identify. They have no reason to know."

"I see," Leonov said, more pleased than ever. "And the part about your President?"

"Ah, the best part," the man said with a fleeting smile. "The new US government, led by our Democratic president, would not share our sentiments. It would fight a return of Russia to its superpower status. That's why the President and his party must be hindered, even disgraced."

"To this end I have an idea. " The man sipped his wine before continuing. "Our President and his wife, who is also a lawyer, have not always followed the tax and business laws of our country. Actually, they have been surprisingly brazen in their disrespect for them. They have an interest in a shady arrangement. It's a real estate deal that is headed south and fast. It needs money to stay afloat. What if some dirty money, drug money for instance, was funneled into the bank that made the original loan? An infusion of drug money will result in political death for the President. Then a more hawkish leadership will take over the White House, an outcome that would benefit us all."

Leonov remained silent as his mind suddenly thought of his daughter, Katya, the only think more precious to him than Mother Russia. He inadvertently smiled: if she only knew the historic opportunity that stood before her father.

"I sense you approve," the man replied. "Can we count on you?"

Leonov did not answer immediately, as he focused on the man before him once again. He considered his host's ideas, feeling no rush to respond. What he had heard made sense. He knew he was the one man in Russia who could pull it off. As head of the SVR, the foreign intelligence arm of the Russian government, he had what it took and then some. He had Everest.

He stared into his host's blue eyes. "Da. Mother Russia will rise again."

1 | Murdered

John Thompson heard the men before the three knocks sounded on his front door. Their approach had not come as a surprise; the noise from their tires rolling over the crushed stones had alerted him. John had not expected anyone, particularly at seven in the morning on a beautiful, sunny summer day.

He swung the door open until it stood wide and stared at his two visitors. They weren't smiling. Cops rarely did.

The sweat of his morning workout cooled against his skin as John glanced past the men to their car and studied the long trail of dust that hovered above the driveway. It reminded him of a snake, uncoiled and striking at its prey.

He returned his attention to the officers. The men were dressed as he would have expected, though their shiny shoes carried a light coat of dust from his driveway. He sensed uneasiness in their demeanor, as if the two were salesmen making the first cold-calls of their careers.

"Are you John Edward Thompson?" the sheriff asked.

"I am."

"We have some bad news, sir. May we come in?"

John noted the sheriff's name, Branson. The deputy's nameplate read Prickett. John said, "I suspect the news won't change whether we stand here or inside."

He did not budge as his steady stare covered the men. "Sir, I'm afraid we have bad news, terrible news really. There is no good way to state it. Your brother is dead."

"Bullshit."

The sheriff spoke quickly. "Sir, this is not a joke, to be sure. Your brother is dead, murdered."

John turned suddenly from the door and rushed to the phone. He dialed his brother's mobile phone number. After six rings he heard a click and was forwarded to voice mail. He hit the Cancel button before his brother's voice had finished.

He stared back at the officers, their eyes firmly on him as they stood uneasily before his door. There could be any number of reasons why his brother hadn't answered. He could be in the shower, on the can, or something equally simple.

The sheriff continued when John had returned. "Yesterday, around 10:00 am, your brother was killed in the J. W. Marriott Hotel on Fourteenth and Pennsylvania in Washington, D.C. An assassin gunned him down. A total of three people died. Tragically, your brother was one of the victims."

John stared uncomprehendingly at the men, his mind reeling—criminal, murderer perhaps, but assassin? He forced his gathering emotions to the back of his mind. He needed to concentrate; he willed his operational side to gain control.

"Assassin, you say?"

The sheriff considered the question. "It appears, sir, that the killer was gunning for a DEA agent."

"And my brother happened to be standing next to him," John said with disbelief. "Who told you that?"

"Ah, no, sir." The sheriff looked at his deputy. "I believe your brother was the DEA agent."

"Bullshit," John repeated as his eyes bored into both men.

"Well, that's what Washington told us," the sheriff insisted, a slight uncertainty in his voice. "I think the TV networks are reporting as much on the morning news."

John barely heard him as thoughts of his twin brother consumed him. Pete had been a talented computer programmer who had dropped out of college after his freshman year, never to return. He had made excellent money from day one and never looked back.

John, meanwhile, had always done well in school. He had graduated from Brown University in Providence, Rhode Island, and like his father had joined the Navy straight out of college. After a year in the service, he had decided to become a Navy SEAL. Six months of grueling effort behind him, John had joined the elite group of fighting men. As a result, he was the one who had taken all the risks. He had been shot at, stabbed, jumped out of hundreds of airplanes, and dived to the bottom of the ocean, and he was still alive.

"What else was reported? Did they capture this so-called assassin?" John asked, anger laced throughout his voice.

"Nothing and no," the sheriff replied.

John looked at the deputy, sending a nervous grimace across his face. He wondered if the deputy had ever been assigned this terrible task. John knew how it felt. He had lost three men while commanding SEAL Team Six. Confronting their next of kin had been a painful experience. Why did the deputy appear so uneasy? And why two police officers? Wouldn't a priest be a better second man?

The sheriff interrupted John's thoughts. "Sir, is it true that you are the only living family member?"

"I am," John said quietly, his anger rising while he struggled to keep his emotions tucked out of sight. Something was wrong, terribly wrong. His brother wasn't a DEA agent. He was certain.

"Well, yes," the sheriff said. "To make a positive identification, the district police would like you to come to Washington. A terrible thing, I know. However, under the circumstances, I don't believe it can be avoided."

"I'll fly down today," John said quickly, as another thought erupted in his mind. They did not seem surprised by his level of control. Did they know his background?

The sheriff reached into his shirt pocket and unfolded a sheet of paper. "All the information is here. A hotel reservation has been made for you, I believe at the Marriott."

John couldn't help himself while his instincts nagged at him. "Is there anything else?"

"No, sir. Again, I am terribly sorry."

John felt like rattling their cages. Something did not add up. He couldn't put his finger on it, but he had learned to trust his gut. "Can I ask you one more question? How did the Washington Metro police find me so quickly?"

"I'm not sure, sir. We got a call from a Sergeant Smith about an hour ago. He faxed us that sheet I handed you and gave us our instructions."

"Instructions?" John repeated.

"Well, you know, he asked us to inform you of the tragedy."

"I see," John said and shut the door.

He made his way back to the dining table, devastated and angry. His brother a DEA agent? Impossible. Informant maybe, but who the hell was he informing on? And now he was dead. How could such a thing happen? John had risked his life countless times; he was willing to die. Had his brother simply stood in the wrong spot at the wrong time?

John slammed his fist on the dining room table, sending the candlesticks and their candles tumbling. His foot shot out, striking the wooden chair to his right and hurling it toward the kitchen.

Fucking Murphy and his law! He was there, always rearing his ugly head. No one could control him, but everyone could count on him. It was a love-hate relationship. SEALs trained for him: never assume anything because Murphy was always nearby.

John fought another realization that lurked in his brain. He had known it before, during his time in occupied Kuwait. Revenge. Someone had murdered his twin brother, if the cops were to be believed. He glanced at the single sheet of paper in his hand. It looked official. Could it be true, his brother murdered by an assassin? Who was the assassin? Could John find him? Dangerous thoughts.

Suddenly John's mind traveled to a time in Bangkok, when his brother and he were young. They could not have been more than eleven years old. They were walking the streets of Pat Pong, a bustling area of town and the center of Bangkok's notorious sex district. Here one could fulfill any sexual fantasy. For young boys the sights were an unreal experience. Pete and John had ventured there only a few times and always when their father was at work at the US Embassy. Their father had warned them to stay away from the area and they had promised never to venture there. It was fraught with danger. Some of Bangkok's least scrupulous men preyed on foreigners and the unsuspecting.

That October, the heat of the day had dissipated and the streets were particularly busy. People from all over the world walked the narrow streets of Pat Pong, fending off street vendors who hawked everything from clothes to duffel bags to watches to paintings. Men posted before the doors of the bars were promoting the sex shows inside. Beautiful Thai women and explicit sexual promises marked their pitches.

That night Pete and John moved through the wave of humanity and were confronted by a very drunken American soldier. He had fallen down and knocked over a watch vendor's cloth-draped table, spilling all his merchandise onto the dirty street. Frantically the vendor tried to pick up his wares before the surging crowd stole them. Pete and John helped the vendor grab some of the watches, but their efforts made little difference. The vendor cursed and kicked the drunken American soldier after realizing that most of his inventory was lost. The soldier seemed oblivious to the vicious kicks. He kept repeating a phrase.

"They put the shit in the dead bodies. They put the shit in the dead bodies."

Suddenly, American soldiers descended on the drunken one. One of them hit him hard, knocking him unconscious, and then they hefted their burden on their shoulders and hauled him away. John had always remembered how hard the other American soldier had hit his drunken companion. Remembering the vicious blows always sent shivers down John's spine. They were given not by a friend but by an enemy. John had instinctively realized this.

During breakfast the next day their father had commented

on an article in the daily paper concerning the death of an American soldier in the Pat Pong district, his throat slashed and his pockets emptied. John and Pete looked at each other. Their father caught their glance. He stared at them until Pete told the story of the American soldier they had seen the previous night. Their father was furious and prohibited them from going to the district ever again. However, John remembered seeing the interest in his father's eyes even as he scolded his sons. The ramblings of the drunken soldier had somehow made sense.

What had made John recall this long-ago incident? It was Pete's naïveté. Pete had never sensed the viciousness of the punches or the deadliness of the secret that the American soldier had spilled. To Pete the incident was a drunken one. He did not see or sense that something sinister was at work. Pete really did not know the ways of a warrior. He had grown up to be a good man who always saw the best in everyone. Evil was something that he did not understand.

John glanced at his watch. It read 7:13 am. It was time to get to Washington, but first he had to make a phone call to the only family he had left.

* * *

Former Lieutenant Commander John Thompson stood in Admiral Sunders' Pentagon office, located on ring E. The office was large even for a flag officer, and filled with memorabilia from a lifetime of naval service. The walls were covered with pictures of SEALs, the quiet warriors of the US military. It reminded John of a patchwork quilt representing the admiral's thirty-plus-year naval career. Previously Sunders had commanded the SEALs. He was now chief of naval plans, policy, and operations, known as OP-06 inside the Pentagon.

As a former SEAL, Sunders knew how the Navy used to operate. The admiral hated politics and preferred action to idle discussions. John knew this disposition created friction in a place where budget numbers and hundred-page reports ruled. It was one of the reasons John liked the admiral.

"At ease," Sunders ordered, gesturing for John to take a seat at a small conference table that consumed the left-hand slide of the admiral's office.

"Thank you, sir," John said from his seat. Seeing the admiral again brought a flood of memories. He missed the grueling days leading men who acknowledged no limits. Winning was everything. He craved the raw energy of the challenge. He realized something else; the admiral had become a substitute for his father.

The admiral, taller than John's father by a few inches, was thin in a fit sort of way. His hair was completely white, his eyes hazel green, and his face leathered from years spent outdoors. Even now, confined to a desk job, the admiral had maintained that rugged athletic demeanor. John's father, on the other hand, had been a little overweight, even chubby, the result of a Navy career anchored to one desk job after another.

"John, you look like hell," Sunders said gravely.

"Yes, sir," he replied, fighting the emotion on the edge of his voice. Memories. Was that all life became, a collection of memories? How probable was it that at thirty-two he had lost his mother, father, and brother, leaving him as the sole living member of his family?

"Sir, do you know what happened at the Marriott?"

"In Washington?"

"Yes, sir."

"Well, only what I've read in the papers."

John started to speak, but a surge of emotion attacked him, and its power shocked him.

The admiral spoke. "Out with it, son. What's on your mind?"

"My brother is dead."

"Oh, my God!" The admiral's face filled with shock. "How?"

"He died at the Marriott."

"What?" Sunders roared. "Three people were killed, but I

had no idea Pete was one of them. Jesus Christ, that's awful."

The admiral stood, heading straight for his desk. He pulled a trashcan from under it and removed a copy of *The Washington Post*. "John, I don't know what to say. I don't remember a Pete Thompson listed as a victim."

John leaned forward and covered his face with his hands. The flight from New Hampshire had been long. Two hours earlier he had arrived at the Ronald Reagan National Airport. Though the Pentagon was only a short distance from the airfield, John had first checked into the Marriott Hotel in downtown Washington, two blocks from the White House.

He had purchased half a dozen newspapers and read the reports of the carnage at the Marriott. The national newspapers had picked up the story, the incident being so close to the White House. The articles all told the same story with a few variations. A tanned gunman wearing green-blue sunglasses and a duster jacket had entered the main lobby of the hotel and chased a man. Officials suspected the gunman, who had used an Ingram MAC 10 submachine gun, was a hired assassin for the Cali drug cartel. The target was reported to be a DEA agent. The agent's description matched Pete's exactly: six-one, two hundred pounds, long brown hair and brown eyes. The two other victims of the attack were considered innocent bystanders: Susan O'Donald from Minneapolis–St. Paul and Bill Edwards from Atlanta.

In the suite that the hotel had provided him, a note asked him to call Sergeant Smith of the Washington Metro police. John had ignored the request. He needed to talk to someone he trusted; the admiral came immediately to mind.

All along John tried to remain calm, but his anger kept building. Every moment he fought to control it. John had left repeated voice messages and e-mails, but had gotten no replies from his brother. That meant one of two things: Pete was missing or he was dead.

The admiral finished scanning the article. "John, your brother is not one of the three names mentioned here."

"I know," John admitted, "but a sheriff came to my door

early this morning and told me my brother was murdered, killed by an assassin. His exact words."

"Have you spoken to the Metro police?"

"My next stop," John confirmed. "But sir, don't you think the description of the DEA agent, Bruce Johnson, is extremely familiar?"

"How do you mean?"

"Look at me, sir."

The admiral paused as he took stock of the young man before him. "I'm sure there is a reasonable explanation."

"Let's hope," John said, hearing the dismay in his own voice.

"John, if there is anything I can do, please let me know."

"Thank you, sir." He sensed the admiral was babysitting him, but why? "Sir, why are the newspapers reporting that the third person, who matches Pete's description, was a DEA agent? I know damn well he wasn't."

"I have no idea," Sunders answered. John thought he heard a note of caution in the admiral's voice.

"The press didn't come up with this on their own," John insisted. "I know how Washington works. You do too. I want to know who slipped them this detail."

"Pure speculation, John."

Frustrated by the admiral's answers, John leaned forward in his chair. He sensed tension in Sunders as the admiral spoke. "I'm sorry, but I need to run, John. I have a meeting with the JC. I will keep my ear to the ground. If I hear something, I'll let you know. Talk to the police. There is a chance, no matter how remote, that Pete is alive and well. Let's not forget that."

John kept his face expressionless, hiding his disappointment that Sunders had so little time for him. However, John knew the admiral could not excuse himself from a meeting of the Joint Chiefs of Staff. He had only promised to squeeze John in briefly between meetings. Why now did John find it unacceptable? Other thoughts ricocheted through his mind, but one in particular infected him. Revenge. John felt it spreading through his veins like a venom.

John remembered how his emotions had led to dangerous consequences while he was behind enemy lines in occupied Kuwait during the Gulf War in 1990. On operations he had witnessed the Iraqis torture innocent people, but he could do nothing without jeopardizing his mission to assist the Kuwaitis in their fight against the Iraqis.

One time in particular he remembered because he had broken this golden rule. It was January, near midnight, the sky cloudless. The air war had not yet started.

The occupying Iraqis enforced a strict curfew on the Kuwaitis. On this particular night, John lay atop a warehouse in the Abrak Keitan section of Kuwait City. He had a good view of the surrounding area, an unoccupied section of the city directly off the King Faisal Highway. His contact was running late.

While he continued to watch, he saw a car pull off the highway and make its way behind the warehouse where he lay. Soon afterward, an Iraqi jeep exited the highway just as the car had. Unlike the car, it drove slowly toward the warehouse. John kept low on the roof and listened as the jeep crept around the facility.

Suddenly yelling voices shattered the quiet night air and the staccato of AK47 machine guns sounded. John counted two short bursts. He crawled to the edge of the warehouse and peered onto the scene below. Four Iraqi soldiers held a family at gunpoint. They were ordering the child to take off her clothes. She could not have been more than twelve years old. Her parents were begging the soldiers for mercy. Their cries went unheard.

Once the child was undressed, the Iraqi officer, a major by the look of his lapels, ordered the woman to undress as well. She did so willingly, hoping that the soldiers would have her and not her daughter. John knew better. The dread in the father was palpable. He too knew the truth.

Without thinking further, John aimed his 9-mm Heckler & Koch MP5 submachine gun. In less than seven seconds, all four Iraqi soldiers were dead.

The father pushed his wife and child into the car; they did

not even bother to dress. Their car sped to the highway and turned right. It quickly vanished into the night air.

It was only a matter of time before another Iraqi patrol came looking for the one that lay in a pool of blood on the asphalt below. John quickly policed his area on the roof to ensure that he left nothing of interest behind.

It took him five minutes to reach the four dead Iraqi soldiers from the rooftop. He dragged each one into the abandoned jeep and then drove the jeep, positioning it over the spilled blood covering the asphalt. Next he booby-trapped the jeep. If anyone tried to move one of the Iraqi soldiers, a quarter pound of Semtex-H explosive would destroy the jeep and anyone within thirty yards.

After John double-checked his handiwork, he walked quietly away and into the desert, his Bedouin robe hiding the MP5 submachine gun from view.

A half hour later, as John made his way through the desert along the outskirts of Kuwait only a mile or so from the Iraqi jeep, he heard a muffled boom. He could not be sure, but he suspected his trap had killed more Iraqi soldiers. At the time he could not have known he was wrong.

As he later learned from a contact in the Kuwaiti resistance, an important member of the resistance had been killed when he had arrived at a warehouse in Abrak Keitan. He and another man had waited the prescribed half hour for their contact to arrive. After the man did not show, the resistance members left. On their way out, they circled around the other side of the warehouse only to find an Iraqi jeep. The resistance leader had jumped out of his vehicle and approached the jeep cautiously while his driver stayed with his charge. The resistance leader saw the jeep was full of dead Iraqi soldiers. He called to his friend that it might come in handy. He would drive it back to their hideout; his friend would follow. The leader opened the jeep and began to pull out the dead soldiers.

The explosion had killed the resistance leader instantly and left nothing but a fiery grave in its aftermath. The driver had not even bothered to get out of the car. He knew the fate of his leader.

He also knew that another Iraqi patrol would come to investigate the explosion.

The man that the resistance leader, Colonel Abu Fouad, was to meet had been John.

Sunders interrupted John's reverie. "I know how you must feel, but revenge is not always as sweet as one thinks. You should know from your time in Kuwait."

John tried to wipe the look of surprise from his face; it was as if the admiral had read his mind. He looked Sunders in the eyes. "I understand, sir."

"Speak to the police."

"Thank you, sir, for your time."

"Think nothing of it." The admiral shook the young man's hand. John returned the firm grip. "Don't do anything stupid," the admiral ordered. "Let the police do their job."

"Yes, sir."

"My door is always open. My home number in case you've forgotten . . ."

John accepted a piece of paper from the admiral. "Thank you, sir."

He hurried through the outer office and into one of the thousands of hallways that made up the maze known as the Pentagon. He needed fresh air. He needed to find out what the hell was going on.

2 | Disappointment Abound

Sergeant Smith sat behind his gunmetal desk, his brown eyes sharp. John surmised the black sergeant was an old hand at homicides, particularly in a city where they were a daily occurrence.

"Sergeant, thank you for seeing me," John said, noting the sergeant's curious stare.

"I only have a few moments, I'm afraid," the sergeant stated in his deep voice as he grabbed a Bic pen.

"I understand," John replied, hiding his surprise. He would have thought the Metro police would be anxious to question him. It was possible, however remotely, that he held a piece of information that could unravel the mystery they were charged with solving.

"How may I help you?" the sergeant asked, his impatient obvious.

"The sheriff in New Hampshire indicated that you needed me to identify my brother's body," John said, trying to keep anger from his voice. "I'm also assuming you might have some questions for me, since I'm the brother."

The sergeant considered John for a moment, his fingers working the pen with practiced movements. "Identify the body. Which body?"

"My brother's."

"Who is your brother?"

"Pete Thompson."

The sergeant leveled his gaze at John, but said nothing. He appeared to be considering the situation.

"Correct me if I am wrong," John continued angrily. "You sent a sheriff to my house in New Hampshire at seven this morning with the express purpose of telling me my brother had been murdered. I fly down here, arrive at the hotel, and find another note instructing me to contact you immediately. Well, here I am and you could care less. What the hell is going on?"

"What are you talking about?" Sergeant Smith demanded. "I don't know who you are. Why would I be sending you notes concerning this crime?"

John pulled the single piece of paper from his shirt pocket and unfolded it. "Are you saying you didn't fax this note to the Ossipee Mountains County Sheriff's office this morning?"

The sergeant grabbed the note from John's outstretched hand and inspected it. "Damn, where did you get this?"

"I already told you," John said.

"Do you have the name of the sheriff?"

"Yes, I remember his name. It was Branson and his sidekick was named Prickett."

"Ossipee Mountains County?" the sergeant repeated. "Do you know the number of the sheriff's office?"

"Do I look like the Yellow Pages?"

The sergeant picked up his phone and punched four buttons. John sensed the man's perplexity with each jab of his index finger. The sergeant spoke briefly and replaced the receiver noisily in its cradle. "This should only take a minute."

Finally the phone rang, and the sergeant lifted the receiver, content to listen. He replaced the headset softly, a deep frown across his face. "Ossipee Mountains County has never heard of a sheriff named Branson. They will check with the surrounding counties."

John dropped his head into his hands, his long hair falling around his face. What the hell was happening? He pictured the sheriff and his partner, realizing his instincts had been dead on.

They were actors. Did this mean his brother was alive? Surely someone hadn't sent the two imposters to his door to lie about something so easily confirmed. And the newspapers, they were real. John decided on another tack. "What can you tell me about Security International Group, SIG?"

"SIG?" the sergeant said as he leaned forward, his large frame pressing against the desk.

"My brother's last contract job was with SIG," John explained.

The sergeant studied the young man. "What exactly are you saying?"

"The dead DEA agent known as Bruce Johnson is really Pete Thompson, my brother."

"How would you know this?"

"Look at me," John demanded. "Don't I look familiar to you? We were goddamn identical twins!"

The sergeant sat back in his chair, the protest of the chair audible above his grunt. He looked angry as he scratched his chin with the tip of his Bic. He opened a folder and leafed through it, removing a number of pictures. He studied each and then thrust three in John's direction.

John grabbed them and stared. There was not much left of the inert figure's face. However, there was enough. He knew with certainty that it was his brother. He even recognized the shoes.

"Is that your brother?" the sergeant asked quietly. John nodded as he forced his eyes away from the sickening pictures. Tears gathered as seconds slipped past. Reality set in. His worst fears were confirmed. His brother was dead. Finally the sergeant spoke. "Tell me about the sheriff."

John started slowly. He welcomed the concentration required to read his mind's eye, plucking the details in their order of prevalence. It took him five minutes to detail the visit. "Something is wrong here, sir. I think you know that."

"What if your brother was a DEA agent using the name Bruce Johnson? That would explain a lot."

"My brother was not a DEA agent."

"I hear you, but nothing surprises me anymore." The sergeant fidgeted with the blue pen again. "I'm not sure your brother would have told you he was DEA. Undercover agents are good at keeping secrets, even from their families."

"I knew my brother," John said emphatically. "I would have known. Please believe me when I say this." He thought for a moment as he wiped his eyes again. "You knew about SIG. How did you hear about it?"

The sergeant sat still for a long moment. "I called a friend in the DEA and asked why they were so interested in the Marriott shooting. That's when I learned the dead man was a DEA agent named Bruce Johnson. My contact said the assassin's description matched a man known to be a hired gun for the Cali cartel. He said Johnson was working undercover for them at SIG."

"Who was first on the scene, your people or the DEA?"

"My men," the sergeant said, squirming in his seat. His chair's creak was less audible this time.

"And the driver's license found on the dead DEA agent," John guessed, "a Pete Thompson from Steamboat Springs, Colorado."

The sergeant simply nodded.

"The DEA told you that was the man's working cover. Am I right?"

The sergeant confirmed with another nod. "You seem to know a lot," the sergeant replied, clearly worried.

John stood and leaned over the sergeant's desk. "Sergeant, I was a Navy fucking SEAL. I know all about undercover agents and government tricks. I also know my brother was not a DEA agent. He wouldn't know a dead drop from a potted plant."

"I hear you," the sergeant repeated, his deep voice increasingly nervous.

"Who is the DEA agent on the case?" John demanded.

"Shields, David Shields," the sergeant said. "Call him. Here's his number."

"You've been very helpful," John stated sarcastically.

"I'm sorry about the misunderstanding," the sergeant said. "Talk with the DEA. They're running this show."

John started to leave but stopped. "Where is the body?"

"The last I heard it was released to the coroner's and cremated."

"You're going to be a very dead asshole if you're fucking with me," John yelled as he wiped his hands across the sergeant's desk, spilling most of its contents on the floor.

The door to the sergeant's officer burst open and two officers stepped in. "Boss, you okay?"

"Mr. Thompson was leaving, weren't you?" Sergeant Smith stood, exposing his full girth, anger in his deep voice.

John stood erect and kept his hands by his side as he moved his weight to the balls of his feet. No one moved. John considered his options. Disabling three Metro police officers would accomplish nothing, though the prospect appealed to him. He wondered when the last time was that they had been subjected to a severe beating. It took all his strengthen to keep himself firmly planted where he stood. "Cremated on whose authority?"

"I wouldn't know," the sergeant replied as a trickle of sweat ran down his forehead. "As I just said, the DEA is running the show. Not a thing I can do about it."

"So I see."

John turned and pushed his way past the two officers before they could react. It was all John could do to keep from turning the sergeant's office into a disaster.

In two minutes he found himself standing on 4th Street in front of the First District Metropolitan Police headquarters. What the hell should he do next?

* * *

The July heat had settled on the whole eastern seaboard. The cemetery in Vienna, Virginia, felt like the jungles of Indonesia minus the rotting vegetation and incessant hum of bugs. Even the birds sought refuge from the exotic heat.

Before him lay the graves of his parents and the post-sized hole waiting for Pete's urn. A small green tent provided a slight respite from the persistent sun. John barely noticed.

The priest had commenced his monologue. Admiral Sunders, his Navy whites catching the faint breeze, stood on John's left. The priest had stationed himself opposite the two mourners. John tried to concentrate on the priest's words, but he could not. Seventy-two hours had passed since his arrival in Washington and he knew less now than he had then.

All his calls to the DEA had gone unanswered. A second visit with the Metro police had gotten him nothing. A trip to the coroner's office had confirmed the sergeant's information. The body of the supposed DEA agent had been cremated. John had demanded to see pictures of the body, which he knew the coroner had taken. The coroner had refused, stating that as far as he was concerned John Thompson did not fit into the family tree of Bruce Johnson. The coroner, like the sergeant, had said the DEA could provide the okay to see the pictures. The only helpful piece of information John did glean from the coroner was the location of the remains, a funeral home in Bethesda, Maryland.

John looked at the urn that held his brother. He felt a bitter smile spread across his face. He had no doubt the DEA was wondering what had happened to the remains of their so-called agent. John had secreted his way into the funeral home late last night and quietly removed Pete's remains. It had been a simple sneak and peek. The security setup at the funeral home was trivial. John had cracked it in less than thirty seconds. The theft had taken no more than ten minutes. He had considered the possibility that the urn did not contain his brother's remains: after all, its tag indicated that the contents were the remains of Bruce Johnson. No matter; he had sent the DEA a message. He hoped they understood.

Before the start of his brother's service, John had recounted his last forty-eight hours to Sunders. The admiral had looked dumbfounded and said he would check into things as best he could. Obviously the matter was out of his jurisdiction, and he made sure John understood that. It was a favor, and he made no guarantees. However, the admiral had learned the name of the managing partner of SIG: George Simpson.

As the priest finished his prayers, John stole a look around the cemetery. It was nearly empty. He saw only one other person, a well-dressed man, maybe near seventy, with a shock of white hair and a mustache to match. He was looking directly at John. When John caught his eye, he bent his head quickly and began scrutinizing a tombstone. John tried to place the face but could not. The man finished his vigil and briskly walked away out of sight.

John's attention returned to his immediate surroundings. He was surprised to see that Sunders had also taken an interest in the man.

"Do you know him?" John asked.

The admiral shook his head slowly. "I don't think so. Do you?"

"No."

John took a deep breath and seized the lone shovel, throwing two spadefuls of dirt onto the black urn nestled in its post-sized hole. Loneliness struck him like a plunge into freezing surf. "Goodbye, my friend and brother." He faced the priest as he tried to ignore his building emotions. "Thank you, Father."

"May God be with you," the priest replied.

John turned quickly as tears started to slip from his eyes. He walked toward the admiral's car, parked a short distance away. As emotions rolled through his body like a thunderstorm, he willed himself to suppress them. He could not allow his feelings to rule. They got in the way. His operational side had to take control, complete control. It was the only way.

The admiral caught up with him after a few minutes and unlocked the car. "To the hotel?"

John nodded, running his hand through his shoulder-length hair. The motion made him think of Pete. He had worn his hair exactly the same way. They both had their mother's hair, thick and brown.

"I'm sorry, John," the admiral said. "As you know, life is rarely fair."

"I know," John replied, looking at the admiral.

"Are you sure I can't give you a ride to the airport? I'd be glad to do it," the admiral offered.

"Thank you, sir. I really appreciate it, but I've arranged for a hotel car."

"Fair enough, off to the hotel then."

3 Motion

The garage door began its ascent. George Simpson was home.

John read his tritium gas–illuminated watch. Its hands displayed 8:12pm. He checked his 9-millimeter SIG-Sauer handgun one last time. The fifteen-round clip was full. He slipped it between the small of his back and his pants, hoping that it would not be required.

After the hotel car had dropped him off at Dulles Airport, John had rented a car, using a false driver's license. He had driven to Virginia, selecting a run-down motel on the other side of the Potomac River from Washington. After paying in advance for one week, he had hit the phone.

It had taken him five calls and a few favors to locate the home address of Simpson, the managing partner of Security International Group. Two hours earlier, with the address in hand, John had driven to Bethesda and had parked his car four blocks from Simpson's house. He had walked the rest of the way.

In a forty-minute search of the house, he had found nothing to suggest that Simpson was anything but an employee of SIG. However, he had found a .38-caliber Colt pistol among an impressive gun collection in the living room. It was displayed with dozens of other antique firearms in an oak cabinet. John recognized it instantly as a very rare gun indeed. He remembered something else: Vincent Foster, the number-three lawyer at the White House, had used such a gun to commit suicide a month earlier. If John's memory served him, the authorities had never found the second .38-caliber Colt pistol, even though it was thought to have been one of a set. John wondered if he had just found it.

After his discovery, he had considered his options for his upcoming encounter with Simpson. He assumed the man would use the door leading from the garage. The carpeting by the front door did not have any footprints on it. Other parts of the carpet did. That told John two things: the cleaning lady had not done her work today, and Simpson was not likely to enter his house through the front door. John assumed a cleaning lady because the house showed no signs of a woman's touch, and there were no wedding pictures to be found.

The house was full of pictures, many from Simpson's days in Vietnam. The pictures made John think that those years of Simpson's life had probably been his best. He had studied the pictures to see if any faces looked familiar, but none had. Simpson was clearly a big man and no doubt very strong, but his years as a civilian would have made him vulnerable. John planned to use his advantage.

He listened as Simpson shut his car door and shuffled along the cement floor as the garage door descended slowly, clattering down its aluminum track.

The kitchen door opened and Simpson entered, using his empty hand to flip on the lights; his other hand held a battered briefcase.

With a powerful jab to Simpson's kidney, followed by a low kick to his right shinbone, John pinned him to the floor, yanking his left hand behind his back. The moves took less than a second, giving Simpson no chance to see his attacker.

"Hi, George," John said. His brother had always said "Hi."

"What the fuck?" Simpson stammered.

"Surprised to hear from me?"

"Who the hell are you, man?" Simpson screamed as John jerked the man's left hand further up his back with his left knee centered deep in his spine. John knew the pain was excruciating.

"Why, I'm surprised you don't recognize my voice," John said, releasing some of the pressure on Simpson's arm. "Have I escaped your memory that quickly? One day I work for you and the next you're trying to kill me. Your company's human resource department is to be commended. Termination from SIG really is just that. I'm surprised more American companies don't employ similar methods. Then again it is illegal, but why should you concern yourself with that detail?"

Simpson tried to catch his breath. John knew the man had guessed that one Pete Thompson had him pinned to the kitchen floor.

"What do you want, man?" whimpered Simpson. "I knew nothing. I was told afterwards."

"Bullshit, George," John replied, wondering just how active a role Simpson had played in his brother's death. He also wondered if Pete called him George. The details could always betray.

"I tried to tell them it wasn't you," Simpson insisted. "Carlos. He's the man. He's convinced you gave the Feds the information."

"What information?"

"The accounting information," Simpson said through gritted teeth. "Let go of me. You're killing my arm, man."

John yanked hard on Simpson's left arm again. "You set me up. I never stole any information from you."

"You fucking bastard," moaned Simpson as he fought to regain his breath. "My arm . . ."

"Me, a fucking bastard!" interrupted John as he delivered another blow to Simpson's kidney. "I should kill you right here. I've kept my mouth shut. I found out early on that SIG was not on the up-and-up. I didn't want any trouble. And how do you repay me? You try and have me killed when some other bastard leaks information to the Feds." John paused. He was guessing. It was all he could do. "You needed a scapegoat to cover the security lapse. You made that me."

"It's not true," Simpson argued. "Carlos came up with your name. It was how the information arrived at the DEA. The web site."

John saw his brother's mistake. A computer geek would use the World Wide Web to send an anonymous electronic mail message. Now what? He racked his brain. Suddenly the rare pistol popped into his mind. Why did it seem important? He decided to take a chance.

"I'm surprised you didn't put a gun in my mouth like you did with Vincent Foster."

"What are you talking about?" Simpson demanded.

"I know you killed Foster."

"You're crazy," exploded Simpson while trying to loosen John's steel grip. "I had nothing to do with Foster's death."

"I hate when you lie to me." John gave Simpson another kidney punch. "You're going to be one of the most hunted men in the world!" John paused to let his words sink in. "I plan to let the world know what a monster you are. I can see it now. The *Washington Post* front page will read "SIG's President Murdered Vincent Foster!" Not only will the Federal government come knocking on your door, but your masters won't be too pleased when the Feds raid SIG from top to bottom. The Feds will rip the place apart. Killing a senior White House official is serious business!"

"What the fuck are you talking about, man?" whimpered Simpson.

"That gun in your collection," John said. "The authorities could never find the matching pistol to the one that killed Foster. There can't be too many of those in existence. I figure it must be the missing gun."

"You're out of your mind," Simpson protested as he tried to squirm from John's powerful grasp. John landed another punch to Simpson's kidney. Simpson went into spasm.

"I really don't care if I am wrong," John replied, anger shaking his voice. "Once I give it to the authorities, they'll have no choice but to hunt you down, particularly after I explain why the Marriott hotel lobby was shot to pieces."

Simpson pleaded. "You've got it all wrong."

"So you admit the pistol is the missing one?" demanded John as he applied more pressure to Simpson 's arm.

"What pistol? I had nothing to do with Foster's death," Simpson repeated. "I'm not a murderer!"

"You're so convincing," John growled as he pulled harder.

"Please," Simpson begged in agony. "Let's make a deal!"

"Make a deal! What, are you crazy?" John exclaimed. "You want me to trust you? What? Do you think I'm that stupid? You could have come to me earlier. Maybe then I could have straightened you out."

"It wasn't my decision," Simpson insisted. "What do you want? Name it. I have money."

"More shit," John replied. "You're full of it. My plan for you is set. Read about it in the *Washington Post* and weep."

"You must want something," Simpson complained, the desperation seeping from each word. "I can get you money. I can find a way to get $250,000!"

"You think you can buy me with $250,000? No way, mister. I want to see the Feds hang you by your fucking balls."

"I didn't kill Foster," Simpson said again. "I had nothing to do with it. It was Petrov, that goddamn Russian. I don't know why he and Carlos are so tight. The Cali's are probably selling drugs to the SVR. It was that bastard Gregori Petrov who gave me the gun and asked me to hold it for him. I had nothing to do with Foster's death."

Holy shit, thought John. Could the Russians have murdered Foster? That couldn't be right. Foster had not been in the White House long enough to be recruited. To top it off, Foster was a nobody from Arkansas. He was new to Washington.

"I don't give a shit," John said, hiding the confusion he felt. "You set me up to die. Fuck Petrov. You're the one I want, you and the fucking Colombians. You bastards are the ones destroying this country. You'll pay!"

"The Colombians are assholes," Simpson insisted, practically spitting out every word, "but I had no choice. They know things about me from 'nam. I had no choice but to work for them. I'm sure that Russian bastard told them. The fucking KGB was all over 'Nam. They had the gooks in their back pocket. I swear, man!"

"Like I said," John declared, "I don't give a shit. Have a nice life." He yanked hard on Simpson's arm, dislocating it. Simpson's scream ricocheted through the house.

With that, John rolled Simpson onto his back. Their eyes met and locked. Fear rolled through Simpson's eyes. John hit him with a quick chop to the head and knocked him unconscious immediately.

John hustled into Simpson's office, down the hall from the kitchen. He started throwing things on the ground, rummaging through drawers and the unlocked filing cabinets. He then moved to the bedroom. He emptied drawers onto the floor. Finally he made his way into the living room, where the impressive gun collection was housed. He took a small canvas bag that he had found in Simpson's closet and started filling it with the guns. When it was half full he stopped. The only gun he kept was the ancient Colt.

Checking to see that he had left no identifying traces, John exited the back of the house through the patio door. He paused and listened to the surroundings as his eyes adjusted to the darkness. He let two minutes pass, jogged quickly to the back corner of the yard, and leaped over the wood fence. He knew it would take him three minutes or less to reach his car, parked four blocks away. His anger fed his strength. The goddamn Russians. Why the hell would they kill Foster? Why were they working with the Cali cartel in the United States? And his brother, why had he not called? John could have helped Pete expose SIG for what it was.

* * *

General Nikolai Leonov was the head of the old First Chief Directorate of the KGB. It had been renamed the Foreign Intelligence Service, or SVR, in 1991, when Mikhail Gorbachev had broken up the world's largest security apparatus. At age sixty-two, the general ran one of the most powerful organizations in post-communist Russia. It was said that the general was very tough with failure, though usually fair. He respected intelligence and despised ignorance, rewarded those who succeeded, but most of all his peers were awed by Leonov's ability to assemble a multitude of apparently random facts into a detailed explanation of events that had actually transpired. He was brilliant at explaining the unexplainable, the perfect spymaster.

General Leonov leaned back in his chair. He had finished reading the latest report from his CIA mole, code named Everest. He was pleased.

Everest had initiated the downfall of SIG right on schedule. Leonov wanted the US government to tear SIG apart. Laid carefully inside its guts was a path of money and deceit that would ruin the US presidency. This was a key component of Leonov's plan, code named Russian Bear.

Everest had apparently devised an ingenious trigger to begin SIG's downfall. It was not what they had originally planned, and Leonov wondered what had changed. No matter, Everest knew that George Simpson worked for SIG and passed information regularly to the CIA. One such tidbit had been SIG's hiring of a contract programmer to build a new accounting system. Everest had used this information to conceive an anonymous way to inform the US government that SIG needed closer attention.

Using the Internet to send an e-mail message, Everest fed a number of government agencies, including the FBI, DEA, and CIA, information they would not be able to resist. In selecting the medium of Internet communication, Everest had assumed

SIG would immediately suspect the programmer. His assumption had proved correct. SIG had killed the programmer in a very public fashion. Stupid on SIG's part, but perfect for his purposes. It would only strengthen the smell of blood in the Americans' nostrils.

Everest had done better than Leonov had hoped, but he always had. He was very clever, and certainly a man who was going places. The only question was how high.

Leonov recollected how Everest had come to serve the SVR. A letter postmarked from Paris had arrived over eight years ago. The letter spoke of a deep resentment for the US government and in particular the CIA. There was no indication who had written it, but the writer promised to forward regular pieces of intelligence that he believed the SVR might find helpful. "Helpful" had been an understatement. The intelligence passed was pure gold.

Leonov had decided personally to handle the new yet unidentified informant, code name Everest. His first task had been to uncover Everest's identity. As he failed repeatedly, Leonov had decided to transfer the focus from identifying the man to making sure that nothing jeopardized him.

As the years passed, everyone in the SVR had marveled at the quality of the intelligence and the ability of the mole to keep his identity a complete mystery. It wasn't until last year that Everest had made a small slip, allowing Leonov to identify the man who had served him so well over the years. Through it all, Leonov never complained. He owed a lot of his success to a man he had never met.

Well, thought Leonov as he pulled himself from his reverie, if operation Russian Bear worked as planned, Everest would find himself on Pennsylvania Avenue by the next election. What a gem that would be!

4 | Estonia's Troubles

Inspector Urams Jürgenson of the Tallinn police, his tie hung loosely around his neck, sat behind a small wooden desk. He was tired. The prisoner looked worse. He sat with his hands bound behind him, squinting away from a powerful light that burned on a tripod. He was naked. The hard wooden chair threatened to tip over at any moment. One of its legs was cut a few centimeters shorter than the other three, making it a precarious perch on which to sit. Jürgenson had lost count of the number of times the prisoner had crashed onto the hard cement floor. The inspector's two helpers must have grown weary; uprighting the prisoner was tiring. The chair had given splinters to past prisoners when they pitched just right. Jürgenson could not tell if his prisoner had experienced that particular delight.

"We know who you are, Mirek," Jürgenson said, wondering if the prisoner wanted a cigarette as badly as he did. "We know you have supplied the people of Estonia with cocaine and heroin. You were caught with both last week. I am losing my patience. I need to know your source."

The prisoner fidgeted. Six hours on that chair naked had not been pleasant. "I just need a name," Jürgenson repeated. "You give me the name now or I will have you shot. It is that simple."

The prisoner spat on the floor defiantly. "You can't have me shot."

Jürgenson sighed inwardly. He had hoped it would not come

to this. He pressed a button by his foot and a moment later the door opened, flooding the tiny room with light from the corridor. Two guards dragged another prisoner into the interrogation room. The guards shoved the prisoner to the ground a few feet from Jürgenson's decrepit desk as another guard banged the door shut again, plunging everything behind the powerful light into darkness.

Jürgenson could see Mirek pulling against his restraints, trying to see beyond the blinding light. The inspector knew the light made it nearly impossible to see anything but rough shadows. However, the desperate pleas of the other prisoner, who had been captured with Mirek, could not be ignored as they filled the tiny room.

"I will now show you what will happen if you don't tell me the name," Jürgenson yelled over the din. He removed his revolver from its holster, stepping in front of the light so Mirek could see the revolver clearly as its barrel pointed at the other prisoner. Without warning the pistol resounded deafeningly in the small room. Jürgenson stalked back to his desk, letting the darkness absorb him as a pool of blood expanded around the other prisoner. Quickly the guards grabbed the dead prisoner and hauled him out of the room, leaving a long smear in their wake.

Jürgenson looked hard at Mirek; the prisoner was in shock. His stare concentrated on the red mess running slowly from the shadows into the light. Jürgenson allowed a few more seconds to pass, giving Mirek little time to digest what he had witnessed.

"Mirek," Jürgenson shouted through the silence. The prisoner whipped his head up and stared at the inspector. "Now you have seen what will happen to you. Answer the fucking question."

"Trubkin," Mirek said in a whisper.

"I didn't hear you!" Jürgenson yelled.

"Trubkin," Mirek said, only slightly more audible. "Nikolai Trubkin."

"Where can I find this man?" Jürgenson demanded.

"I don't know," Mirek insisted, "Believe me, I don't . . ."

"Bullshit." Jürgenson stepped closer to the prisoner, shielding him partially from the blinding light as he removed his revolver again.

"I don't know, I swear," Mirek pleaded. "I get all my instructions in dead drops."

The inspector continued to raise his pistol, his movements measured. With each second Mirek started to shake more violently. Suddenly a pool of urine puddled on the floor directly beneath the prisoner. Jürgenson took another step closer to Mirek.

"I know nothing more. For God's sake, I know nothing," Mirek pleaded as he desperately tried to back away from the pistol's aim. In his haste, Mirek only managed to tip over, causing him to crash roughly on his shoulder amid his urine.

Jürgenson considered the scene before him and made a snap decision. He returned to his desk and pushed the buzzer. One of the guards entered. "Yes, sir."

"Get me a detailed map of the city," Jürgenson ordered. "Quickly." Jürgenson returned his attention to Mirek as the guard retreated. "I will give you a half hour to mark the map with all the dead drops that Trubkin uses to contact you. Do not leave any out. Also, I want to know the exact markings you leave for each drop."

The guard reappeared with a map in hand.

"Watch him," Jürgenson ordered. "He has a half hour to identify all the dead drops. If he tries anything funny, shoot him in the kneecaps. Also, have someone clean up this mess."

"Yes, sir," the guard replied. Jürgenson turned and exited the room. He walked down to another office and opened the door. He found his officer cleaning himself.

"Did you ever consider acting school?" Jürgenson asked. "That was quite a performance."

"Thanks," the officer replied as he lit a cigarette. He offered the inspector one.

"No thanks," Jürgenson said. He had not smoked in years, but during interrogations the urge struck him like a guard's nightstick. Even now he wanted one, but he would not allow himself the simple pleasure. He considered his officer again. The man had been undercover, working by Mirek's side for the last year as a welder's assistant. He had done an admirable job. "Be sure that Mirek does not lay eyes on you. Also, stay off the streets for a few days. Take a week's vacation. Get out of sight. How's that sound?"

"Great, sir."

"See to it then," Jürgenson ordered. He left the room and closed the door.

Jürgenson's mind was working fast as he walked to his office and settled in his chair. The use of dead drops indicated that Trubkin probably had an intelligence background. Maybe he was an active agent gone sour. It happened all the time these days. In either case, Jürgenson had to be careful. Those from the intelligence area had many contacts. He had no illusion that these agents were operating with their superior's consent. In the case of Trubkin, Jürgenson believed he was well connected. The quality and volume of drugs being distributed through Mirek were substantial. Also, Trubkin probably lived in Russia. The inspector doubted that he was a local boy.

The question now was what to do with Mirek. Jürgenson had not wanted to arrest him, but his officer, the one whom Jürgenson had used to stage the fake execution, had suspected that Mirek was on to him. From Jürgenson's time with Mirek, he could not tell. Jürgenson had felt he had no choice but to arrest Mirek before he identified his officer as an undercover operative. Also, Jürgenson's boss had been pressuring him to make an arrest to show the citizens of Estonia that the police were on top of the growing drug problem. Politics, always politics.

Nevertheless, if Jürgenson could catch Trubkin in Estonia after Mirek's confession, he might have a chance. Jürgenson was not an investigator who liked to fail. He rarely did. Maybe his lack of experience with failure was the reason he detested it so much.

* * *

Nikolai Trubkin finished toweling himself off as the phone interrupted his thoughts. He wrapped the towel around his lean, muscular body and marched into the living room of his hotel suite. The view from his window of Place du Parvis, the open plaza across from Notre Dame, was beautiful, but Trubkin did not notice. He answered the phone.

"Oui," he said in French.

"I have bad news for you," the voice said. Trubkin recognized it and knew it was serious if Zaitsev needed to call him in Paris.

"And what news is that?" Trubkin asked in Russian.

"Mirek was arrested late last night," Zaitsev explained. "He is being held by an investigator named Urams Jürgenson. The investigator is very good."

Damn, Mirek. Trubkin wanted to ask Zaitsev the circumstances of the arrest, but he knew better. He would find out in good time. The message from Zaitsev was clear. Mirek was a liability. It was Trubkin's job to take care of the problem.

"I understand," Trubkin said. "I'll handle it."

"When will you return?" Zaitsev asked.

"Friday," Trubkin said.

"Maybe I should send someone else," Zaitsev suggested.

"No," Trubkin said harshly. He wanted to deal with Mirek himself. "I will take care of it. He knows nothing. If he spends another few days in a cell, it will do us no harm. Just make sure no one uses any of the dead drops. I am sure they're being watched, particularly if this inspector is as good as you suggest."

"The order has already gone out," Zaitsev confirmed. "Call me when the problem is resolved."

"I will," Trubkin promised. He heard the click on the line as Zaitsev ended the conversation.

Trubkin started to consider his options. He knew the syndicate's business was safe. Mirek knew nothing that could hurt the syndicate, but Mirek did know Trubkin's name. Trubkin did not like that one bit, and Mirek would pay for his mistake.

* * *

Trubkin walked into the Tallinn police station in the uniform of the Russian Federal Police, a unit based in Moscow and responsible, among other things, for handling the growing drug problem that plagued Russia. Trubkin thought the uniform fitted him well. The insignia indicated he was a colonel. He walked directly up to the sergeant seated at the reception desk.

"I am here to interview the prisoner, Mirek," Trubkin said in an authoritative voice.

"Say again," the sergeant asked.

"When you address me," Trubkin demanded, "you will call me 'sir'. Now take me to the prisoner Mirek immediately." The sergeant started to pay attention.

"Sir, I was not informed that anyone from Moscow was to interview the prisoner."

"I spoke with Inspector Jürgenson earlier," Trubkin said. "He wanted me to question the prisoner. As you know, we combat the drug problem like you, but in Russia. This prisoner is involved in drugs, no?" The sergeant looked down at his papers and shuffled a few of them. He obviously did not know what to do. Trubkin could just picture what was passing through his mind. Jürgenson had the day off and the sergeant certainly did not want to disturb him at home, assuming Jürgenson was at home. Even if he did call Jürgenson, it would take time. The sergeant did not want to keep Trubkin waiting. Trubkin had no doubt that the sergeant despised Russians, and he figured the sergeant still feared them, as well he should.

"Have him brought to the first interrogation room," Trubkin ordered. "I will wait for him there."

"Sir," the sergeant began, "I'm not sure I can help you."

"Damn it, Sergeant," Trubkin said, "do you want me to call Inspector Jürgenson at home and tell him how uncooperative you have been? I did not make the trip from Moscow for fun. I suggest you bring Mirek to the first interrogation room immediately. I do not have all day to listen to your shit."

"Yes, sir," the sergeant said as Trubkin turned and headed to the first interrogation room. The detailed information he had received in Vienna before flying to Tallinn included a complete layout of the police station. He had memorized it.

It took only ten minutes for Mirek to be brought into the interrogation room. As soon as Trubkin heard the door to the tiny room open, he turned his back and looked out a filthy mesh window. He did not want Mirek to recognize him until the guard had left. Trubkin heard the prisoner sit in the chair. Without turning around Trubkin said, "That is all."

"Yes, sir," the guard replied rigidly. Trubkin heard the door shut and turned around.

The surprise on Mirek's face was total as he stared at Trubkin. The man's fear consumed him.

"This is quite a mess you've gotten yourself into," Trubkin began. "I don't pay you to languish in jail cells. What happened?" Mirek explained, and Trubkin listened without interrupting, even when Mirek explained how Jürgenson had killed the other prisoner. Trubkin instantly saw through that scene.

"You gave Jürgenson my name, didn't you?" Trubkin demanded.

"No way, boss," Mirek said in a pathetic voice. "I would never do that. I swear!"

Trubkin snatched his pistol quickly from under his jacket and placed one subsonic round into Mirek's head. The silencer on the Italian-made Beretta .380 pistol reduced the shot to a pop. The pistol was a small-caliber automatic, and he liked it for its accuracy and compactness. It had elegance, not that Mirek would have noticed. The prisoner sat in the chair, his eyes still open but staring at nothing.

Trubkin exited the room quickly. The guard was standing just outside.

"Guard the door," Trubkin said. "I'll be right back. I want

the prisoner to sweat it out." The guard nodded, and Trubkin walked down the hall.

"Thanks for your help," Trubkin said as he passed the sergeant at the reception desk. Once outside, he walked quickly to a waiting car. He jumped into the back seat, and the driver gunned it. He had succeeded, but he did not like the fact that Mirek had failed him in more ways than one.

* * *

The guard stood by the door and wondered how long the Russian officer would make the prisoner wait. It was past the guard's break time and he wanted to leave, but he could not leave the prisoner unattended. It was damned unusual to leave a prisoner in the interrogation room by himself in the first place. Damn Russians, they screwed up everything. At that moment the guard heard a thud. The guard drew his pistol and quickly opened the door. One look at the prisoner and he holstered his gun. The prisoner's blank stare said everything. Christ, heads were going to roll when Jürgenson learned of this screw-up. His own head would no doubt be one of them. The guard started yelling for help.

* * *

Jürgenson stood next to the single mesh-covered window in the first interrogation room. The body of Mirek had been removed; the blood hadn't. He could not believe it. A man posing as a Russian policeman walks into an Estonian police station in broad daylight and executes a prisoner while everyone in the station has their thumbs in their ass. Jürgenson already had the police artist working on a sketch of the man. Hopefully the sergeant would not fuck that up also.

He considered how Mirek had come to his attention, an unexpected tip from the American CIA. It was a good tip. Damn, how could it end like this?

Now the big question was what to do next. He could run Trubkin's name through Interpol, but Jürgenson had no doubt that Trubkin would learn of this search immediately. Trubkin would assume that Mirek had revealed his name, particularly if Mirek had told him about the staged execution. If no search was done, Trubkin might think that Mirek had not given his name after all. That could work to Jürgenson's benefit. Nevertheless he still needed to learn more about Trubkin. It was obvious from Mirek's death that Trubkin's organization was well connected. The assassin had known that the inspector was out of the precinct for the day. That might have smelled of an inside job, but such information was fairly easy to obtain. Even a simple phone call could glean these details from his unsuspecting men.

A thought occurred to Jürgenson. Maybe the impostor was Trubkin. His masters would hold him responsible for Mirek's actions. He had had no choice but to solve the problem himself–a true leader, reflected Jürgenson, and no doubt a very dangerous man.

Jürgenson decided he had one option: use the artist's drawing to start a search and attach no name to it, maybe leading Trubkin to believe Mirek had not given his name after all. It was a slim chance, but it was better than nothing.

Whoever Trubkin was, Jürgenson was going to find him. He turned to leave the room. It was time to tell his commander what had happened. There would be hell to pay.

5 Path to California

Most of the guests at this fancy California gala were in their fifties and sixties. They, no doubt practiced at this type of social event, were dressed in black tie and long evening gowns. John had gone to any number of Navy social events, but they were nothing like this one. Here money was the power base. In the Navy, position held the heavy stick.

John saw a young woman make her way along the pool, draped in a red dress that hung from a pair of thin straps arched across her tanned shoulders. The silk fabric showed her California figure in exquisite detail. Heads turned, admiring her as she sauntered along the pool's edge. Even her reflection on the blue surface invited a second glance. It was time to drop into the lie. He approached her. "Hello, I'm Pete."

She smiled, her green eyes studying him. "Betsy. Nice to meet you."

"May I escort you to the bar? I believe your drink is in need of attention." John hoisted his beer to indicate the direction. "I think the bar is over there."

"I like the way you think."

John opted for another Corona, Betsy for a glass of Mondavi Chardonnay. With drink in hand Betsy led him back along the pool side.

"Have you known the Davenports long?" he asked.

"For years," Betsy said, "ever since they've owned this island. It's called Santa Cruz. It's a working farm, beautiful, if remote. Mr. Davenport bought it fifteen years ago."

"It must have cost a bundle, the island I mean."

"I'm sure it did, but Mrs. Davenport was loaded."

"Was?"

"Yes, she died three years ago. Breast cancer."

"Breast cancer?" He added, "My mother died when I was one. I never really knew her. Cancer took her too."

"I'm sorry."

"Thanks," John said, suddenly sad as his mind jumped to thoughts of his brother. He pushed them away. "It looks like a beautiful place to live."

"Yes, it's beautiful," Betsy agreed, "but it's too inconvenient for me. I like people, parties, traveling. Living out here makes all that tougher."

"I can see that, but what a great place to retreat to."

"I'll agree with you there," Betsy said. "It's a great hideaway."

"It's magnificent. I guess you met the Davenports through your parents?"

"No, Logan and I grew up together."

"Logan?"

"Mr. Davenport's daughter." She looked oddly at John. "I take it you don't know the Davenports well."

John shook his head. "I'm here on business and was invited. You're the only one I know at this affair."

"Lucky me." Betsy smiled and took a sip of her wine. "Logan has lived here for the last five years. Before that she lived in San Francisco after she finished up at Stanford in '86."

"What do you do?"

"I sell houses," Betsy said with a professional smile. "Do you want one? I know this great house just outside of town. It's selling for $1.2 million."

John laughed. "Sounds too small for me. Got anything larger?"

Betsy looked at him suspiciously, and John smiled. They both laughed. "What brings you to town?"

"Business."

"What type of business?"

"I'm a consultant," John said, not wanting to be more specific. The hard part about taking on someone else's identity, even someone he knew as well as his brother, was knowing enough. John was a very sophisticated computer user. However, he was not a computer programmer like his brother. John doubted Betsy knew a great deal about the machines, but others might. The more vague he could be, the better.

"And the party, is it business too?"

John studied Betsy for a second. "No. A friend in Washington thought I might enjoy it."

"Who you know is what life is all about," Betsy observed. "Don't you think?"

"I suppose," replied John as he eyed the blue water of the pool, realizing that its curves were not as graceful as hers, "but I'd like to think there is more to it than that."

"Like what?" Betsy asked.

"Nature, love, friendship." John turned his focus to the evening sky as the sun closed on the waters of the Pacific. It made him think of Japan. What sank here rose there as a new day—the morning sun, *Asahi*.

Betsy smiled. "Don't tell me you're a romantic. I don't think I've ever met one."

"I find that hard to believe," John said. "You must have more men chasing you than you could possibly know what to do with."

"Maybe, but they're all fifty and lecherous."

They both laughed again.

"Let's get another drink," she insisted. "I'd have a dozen of these if I could."

"I'll get them," John offered. "I'll be right back."

John scanned the crowd as he waited for the bartender to fetch the drinks. He did not recognize anyone; just as well, he thought. As he waited, he realized his brother would never attend a party again, or see a sunset. The pain of the thought towered above him like a huge sea serpent.

"Sir, your drinks."

John turned to the bartender. "Thanks."

With a drink in each hand he looked for Betsy. She was talking to a lady whose looks reminded him of Barbara Bush. John joined them. After a few moments of small talk, he said, "Why don't you introduce me to the host of this party? It would be rude not to meet him."

"Right you are," Betsy agreed. She spun around and scanned the crowd. After a few moments she grabbed John's hand. "This way."

They found the host standing near the edge of the swimming pool, in conversation with an elderly couple. Alex Davenport looked like the billionaire he was. His penetrating blue eyes gleamed with confidence in his tanned face. His fifty-five-year-old physique looked ten years younger, and his perfectly tailored black tuxedo spoke of wealth. He also looked vaguely familiar.

All three turned as Betsy and John approached. They recognized Betsy and gave her a warm welcome.

"Who is your friend?" Mr. Davenport asked, extending his right hand in John's direction.

John shook it, wondering how much Mr. Davenport knew about his visit. "My name is Pete Thompson, sir."

"Alexander Davenport."

"It's a pleasure, sir."

"Pete, please meet Bill and Sarah Sinclair," Mr. Davenport said. John shook the couple's hands. "By the way, none of this "sir" crap. My name is Alex and the Sinclairs' are Bill and Sarah."

John smiled. "Okay."

"Now where did you find Betsy?" Alex Davenport asked. "Did she try to sell you real estate as soon as she met you?"

Betsy punched Davenport lightly on the shoulder. John could tell that she was considered family.

"Young man, I can only warn you now. This young lady is trouble." He laughed. "Actually, women are trouble; don't you agree, Bill?"

"Now that you mention it," Bill Sinclair replied with a chuckle, "I think you have a point."

Betsy and Sarah made a loud protest.

"What brings you to this lovely part of the world?" Sarah Sinclair chimed. She obviously felt a change of subject was warranted.

"A little business," John replied. "I have a meeting and plan to fly back to Washington, DC, tomorrow morning. Unfortunately it's a quick trip."

"That is most unfortunate." Sarah spoke as though they had been long-time friends.

"What business are you in?" Davenport inquired.

"I write computer software."

"You don't look the type," Davenport said with confidence. "I thought computer guys were nerdy and wore glasses."

"Alex, really," Mrs. Sinclair cried.

"And what exactly do you do with computers?" Davenport pressed.

"I write database applications for small clients," John answered, noting Davenport's interest. "A one-man consulting show. Not much really."

"Hello."

Everyone turned. The young woman's beauty was breathtaking. Her dark hair fell to the top of her bare shoulders. A black dress with thin straps hugged her figure delicately, stopping just above her tanned ankles. A long slit down one side flashed glimpses of her dark, long legs. But amazing as her body was, her blue eyes captivated John the most. They stood out strikingly in her beautifully tanned face. Her eyes resembled her father's, warmer but somehow more wary.

"Pete, I'd like you to meet my daughter, Logan."

"A pleasure," John said awkwardly. The strength of her

handshake surprised him as he peered into her eyes. He recognized a deep intelligence.

"Pete was just telling us about his business," Sarah Sinclair said. "It sounds very exciting. He writes computer software."

"Really," Logan said. "You don't strike me as a computer programmer."

"It must run in the family. Your father said the same thing," Betsy said as everyone chuckled.

Logan smiled graciously.

"How did you learn about computers?" Bill Sinclair asked, mixing his drink with his index finger. John noted the man's hands were nicely manicured, which made him realize his hands were too rough to be a computer programmer's. The details—how revealing they could be.

"Self-taught, mostly," John answered. "The applications I write are very simple. I don't consider myself an expert. I'm just a decent problem solver."

"Are you based in Washington, DC?" Sarah Sinclair asked.

"No, I live in Steamboat Springs, Colorado. My current client is in Washington."

"What business would a computer specialist working in Washington have in Santa Barbara?" Davenport asked.

John smiled. "I'm afraid I can't say. Client confidentiality."

"Are you sure you can't give us one hint?" Sarah asked. "We can keep a secret."

"I'm sure you can, Sarah."

"Pete, you trust us," Betsy insisted.

John nodded. He doubted it made any difference and suspected Davenport already knew whom he was meeting and would undoubtedly know about the late addition to his guest list. In Arabic John said, "I hope to meet the former ambassador of Colombia tonight."

"What was that?" Sarah asked.

"Arabic," Logan said.

John hid his surprise. "Do you speak Arabic?"

"No," she replied coolly. "Just a lucky guess."

John wondered. He continued in Arabic. "You are the most beautiful woman I have ever met, and I'd like nothing more than to spend the night with you." He watched her, and she did not blush.

"What are you saying?" Betsy demanded.

John shrugged his shoulders. "I really can't say. I'm sorry. My client's boss is a tyrant."

"Come now, that's just not fair," Betsy insisted. "Tell us."

John smiled. "Okay, I told Logan that the sock clinging to her beautiful dress is most becoming."

Logan gave herself a quick once-over. She frowned at him. "I thought there were two. Damn, I must have lost one."

Everyone laughed.

"What other languages do you know?" Bill Sinclair asked.

"Besides Japanese and Arabic, I also know a little bit of Thai," John replied. He did not mention Russian. He wouldn't be able to explain why he knew it unless he mentioned his years in the Navy.

"That's a very interesting combination of languages," Logan commented, her eyes steady on John. "Do they come in handy in your line of work?"

"Not really," John lied.

"Good linguists are hard to find," Davenport added. "I'm surprised you don't work for the government."

"I've had offers," John answered quickly. His performance tonight was less than his best. He needed to start thinking and slow the booze intake. He had always liked to drink, but tonight he felt reckless. His emotions were tugging him in a new direction, one he could not afford to follow. "But I'm not the type."

"Really," Davenport insisted.

"Speaking of Washington," Sarah Sinclair said, "how about that shooting right next to the White House?"

"A terrible affair," Davenport confirmed.

John took a sip of his drink. This was one topic he did not want to discuss. He did not trust himself.

Mrs. Sinclair started to ask another question, but Davenport interrupted her. "Pete, I'd like to show you something, if you have a minute. I think you will find it interesting."

"Sure," John replied.

Davenport turned to Betsy. "My dear, do you mind if I borrow Pete for a few moments?"

Betsy took her cue and shook her head. "No problem. I'll see you when you get back. You will bring him back, won't you?"

"Don't worry, my dear," Davenport said with a wealthy smile. "I have no evil plans for him."

"Don't believe everything he tells you," Logan added.

"That's not very reassuring," John replied. She was so beautiful, but there was more. What was it?

John walked with Davenport as they followed the flagstones, which led to the large stone house that graced the island. They did not speak as they made their way. John was curious. What could the billionaire possibly have to show him?

Davenport interrupted John's thoughts as they stepped into the house. "How long have you been a computer programmer?"

"Six years," John answered as he noted his impressive surroundings. The paintings were particularly grand. "I never went to college. I got an early start in the industry. What's your line of business?"

"I was in the Army during the Second World War," Davenport said. "I spent a great deal of time in France. It was ugly. You never knew whom you could trust; even family members turned against each other. It was sickening. I hope the world never faces such a nightmare again. I'm not sure it could handle it."

They entered Davenport's office through a pair of glass French doors. The office had an excellent view of the pool. An arrangement of tables and chairs sat just under the windows outside. It looked like a great place to take breakfast, where the rising sun would shower morning light onto the patio. Now the view was filled with the twinkling lights of Santa Barbara in the distance and the lit pool glowing blue, surrounded by guests in black tie.

John chuckled silently at the idea that struck him; he could not imagine what would happen if the guests started to throw each other into the pool. John asked, "What did you do after the war?"

"I worked with Donovan for a few years," Davenport answered.

"Who?" John asked. He knew Davenport was referring to Major General William Donovan, the director of the OSS, the CIA's predecessor; however, a computer programmer would not have heard of him. Davenport was testing him.

"He ran the OSS, the Office of Strategic Services."

"Oh, and then what did you do?"

"Many things," Davenport replied evasively. "But I didn't ask you to join me to discuss my past. I hope there will be other times for that. No, my reasons for pulling you aside are much more selfish."

John locked eyes with Davenport. What had he meant about "other times?" He tried to read Davenport's eyes, but he could not. The man's eyes reminded John of Admiral Sunders' even though the admiral's were hazel. Both men had eyes that could show many emotions; both had a remarkable ability to control which emotions were displayed.

"Pete, please take a seat," Davenport said. John sat down on a sofa before Davenport's large mahogany desk. The desk was bare except for a multi-line telephone, a blotter, and a Carter penholder with two pens. Davenport walked to the wet bar. "Another drink?"

"A rum and Coke if you have it," John said. He had had enough beer and did not particularly like rum. He could slow his pace without being rude.

"I think I can handle that." Davenport busied himself with the task. John found himself studying the office. The walls were filled with books and pictures. The pictures included shots of Davenport with famous people, particularly from Washington. John saw several presidents, lots of senators, and other power brokers who inhabited Washington's corridors of influence. Clearly

Davenport was a player. He knew the people who made Washington work.

"Your drink," Davenport said as he handed a glass to John and took a seat on the small sofa. "To your health."

John raised his glass and waited for Davenport to begin.

"I am the most doting father. I worry about her constantly." Davenport looked at John as he took a healthy sip from his drink. John wondered where this conversation was headed.

"Several years ago Logan's husband was killed in a horrible automobile accident, a real inferno," Davenport began, his voice sad with the memory. "She could have been in that car. Only fate saved her. She had a flat tire on her way home. She called Greg. He was waiting at home. She told him to go to the cocktail party and not to wait for her. She wanted to take a quick shower. She was dirty after changing the tire. He said he would wait, but she insisted. She has a way of doing that. On her drive to the party she took the same route that Greg had. She arrived on the scene only a few minutes after they extinguished the fire. She saw what remained of Greg sitting in the driver's seat. I don't need to tell you, it was not a pretty sight."

Davenport continued with a deep sigh. "As you can imagine, she was utterly devastated. Who wouldn't be?"

"Life can be so cruel," John said with heart.

"I take it you have seen death," Davenport said. "It wears an ugly face."

John lied. "I've lost a few friends to car accidents; however, none so terrible as your daughter's."

Davenport nodded. "Too many young people die in this life. Life is fleeting in many respects. It's all a matter of timing and perspective."

"I agree," John said, wondering again where this conversation was headed. He had a sense that Davenport was testing him. It struck him as odd.

"I think she likes you," Davenport said in a matter-of-fact tone. "I can tell."

"Excuse me, sir," John said. "Who likes me, Betsy?"

Davenport stood and wandered behind his desk. "Oh, Betsy. Yes, I'm sure she likes you too. She is easily impressed. But I was not speaking of Betsy." He paused. John held his stare. "Logan, she likes you."

"Sir, your daughter and I just met moments ago," John replied. Where was Davenport going with this line of conversation? "Pardon me, but I'm a little confused."

"I know," Davenport said. "I've been a bit forward. Please accept my apologies, but I am a man who likes to get to the point. I think it saves time. You strike me as the same type of individual. We don't have time for bullshit." John just nodded, noting that Davenport had not touched his drink again.

"What exactly are you doing in Santa Barbara?" Davenport asked in a more businesslike tone. John set his drink down on the small coffee table. Davenport was enigmatic. What did he really want?

"You heard what I said."

"I certainly did, Pete, but I am very curious."

John realized that this man was a master of the little details. He thought back to the day after his encounter with George Simpson, when he had decided on his next step. He had called US Senator William Bennett, who represented the State of California. The senator was a powerful member of the Select Intelligence Committee, which provided congressional oversight of the US intelligence community. John had met the statesman several times while leading SEAL Team Six. From time to time, John had briefed the committee on Navy SEAL operations. The senator had always taken John's advice to heart and had come to trust his blunt answers. John had noticed his picture among those on Davenport's office wall.

John knew that Bennett worked with all the key players in Washington and certainly those in the State Department. That had been John's reason for requesting the meeting. He wanted the senator to introduce him to someone in the State Department who knew Colombia, and in particular Cartagena, the home of the Cali cartel. The senator wanted details, but John indicated he could not provide any. He asked the senator to trust him. The senior statesman agreed and offered a candidate, the former Colombian Ambassador Alan Maxwell.

Senator Bennett indicated he had known Maxwell for years and considered him a true Colombian expert. The senator called Maxwell and told him he had a friend in need. He wanted the former ambassador to meet this friend as a personal favor. The friend's name was Pete Thompson. Now, thirty-six hours later, John was in California, attending a charity gala at which the former ambassador would be present. Washington had its ways.

"Yes, sir, I can see that you are."

"Please, call me Alex. I insist."

"Sorry, Alex."

"I'm interested, that's all," Davenport remarked. "I never did like Maxwell. I knew his father. He was a piece of work. He had his fingers in all the pots. I'm sure the younger Maxwell followed his father's lead. Money will do that to men. You'll see."

John needed to make a decision. Could he trust Alex Davenport? He knew nothing about him, and the more he learned, the less he felt he knew. Something intangible about him made John leery.

Davenport chuckled as though he sensed John's uneasiness. "I'll leave it be. I'm sorry I was so nosy. Some habits are hard to change. Why don't we rejoin the other guests? I'll introduce you to the former ambassador. Feel free to use my office if you need to."

"Thank you, that's very kind." John stood and followed Davenport back to the patio.

Davenport stopped at the door of his office. John sensed the billionaire had just made a decision. "I hope my daughter gets a chance to know you."

"I'd like that," John said.

* * *

GILL

"Mr. Ambassador, it's a great pleasure to meet you." John shook the former ambassador's hand. Maxwell's grip was firm.

"I'll leave you two," Davenport said. John did not like his look and he suspected that neither did Maxwell. There was no love lost between these two men. John wondered why, believing Davenport's earlier explanation fell short of the truth.

The former ambassador gestured toward the ocean. "Should we take a walk to the point?"

"Certainly, sir," John agreed.

As they reached the end of the gravel walkway, both men paused and faced the dark waters of the Pacific. A few moments passed before either spoke.

"I am an old man who sits on his porch and watches the Pacific display its many faces. It fascinates me."

"It's both beautiful and dangerous," John answered. "My respect for it is complete."

"Well said and spoken like one experienced in its ways," Maxwell replied. "What else do you do besides write computer applications?"

"Write computer applications."

"I see."

Silence fell again as they both absorbed the view of the Pacific.

"To the view," John said as he held his drink high, silently toasting his brother.

"To the view," joined the former ambassador. Each man sipped his drink. "How is the senator?"

John reminded himself of what his instructors in the Navy had drilled into him: always mix a part of the truth into the story. "I don't know him very well. I didn't know who else to turn to. My father introduced me to him long ago."

"I see. Bill and I go way back," Maxwell explained. "He told me you are in some kind of trouble. How can I help?"

"I'm interested in Gregori Petrov. He seems to have some dealings with Colombians."

"I believe you mean Aleksandr Petrov," the former ambassador replied.

"Yes, Aleksandr," John replied smoothly. Had Simpson deliberately lied to him, or did he truly think Petrov's real name was Gregori? John decided not to bother Maxwell with this detail.

"An interesting fellow if I do say so myself," Maxwell added. "What does a computer consultant have to do with him?"

"I recently escaped an attempt on my life," John said carefully. "I confronted the man who set me up. He mentioned this man's name."

Maxwell absorbed the information for a moment, while John considered what he knew about the ambassador.

"What do you want to know?"

"How well do you know Petrov, for starters?"

"Personally, not well. He seems to manage the relationship between the Cali cartel and SVR—the KGB's old first chief directorate."

"The what?" asked John, remembering his role as a computer programmer.

"The CIA of the KGB," Maxwell explained.

"Really? Who runs the cartel?"

"Señor Anastasio, or El Gordo, as he's known."

"Do Petrov and El Gordo work together?"

"Now that depends on who you're talking to. The public line is that they've only met socially and superficially. However, the private skinny is that they do business together."

John probed. "How do you mean?"

"I heard it said that El Gordo sells the SVR its drugs. Petrov is the main contact for his masters in Moscow."

"In a time of budget cuts, is the SVR forced to find alternative sources of money?" John asked.

"It's something like that," Maxwell said, "but it goes deeper, I believe. Mind you, I'm just speculating. Certainly the SVR needs the money. What government agency doesn't? The SVR is also in the business of spying. What better way to spy than to do business with whomever you're spying on? Do you see my point?"

John nodded. "So money and information are the goals?"

"Yes. Let me give you a scenario," Maxwell suggested. "Mr. X, who has an important position in the State Department, has a drug habit. He wants to be discreet, so he deals with some big-time Colombian rather than the street punk dealers. He knows the Colombian because he sees the intelligence reports from the area. If you were the SVR, would you want this information? You bet you would. The drug lords deal with a lot of interesting people all over the world. The SVR plays in the game to get information, valuable information, while undoubtedly making a great deal of money."

"I understand," John said. "Who do you think controls Petrov? Moscow or El Gordo?"

"That's a good question, but I have to believe Moscow does. Petrov is a smart man, but not particularly courageous. He's a plotter who knows how to use flattery to his advantage. Actually, if there is one thing that Petrov can do well, it's flatter people. He's a master. Personally, I don't know how his superiors put up with it. I would tire of his bullshit in moments."

The former ambassador paused before he continued. "Now if I may ask a question. Why are you interested in Petrov?"

"I thought Bill told you why I went to him," John said with a feigned look of surprise. Maxwell raised a skeptical eyebrow. John knew that the senator had told him nothing. John waited for the former ambassador to break the silence, as his eyes swung toward the party. Logan was nowhere in sight, and he wondered where she'd gotten to. The distraction surprised him.

"Bennett's such a secretive bastard. It's as though he doesn't trust me after all these years."

"I doubt that, sir," John said, as he forced himself to concentrate. This wasn't the time to be thinking about Logan, far from it. "I thought he would have told you why I'm here."

"He gave me an outline, but he said you would fill me in."

Sneaky, thought John. The former ambassador was playing him. He obliged. "Someone tried to kill me last week. I escaped by the narrowest of margins. I know who set me up. I had a little heart-to-heart with that man. He gave me Petrov's name and mentioned the Colombian connection."

"You've already said as much," Maxwell said. His brow tightened with his thoughts. "Do you think these men are responsible for the attempt on your life?"

"Yes," John said quickly. "Can I ask you one more question?"

"Certainly," Maxwell said with a note of frustration.

"Do you think Vincent Foster was murdered?"

The former ambassador looked John directly in the eyes. John saw an intensity he had not noticed previously. "You mean the White House counselor who committed suicide in July?" John nodded. "An interesting question, but what is its relevance to our discussion?"

"None really," John said, as he glanced at the ground. "His name came to mind after I stumbled on a 1913 .38-caliber Colt pistol when I visited the man who set me up." John paused for a moment while the former ambassador considered at the Pacific.

"Do you think he was murdered?" John repeated.

"Who knows?" Maxwell answered after a few moments. "Washington has more mirrors in it than a haunted house at a carnival. Anything is possible. Personally, though, I bet it was a simple suicide. The man had never worked in Washington. He was unprepared for all the pressure. It got to him. He took his life. End of story. It has happened before and will happen again. Washington can do that to people."

"I can't believe there are many guns like that floating around," John persisted.

"I imagine you're right," Maxwell said. "Do you have any other questions?"

"Have you ever heard of a company called Security International Group?"

"It sounds familiar. Have they been in the papers recently?"

"Well, yes," John replied, as he tried to gauge how much Maxwell knew. "I believe they were involved in that mess at the Marriott in Washington."

The ambassador stared at John. "Horrid, that crime. Two blocks from the White House. What might be next?" He stopped in mid-sentence. "You were there, weren't you?"

"Yes," John confirmed, "and lucky to be here."

"Your client, it was SIG?"

John noted Maxwell's use of the company's initials. He knew more about the company than he was letting on.

"Bingo," John said. "Does El Gordo own SIG?"

"I wouldn't know," Maxwell answered. "Do you have any more questions?"

"No, sir," John answered. "Thank you for your time. I'm sorry to have intruded on your evening."

"Really, no problem at all," Maxwell said. "Let me know if I can help you in the future. My door is always open for a friend of Bill's."

John thanked the ambassador again as they joined the rest of the party. The conversation had gone as expected. Nevertheless, unless John was entirely off base, Ambassador Maxwell had lied to him more than once. The question was why.

6 | Friend or Foe

Logan stood by the reddish-brown horse, a brush firmly in hand. She could feel the animal's body heat as the morning sun rose suddenly above the horizon. She liked the early morning, its freshness—a new beginning.

She had slept little during the night, being haunted by her past and scared by the present. She did not know what it was about him that drew her in—his shoulder-length hair, his firm body, or his dark brown eyes. Maybe it was his smile and the warmth it brought. She could feel intensity radiate from him. Like her father, John was a man of action and so different from Greg.

A chill ran down her back at the thought. Her Greg. He did not deserve to be burned alive. What God could subject a good man to such a terrible end? Why?

Logan tried to focus on her horse and the rhythm of his breathing. Sunrise was a special animal and Logan doted on him. She leaned forward and whispered in his ear. He rolled his ears backward while he chewed his hay, content to listen.

Logan sighed. "If only you could speak."

She realized it was nearly five years since she had been with a man. The thought frightened her. She had always wanted children, but after Greg's death she had abandoned the idea. How could she bring children into a world that was so cruel? It wouldn't be fair.

And now she found herself excited by a man. Why? What

was it about Pete that had awakened this need in her? She readily admitted to herself that he was beautiful, but she could not quite figure out the awkwardness in his manner—sadness perhaps. She wondered if, like her, he had been damaged by a tragedy. Was that what pulled her toward him?

What would Greg think? He had always given sound advice, a sure hand in difficult seas. She set the brush down. It was time to fetch some oats.

* * *

Davenport sat behind his large mahogany desk, which was littered with papers from his morning efforts. He had started his day, as usual, at four o'clock in the morning. He would have liked to say his years in the military had taught him the benefits of waking before dawn, but the explanation was much simpler. The Asian countries where he handled most of his business were nine to thirteen hours ahead of California. To communicate with them before the close of the business day demanded that he get an early start. After spending a few hours working with Asia, he was ready to handle his business dealings in Europe and finally on the East Coast, just three time zones away.

He had always been a workaholic. His friends had wondered why, particularly since he had married an exceptionally rich woman, his late wife Susan Rosenburg. He could have chosen a life of idle play, but that was not his style. He hated the idea of relying on anyone. The decision to marry Susan had been tough. He desperately wanted access to her money because he knew he could use it to make a lot more money for himself. Nevertheless he loathed the idea of having to rely on it. In the end, he had reconciled his feelings by convincing himself that his marriage with Susan was no more than a business deal.

In the beginning, that was all it was. However, time has a habit of changing things. The first few years of their marriage had been rocky. Davenport was always traveling and spending little time with his beautiful wife, but that had slowly changed. As he started to make real money for himself, and his daughter Logan began to grow, he realized that making money was only a small part of being successful. He started spending time with his wife and daughter. It was the best thing he had ever done. When Susan had died of cancer three years earlier, Davenport had been devastated.

The last five years had been tough, beginning with Logan's husband's death, which had chilled him. Davenport had not cared a great deal for Greg, but he knew Logan was devoted to him. Arriving on the scene had traumatized her.

While Susan and he tried to help Logan, they learned that Susan had breast cancer. It had been a blow to them all. Susan had deteriorated quickly. The irony was that in Susan's sickness came Logan's strength. She had pulled her life together as she helped her mother through the last two years. Davenport missed his wife terribly. She was a good woman who had shown him a side of life he never would have known otherwise.

The telephone rang and he answered it.

"Hello."

"Alex, it's Sherm."

"How are you, you old fox." Davenport leaned back in his director's chair. Sherman Spencer was President and Chief Operating Officer of Pacific Rim Air, based in Singapore, a wholly owned subsidiary of Hong Kong Transportation Limited. Davenport had started both companies, and others, in 1966. They had all started as shell companies to hide his drug-smuggling operations in Asia. As time passed, Davenport had realized he could not stay in the drug business. Yes, it was profitable, but it held many risks, particularly to one's person and family. Slowly Davenport had invested in legitimate businesses and, by the mid-seventies, found his drug business contributing less than thirty percent to his overall annual profits. This change was largely due to the success of Hong Kong Transportation Limited. Davenport had taken this diversified air cargo company public in 1974 and made over fifty-five million dollars. Today it was a $3.5 billion multinational conglomerate, operating in thirty-seven countries. Davenport still owned thirty-five percent of HKT.

Davenport had met Sherman in Bangkok in 1967. Davenport was then working full time for the CIA, using a position with Shell Oil Company as his cover. Sherman was on his last tour in Vietnam and was anxious to get back home to the United States. He had had enough of Vietnam. He was disgusted with his government's prosecution of the war. The two men had met by chance at the Oriental, a five-star hotel on the banks of the Chao Phraya River in downtown Bangkok. Both men had taken seats by the pool, sharing shade provided by one of the umbrellas on the verandah. Each was absorbing the unobstructed view of the river, watching the heavy traffic on its dirty brown waters. Davenport had introduced himself to Sherman. They had hit it off immediately.

Davenport learned quickly that Sherman's language skills were excellent. He told Sherman to call him when he left the Army. Davenport indicated he was in several businesses, and that a man with Sherman's skills could come in handy. Sherman said he would call and, good to his word, did so three months later. Now, almost thirty years later, Sherman was running one of HKT's most profitable businesses.

"You're still at the office?" Davenport asked. He knew there was a thirteen-hour time difference between California and Singapore. It was 7:18 am in California and 8:18 p.m. in Singapore.

"Yeah, just finishing up some numbers for a meeting with the Chinese," Sherman answered. "Those bastards always want a deal. It never changes."

"You're right on that score. What can I do for you?"

"I'd like to send you the numbers and have you review them. Something isn't right about them. I thought you might see the problem right away. I'd certainly appreciate it."

"Sure, send them over and I'll have a look at them before I

head down to Los Angeles for a lunch meeting." Davenport consulted his Rolex watch. His helicopter left in three hours.

"Thanks, I appreciate it. I'll send them as soon as we get off the phone," Sherman said. "By the way, I had an interesting call today. Do you remember George Simpson from 'Nam?"

Davenport sat up at his desk. He certainly did.

"Yes, I remember him. What's he up to?"

"He's looking for a little help. It appears some Colombians are after his hide."

"Really? What has he done?" Davenport asked.

"Apparently he ran an operation in the US called SIG. It's some kind of security concern that fronts for the Cali cartel. He didn't give me all the details, but it appears the operation has sprung a leak. The Feds are investigating; at least George thinks so. That's why he's planning to split. He said the henchman, Carlos, recently tried to kill a programmer named Pete Thompson who exposed SIG to the government. George thinks they missed their mark on the Thompson guy, and he passed some hot information to the Feds."

"You said the programmer's name was Pete Thompson?"

"Yeah, Pete Thompson," Sherman repeated. "Do you know him?"

"No," Davenport lied. He did not want Sherman to realize, at least not yet, that the information he possessed was significant. "What did George want?"

"A safe house until he can get his life in order. He understood he was asking a lot, but he reminded me of all his efforts on our behalf in 'Nam."

"Did you give him one?" Davenport asked.

"I told him he could have the Silk House for a month. It's the least I could do. He saved our bacon once or twice, maybe more. I never did like those Colombian thugs anyway."

"Interesting. Keep me posted and give George my best," Davenport said. "I'll have those numbers back to you in a few hours. I'll talk with you tomorrow."

"Great," Sherman said. "Thanks for the help." Sherman broke the connection, and Davenport replaced the headset in its cradle.

Davenport did not believe in coincidences. Senator Bennett had called personally to ask if a Pete Thompson could be added to the guest list of the gala. At the time, Davenport had never considered the possibility that the senator was talking about Bill Thompson's son. Davenport had assumed the friend must be important: someone older, someone the senator needed.

He had immediately recognized Pete as Bill Thompson's son. Surprise had overcome Davenport when he was introduced to the young man. What would Bill Thompson's son and the former ambassador have to discuss?

Pete had indicated that he was a software programmer and had a client or clients in Washington, DC. Davenport had wondered on and off if Pete was CIA or ex-military: his manner, speech, and particularly his eyes suggested a killer. However, he appeared to be an awful liar. It was clear that he wanted to hide his purpose for attending the party, and yet he had all but given it away. Pete was either an expert or a novice. Davenport felt uncomfortable that he did not know; he had come to expect certainty from himself about such matters.

And now this new piece of information, in which a computer programmer had stolen information from SIG, given it to the Feds, and consequently had an attempt made on his life. Maybe the senator thought Maxwell could help the young man because of a Colombian drug cartel's involvement. But why have the meeting on his island?

Something was afoot. What, who, and why? These three questions needed answers. A plan came to mind. Davenport made a quick decision. He picked up the phone and dialed the operator.

"I'm looking for the number of the Santa Barbara Inn."

A few moments later the phone began to ring.

"Pete Thompson, please." He held while he was connected. He hoped he had not missed him.

"Hello."

"Pete, Alex Davenport."

"Alex, you just caught me," John said, surprise in his voice.

"Yes, well I'm glad. I had hoped we could have dinner tonight, say around 7:00 p.m."

"I'd like that very much," John replied, "but I have a 9:30 am flight to catch."

"I understand, but maybe you would consider rescheduling. I believe if would be worth your time."

"Let me check on my flight alternatives and I'll get back to you. What's your number?"

"Pete, I'll have my assistant handle that. I'm sure she can get you on the same flight to Washington tomorrow morning."

John paused. "Okay, how do I get to the island?"

"Wait on the wharf where you met the boat last night. I'll have my helicopter pick you up. Let's say at 6:30 p.m. I have a meeting in LA or I'd suggest an earlier time. You can stay on the island tonight. I'll tell Maggie to make a bed for you."

"It's very generous of you."

"My pleasure," Davenport confirmed. "I'll see you then."

Davenport sat back in his chair and pondered the balls in the air. The Feds apparently were after SIG, and by extension the Cali cartel. The attempt to kill Pete Thompson appeared to be the trigger. Why? What did Pete Thompson mean to the government? What had led Thompson to Maxwell? Was it really the senator?

If Davenport had learned one thing over the years, it was that shit rolls downhill. Once a ball starts moving, it is very hard to stop. The key is not to stop the ball, but to force it in a direction that will reap the biggest benefit or limit the damage. Davenport had too much at stake to fail now. Somehow he had a nagging sense that these events related to his plans more than he cared to admit. There was no direct line visible, but that meant nothing. Some lines were not that obvious.

Davenport looked through the French windows of his office, absorbing the breathtaking view of the Santa Barbara Channel, which twinkled as the morning sunlight danced on its undulating surface. He still could not believe that one of Bill Thompson's sons had just stepped into his life. And why now, of all times? And why, of all the men in the world, had this young man awakened something in Logan? Davenport had seen it instantly. Logan's look had said it all. His conclusion had been confirmed while Pete and Maxwell spoke. Logan had repeatedly focused her attention toward the place where the two men stood.

He sighed deeply–time to get back to work. His plans required all his attention and abilities. He was going for the ultimate power grab. The risks were huge; however, what else did he have to live for? He loved Logan more than he could articulate, but he needed to challenge himself. He needed to prove to himself and everyone else that no boundaries existed that he could not leap.

7 | Another Visit

Logan greeted John as he stepped from the helicopter. She wore a white buttoned-up blouse, blue jeans, and a pair of leather sandals. Her dark brown hair danced in the downwash of the helicopter. All her attempts to keep it in place proved fruitless.

"Hello, Logan," he yelled above the noise as the helicopter blades spun down.

"Hey, Pete," she said. Guilt swept through his insides. He hated the lie.

She led him from the helicopter and away from the house. "Dinner isn't for a half hour. I'd thought you'd like the view from the point."

"Trust me, I will," John replied after his eyes had completely covered Logan. She blushed at his silly comment. Couldn't he think of anything wittier to say?

Soon they were standing on the point, facing west and watching the sun close on the waters of the Pacific in the inevitable daily dash. The last rays painted the rolling surface of the ocean brilliantly. Seagulls glided overhead as the ocean crashed onto the boulders that dotted the small beach below the fifty-foot-high point.

From his visit the previous night, John knew that around to the right were stone steps leading to the island's dock, a facility that resembled a small marina. As John considered his surroundings, he suddenly felt an appreciation for what money could buy.

The thousands of acres that made up Davenport's private island were almost too beautiful to be believed.

"It's beautiful here," John said.

"It is," Logan readily agreed.

He could smell her by his side. Her scent was sweet and natural. He fought a strong urge to pull her close, to feel her warmth, and to stare into her beautiful blue eyes while the fading light of day washed over them. Uncertainty filled him. He didn't even know Logan. What made her so attractive? Had the death of his brother and the resulting loneliness heightened his emotions, or was something else at work?

John looked at her, his brow bunched with thought. Logan noticed his discomfort. "Are you okay?"

Their eyes locked. "Is it that obvious?"

She smiled. "You have the same look on your face that you did last night."

"Really?"

Logan paused a moment before she continued. "Yes, when Sarah mentioned the shootings in Washington, your whole persona changed. You seemed upset, angry."

John did not respond immediately as his eyes returned to the breathtaking view of the Pacific. "You are a very perceptive woman."

Logan's hand quickly landed on John's arm, the touch gentle. "You're embarrassed."

"I am," John replied as he felt the richness of her touch. He struggled with his next words. He wanted to jump from the lie he had created and to tell her the truth, all of it. His operational side nagged at him, warning him.

Finally he spoke. "You like the truth, don't you?"

"Don't you?"

"I live by it, but sometimes things are not so simple."

"What are you so scared of?"

John could not believe he was having this conversation. Logan was even brighter than he had thought. The urge to sweep her into his arms and never let go rushed over him again like a sudden gust of wind. But following the first gust was another equally strong; his operational side screamed at him to be careful. John didn't trust her father, so why did he think he could trust her?

He said suddenly. "You're very beautiful."

Logan looked away and said nothing. He felt her awkwardness and fought for something neutral to say.

"How long have you lived here?"

She smiled. "My father and mother bought the island nine years ago. I've lived here for the last five."

"I'm sorry about Greg."

Logan turned sharply and stared at John. He immediately recognized his mistake. "Your father…"

"My father had no business discussing Greg with you."

John ran his hand through his hair as grief blew over him. Why did he care so? Why did he feel that each word mattered so much? He fought his frustration and said, "Let's try again. It's a lovely day, don't you think?"

Logan could not help but smile. "Beautiful."

"What did you do today?"

"Rode my horse, Sunrise, and took a swim in the ocean. And you?"

"I walked the city streets of Santa Barbara, bought some clothes—I needed something to wear ¯ and I thought about you."

Logan blushed. "Are you always so forward?"

"No, but awkwardness makes a man do funny things."

"You don't strike me as the awkward type."

"Normally, no, but then again I've never met you before."

She shook her head. "You're a rather strange man."

"Funny, maybe, but not strange."

"We better head inside," Logan suggested. "Dinner will be served soon."

"I'm sorry about earlier," John said. She nodded as their eyes met. He saw her pain.

"I know. I'm sorry too. I loved Greg."

* * *

The table was set for three. Logan, John, and Davenport took their seats.

The billionaire sported a dark blue Giorgio Armani jacket. His white button-down shirt, opened at the collar, revealed a tanned chest. The white and blue combo went well with his eyes and white hair. His slacks were gray and pleated. On the other hand, John wore khaki Dockers pants, purchased in Santa Barbara that morning. He had not brought a jacket, no doubt a social faux pas in the eyes of Davenport, a man who appeared to take his dress seriously.

Davenport sampled the red wine poured by the servant. "That's great, Jean."

"A beautiful place you have here," John commented.

"I'm glad you like it," Davenport said. "I think you'll like the wine too. It's Jordan 1992 Cabernet Sauvignon from Alexander Valley." Davenport placed his napkin on his lap as he looked at John.

"I know very little about wines," John said. "My father enjoyed them, but I was too young to pay a lot of attention."

"Never too late to learn." Davenport took a sip from his glass. He looked over the top, his attention focused on John. "Logan, I hope you gave Pete a small tour."

"I did my best, father."

He smiled at her, then returned his attention to John. "I'm glad you could make it for dinner tonight. Logan and I are both delighted."

"Thanks for asking," John replied, reflecting on how he had come to be at their dinner table. He looked at Logan and she smiled.

"Do your folks live in the Washington area?"

"They used to," John said slowly.

"Pardon me for asking," Davenport said delicately, "but the way you just said it leads me to believe they are both dead."

"Father," Logan pleaded, her tone firm. "What an awful thing to say."

John took a forkful of his salad as the servant who had poured the wine retreated to the kitchen. He considered his response as he chewed. He sensed that Davenport already knew his parents were dead. How would that be? He looked at Logan. "It's okay. My father died in a car accident in West Virginia six years ago; he plummeted off a roadside cliff. It was a rainy night. And my mother, well, she died of cancer, breast cancer."

"I'm dreadfully sorry," Davenport said, genuine concern in his voice. "What line of work was your father in?"

"The Navy," John replied, "though I can't remember him ever setting foot on a ship. His assignments were usually at our embassies. I suspect he worked for the Defense Intelligence Agency, though I never asked. He was a secretive man."

"Very interesting," Davenport commented. He ate a forkful of salad before continuing. "As I said last night, I worked for the CIA a long time ago. I got out in 1954 after a meeting went bad. I was wounded and lucky to live."

"Wow. Where was that?" John asked. His brother had been fond of that word.

"Berlin. It was a difficult time. The Stazi was everywhere."

John knew the Stazi had been the name for the East German secret police. They were notorious for their ruthlessness. Now that Germany was a unified country with no legitimate place for the Stazi or its members, the old institution had been dismantled. It was hard times for ex–Stazi officials, and consequently many members found work in less than legal occupations. Quite a few of them were hired guns now that the Berlin Wall had come tumbling down.

"What embassies did your father post to?" Davenport asked. He seemed anxious to change the topic away from himself.

"I'm not sure of them all," John said as he glanced at Logan. She concentrated on her salad. "When my mother was still alive, we stayed in the States, as best I can remember. After she died our father took us with him. We spent five years in Tokyo and then another three in Bangkok and finally five in Baghdad. We returned to the States in 1975 and lived in Arlington, Virginia."

"Where did you go to school?" Davenport asked.

"I went to Taft, in Connecticut. I graduated in 1981. I only made it through one year of college."

"Your mother must have died when you were only one," Davenport speculated.

"You're correct," John acknowledged, as he took a long sip of his wine. It was very good, as was Davenport's math. John realized the billionaire was committing each detail to memory. He suspected Davenport was the type to check a guy's background, but John doubted it meant a search all the way back to year one. Had something triggered a deeper interest? John could not help but feel suspicious of Davenport. His eyes were cold and calculating, so unlike Logan's. She had her father's eyes, but hers were warm, if cautiously so.

"You've done so much," Davenport insisted.

"We've been fortunate," John replied.

"You said we?" Davenport said after he sipped his wine. "Do you have a sister?"

John sat back in his chair to give the servant more room to clear his empty salad plate. The action gave him a few moments to think. The question was an interesting one. John doubted a man like Davenport would assume a sister before a brother. Maybe he was reading too much into the question; Davenport did, after all, have only a daughter. No matter, John's sonar had just gone active.

"Actually, I have a brother. His name is John."

"What does he do?"

"He's an ex–Navy SEAL and commanded SEAL Team Six."

"If he was a commander, he must have gone to college," Davenport stated. "Where did he go?"

"Father, why don't you ask him to write a biography before dinner."

Davenport looked at his daughter, a thin smile on his face.

"Logan, you should know me better. People's backgrounds fascinate me."

"I do know you, father, and that's the point. I believe our guest had hoped for a more lighthearted discussion."

"Logan, it's okay," John said, realizing it was not okay. She was mad at her father. John wondered how the elder Davenport would react.

"Logan, what did you do today?" her father asked.

John and Logan looked at each other.

"What's so funny?" Davenport demanded.

"Nothing, father," Logan answered, a smile still on her face. "I spent the morning with Sunrise and took a swim. It was such a beautiful day, don't you think?"

"Well, yes it was," Davenport said, still unsure of their reactions. John could see the elder man's frustration. He clearly liked to be in control.

"Pete, after dinner I was hoping we might have more time to chat," Davenport proposed.

"I'd enjoy that, sir."

"All business, that's my father," Logan remarked.

"Dear, please, we have a guest," Davenport said with a smile. "Pete, she can be so difficult."

"I can see that," John said.

* * *

"A drink?" Davenport asked as he shut the study's French doors.

"No. I'm fine," John replied.

"It was good of you to come."

"It would have been a hard offer to refuse."

"I suppose," Davenport said as he took a seat next to John on the small sofa. "I'm a man who likes to get his way."

John wondered if last night was just a dress rehearsal. "Nothing wrong with that."

"No, I suppose not," he agreed, "but I didn't ask you here to discuss me. So let me get right to the point. Pete, I sense you are in some kind of trouble. I'd like to help."

John studied Davenport closely. This man wanted something. As he had said, he was a person who liked to get his way. What did he want? What could John possibly mean to him? Maybe Davenport just wanted to know why he had met with Maxwell.

"Is it money, Pete?"

"No, sir."

"Please, call me Alex."

"Sorry, Alex."

"Pete, you had Senator Bennett set up a meeting with Maxwell. For some reason the senator insisted on my gala. I definitely know it was not Maxwell's idea; we don't exactly like each other, but that's another matter. Pete, I can help if I know what is going on."

John considered what Davenport had said. Maxwell and he hated each other and the senator knew it. That was an interesting piece of information and confirmed his suspicion. He wondered if that was what had piqued Davenport's interest.

"You're quite perceptive," John said. "I find myself in a tight spot."

"Is it money?" Davenport asked again.

"No, it's not money," John replied. "I did something that almost got me killed." He paused, hoping to give Davenport the impression that the topic was difficult for him. Finally he continued. "Until last week I had a contract with a firm named Security International Group, better known as SIG. You would have no reason to know them. It's a small firm by your standards. Anyway, I thought they were a company providing personal protection to the rich and famous. While programming a new accounting application for them, I stumbled on data that gave me cause for concern. I passed it on to the police."

Davenport nodded. "What type of information?"

"Accounting information that strongly suggested that SIG did a lot of business with a drug cartel."

"What did the police say when you handed them the information?"

"I e-mailed it to them anonymously. I never spoke to them. The next day I was at my hotel and a gunman started shooting. People were killed. I was lucky to survive."

"This happened in Washington, didn't it?"

John confirmed with a nod.

"I read about it. The Marriott Hotel on Pennsylvania Avenue. My God, all the reports said it was a massacre. Are you sure the gunman was after you?"

"I think so," John replied.

"If my memory serves me right," Davenport said, "I believe a DEA agent died in the attack. Couldn't the gunman's target have been this man?"

"Maybe," John said, as he realized that Davenport had done his homework. "I just don't believe in coincidences of this magnitude."

"Neither do I," Davenport agreed knowingly. "Neither do I. Did Maxwell help you?"

"Yes and no," John answered. "The senator told me Maxwell had a deep knowledge of Colombia. I had hoped he could shed some light on the people I'm forced to deal with."

"Nasty bastards, I suspect."

"I agree."

"What do you plan to do?"

John sighed. "I don't really know."

Davenport nodded as he looked away from John, apparently in deep thought. John did not trust the man for a moment, but that did not mean he could not be extremely useful.

"Where is your brother now? He sounds like the safest person you could have by your side."

"I don't want to involve him," John insisted. "It's my problem, not his."

"Noble of you, but what are brothers for?" Davenport pressed.

"If he led SEAL Team Six, you have one helluva brother, a trained killer really."

John considered Davenport's comment. Was he trying to piss off Pete, or John? He had a nagging feeling that Davenport already knew John was pretending to be Pete, as unlikely as that seemed.

"Yes, I suppose he has killed," John said coolly.

"Killed," Davenport repeated. "Son, that's what Navy SEALs do. They kill people for the US government in all the godforsaken places on this earth. They are this country's elite warriors, one of our lethal weapons."

John decided it was time to do what he had planned ever since Davenport had invited him back to the island. "Pete's dead."

"Excuse me?" Davenport stared at him. John could tell that Davenport had not expected the truth so quickly.

"I'm John. Pete is dead, killed at the Marriott."

"A Pete Thompson was not listed as a victim as far as I'm aware," Davenport said, his face emotionless.

"You've done your homework," John replied. "The DEA agent, he was really my brother."

"Your brother worked for the DEA?" asked a surprised Davenport. Now it was John's turn to nod, a small lie wrapped in the truth. Let Davenport learn if it was a lie. Maybe it would lead him to those in the government who were creating the fiction.

"Very interesting." Davenport stood. "I take it you don't believe your brother's death is an end of things. How come?"

John took a moment to answer. "The DEA wouldn't allow me to see the body. It was cremated almost immediately. Also, they won't return my calls."

"Most unusual. So you think your brother is still alive?"

John ignored the question. "I do know a thing or two about government dirty tricks. I'm sure you do too. Something smells."

"You might be right," Davenport acknowledged. "What can I do?"

"Alex, it's not your problem."

"Bullshit, John. I can help you, and you're going to need it."

"But really, it's my problem. Maybe I'm wrong, and the DEA performed a bureaucratic miracle and had my brother's body cremated in less than twenty-four hours. I just don't know."

"I understand, John, I truly do. Please accept my offer. I know everyone in Washington who is anyone. Ask the senator if you don't believe me. If I had to guess, I bet the senator hoped you and I would have a chance to talk. Maxwell was just an excuse to get you here. That's why the senator insisted the meeting take place here on the island."

John had not considered that angle. No matter, John gave in to what he'd wanted all along.

"Alex, I'd appreciate your help."

"May I make another suggestion?"

"Sure."

"Stay here for a few days. Let me make some calls. You'll be safe here and out of harm's way."

John liked the idea for more than operational reasons. He was slightly angry with himself. He needed to stay focused. "That's very generous of you."

* * *

John left Davenport in his study and started to make his way to his room on the second floor. He was content with how the meeting had gone. Davenport had said he would help. He hoped the man's help would bring some benefits. He did not trust him, but maybe John would learn something. However, that was only the half of it.

Davenport now knew the truth and Logan didn't. She must not learn the truth from her father. John heard a TV down the wide hallway of the house and headed in that direction. He did not know how this would go, but he had to do it. Maybe she would hate him for it. In a way, it would make things easier.

The door to the small study was open, and he could just see Logan's head above the top of the sofa. An unfamiliar movie played on the screen.

"Logan."

She craned her head in his direction and smiled.

"Sorry to disturb you."

"Don't be ridiculous," Logan insisted. "Have a seat."

He did so, wondering where he would start.

"Did you and father have a good talk?"

"Yes, I guess we did."

She did not say anything for a moment. "What's wrong, Pete?"

"I've lied to you."

She looked at him, trying to read his expression. It was time to dive in. He wondered how cold the waters would get.

"My real name is John Thompson. My brother Pete was killed a few days ago in the gun battle at the Marriott."

John looked at Logan as she pretended to watch the movie. He could not remember a time when he had felt so awkward. "I'm sorry."

"You've said that a lot today."

"I guess I have."

"Did you tell my father this?"

"Yes."

Logan faced John and reached for his hands. "I'm sorry about your brother."

John tried to imagine what she was thinking, suspecting her mind was filling with her husband's death. "The pain, it comes like waves. It's unexpected."

She nodded knowingly.

John pulled her close, wrapping his strong arms around her waist; she did not resist. She studied him intently at close range. "I'm afraid I don't understand you."

It took John ten minutes to explain the events of the past week.

"And what did you do in the Navy?"

"I was a SEAL."

"You've killed people."

"Only when absolutely necessary."

"But you have killed?"

"Yes."

John watched her eyes as she considered his answer. He saw a mixture of fear and worry.

"Logan." John stopped, unsure how he should continue. "Look at me."

Their eyes locked. "Logan, I'm sorry. I'm not thinking clearly. I..."

"It's okay."

"No, it's not."

A tear ran from her eye, and John used his thumb to sweep it from her face. He pulled her closer, feeling her warmth radiate through him. Human touch could be magical. Until that moment he did not realize how much he had yearned for it. Minutes passed.

John broke the silence. "I wish we could have met under different circumstances."

"At least we met," she said after a moment. "God knows why, but I'm drawn to you."

John did not know what to say as he felt the pressure of her hug. He hugged her back. Logan lifted her head and looked John in the eyes.

"Logan, I don't know what to think."

She ran a hand down the side of his face. "Neither do I."

"It's late. I should go."

She nodded. "You're not leaving tomorrow, are you?"

"Your father suggested I stay. He plans to make a few inquires in Washington for me."

"Do you want to go sailing tomorrow?"

"I'd like that, but I'll need to find some shorts."

Logan smiled. "I'm sure we can make do. By the way, you do know how to sail?"

"I've done it once or twice." John smiled and stood. "Thanks for listening. I needed to talk with someone. I'm glad it was you. Goodnight."

"Sleep well," Logan said.

She watched John leave the study. His revelations had shaken her. She had felt his awkwardness almost immediately the previous night and again as they had stood on the point. Both times it had struck her as odd. Repeatedly she had asked herself what drove a handsome, intelligent man to moments of insecurity. Now she knew. Someone he loved had been viciously taken from his life. She could feel his raw pain, so similar to hers. She shuddered as she brought her legs tight to her chest and wrapped her arms about them. The pain came in waves, striking at any time and without warning. If only it could be predicted, controlled.

As she rocked back and forth, attempting to comfort her own mind, she realized something deeper. Five years had passed since Greg had died, five years she had spent in self-imposed exile on the family island. In all that time she had never once felt as she did now. The craving, she'd thought she might never feel it again. She was falling in love with John. It seemed so silly. She hardly knew him. He had lied to her, and he represented many things that she despised—guns and killing. And why now? She still loved Greg. Could she love two men? Was that fair to either of them?

She leaned into the soft pillows of the couch as a few tears wandered from her eyes. The pillows felt soft, comforting. She wished that they could reach out and hug her, the way John had. She could still smell John on the fabric, still feel his strong arms locked around her. His chest was hard with muscle, his hair soft, and his eyes sharp. She pressed her face deeper into the pillows. Why did things have to be so complicated? Her spirit cried out for simplicity, for order instead of the madness all around, but life continued to deliver something different.

8 A Meeting in Paris

The view from the bluff was breathtaking; she had always thought so. Several constellations dominated the night sky: the Big Dipper and the Northern Cross were two she recognized. She watched him for a moment as she listened to the water break against the rocks on the beach below. His concentration appeared locked on the star-filled sky.

Even from twenty feet a formidable feeling emanated from him. His hair fell lightly onto his broad shoulders, which were covered by a thin white T-shirt. During their day of sailing he had removed his shirt. His powerful body had aroused her. His movements were precise and measured. He certainly knew how to sail, but there was more. He was funny, even though he never quite lost his air of seriousness.

Now, as they stood on the bluff, she wondered what he was thinking. Did he relish the peaceful, private island she called home? Did he sense that she was hiding from the world here, paralyzed by her memories of Greg? Did he realize he had awakened a part of her that had all but disappeared?

Her thoughts turned to Greg. In the five years since his death she had only determined that the event had been an end. She knew for certain that her life had changed. How was the only remaining question. She found herself staring down a path, not necessarily of her choosing. Or was it?

He interrupted her thoughts. "What a great view."

"It is," she replied, excited that he felt that way. The silence fell again. Minutes passed until John turned and looked at her. She brought her eyes up to meet his.

"What a day. Thanks."

She smiled in the darkness. "I'm glad you feel better, at least a little."

"I do, but . . ." He hesitated. "I can't believe my brother has been dead only a week."

She felt a frown cross her face; she did not want him to think about his brother, not now. John reacted to her expression and instantly she regretted her thought. It was selfish. She reached out for him.

"I'm running a little scared," he said, a hint of awkwardness in his voice as he pressed against her.

"I know and it's okay," Logan said. She considered his face. Her hand ran through his brown hair. "You're still not telling me everything, are you?"

She watched him look past her toward the Pacific. Seconds passed. "Am I that easy to read?"

"No," she answered quickly, afraid to scare him. "I just have a sense. I'm being nosy. That's all."

Logan felt his warmth, his strength, and his beauty, relishing them all; even his fears gave her strength. He needed her and she needed him.

He returned her gaze for a while before speaking. "I'm having a hard time understanding how I could meet someone like you under such conflicting circumstances. I must uncover the truth about my brother's death and yet I'm so drawn to you."

His pain troubled her. She knew how it felt, but she had a sixth sense that his brother's death wasn't the only thing burdening him. She wondered if she was part of the problem. She desperately wanted to know, even though the truth scared her. "Tell me, what's really bothering you?"

She felt his arms tighten around her waist. She welcomed his strong grip. He gave her a pained look. "I don't know if you're friend or foe."

She stared at him, unsure of what he meant. Friend for sure, she thought. "Me?"

"Yes."

She stared at John. "Do you work for the CIA?"

He shook his head. "You know the truth. I've hidden nothing. I'm just an ex–Navy SEAL. That's all."

She realized again how much he needed her and it excited her. Her hand stroked his hair again, pushing it behind his ear. "I didn't know military men had such long hair."

He smiled. "Our team had a broad latitude when it came to grooming. The less we looked like military men, the more effective we were in hostile situations. Many of our operations required that we sneak into a country, perform surveillance, and hit the target–tangos, we called them. I've kept the look."

"Sounds dangerous," Logan said, wondering how many men he had killed. The thought sent a shiver through her, but she focused her attention on his hair, afraid her eyes would reveal her thoughts. "Why did you get out of the Navy?"

"That's a long story."

She realized she wanted to know everything there was to know about him. She wanted to help him, love him, and kiss him, but what about Greg? He'd understand, wouldn't he? This man needed her love. Resolve washed over her. "We have all night, don't we?"

Surprise registered on his face. He looked into her eyes, and she returned his steady gaze. He moved gently, kissing her on the lips, the sensation overwhelming as he reached behind her head and drew her tight. After a few moments he pulled away.

"I'm so glad you're here," Logan said, unable to control herself any longer. She kissed him again, savoring the viselike grip that lifted her off the ground. Her need grew stronger.

"I'm scared," Logan confided. "Something draws me to you and yet you represent everything I loathe. Violence is so ugly."

He looked deeply into her eyes. "I am very good at what I do. I have killed men. It was my duty; my survival depended on it. I'm a warrior. I don't fear death. It's important that you understand these things. But I can love and want to love. I'm loyal to the bone."

Logan pushed away from him gently, knowing what she wanted next. "Let's take a walk on the beach. Follow me." She started to run. He did not follow her immediately, but when he did he caught up to her quickly with his powerful strides. She was very excited.

* * *

John found his mind wandering as he held the newspaper, having managed only to read the first few pages of the *New York Times*.

Logan and he had just spent their third day together. He was completely enthralled by her. They had spent the three days sailing, swimming, and making love. He felt both overjoyed and appalled by the relationship. He knew he was falling deeply in love with Logan and she with him. That excited him, but it was happing so quickly and so soon after his brother's murder. Guilt enveloped him.

They had established a routine: breakfast outdoors, soaking in the morning sun on the patio that stood a short distance from the beautiful S-shaped pool. The patio offered an unobstructed view of the Santa Barbara Channel to the east. Behind lay the house and the windows of Davenport's office. John greatly enjoyed this setting and Logan's company. He enjoyed reading the *New York Times* as he ate breakfast, Logan's beauty silhouetted against the magnificent surroundings, but the situation had become complicated. From where he sat, he could frequently overhear Davenport's phone conversations.

John's mind returned to his immediate surroundings as his ears picked up Davenport's voice again through the office windows. The man was speaking Russian. He listened, the words unmistakably clear. Suddenly his worst fears were confirmed.

John folded the newspaper and placed it on his lap. He had always known he could not stay on Davenport's island, glued to his daughter like a high school sweetheart. He had business to attend to. He had to find his brother's killers and anyone else who had had a hand in Pete's demise. How would Logan react when he decided to leave? And now John feared the worst; her father was somehow involved. His stomach turned with anger.

Logan looked up from her reading and saw his grim face. He cursed himself.

"What's wrong?"

A thousand thoughts raced through John's mind, all searching for an explanation of why Davenport would be speaking to a Russian general named Leonov. None of the explanations made John feel comfortable, especially considering what he had just heard.

John was not surprised that Davenport spoke Russian. Many CIA operatives, especially those working against the KGB's efforts in Asia during the Vietnam War, had needed the skill. John felt certain Davenport fell into this category. The question, however, was what business Davenport had with a Russian general.

"Nothing's wrong." John held up the newspaper. "Just the news."

"Oh," Logan said.

* * *

John knocked on Davenport's office door.

"Come in."

"Alex, I'm hope I'm not intruding."

"Don't be ridiculous," Davenport insisted. "Having fun?"

John hesitated, caught between his feelings for Logan and his desire to hunt his brother's executioners. His hesitation gave him time to examine the many papers on the billionaire's desk. One caught his attention as he said, "Yes, but I'm feeling a little anxious."

"About what?" Davenport inquired.

John moved closer to Davenport's desk. "My brother. Have you learned anything yet?"

"No, not much," Davenport answered. "What I know so far matches your findings. I do have calls in to a few people, but they have yet to call back."

John considered Davenport's response; it was wrong. When a man like Alex Davenport called, people returned his calls promptly. The man was lying to him. As John considered his next step, his eyes studied a printed e-mail message lying on Davenport's desk. It was in Russian. John took a chance and picked up the memo.

"Alex, is this Russian?"

Davenport reached quickly, grabbing the piece of paper from John's hand. "Yes," Davenport replied, his tone indicating his anger.

John responded quickly. "I hear that's a tough language."

"I suppose. I hate to be rude, but I must make a call. I'll keep you posted, John. Just relax and enjoy yourself."

John nodded. "Thanks, Alex."

He let himself out of the man's office and exited the house through the same French doors through which he had stepped into Davenport's world four nights earlier. John was not surprised. He had never trusted the man and had only enlisted his support to ferret out the players in the US government who had taken a keen interest in Pete's affairs.

John considered the contents of the memo, the two sentences easily visible in his mind's eye—a meeting in Paris, six days from now, between a Russian named Trubkin and an Arab named Yousef. John recognized both names. No matter how hard he tried to convince himself that the two men could be anyone, he knew this was not the case. It would be too great a coincidence.

John's thoughts jumped back to his last assignment as a Navy SEAL.

From John's perch three hundred yards away, he watched the two men step into his view after giving the chefs their instructions. This was tradition at the Fish Market, one of Bangkok's finest restaurants.

John had eaten at the Fish Market many times and knew the restaurant's routine well; it was one of his favorite restaurants in the city. The freshness of the food was hard to beat and the chefs were recognized as some of the best in all of Bangkok. He and his brother had spent memorable nights with their father in the restaurant twenty years ago.

He shook these thoughts from his mind as he peered through the scope mounted on his 7-millimeter Remington Magnum sniper rifle.

John lay prone on the third floor of an unfinished building. It stood across the street from the Fish Market. The building, a nondescript cement structure typical of Bangkok, was in the midst of refurbishing and offered a perfect place to stage his mission. He had an unobstructed view of the restaurant dining area, which was outdoors except for the tentlike roof. Sukhumvit Road ran southeast from this point and created the expanse that separated John from his quarry.

The street was busy with the usual Bangkok traffic, a collection of automobiles, taxis, tuk-tuks, and buses that belched black smoke. The grime of the city stuck like a layer of plaster. John welcomed the dirt and constant din of Bangkok life. It was the perfect city in which to dispatch his quarry to Allah.

He brought his target into focus. He made a slight adjustment, and the image cleared. His target, Abdel Khabbani, an accomplished Arab terrorist who had preyed once too often on American citizens abroad, took a seat. John considered it his luck that the target had chosen a restaurant he knew so well. It made his job easier.

He focused his attention on his target

John was ready to take the shot. The distance was less than three hundred yards and there was little or no wind. However, he altered his aim and his scope's eyepiece filled with the features of Khabbani's guest.

The guest was a well-built man, probably in his early forties. His dark hair was cut short and he had a military bearing. His suit, John guessed, was from London; it had that look and cut. The man's Slavic face was tanned, his eyes black. John attempted to read his lips. He thought the two men were speaking French, but he could not be sure. He knew only a smattering of French, a passable amount at best.

These things did not interest him as much as the tattoo on the inside of the man's right arm. John recognized it as a tattoo worn by Russian mob members. He could not recall the mob. Nevertheless, he would remember the face. That would be enough for the debriefers in Virginia Beach.

John adjusted the scope and increased the magnification until he could look into the Russian's right eye. He made the adjustments with practiced movements. He did not like what he saw. What would an Arab terrorist and a member of a Russian mob have in common? Weapons? Conventional or nuclear? Not a pretty thought. Old Ivan could never be trusted, especially in today's Russia of economic anarchy.

John contemplated ending the Russian's life, but his orders did not allow it. Besides, hitting two targets would significantly increase the difficulty of the mission, a risk he was not willing to take. His mission in Bangkok was straightforward: send Khabbani to his maker. It was time.

John recaptured Khabbani in his sights with the smallest of movements, selecting a spot a half inch above the terrorist's left eye. A half inch was the amount the bullet would drop on its 0.03-second journey across the expanse that lay between John and the restaurant. He felt sweat trickle down the side of his face. He let his breath out slowly. His body was perfectly still. With practiced precision, he applied six pounds of pressure to the trigger.

Khabbani's head exploded like a watermelon dropped from a third-floor window. Blood bathed the Russian and diners at two adjacent tables. Chaos filled the restaurant as the patrons realized it was blood and not food that had flown through the upscale eatery. John watched the Russian react. He was quick, dropping to the floor and rolling away from the table, finally coming up on one knee behind four patrons who were still trying to understand what had happened. The Russian was looking directly at John. He had instantly guessed where the sniper lay. John knew without a doubt that he was looking at another professional. Time to leave.

John rolled away from his perch toward the back of the building. When he knew he was out of the line of sight, he stood. He ripped off his shooting suit. Quickly he jogged down the four flights of stairs and exited into a dark alley that cut behind the building. As he reached the alley, John dropped the gun in a grimy dumpster positioned a few feet from the building. A single spent shell casing followed the gun. The Mossad, the Israeli intelligence agency, favored both items for such assignments. They had been selected for precisely that reason.

John continued jogging until he reached the sidewalk of Soi Asoke, a street that ran perpendicular to Sukhumvit Road. He slowed to a walk so as not to attract unwanted attention.

Waiting on the curb was a tuk-tuk, a local three-wheeled taxi, a common sight in Bangkok. Its driver was another Navy SEAL, seaman first class Eddy Mothers, known as Mother. He was dressed in local attire, while John had the look of a western tourist. Mother's build was small and wiry, much like a Thai's, and his skin was dark, a sign of his Puerto Rican descent.

John climbed effortlessly into the back of the tuk-tuk. Mother gunned the engine, and the tuk-tuk shot into the traffic with a roar.

The mission had gone perfectly to plan, John reflected, and now it seemed that Trubkin was at it again.

Nikolai Fyodorovich Trubkin was an ex-KGB colonel who offered his talents to the criminal elements of Russia. He had been Adbel Khabbani's dinner guest in Bangkok. He was a worthy adversary and one in whom the US government had taken a keen interest. The government suspected that Trubkin had maintained close ties with his old KGB masters, now the SVR. The memo confirmed that possibility, and John suspected he now knew the name of Trubkin's real master–a General Leonov.

The other party scheduled to attend the Paris meeting was Ramzi Ahmed Yousef, a Pakistani. No one but he knew his real name and for whom he worked, but one thing was certain: he was a practiced terrorist. The US government believed Yousef to be the mastermind of the World Trade Centers bombing the previous year. Five people had been killed in the blast and hundreds injured.

John turned his mind to a larger question. Why was Davenport interested in this meeting, and what did he and the general have brewing? Nothing that came to mind made John relax. Nothing good could arise from a relationship involving a Russian general, an Arab terrorist, an ex-KGB agent, and Alex Davenport.

John considered his next move. It was obvious. Paris. However, he first needed to stop in Washington. He needed to attend to a few details there. And Logan—how would he explain his quick departure to her?

* * *

Logan felt the twenty-five-foot Boston Whaler rise as she moved the throttle forward to its stops, the powerful twin Mercury engines grinding through the salt water. She glanced once over her shoulder, catching John standing at the end of the Santa Barbara pier, his small travel bag at his feet, staring after her. She did not wave as the wind broke over her forehead, making her hair snap around her head. Its small lashes were a welcome distraction from her troubled thoughts.

She felt angry, cheated. Damn him. After four incredible days—breathtaking days—how could he suddenly get up and leave without any notice? What had changed? What could drive a man to such a sudden act?

She desperately wanted to turn the boat around, crash it into the dock if necessary, and follow John to wherever he was headed. It made her so mad. What was it about him that unleashed such thoughts? Yes, he was gorgeous, incredibly strong, intelligent, caring, and a man, but what drove her emotions to these unknown heights? What if she never saw him again? The thought horrified her, paralyzed her.

Suddenly she pulled the throttles back as her eyes filled with tears. It was too much.

When she finally looked up, she had no idea how much time had passed since she had halted the boat's dash across the smooth surface of Santa Barbara Harbor. She looked back toward the city, but the dock was a speck among many others. She knew John was long gone. The thought sent another wave of sadness through her, rocking her to her core. She was in love with a man she barely knew. What had she done?

9 | Positioning

Dan Myers sat across from James Lewis, the director of the CIA. He noted the grim look on the director's face. Dan was not surprised as he ran a finger along his white mustache. The pressure was building, as it should be.

Dan had never eaten at La Chaumière, an elegant French restaurant a few short blocks from the center of Georgetown. Their table was pushed back in a corner, making it hard for anyone to notice them without approaching directly. Dan assumed that Director Lewis had requested this particular table for this very reason.

The DCI took a long sip from his Scotch as Dan attended to his gin and tonic. The scene reminded Dan of the meeting they had had only ten days earlier. On that day, Lewis had called him at home, requesting a meeting at another discreet restaurant. The director had claimed that he had a particularly difficult problem requiring Dan's expertise.

Before that call Dan had been resting comfortably in the confines of retirement. He had retired sixteen months earlier, ending a thirty-seven-year career at the CIA, the last ten years as Deputy Director of Special Operations. The last six months had been particularly difficult after he and his wife had learned that she had cancer. At first they had thought she might recover, but after a few months of chemotherapy it had become apparent that her time was limited.

Dan had made his decision to leave the CIA suddenly. His

wife needed him, and he could not leave her alone while she suffered a painful end. Also, the new administration had been elected, and he did not enjoy the prospects it would bring to Washington and the agency. Enough was enough.

Dozens of senior government officials from a variety of agencies had urged him to take a leave of absence so he could return after his wife recovered, though they all knew she would not.

He still thought of her every day, wishing he had spent more time with her. His dedication to his job had cost them valuable hours together. He knew he had cheated his marriage in this way. She had always stood by his side no matter what ungodly demands the CIA placed on him. He hated to admit it, but the job had always come before his relationship with her. She had deserved better, particularly after Tim had died in Vietnam. She had always carried sadness with her after learning of her son's death. The news had devastated them both. Dan's only salvation lay in his role at the CIA, which allowed him to strike back at the evil in the world. It could not replace Tim, but at least it was something. His wife had never enjoyed such an outlet.

And now Dan found himself working again, running a secret operation way outside normal channels. The death of a young man named Pete Thompson two blocks from the White House had given the CIA cause for concern. In Dan's eyes the young man's death marked an end of a ball of string. Once someone started pulling on it, it was only a matter of time until the whole ball unwound.

"Sir, I appreciate your seeing me on such short notice," Dan began. The director nodded. "I need a favor, but first please read this intercept."

He handed the director the fax he had received from California.

TOP SECRET

TO: 011-57-53-656-447 **Doc #:** AZL-234-873H

FROM: 310-547-3210

Date: 09/03/93 **Copy:** 1 of 1
Time: 07:08 PST
Duration: 2.54 Minutes
Translator: 3426

Maxwell: ¿Señor, como está usted?

El Gordo: Estoy bien. ¿Y usted?

Maxwell: I am well. Unfortunately I am calling on a small business matter. It came to my attention, and I thought you might be interested.

El Gordo: Please continue.

Maxwell: I spoke with a young man two nights ago. He was from Washington. He was interested in knowing about your relationship with Petrov.

El Gordo: We are social friends, Petrov and I, no?

Maxwell: He suspects differently. He knows Petrov is SVR. He thinks you are selling drugs to the SVR.

El Gordo: (Pause) That is most unfortunate. Who is this individual?

Maxwell: Pete Thompson.

El Gordo: Pete Thompson?

Maxwell: Yes, Pete Thompson. It appears that someone tried to kill him last week. He spoke with the person he believes set him up. He says this man mentioned your name and Petrov's. He was asking me for background information.

El Gordo: How did he get your name?

Maxwell: That's interesting too. He appears to have a friend in Washington, a Senator William Bennett. He and I have been friends for a long time. He asked me to meet with Pete as a personal favor. I could not turn him down.

El Gordo: (Pause—2 Sec.) I see. What did he look like?

Maxwell: He was six foot, two-ten, or thereabout. Brown

eyes and long brown hair. Athletic looking. Intense. Angry. What's this all about?

El Gordo: I don't know. I don't know a Pete Thompson. I will have to ask around. If he is interested in me, then I must be interested in him. You said he thinks I tried to kill him?

Maxwell: That's what he said. Seems difficult if you say you don't know him.

El Gordo: I appreciate your call, Alan. The information could be useful. I must go now. Thank you again. When is your next trip to our country? Soon, I hope.

Maxwell: There was one other thing he said.

El Gordo: And what was that?

Maxwell: He believes SIG had a hand in the death of Vincent Foster.

El Gordo: (Pause—6 Sec.) How can that be?

Maxwell: I said as much.

El Gordo: (Pause—3 Sec.) Thank you for the call. It has been most enlightening. I hope to see you soon.

Maxwell: Yes, certainly, soon.

"So John spoke with Simpson?" the director asked after he finished reading the conversation for a second time.

"Yes, I believe he did." Dan did not elaborate that he had had Simpson under surveillance and knew that John had scared the hell out of the ex–Army sergeant. The whole conversation was on tape, thanks to a neighbor living across the street who had agreed to let a team of DEA officers use his living room. They were not really DEA officers, but the neighbor never knew the difference.

"That part about Foster seemed to catch El Gordo by surprise," the director added.

"I had the same impression," Dan agreed. "I think it's valid to assume El Gordo is upset. He was not pleased to learn that people outside of SIG suspect the cartel had a hand in Vincent

Foster's death." Dan paused for a moment. He appeared to think out loud. "The logical question is, what did Foster do that affected the Cali cartel?"

"Foster had something to do with Whitewater," the director said. "He was the First Lady's lawyer. Real estate deals, even failed ones, require money. Maybe the cartel, through a front company or two, somehow became involved in the deal. Maybe they laundered money through one of the S & Ls that were involved. Remember, we saw McDougal's S & L listed on Thompson's e-mail that he sent the DEA."

Dan nodded. The same thought had occurred to him, but for different reasons. Ever since the Director Lewis had pulled him from retirement, Dan had given a great deal of thought to the CIA's predicament.

The director had been appalled by the possibility that a CIA informant working at SIG had had a hand in the death of Vincent Foster, the number-three legal counsel at the White House. The e-mail received by the authorities had mentioned a 1913 Colt .38-caliber pistol. A similar pistol had been used to end Foster's life. The pistol used to kill Foster had been one of a set, the second one having been recovered at Foster's house. However, as the director had explained in their first meeting, the second pistol had gone missing.

In addition, the e-mail had contained a list of SIG's customers, one of which was Madison Guarantee Savings and Loan. That particular institution had been mentioned in connection with the growing Whitewater scandal in Washington.

From the director's point of view, the whole scenario spelled trouble for the agency. Therefore the director had pulled Dan out of retirement and asked him to run a secret operation to uncover the truth.

"So it looks like they believe Pete is alive?" the director added, pulling Dan from his thoughts. "Would you agree?"

"Yes. The description given by Maxwell is the first convincing proof they've had that Pete is still alive. Simpson's encounter also suggested Pete is alive. Now they have someone they respect, who has no reason to lie, claiming that Pete Thompson visited him.

"In addition," Dan continued, "it appears John is using his brother's credit cards. I suspect he called the credit card companies, pretending to be his brother, and said he lost his wallet. They've obviously sent him replacement cards."

"I agree. He's leaving a deliberate trail. To anyone who's looking, it appears that Pete Thompson is alive and well."

" Interesting. Where is John now?" the DCI asked.

"Still in California," Dan said, a note of caution in his voice. "He missed his flight a few mornings ago. He made a reservation today for a flight back to Washington."

The director raised an eyebrow. "Do we know why?"

"Davenport's helicopter flew him to the island four days ago. He was there until this morning."

"Do you think Davenport offered to help him?" the director asked. "He certainly has the resources and the know-how to lend a hand, that is, to John."

Dan sensed the director's hesitancy. "Something bothering you about that?"

The director paused. "Just giving that possibility some thought."

"How well do you know Alex Davenport?"

"I've met him a number of times. Who in Washington hasn't? I know he is ex-CIA; however, that's about all."

Dan nodded but added nothing. The DCI changed the subject again.

"This Petrov guy, SVR. What do you make of that?"

"I'm not sure," Dan said. "Petrov is a common Russian name. I'm checking a number of sources now. We'll have to wait and see. Drug money is bad enough, but SVR involvement is something entirely different. I really don't see how they fit."

"But they might," suggested the director.

Dan had thought about this point. It was the real reason he

did not think the cartel had anything to do with Foster's death. If El Gordo had wanted Foster dead, he would not have used the SVR to kill him. He would have used one of his own or a contractor, as he had done for the hit on Pete Thompson. That meant that El Gordo had not had Foster killed. The SVR had.

"And what's the next step?" Lewis asked.

"I'd like to have the NSA monitor all calls made to El Gordo's private number listed on this transcript," Dan said as he turned his thoughts back to the conversation. "I need your help on this one. I could call a friend or two at the NSA, but I think it would be best if you made a quiet request to General Field."

The director took a moment to consider Dan's request. "I can arrange that, though I hate the thought of broadening the circle on this one. Do you want a search done against El Gordo's voice pattern on back tapes as well?"

"No, not yet," Dan replied. "I think things are developing. If we get nothing in a week or two, then let's consider that option. We don't want to get the NSA too excited. General Field isn't too close to the President, but no reason to push him."

"I know," agreed the director with a frown.

George Field was a three-star general who headed the National Security Agency, the heart and soul of the United States' sprawling signal intelligence operation.

"If he learns that we're sniffing around Foster's death," Dan suggested, "he could put a bug in the President's ear. We don't need that for a variety of reasons."

"That's for sure. Any suggestions?"

"Tell him you know SIG had a hand in killing the DEA agent," Dan suggested. "He'll never know an agent by that name died in Turkey unless he really digs. I doubt he will. Also, he'll know, or he can certainly find out, that SIG is closely linked to the Cali cartel. Tell him you would consider it a favor. He'll like the idea of you owing him one."

"It's a little out of our jurisdiction," the director complained. "It is unusual."

"A good point," Dan agreed, "but keeping an eye on the Cali cartel is not. They are a foreign threat, after all. I'd suggest pressing that angle."

"Your plan has merit, but I don't like the part about owing a three-star general." Lewis spoke with the required amount of political sarcasm. "I'll make the call today."

"Good," Dan replied. "I suggest that any conversation they catch be forwarded directly to your office, *eyes only*. I want everything, even the conversations about his latest female companion or pickup truck."

Dan knew the NSA could send information to the CIA, cross-decked by fiber optic cable, into Mercury, the CIA's communication facility, and then forward it to the CIA's operation center, Room 7-F-27 in the old headquarters building.

"Consider it done," Lewis said.

"I suspect we'll learn some interesting tidbits in the coming weeks. As the pressure builds, conversations will happen. We'll wait and see where they lead."

"Okay, I'm with you," the director of the CIA declared.

* * *

Admiral Sunders sat in Dan's home office, a cramped space filled with hundreds of books. The man behind the desk was sixty-five, had a strong handshake, sharp blue eyes, a broad white mustache, and a presence that could be physically felt. He wore a blue button-down shirt with his initials, DWM, monogrammed on the front pocket. His pants, white Dockers, hung loosely to the top of his expensive loafers.

"Read these," Dan ordered.

Sunders looked at the documents closely and immediately recognized them as intercepts. One was John's encounter with Simpson; the other two were El Gordo's phone conversations. Sunders read the first two and then started with the third one.

TOP SECRET

TO: 011-57-53-656-447 **Doc #:** AZL-235-874A
FROM: 310-547-3210
Date: 09/05/93 **Copy:** 1 of 1
Time: 09:18 PST
Duration: 4.14 Minutes
Translator: 3426

Unknown: Diga.
Davenport: El señor, por favor. (2.11 Min. pass until Gordo speaks.)
Gordo: ¿Sí?
Davenport: It's Davenport. How are you today?
Gordo: Así, así. The normal shit. And you and your lovely daughter?
Davenport: We are well. Thank you for asking. How is your family?
Gordo: All are well, thank you. How can I help you?
Davenport: I have a piece of information that you might find valuable.
Gordo: Really?
Davenport: It concerns George Simpson. I believe you are looking for him.
Gordo: Yes, we are still looking for him.
Davenport: I think you will find him in Singapore, staying at a house called the Silk House. If you would like, I can deal with him.
Gordo: You are very kind, but it is our business. We must attend to it. I'm sure that you understand. I hate to involve you more than you already are. I'm already in your debt.
Davenport: Do you want the phone number?
Gordo: You are, as usual, very thorough. Thank you, but I don't think the number will be necessary.
Davenport: My information tells me that he does not plan to move in the near future. You have a few days to make the arrangements. I'm confident that he will still be there. Are you sure I can't help further?

> **Gordo:** No, you have already helped enough. We must handle the rest of this ugly matter by ourselves. As you know, it is a matter of honor.
>
> **Davenport:** As you wish.
>
> **Gordo:** Buenas noches, Señor Davenport. Muchas gracias.

"This is serious," the admiral concluded. "Where is John now?"

"He left for Paris this afternoon from Dulles, using his brother's passport."

"Any ideas why?"

"No."

"I don't like it. He's running blind," the admiral insisted. "You need to bring him in, talk to him. Explain the bigger picture."

"Maybe, but I think it's too early. He's just beginning to stir the hornet's nest without our help."

"Dan, at least he should know about his father and Davenport," Sunders argued. "I don't think we want him to learn about that on his own. Let's face it, Davenport must know who John is. He might even suspect that John's visit was the beginning of an action directed against him."

"Possible, but John was close to him and nothing happened," Dan pointed out. "I suspect Davenport has discounted the possibility and is looking for another."

"Do you think Davenport sent him to Paris?"

"A possibility."

"Do you know where John is staying in Paris?"

"Not yet."

"You may never, if he starts using another passport," Sunders said. "Let's not forget who he is. He knows all about fake documents and how to obtain them."

"That concern has crossed my mind."

"We should bring him in," the admiral pressed.

"No, not yet," Dan answered coolly. "He couldn't handle it. He's struggling with the knowledge of his dead brother. That's enough."

The admiral did not like Dan's look. "What else do you know that you haven't told me?"

Dan did not answer immediately. "There is something else, you're right," Dan agreed. "I think John has fallen for Logan."

"What?" the admiral exclaimed. "You must be joking."

"I'm not certain yet," Dan said slowly, "but look at these pictures." He handed them to the admiral.

"This is unbelievable," the admiral declared with shock, as he tossed the pictures back on to Dan's desk. "How could you possibly send him to Davenport's? What were you thinking?"

"I haven't told you everything, nor can I," Dan explained. "All I'll say is that Davenport's fingerprints have been on this hot potato from the beginning. Do you know what's most interesting?"

"No."

"Davenport knows about his daughter and John. Now I find that downright curious."

The admiral leaned back in his chair and ran his hands through his short-cropped hair. Possibilities flashed though his mind. "Things are out of control."

"It's the nature of the beast."

The admiral insisted, "This is absurd. Let's pull him in."

"Too soon."

The admiral changed his tack. "He definitely knows someone is watching him."

"Yes, he is leaving an obvious trail," Dan agreed.

"Davenport must be pissed," Sunders said.

"I'm sure he is," Dan said. "Think of what must be going through his mind. He's the type to keep a close eye on his possessions. Think how he must have felt when he learned she was in love again and that person was Bill Thompson's son. It must have given him apoplexy."

The admiral nodded with a thin smile. "I guess he can't interfere without giving himself away."

"Exactly. He has bigger fish to fry. He has to allow the relationship to continue, otherwise he'll spook John."

"You're probably right," the admiral agreed. "Also, it would only drive his daughter away." The admiral paused for a moment. "Don't you think Davenport must have known why a Pete Thompson was added to the guest list?"

"No, I gave Senator Bennett strict instructions on that point," Dan explained. "I wanted to complicate things. At some point, Davenport realized John or Pete was at the party to meet Maxwell, whom he despises. It will only be a matter of time until he puts some pressure on the senator."

"You're a bastard, Dan, a real bastard."

"This is business, Admiral, and you know it. Davenport only plays in the stratosphere. We must know what he is up to."

"This thing is just too damn complicated," the admiral repeated.

Dan shrugged his shoulders.

"Mind you, if anything happens to John, I will hold you personally responsible. He's a good man, and he does not deserve to be a victim of your sorcery." The admiral stood.

"Trust me, Admiral."

"I almost wish I didn't," the admiral said as he turned to leave. "I'll be in touch."

10 A Paris Night

Rue St. Antoine was busy with the after-work crowd, which suited John perfectly as he sipped his coffee.

He had spent the last three hours sitting at Hippopotamus on the corner of rue de la Bastille. His attire, faded black pants, a brown turtleneck, and a black leather jacket, came from second-hand stores in Paris' Latin section, located along the boulevard St. Germain. He looked decidedly French.

He had spent his second day in Paris watching the area surrounding the Brasserie Bofinger, the oldest brasserie in Paris, careful to note the faces and the routines of those surrounding it. His Navy SEAL training was second nature to him, and it served him well. He realized that he had never stopped thinking from a SEAL point of view. He saw a building not as a thing of beauty, but as an obstacle to climb or destroy. His eighteen-month hiatus had done little to dull his operational skills. All those years of grueling training had left their mark. On his own he had kept up with his shooting and a rigorous exercise schedule, not at the same rate as when he was an active SEAL, but hopefully enough in his current circumstances.

He felt confident that his interest in the area had gone unnoticed. He looked like a young man with a lot of spare time, a drawing pad in his hands. His role was that of an American trying to be a French artist, living off his parents' wealth while despising them at the same time. It was a common enough story. The cover gave him the ability to wander aimlessly around the area, making sketches along the way. His drawings would win no prizes.

As the second day progressed, he began to learn the routines of the various storekeepers and restaurant workers making their living on the rue St. Antoine. It was a quiet thoroughfare just off the busy Place de la Bastille, a large circular intersection centered around the "Genius of Liberty" atop the Colonne de Juillet. On the other side of the intersection from the Brasserie Bofinger was the Opéra Bastille, a large glass structure that was a far cry from Paris's original opera, Opéra de Paris Garnier. The sidewalks of the café ebbed and flowed with people and gave him an unobstructed view of the brasserie and the intersection. The restaurant did a brisk business even though it was tucked away on the quiet rue de la Bastille. Unlike most Parisian brasseries, it did not have the space for an outdoor eating area on the sidewalk that ran by its front door. As a result, John had realized immediately that the meeting would take place inside the restaurant.

Throughout the two days, he had kept a watchful eye out for other individuals taking an interest in the Brasserie Bofinger. It was entirely conceivable that other parties knew about the meeting. A sophisticated crew of three to ten people would be hard to spot, particularly if they had leased a room in one of the surrounding buildings. The only hotel on the street, the Spéria, was next to the brasserie and faced the same way, making it an unlikely spot from which to set up a surveillance team. That left leasing an office or apartment in the buildings across the street. He had no such luxury, and he did not believe other interested parties did either. John doubted the meeting had been set up that far in advance.

He had concluded that he could not complete the "op" successfully by himself. He planned to listen and record the meeting and to apprehend Yousef, letting him know that the authorities had his number. He could think of no better way to scare the Russians away from the deal.

He had thought hard about this problem. He had little hope of finding Yousef before the meeting and only slightly better odds of following him afterward. The only time he would know Yousef's exact whereabouts was at the meeting itself. Also, he had to confirm the meeting's participants and the topic of discussion. Nabbing Yousef beforehand was not only logistically unlikely, but made no sense. The only possible times were near the end of the meeting and before Yousef left the brasserie.

The restaurant had three entrances, only one of which John could cover. That meant that even if he had had enough men to cover them all, he still did not know which entrance the TIQ, the tango-in-question, would use. That left the restaurant itself. The grab had to happen inside. How much simpler to double-tap the bastard, a quick two shots to the head, sending the miserable Pakistani to Allah's side. Bottom line, the grab would be at least a two-man job, preferably three—two men to do the snatch and one to drive the getaway car.

In this case, John lacked essential elements of intelligence. In addition, Mr. Murphy could all too easily decide to pay a visit. All things considered, he needed help. John turned and made his way down rue St. Antoine. It was time to call a friend.

*   *   *

The telephone rang, and he set the map down on his bed.

"Oui?" John answered. He was expecting only one call.

"Henri's dress shop," came the reply.

John smiled. "I didn't order a dress. You must have the wrong room."

"But that fat whore you bedded with last night," the voice began, "she ordered this dress from your room."

"Maybe it was you who were bedding the fat whore."

Both men laughed.

"Good to have you in town," Claude said. "How long you here for?"

"That depends," John replied.

"On?"

"Can we meet," John asked, "in twenty minutes at Le Café Marly in the Richelieu Wing of the Louvre?"

"In a hurry to start drinking?"

"You could say."

"The drinks are on you," Claude insisted. "I'll see you in forty-five."

"Thanks."

Fifty minutes later, both men were seated at the far end of Le Café Marly, named for the Marly horses on display in the Richelieu Wing of the museum directly behind them. I.M. Pei's Pyramid Entrance to the Musé du Louvre dominated the center courtyard of the old palace directly in front of them, where French kings had ruled the country for over 400 years.

"To my friend, the French dressmaker," John toasted as he raised his glass.

"Bastard," Claude exclaimed as he took a long sip of his Scotch. "What brings you to our fair city?"

"A little TTS," John replied, using a SEAL expression–tap em, tie em, and stash 'em. A smile spread across Claude's face.

Claude and John went way back. Claude was an ex-member of the French counterterrorist group GIGN, an organization similar in some ways to Navy SEAL Team Six. They had first met in 1982, when John and a SEAL team of eight men had been charged with infiltrating a French nuclear power station.

After Charles de Gaulle had pulled France out of NATO, the US government had felt compelled to keep a close eye on the French nuclear capabilities. The unwillingness of the French to share any information with their former allies concerned Washington. Washington's nightmare was a French nuclear plant falling into Soviet hands. As a result of this fear, Washington frequently used SEAL teams to infiltrate French nuclear sites and gather intelligence on their abilities. Of particular interest was whether a reactor was a breeder–one that could produce materials for making nuclear devices. Also, the operations helped identify the best means of destroying such a reactor should the need ever arise.

On this particular sortie into the French nuclear establishment, John's team had had a different mission. They were working with the French government to test security at a reactor outside Nice, known as Installation Number 12 in Washington. Concern about a French-built reactor in Iraq had led the French and Americans to conduct a joint exercise to develop a plan for destroying that reactor, which was modeled after the Nice installation. Simulating an attack on Installation Number 12 seemed the best way to perfect such a plan. Claude had been a member of the French team. During the six-day joint exercise, Claude and John had become friends and had kept in touch on a more or less regular basis.

"Who are you sneaking on?" Claude asked.

"A few nasties," John replied. The waiter approached and John ordered two more Scotches.

"Can I come along for the ride?"

John smiled. "You didn't think the booze was free?"

"Not by a long shot," Claude replied. "Americans are cheap bastards. But seriously, what's up?"

"I can't tell you much. This op is way off the books and I mean way off. If things go south, there is no one to help us. No one."

"It's not against France?"

"No, France will benefit, but you know how official France feels about Americans operating on their turf." John gave Claude a quick report of the planned meeting and his surveillance of the Brasserie Bofinger.

"They just don't know fun when they see it," Claude replied. "Count me in."

"You're sure? It could be hairy, and if Mr. Murphy displays his puss-ass, there could be a lot of explaining to do."

"Are you saying you're having second thoughts?" Claude asked with a wicked smile.

John shook his head as he gave Claude the finger. He was a man to be trusted, both in the heat of the battle and afterward. A secret was safe with him. It was time to get down to business; there was a lot of planning to do.

* * *

John and Claude crossed the street quickly to avoid the rush of cars, their eyes scanning, looking for anything suspicious. It was a little before seven o'clock and darkness approached. They had prepared as much as possible, reviewing their plan again and again in search of refinements, but that time had passed; it was time to execute.

They entered the restaurant through an old wooden door to the right of a revolving one of similar vintage. The small bar lay directly ahead, and to the left of the revolving door stood the maître d's podium. Claude approached.

"Good evening," the maître d' said in French.

"And to you," Claude replied, also in French. "May I speak with the manager concerning an urgent matter? I'm from the Deuxième."

The maître d' did not seem surprised, as John and Claude had expected. During the last three days of surveillance, they had noticed that a man had taken an interest in the restaurant. Claude had followed the man. To their surprise he had returned to the Deuxième, the French agency charged with handling terrorists and antiterrorist matters.

They had discussed the possibilities at length, but had finally settled on the "Washington factor." Because the surveillance was never more than a single person, they had concluded that someone had whispered unofficially in the Deuxième's ear. That someone had to be the same person in Washington who had his eye on John, so whoever it was probably knew John was in Paris. The surveillance by the Deuxième had to be an attempt to understand his presence there. If the Deuxième had already known about the meeting and its participants, there would have been no reason to place the brasserie under surveillance. On the contrary, the Deuxième would have stayed as far away from the building as possible for fear of revealing its knowledge to the TIQs. Only on the night of the meeting would they have put someone in place. After their arrival the entire area would have been sealed, making escape impossible. Yousef's capture offered immense political capital, and that was not to be wasted. The French might be soft on terrorists, but they were excellent politicians.

The manager appeared almost immediately. He was of medium size, in his forties, and dressed flawlessly in a suit. He nodded at them both but did not ask for their identification, not that it mattered. A friend of Claude's had made two Deuxième IDs.

"I thought all the arrangements were made," the manager said.

"Some last-minute changes," Claude informed him. "Can we speak somewhere a little more private?"

"Certainly, follow me."

In a few minutes they found themselves in the manager's office. Claude reached into his sport jacket and removed a saltshaker identical to those used by the brasserie. John had stolen it earlier in the week. They had secreted a transmitter into its lid. It would ensure that any conversation within a couple of feet would find its way to the tape recorder in John's jacket pocket.

"Please make sure this is put on their table," Claude ordered. "You and the maître d' have memorized the description of the two men?"

The manager shook his head. "No one has given us a description. We were told that your man posted behind the bar would point out which table you were interested in once the men took their seats. If I recall, it was an issue of security."

John and Claude kept straight faces, but their suspicions had been confirmed. The Deuxième had no idea who John planned to watch.

"Yes, but now it's time," Claude explained. "Get the maître d' and I'll give you both detailed descriptions of two men. Also, have him bring tonight's list of reservations and a layout of the tables."

The manager picked up his phone and spoke briefly. "He will be here in a moment."

John and Claude waited in silence. The manager was clearly nervous. Three minutes later the maître d' appeared, and in ten minutes Claude had explained in detail what was expected of the two men.

"Any questions?"

Both men shook their heads. John and Claude had left nothing to chance. Their instructions had bordered on anal retentive.

"You've been most cooperative," Claude commented. "Now if you could show us to our table."

The table was perfect, giving them an excellent view of the brasserie's ground floor and its entrance. It was in the left corner, far back, and allowed them to come and go without a waiter's help. Many tables were so closely crowded together that they required a waiter's assistance for those patrons seated against the wall, which was ringed by comfortable banquette seats. Three of the walls in this section were completely covered by mirrors. The last, straight ahead, was only a half wall that divided their section from the smoking section in the front of the establishment. A thick glass partition lined the top of the divider.

They had selected a table for Yousef and Trubkin in the same section of the restaurant, directly in front of a walkway in the center. Nearby a small set of stairs led to the wash closets. The atmosphere of the table was fine, but for a trained intelligence professional and a terrorist its location would ring a few bells. One person would be forced to sit with his back to over half the patrons in the section, though he would have a good view of the brasserie's entrance and an adequate view of the sidewalk and its foot traffic. The other seat faced the back of the section. Its only saving grace was the three mirrored walls. One could use them to keep a reasonably good eye on the coming and goings of the restaurant. There was always the possibility that the TIQs would complain, but Claude's instructions to the manager had been specific; the men sit at that table, period. The brasserie would be very crowded, with a long list of reservations. It would be easy to claim all the other tables were reserved. The only disaster lay in the possibility that the men would insist, and, not getting their way, might leave the restaurant altogether. It was a risk, but John suspected neither man was interested in causing a scene that might help someone remember him. No, he suspected they would take their lumps, believing no one knew they were there in the first place.

After a few moments a waiter appeared and offered a wine list and a menu. They accepted both, and the waiter departed as quickly as he had appeared.

"A bottle seems appropriate," John said in French as they opened their menus. "Too bad we can't enjoy it."

"A shame, yes, and it's our *francs* paying for this ritzy establishment," Claude remarked as studied the wine list. John's eyes continued to traverse the restaurant.

Over the next forty-five minutes they ordered appetizers and meals. Both men agreed the food was excellent, though they ate little. The job at hand went best on an empty stomach.

As time passed, John became anxious. Maybe they had missed the meeting. With the exception of two tables, the one they had specified to the manager and one other, the restaurant had filled with a mix of people, none matching John's mental profile of either TIQ. Had Murphy visited so soon?

Finally a man arrived who looked Arabic. The maître d' greeted him and gestured toward the back of the restaurant. The maître d' looked nervous as he began to walk. John worried that Yousef would notice.

He recognized Yousef from the photos he had seen. SEAL Team Six maintained detailed intelligence on all known terrorists. It was part of their ongoing training to know the traits and habits of the men and women they might face. John still could not believe that his brother's death had led him to Paris, seated only a few tables away from one of the most wanted tangos in the world. Many of the pictures John had seen of Yousef showed him dressed as one would expect a fanatical Muslim terrorist to look. For this meeting he had abandoned the scruffy fanatical look. He was clean shaven and wore a two-piece European tailored suit. He looked every bit the successful businessman.

John and Claude could see that Yousef was not entirely happy with the location of the table. He took the better of the two seats, the one facing the front of the restaurant. Trubkin would have to face the back.

Five minutes later, a large, well-built man in his mid-to late forties entered the brasserie. His blond hair, blue eyes, and Slavic face went well with his charcoal gray suit. He looked Russian, even KGB to the trained eye. His actions and particularly his eyes marked him as a professional; they never stopped roaming the restaurant as he approached Yousef. John and Claude stared at their dinners lest Trubkin should notice their interest.

"Is that him?" Claude asked.

"I think so. His hair color is different. It was not blond nor were his eyes blue. The hair is longer too."

"All things easily changed," Claude pointed out.

"Let's assume it's him."

John felt the .40-caliber 92/96G Beretta that Claude had supplied at the small of his back. He knew the pistol had been developed specifically for the needs of the French gendarmerie and other law enforcement agencies worldwide. The G models differed from the others in that the hammer drop lever did not function as a traditional safety. When the lever was released after being activated, it automatically returned to the ready-to-fire position. Claude packed the same pistol. They had picked the Beretta because the Israelis favored it. Claude had grumbled about the choice because the French also favored them. In the end John had prevailed. As far as he was concerned, if things went wrong, who better to blame than the Israelis and the French?

They had solved their transportation problem by parking a car illegally a half block from the restaurant. The car had diplomatic plates that they had lifted from a car outside the Swedish embassy two days earlier. They were fairly confident the French Urbaine would let it be and not pay too much attention to the number of the stolen plate. However, if something happened, they planned to double-tap Yousef on the spot. It was their only choice. Down deep John knew the real reason he wanted to capture Yousef; he wanted to uncover the secret hand in Washington. Yousef would be the perfect bait. The recklessness of the idea appealed to him.

John took a few more bites of his dinner. It was very good, but that fact was lost on him now. His mind focused completely on the two men seated only a short distance from him. John was a man of action. He appreciated surveillance, but at some point surveillance only paid dividends if action followed—swift violent action in the case of tangos. John knew the score: some chances came only once. He looked at Claude. He knew his friend was thinking exactly the same thing.

* * *

"A wonderful meal," Trubkin commented. "You certainly know how to select a restaurant."

"Thank you for the kind compliment," Yousef replied in perfect English. He had not spoken it much since February 26, 1992, the day Salameh and he had driven the rented van into the garage of the World Trade Center and set the detonator. He had caught a flight to Geneva later that day, leaving the other conspirators to occupy the American authorities. The gracious smile he wore on his face hid his contempt for the Russian. He disliked Russians and particularly KGB agents, which he suspected Trubkin to be even though he was known to work for the Chechens. The Russian actions in Afghanistan had been murderous, and his Mujahadeen brothers had suffered greatly at the hand of the Russian monster. Considering how many Chechens the Russian had killed over the years, Yousef was surprised they would tolerate the likes of Trubkin in their midst. The reasons had to be terribly compelling, thought Yousef. He wondered, not for the first time, what they were.

Now he was forced to deal with the Russian. That worked against all his principles. The Chechens he welcomed, but for the Chechens to send a Russian as their emissary struck a sour note. Allah worked in mysterious ways. Yousef's training had begun in the rough foothills of Afghanistan, fighting the Russian barbarians. He had killed many of them and was proud of it. Nevertheless his current duties required him to mask his hatred. This man Trubkin was just a means to an end.

"A perfect meal to prepare one for a business discussion," Trubkin continued, unaware of his guest's thoughts. Yousef nodded in agreement.

"I can get you two of the items that you want," Trubkin said. He did not like the Pakistani and doubted that the Pakistani liked him, but doing business together had nothing to do with personal feelings. The Pakistani represented an interested party, and that party was actively trying to acquire atomic bombs.

"What size?" Yousef asked after a moment's pause.

"One hundred," Trubkin said, referring to the number of kilotons the bombs could produce. "I'm sure that size is more than adequate for your purpose, wouldn't you agree?"

Yousef nodded. "And the cost that you propose?"

"One hundred and fifty US," Trubkin said with a steady stare.

"Ridiculous," Yousef countered. "You must be joking."

"That includes delivery," Trubkin added, hiding his hatred. Expensive! It was a bargain price compared with developing such effective devices on their own, not that the Arabs could, pathetic bastards that they were. He remembered working in south Yemen in the mid-eighties. The heat, coupled with the Arabs' lack of mechanical prowess, was enough to break any man's faith in supporting such a backward and unthankful nation. Not only were the Yemenis impossible to work with, they continually showed an uncanny ability to ruin the best equipment. After three years in Yemen, he had concluded that Arabs were a worthless lot.

"The price is very reasonable. If you made the items yourself, you would spend ten times that amount, and it would take you years. I suspect your timetable does not give you such latitude."

Yousef was quiet for a moment. He had authorization for $100 million for each nuclear bomb, though he suspected his superiors would pay twice that amount for each. "Ninety-five each," Yousef parried. "That's my offer."

Trubkin removed his napkin from his lap and placed it on the table. "I'm afraid then that we have little else to discuss," he said in a curt tone. "You obviously have a great deal of confidence in your people to make these items." Trubkin saw the reaction in Yousef's eyes. The Arab did not like that comment one bit. Who cared, he hated all Arabs anyway.

"I understand your feelings," Yousef said, acknowledging Trubkin's comment. "Allow me to discuss the matter with my client. I will leave a message for you in the normal manner in a week's time. Is that sufficient?"

"Certainly, Ramzi," Trubkin replied. He suspected that Iraq was Yousef's client, though there was an outside chance that Iran was pulling his strings. Trubkin did not care. His job was to sell the bombs and get the money. His masters appeared not to give a damn who got the bombs. Trubkin felt this was a little shortsighted on their parts, but it was not for him to comment.

"In a week then," Yousef repeated as the waiter approached the table to retrieve the American Express card that Trubkin had placed on top of the dinner table. At least the Russian had the decency to pay for dinner.

* * *

"It's almost time," Claude said. They watched the waiter hand the TIQs their dinner bill.

"You know the drill," John said. "I'll approach their table and ask Trubkin in Russian if he knows who the fuck he's dining with. As soon as Yousef makes a move, disable him. I take care of Trubkin. I'll approach from the bathroom. You ready?"

"Sure, but watch yourself. That Russian is no slouch, he's a professional."

"I know." John remembered how the Russian had moved after he had fired the shot in Bangkok twenty-six months earlier. The world was a very small place. "Let's do it."

John stood up and headed to the men's room, its entrance down a small set of steps a few feet from where the two terrorists sat. He passed directly behind Trubkin as the man removed a credit card to pay for the meal. It looked like an American Express card. John saw an unexpected opportunity as both men watched Trubkin's action. He nodded to Claude and made his move, pulling the Beretta from its hiding place. Claude was equally quick and covered the thirty feet between their table and the terrorists' in less than two seconds. Before either man could respond, John had his gun pointed at the Russian's head and Claude had his aimed at Yousef's.

The restaurant fell silent. Claude yelled in French for everyone to stay calm and no one would get hurt. John could see the maître d' standing by his podium, shock on his face. This was not a part of the agreement. They figured they had less than five minutes to get Yousef out of the restaurant and into a car before the police arrived. That was not much time if these men became uncooperative.

"Everyone, please remain calm," Claude ordered in a booming voice. "These men are wanted criminals and are extremely dangerous. For everyone's safety, please stay in your seats. Anyone moving will be considered a threat." The silence in the restaurant was palpable. No one moved. John and Claude kept their attention on the two men, their pistols aimed steadily at the TIQs' heads.

In Russian John said, "Feel like Bangkok all over again?"

Trubkin turned his head like an owl in John's direction, pure hatred in his eyes. John returned his glare with a thin smile and motioned for him to face his dinner guest. John had raised his pistol to strike Trubkin in the back of the head when the silence was shattered.

From the front of the restaurant John heard glass break. Two gunshots followed in quick succession. John saw Claude spin to his left and stagger back as a shot caught his right forearm. His pistol fell from his hand. Yousef started to dive for Claude's dropped gun. John's left foot shot out savagely and caught Yousef in the chest. The kick sent him sprawling backward into the island fixed in the middle of the section. A five-foot vase, decorated with a fine blue heron along its stem and containing a beautiful arrangement of flowers, came crashing down on the patrons next to Yousef. Screams sounded throughout the restaurant.

John's kick gave Claude the seconds he needed to retrieve his gun with his left hand. Another shot sounded, missing John by the narrowest of margins. John could do nothing until the shooter outside the restaurant was gone. He aimed his gun at a spot above and to the right of the hole in the shattered window, assuming the gunman was right-handed. He squeezed off three quick shots. More glass shattered, and he heard rather than saw a figure crash against the broken glass. He knew without seeing that his three shots were tightly spaced. They would have fitted neatly on a small five-by-three index card. His training dictated no less.

While he was shooting, Trubkin had started to move. John felt rather than saw the punch. His kidneys screamed with pain, which instantly spread through his right side as he stumbled forward from the force of the blow. He fought the blurring that started to spread across his vision and began to spin toward his attacker, but not in time to miss a vicious blow on his hip, delivered by a powerful roundhouse kick. It sent John tumbling against the waiter's station. A waiter and countless plates crashed in a ruinous pile on the floor with John sprawled helplessly on top. Trubkin started to move, his eyes fixed on John, but stopped as John raised his gun. Trubkin dived for the opening that led to the front of the restaurant, leaping out of John's line of fire. Coming out of his barrel roll, he fled in the direction of the kitchen.

John took an instant to look at Claude, who was rising to chase Yousef. As Yousef sprang past him, John attempted to untangle himself from the destroyed waiter's station. Yousef, headed to the entrance of the brasserie, had a good three steps on Claude, who was just emerging from a crouch, his gun in his uninjured left hand. John commanded his body to move. In two seconds he and Claude were up and running. Yousef now had five to six steps on them as he entered the revolving doors. John raised his gun and fired two more shots. The first one grazed Yousef in the right shoulder; the second shot went high and sent wood splintering across the entrance as the bullet lodged in the ornate woodwork of the revolving door. Yousef grabbed his shoulder briefly, but he kept moving. In seconds he was out the door, leaving John with no shot.

John beat Claude to the swinging doors and exited onto the street. The normally quiet rue was filled with desperate people, all trying to avoid the firefight engulfing the brasserie. As John passed through the doorway, two shots ripped into the open door of the restaurant. He ducked and found shelter near the entrance. Claude did the same. John peeked around the corner of the doorframe and caught a glimpse of Yousef fleeing down the rue de la Bastille, away from the Place de la Bastille. John and Claude could not return the fire; there were too many people on the street. John noticed the body of the man he had shot through the window, his lifeless hand still clutching a nine-millimeter SIG-Sauer P226 pistol. John took a deep breath–no time to think about him, it was time to move.

John willed his body to act. He rose from his crouch and started to run after Yousef, down rue de la Bastille, to where it T'd into rue des Tournelles. Yousef had turned left past Bistro du Dôme on the corner. John could just see Yousef through the crowd as Claude and he gained on the Pakistani terrorist. Yousef crossed rue St. Antoine, bringing a loud flurry of protests from angry motorists.

For a moment John lost Yousef as he ducked behind a truck on the rue. Seconds passed, then John saw him again. He was opening the right back door of a black car parked before the church on the far side of rue St. Antoine. John and Claude ran into the small triangle area flanked by St. Antoine and Tournelles, their guns in hand, ready to fire. More horns blared, people screamed, sirens neared. It was bedlam. John heard rather than saw a car rev its powerful engine. The black Citroën tried to forge a path in the snarled traffic, but it instantly struck another car. John stopped and aimed his weapon at Citroën. He squeezed off four shots. They shattered the window screen, bringing the vehicle to a lurching halt as it attempted to disengage itself from the other car. The back right door of the Citroën opened and Yousef scrambled out. Running again, Claude and John raced after him. He was in their sights.

As Yousef cut down the small side street known as rue Castex, heading in the direction of rue Henry IV, police cars arrived on the scene. Policemen jumped out of their cars, guns drawn. John felt Claude's powerful hand grab him and pull him to a stop.

"Enough," Claude yelled. "Put the gun away. Let's get out of here. Yousef is gone. We've lost this round."

John stared hard at Claude and knew he was right. How could they have known that Yousef had a shooter stationed outside the restaurant? Murphy's Law, what can go wrong will go wrong. John stuck the Beretta in the small of his back. He could feel the hot steel through his shirt. Claude did the same. They should have thought of the possibility, fuck.

"Let's get out of here," Claude ordered. "The Bastille Métro station is this way. Hurry." Claude and John did not run, which would have drawn unnecessary attention, but they did not dally either. As they hurried through the crowd that had gathered around the area, John took a look at Claude's arm.

"Clean through?" John asked. Claude nodded; he had been very lucky.

One minute later they were jogging down the steps of the Métro station. Claude had removed a bandanna from his pocket and wrapped it around his arm. John pulled it tight, stemming the flow of blood. The bandanna also helped hide the wound from any prying eyes. They came to the turnstiles and inserted their tokens, which they had purchased in advance on the out chance that they would need the Métro for a quick exit.

A train was boarding as they reached the platform. They sprinted and made it. As the Métro pulled away from the station headed toward Place d'Italie, they could see two policemen reach the platform. John and Claude turned to hide their faces. As he did so, John saw one of the transit policeman reach for his radio. He was obviously calling ahead to the next station. As soon as the train hit the dark tunnel, John and Claude started running to the front. They could not afford to be trapped on the train. The police would surely catch them.

Two minutes later the Métro popped out of the dark tunnel and into the well-lit station at Quai de la Papée. John and Claude stood on the far side of the train away from the platform, each canvassing the platform for signs of the police. They saw three standing by a set of turnstiles, but they did not seem overly concerned. John looked at Claude and he nodded. "Let's stay. They obviously don't plan to search the train."

"That was too close," John insisted.

"You got that right," Claude agreed.

* * *

Trubkin paced back and forth in his hotel suite. He was not happy. What the hell had happened in the restaurant? What a *razebaistvo*, a fuck-up! One minute he was paying the bill, and the next he had a gun pointed at his head. Who were those men? He walked to the wet bar and poured himself another vodka, drinking the fiery liquid in a single gulp. He needed to think. The gunman had mentioned the meeting in Bangkok. This meeting was the second that had ended badly and it angered him. The fucking Arabs, he hated the bastards. He'd rather kill them than work with them.

First, the two gunmen were professionals. That much was clear. Everything from the way they held their guns, 9-millimeter Berettas, to the kick the one had given Yousef, said as much. That kick was one of the quickest moves he had ever seen. Who did they work for? The one with the gun trained on Yousef spoke perfect French and probably was a native. The other one spoke perfect Russian. He dressed like a Frenchman, but something told Trubkin that he was not French. American had a better feel to it. Second, they seemed interested not in him but in Yousef. When he had headed in a different direction, there had been no hesitation as to which man they would follow. However, the American gunman had recognized him.

Had Yousef been followed to the meeting? It was always a possibility, but unlikely. Yousef had not stayed free from the long arms of western justice, which pursued him relentlessly, out of pure luck. He was good and would have been extra cautious about tonight's meeting. Its success meant too much to him and his Arab brothers. He wouldn't have taken any chances. Also, he had had two men with him, one driving the car and the other watching the restaurant. It had been the latter who had taken the first shots. He had grazed the Frenchman and missed the other gunman, a mistake that had cost him his life. Three perfectly placed shots by the American gunman and he was on his way to Allah. Trubkin had to admit he would have been hard pressed to make three better shots. That had been another part of his decision to flee rather than to fight. He had learned long ago that fighting is a dangerous business, particularly when one's adversary is highly skilled in the art of killing. This man obviously was.

After Trubkin had exited the restaurant through the kitchen, passing the panicked chefs, he had circled around the block and returned to the rue St. Antoine where it entered the Place de la Bastille. He reasoned that since he was not the men's primary target, he was relatively safe to watch the outcome of their pursuit. He also needed to know more about the gunmen. Though out of breath when he reached the corner of the rue St. Antoine and Place de la Bastille, he had been in time to see the shots into the black Citroën. They had stopped the sedan in its tracks. Trubkin had watched the two men race after Yousef as he exited the crippled car. He had seen that Yousef was in trouble. His two pursuers were big, strong men. Unless he could disable one of them, Trubkin believed the two would be too much for him.

Trubkin had barely finished the thought when the two gunmen had stopped in their tracks, ending their pursuit of Yousef. At first Trubkin could not understand what had caused the two men to stop. They were gaining on Yousef and had the advantage. Then it had dawned on him as he watched them turn briskly toward Place de la Bastille and hurry down the Métro stop. It was the flood of police cars filling the area that had caused the men to cease their chase. Were they fugitives too?

It was totally unexpected. He reasoned that these men were not operating for the French government or a government that considered France its friend. That could be the only answer. He had considered following the men. However, he knew they were focused on possible pursuers, alert, with every sense operating to full capacity. He knew the feeling, the power and the rush. He had no choice but to let them go.

Trubkin glanced at his watch. His Air France flight to Moscow left at 9:35 am tomorrow. It arrived at 3:10 p.m. His meeting with General Leonov was set for 5:00. What would he tell him? He knew nothing about tonight's events. The meeting with Yousef had gone as expected, and Yousef had seemed relaxed, confident. His face had registered total surprise when the gunmen had sprung their attack. The general would want more; the two gunmen had to be identified. Trubkin sighed in frustration. At least he had good news about Tallinn. That operation had been a total success.

* * *

John and Claude relaxed on Claude's houseboat, a pleasant craft moored on the north shore of the Seine, just east of the Pont Alexandre III. The converted barge had been made into an elegant home. The outside still looked as it had originally, except for a better paint job and some flowers on the deck, but the inside was something else. It was the perfect place to hide from the authorities and live a life of anonymity. The living area was filled with deep armchairs and a matching couch. A sophisticated sound system brought the ambiance to its peak. A twelve-pack of Heineken lay half empty between the two men.

"It's great to drink with a Frenchman who appreciates beer," John said as he set down his empty bottle. He glanced at his watch. It read 2:37 am and they had just finished discussing what they had heard on the tape. The conversation between Yousef and Trubkin had disturbed them deeply. "Most of you Frogs spend too much time hugging a wine bottle."

"Too bad you Americans can't make a wine worth hugging," Claude countered with a big grin on his face.

"I best be on my way," John said. "I need to decide what to do next."

"You're welcome to stay here for the night," Claude said. "The couch has your name on it. It's probably safer than the hotel."

"Thanks." John smiled. "I'm tempted to take you up on the offer, but I have a hunch I need to follow."

"The Deuxième?"

"Yeah. I need to learn who in Washington is pulling the strings. This might be a thread I can follow."

"You need a change of clothes," Claude suggested, his professional eye considering John. "Take a shower, shave off that stubble, and put a suit on. It will make you respectable, at least on the surface. You know where the bathroom is. Have at it."

"You're right," John agreed. He started to make his way to the bathroom.

Claude laughed as the look of frustration flashed across his friend's face yet again. John flipped him the bird.

"And fuck you too."

"Thanks for your help tonight. I owe you one. I fucked up. Trying to take Yousef was stupid."

"Bold it was, but not stupid. We had an even chance. This time it did not go our way."

"Maybe," John agreed. "But my reasons behind this one are real personal."

Claude stared at his friend. "I know." He opened another beer bottle with his teeth. "It is I who owe you. I was bored and needed some excitement. Besides, it's Yousef who's at fault. His shooter ventilated me and I hold him responsible."

"I knew there was a reason I liked you," John said. "You're as stupid as I am."

Both men laughed again, and John headed to the shower.

* * *

The hot water struck his weary body. He had rerun the evening in his head dozens of times. Nothing new sprang to mind. He wondered what he should do next. Should he pursue Trubkin, Yousef, or Washington? He just did not know. He was missing too much of the big picture. What was afoot? Who was behind it?

He quickly turned the hot water off, and ice-cold water slammed his body. He forced himself to endure its agony for a full minute. Finally he shut the water off and fetched a towel. Logan sprang into his mind. He wondered what she was doing. He wanted to call her, but she would only ask questions that he could not answer. Lying to her was not an option. He had done that once, and that was enough. Their relationship could not survive more. He even wondered if it would survive, period. They were from different worlds, and now the chances were strong that her father was an evil part of the plans unfolding before John's eyes. Anguish swept over John at the thought that he would be Davenport's executioner.

11 | A Washington Touch

A taxi deposited John in front of the Opéra Paris Garnier, a few blocks from his hotel, the Hôtel Ile de France Opéra. The large round opera house basked in lights set around its base, and the light radiated from the building into the large intersection, which at that hour lay empty. The walk to the hotel would only take minutes, but John wanted to be sure that the police had not placed it under surveillance. There was no reason to invite Mr. Murphy; he had shown his ugly head once too often.

A half hour later, he was comfortable that no one was watching the hotel from the outside. The police could be waiting inside the small establishment and there would be little he could do, but he suspected the Deuxième presence tonight had been unofficial, at least until John and Claude had drawn their guns.

The man behind the desk handed him his room key without a word, a nervous look in his eye. John knew instantly that he had guests.

"Any messages for me?" John asked. He kept a steady stare on the man, who seemed to melt with the question.

"Non, Monsieur."

John nodded and walked the short distance to the stairway. As soon as he was out of sight of the front desk, he removed his pistol from his belt. Then he thought better of it. He slipped the pistol back into hiding. Quietly he stepped up the narrow, winding stairs; his room was on the third floor. There were only four rooms on his floor.

He listened for a moment and realized he could smell his visitor; the odor of cigarettes hung heavy in the air. John almost decided to make a run for it, but he was intensely interested in who had decided to pay him a visit. Even if someone had given the police a good description of him, it would take them a while to match photographs from the airport's cameras to a police drawing. Once they had a name, they would still have to locate the hotel. In the five-block area there were over seventy hotels. John doubted four hours would have been enough.

He unlocked his door and swung it open. John stepped into his tiny room. A man was seated in the lone chair. John shut the door and hit the light switch with his left elbow. The man was in his mid-forties and wore a neatly trimmed mustache on his long French face. His eyes caught John's attention, their intelligent obvious as they considered John. The man had not bothered to remove his trench coat, and he had "cop" written all over him.

A heavily accented French voice filled the room. "Good evening, Monsieur."

"And who are you?"

"I am Henri Maitrot, an inspector with the Deuxième."

"A little late for house calls," John said. Under normal circumstances he would have expected the Urbaine, the French police. The Deuxième handled terrorist and counterintelligence operations in France, and a homicide in Paris was hardly their beat.

"Oui, and how was dinner?" queried the inspector.

"Interesting."

The inspector seemed at ease. "You look familiar. Have we met before?"

"I don't think so. I come to Paris rarely. This trip is for pleasure, a chance to be alone and put some thought to a new business idea."

"You Americans are always thinking about business, even on holidays. An unhealthy habit, I think."

"Working until four in the morning cannot be much better," John replied.

The inspector smiled. "You have a point. A good hotel, the Hôtel Ile de France Opéra; most American tourists are not familiar with it. A real find if you ask me."

"A friend of mine recommended it," John said. He was concerned. This inspector was smart, and John believed he had a reason for asking each question. The man had to have backup, unless he knew more about John than he was letting on.

"Who were those murderous men in the restaurant?" John asked. The inspector looked at him, his dark eyes pinned on John.

"We're not sure," the inspector said. "One man dead outside the restaurant, another dead in his automobile. Two more injured, by witnesses' accounts; however, they escaped."

"Drugs," John suggested.

"I doubt it," the inspector answered. He seemed lost in thought for a moment. "Do you know who the gunmen were?"

"Excuse me?"

"Your looks match closely the description of one of the gunmen," the inspector remarked.

"Really," John replied as he tried to figure out the inspector.

"Your information could help," the inspector insisted. "To be honest, I do not think you are a tourist or even an American businessman." He paused to look at John, a hint of frustration in his voice. "But let me tell you what I do know.

"Terrorism is a serious threat in France. We cannot do enough to prevent it. It is sad to say, but in some ways it has become a fact of life. My job is to protect France from terrorists. That's what the Deuxième does. We are much like your counterintelligence department in the FBI. I'm sure you know all these things, no?"

"All Americans have heard of the FBI," John said.

"Please, what were you doing in that restaurant tonight?" the inspector asked, his tone firm.

"Listening," John said.

"I gathered that," the inspector said with an edge of annoyance. "I'm interested in whom you were listening to."

"Ramzi Yousef," John said.

The inspector sat quietly for a moment. "How did you know he was going to be there?"

"A last-minute tip," John said.

"Ah, a last-minute tip," the inspector repeated. "So our friends across the Atlantic didn't see it fit to give us a call? We at the Deuxième could have provided some help. Maybe Yousef would be in a jet flying across the Atlantic as we speak. What do you think?"

"A valid point, Inspector," John said, "but circumstances did not permit it. God's honest truth."

"I believe you," the inspector said after a moment. He reached into his jacket. John watched his every move, ready to spring on the man at the first sign of trouble. With an economy of motion, the inspector withdrew a single sheet of paper, as if sensing John's concern. He held it and John stepped forward, retrieving it from the inspector's grasp.

It was a photocopy of a drawing made by a police artist, a man dressed in some kind of military or police uniform. John looked at the inspector with surprise.

"You recognize that man?" the inspector asked.

John thought he had seen a smile flicker across the inspector's face. "Yes."

"His name, if you please."

"Nikolai Trubkin."

"Yes, I thought so too. This picture came across the wire at Interpol a few days ago. An inspector in the Tallinn police force placed it there. I believe his name is Urams Jürgenson. I thought you would be interested."

"There is a lot you aren't telling me," John said.

"I could say the same to you," the inspector reflected. "Here is my card. I expect a call the next time. You know one favor deserves another, even in our line of work."

"You have my word," John said, hoping his relief was not too obvious.

The inspector stood, and John stepped away from the door.

"May I ask you one other question?" the inspector queried.

"Certainly."

"How could you have missed him?"

"I have asked myself the same question. Maybe he's a cat?"

"Oui, maybe he has just used his ninth life."

"Let's hope."

"Don't forget our little deal," the inspector reminded John. "If you find yourself in France again, I expect to know and before the fact."

"You will," John said. He had a thought, a way to ease the inspector's conscience. John knew the inspector was taking a risk, whether someone from Washington had called or not. "By the way, I have a friend in the Deuxième, Pierre Bulat. Tell him a dolphin sends him his best."

"A fine man," the inspector nodded. "I will give him your best, Mr. Thompson."

"Please," John replied.

"Au revoir."

"Au revoir, Inspector."

The inspector closed the door quietly, and John let out a sigh of relief. It had been dumb to return to the hotel. However, at every turn it seemed someone in Washington pulled a few strings for him. He wondered how long he could count on this factor, especially after his actions tonight. He suspected they might give Washington cause for concern—well, all the better.

He glanced at the drawing of Trubkin again. An inspector in Tallinn, Estonia, wanted Trubkin for unspecified crimes. John needed a reason to talk to this man, since he held no official capacity. Saying that he had gotten the picture from an inspector in the Deuxième simply would not float; there was no reason for the inspector in Tallinn to believe him, and he certainly did not want to impose on Inspector Maitrot again. John figured the inspector's debt to Washington was paid in full.

* * *

The phone rang and Dan answered it. “Hello.”

“Dan,” Inspector Maitrot said.

“Henri, how are you?” Dan asked in French.

“A busy evening in Paris tonight. Your man has caused quite a stir. It is not at all what I had anticipated from our earlier conversation.”

“Really. Can you tell me what happened?” Dan asked with deliberate surprise in his voice.

“Oui,” the inspector said, and he told Dan what he knew.

“Ramzi Yousef and Nikolai Trubkin,” Dan said, as he considered the ramifications. "And the tapes?”

“Oui, I have already given them to the man you sent,” the inspector confirmed. “What do you suppose John would have done with Yousef?”

“I’m not sure,” Dan answered, “but from what you’ve described he was planning to take him hostage. The car with stolen diplomatic license plates was probably their getaway vehicle, as you suspect. Have you identified the dead men yet?”

“That will take a few days,” the inspector said. “Dan, we go way back, and I have done what you have asked. However, if I had any idea of the magnitude of your small favor, I’m not sure I would have agreed.”

“Henri, if I had known Yousef was involved, I would have told you. We would have had an excellent chance to nab that bastard.”

“Water over the dam, I’m afraid. It is late here, and I must go.”

Dan hesitated for a moment, but he decided to ask anyway. “Henri, I have a thought.”

“Oui?”

“You mentioned that John and his partner used Berettas, a gun favored by the Mossad. Maybe it would be good to let the Russians and Yousef believe the Israelis were behind tonight’s raid. They might already be thinking that. I mean, it was clear that their two assailants were not working with the French police."

"Interesting, but why?"

"Just a thought. It might make the Russians nervous. The Mossad is very active in Russia. We both know that."

"And?"

"You might see if the information gets back to them."

The inspector was quiet for a moment, considering the ramifications of Dan's point. "No promises, but I will consider it. Au revoir."

12 Baltic Sea Secrets

Jürgenson sat at his cluttered desk. The search for a single scrap of paper on which he had written a phone number had proved fruitless. He knew it was there, but for the past five minutes it had eluded him. It must be nice to have a secretary to organize an office, but the Estonian police could not afford such western luxuries.

A sharp knock on his office door interrupted his thoughts. "Come in."

His desk sergeant moved his large frame through the door, with effort, Jürgenson noted. Had the man gained even more weight? He already weighed 135 kilos. Disgusting. Jürgenson had told his wife that, should he ever show the slightest tendency toward obesity, she should not hesitate to use the gun in the bedside table.

"What is it?" Jürgenson asked with impatience. He really did need to find that scrap of paper.

"There's someone here to see you," the sergeant said. He paused, uncertain of himself.

"Come out with it," Jürgenson ordered. "I haven't got all day."

"Yes, sir. He's an American," the sergeant replied. "He is very insistent that he speak only to you. He claims you and he have a mutual friend. A Russian."

Jürgenson looked up from his search. "What did you say?"

"He wants very much to speak to you," the sergeant repeated.

"I heard that part," Jürgenson said. "The next part."

"Oh, the Russian. He says that you and he have a friend who is Russian."

"Is that so," Jürgenson said. Was this man a crazy tourist? The last thing he wanted was to spend time listening to an American tourist explain a petty robbery, though the fact that the American had asked for him by name suggested the visit might be significant. Was the CIA sending another gift? They would know there was one Russian in particular he wanted to find. "What does he look like?"

"Brown eyes and hair, which is long. About two meters tall, I think. Casually dressed, no camera, well built, probably ex-military. He has that bearing, though he hides it well."

"Anything else?" Jürgenson inquired.

"Well, his eyes, sir. I felt like they could see right through me. Also he speaks very good Russian."

"How do you know he's American?" Jürgenson asked.

"He showed me this, sir." The sergeant handed John's passport to Jürgenson, and the inspector paged through it. "I called customs, and they said he entered the country on a one o'clock SAS flight from Stockholm."

"Show him in," Jürgenson ordered. "After five minutes, call me. I will use it as an excuse to get rid of him. You understand?"

"Completely, sir." The sergeant turned and left, closing the door behind him.

Two minutes later another knock sounded on Jürgenson's office door. The large sergeant opened the door. He gestured for the American to enter.

"Inspector Jürgenson, I appreciate your willingness to see me on such short notice," John said in Russian. John did not speak Estonian and did not want to risk the inspector's English being imperfect. Considering the history of the two countries, he figured the inspector knew Russian as well as he did Estonian. Hopefully, the inspector would be willing to speak it. John suspected that the inspector had no love for the Russians; few Estonians did. He offered his hand, but Jürgenson gestured for him to take a seat in the lone wooden chair that stood before his desk. The small affront did not bother John, and he did as instructed.

"Sergeant, you may leave us now," Jürgenson ordered. The door closed softly behind the man's immense frame.

John watched as the inspector paged through his passport and its extensions. John had traveled widely in the last nine years, though most of his travels were not documented in his passport. On most clandestine operations, he and his men had used forged passports or simply traveled on military transportation. John would have felt more comfortable now with a forged passport, but the fake identity he had purchased in France was not that of a private investigator, the role he planned to assume with the inspector. With his own passport, he would be exposed after the operation ended. However, he doubted that would matter. All the combatants knew who he was and where he lived. His only safety lay in removing them from the face of the planet.

He noted that Jürgenson's desk was a mess, like the rest of his office. However, the man's eyes showed a deep intelligence.

"Is it your first time to Estonia?" Jürgenson inquired.

"Yes, it is," said John.

"What were you doing in France?" Jürgenson asked. He agreed with his sergeant's assessment: John Thompson had been in the military at some time, his long hair notwithstanding. His dark brown eyes were bottomless. He was not a man to be taken lightly.

John removed the artist's drawing from his jacket pocket, unfolded it, and handed it to Jürgenson. After a quick glance, the inspector looked up and studied John closely. John returned the steady gaze.

"Where did you get this?" Jürgenson asked as he placed the drawing on his desk. He focused his attention on John's passport.

"I saw a man who looked very much like that one in Paris two nights ago," John answered.

"Your Russian is very good," Jürgenson observed. "Where did you learn it?"

"My father was in the military," John said. "We traveled a great deal."

"Have you lived in Russia?" Jürgenson asked.

"No, I have not," John said.

"Your Russian is very good for not having lived there," Jürgenson confirmed. "Do you speak other languages as well? I can see you've traveled widely."

"I speak Japanese and Arabic fluently," John revealed.

"Impressive," Jürgenson said, more to himself than to John. "What can I do for you?"

"I'm interested in that man," John said, as he pointed to the drawing.

"You don't say?" Jürgenson allowed a little surprise to enter his voice as he looked hard at John. What did this American want? Hadn't he just seen the criminal in Paris? Why did he need Jürgenson's help to find him again? Was he from the CIA?

"Who are you?" Jürgenson asked. "In what capacity have you come here?"

"I am a private investigator." John produced the business card that he had had made in Paris. Because of the rush, the cards had cost him a small fortune. "I have a client whose husband was murdered. She is a wealthy woman and will spare no expense to identify her husband's killer. It is my job to find him."

The phone rang and Jürgenson answered it. He listened for a moment. "Thanks, Sergeant. That is all." He replaced the phone in its cradle. "You think this man killed your client's husband?"

John guessed the inspector did not believe him. "I think he was involved."

"What do you expect from me?" Jürgenson asked.

"As I said, my hope is that we can work together," John suggested. "The man in that picture is Nikolai Trubkin, an ex-KGB colonel who works with the Chechen mob and has maintained close ties with his former masters."

Jürgenson paused for a moment as his eyes scanned the drawing. "What else do you know about this man?"

"Not much more," John said, "except that he's very dangerous and killing comes easy to him. You might say he even enjoys it."

"What can you offer me?" Jürgenson asked, hoping to discover whom this American really worked for. "You are only a private investigator from America."

"Yes, but I have many contacts, as you can tell by my possession of your drawing."

"Tell me something I don't know," Jürgenson demanded. He wanted to trust this man, but he needed a reason, a very good reason.

John thought for a moment. He could not come completely clean with the inspector, though his instincts suggested he do so. He liked Jürgenson and had a gut feeling that the man could help.

John reached out and put his hand on the inspector's letter opener, which lay at the edge of his desk. "May I?"

Jürgenson nodded. In a blink of an eye, John threw the letter opener. It sped across the fifteen-foot office and lodged itself in a large wall map of Europe. The blade split the city of Paris cleanly in two.

"I was a Navy SEAL," John said. "My training included many things. I know how to hunt a man. Trubkin is a bad man. He must be stopped, and I will not sleep until he is behind bars or dead. I suspect you feel the same way. Let's work together. Tell me all that you know about him. Why do you want him? What crime did he commit?"

Jürgenson looked at his letter opener. Its point marked Paris exactly, while the handle stood perpendicular to the wall. It was a perfect toss. The speed had amazed him. Jürgenson grudgingly realized that he could have been this man's victim just as easily. He was getting too casual in his old age. He had considered retirement on his fifty-fifth birthday in January, but had decided against it. Maybe it was time to reconsider.

"Maps like that are not inexpensive," Jürgenson said tersely. He was not about to reveal his actual thoughts.

"My apologies," John said. "I've watched too many American movies."

"So you're an investigator?" Jürgenson asked again. He was not convinced.

"Yes, I am an investigator," John said as their eyes met.

It took Jürgenson fifteen minutes to tell the story. He started with Mirek's capture, his confession, and his death. John listened closely. The story he told was unbelievable.

"So you think he is in the drug business?" John asked.

"Yes, among other things," Jürgenson replied. "Russia is a country run by gangsters. Everything is for sale: wood, minerals, military goods, even tanks. It's one big sale."

"My investigation started with another Russian. He works closely with a firm called Security International Group, SIG. They are owned by the Colombians, the Cali cartel, to be exact." John paused to let Jürgenson absorb what he had said. "I suspect the Colombians are supplying the SVR with drugs, which they are bringing back to Russia and probably here. Running drugs is a way for the SVR to make money and to trap new spies. The fact that its citizens use the stuff makes no difference."

"Interesting," Jürgenson said. "So you think the drugs are coming from South America?"

"I think it's a fair guess in light of what you've told me and what I know," John answered. From Jürgenson's expression John figured the inspector thought differently.

"What does this have to do with the murdered husband?" Jürgenson pressed.

"It is all related," John answered. "The husband was no angel. He moved suspicious cargoes."

Jürgenson stared at him for a moment and then started to search through the mass of paper piles on his desk. It took him two minutes until he removed a folder from one of the stacks.

"Mirek worked in the grain terminal, east of Tallinn. It's called

Muuga Sadam," Jürgenson began. "My officer spent a year working by his side as a welder. That was until two weeks ago. Mirek was transferred to a grain ship called the Sadko. My officer was not. That's when we suspected that someone had spotted my officer for what he was. Until that point they had worked as a team, always together. In hindsight I think we were wrong. Anyway, the ship is registered to a firm in Asia called Hong Kong Transportation Limited."

John sat forward; Jürgenson noted his interest.

"Do you know this ship?"

John shook his head. "No, but I've heard of HKT."

"I have tried to learn more about the company. A man named Davenport owns it, or at least a very good part of it. It is a publicly traded company on the Hong Kong Exchange. I believe he is an American billionaire."

"He certainly is," John agreed.

"Do you know him?"

"Actually I do."

"How do you know him?"

"He knows the widow well."

"What's her name?"

"Sarah Sinclair. She lives in Santa Barbara, as does Davenport. Actually he owns an island just off the shore from Santa Barbara, called Santa Cruz."

"I see," Jürgenson said. "Did this late husband happen to work for Davenport?"

John smiled. He liked the way Jürgenson thought and was half tempted to confirm his idea. However, good lies were simple ones that matched the truth as closely as possible. "No, Inspector, he did not. As far as I know, they only knew each other socially. Santa Barbara is not that big a city, particularly for the super-rich."

"Yes, I see."

"What about this ship? Is it still in port?"

"I believe it is," Jürgenson replied, "but I'm not sure it matters."

"How so?"

"I've done a little digging and have learned that the grain ship is under contract to a firm in Istanbul, name Aegean Exporting. Its next destination after it finishes unloading its grain is Istanbul. I think unloading will be completed in another ten days."

"And?" John pressed.

"And I think a visit to Istanbul might lead us to whoever is shipping the drugs to Estonia."

"So you think the grain ship brings drugs back after it delivers the grain?"

Jürgenson shook his head. "No, most of the ships that arrive at this port bring grain and leave empty to their home ports. Some unload part of their cargo here and then sail to St. Petersburg. St. Petersburg cannot handle a ship that drafts more than fourteen meters. The port here can handle eighteen meters, though most ships take less since the strait around Denmark can only handle sixteen meters. Only a few ships load grain here and take it somewhere else.

"So ships are generally full when they arrive," Jürgenson continued. "For a big ship, it can take almost two weeks to unload. That gives the thieves a large window of opportunity to unload their contraband.

"I had one of my men take a look at the Sadko before I arrested Mirek. I have a number of men on my payroll and this one is attached to the customs office. He got a look at the number three hold, and you know what he found?"

John shook his head.

"A large compartment cleverly concealed in the hold."

"A compartment," John repeated as another, dangerous, thought occurred to him.

"The hideaway is plenty big; it could hold millions of dollars in heroin or other contraband."

"So you think the lead in Istanbul is worth pursuing?"

Jürgenson nodded. "I have very limited resources. You say you can help; maybe you can. We need to learn who the supplier is and then we can involve Interpol."

John thought for a moment; what Jürgenson proposed was reasonable. The agent in Istanbul might have paperwork that made a direct connection between Davenport and Leonov. However, John wondered whether the compartment was designed to hold drugs or something else. Since the Russians had been shipping drugs for a while, it seemed unlikely they would need a new compartment to hide them in. More likely, an existing compartment would need enhancements to carry its new cargo. Drugs were a corollary to this caper, and the question was not what was being shipped from the Middle East to Estonia, but what was being shipped from Estonia to the Middle East.

John was not about to tell the inspector any of his conclusions. A trip to Istanbul still fitted his overall plan to attack Davenport from all angles, but first he would take a closer look at the Sadko. She held secrets that John wanted to know.

"I'll go to Istanbul in a few days," John said, "and I'll visit the firm. Meanwhile I'll need two favors from you."

Jürgenson did not answer immediately. "Specifically?"

"I'd like to take a closer look at the ship and her modified grain hold at night. Before I can do that, I'd like to see what I'm up against. I wonder if you can arrange a daytime tour of the facility."

"What importance could the ship possibly have to you?"

John knew Jürgenson was no dummy. "My widow's husband was a bad man from what I can tell, and he was a small-time player in the arms business."

"You think the hold is for arms and not drugs?" Jürgenson asked.

"I'm not sure," John replied. "It's a long shot, but maybe Davenport and her husband were more closely linked than I thought. It doesn't make sense for the compartment to be empty on one leg of the trip."

Jürgenson's face tightened in a scowl. "You ask a lot. What aren't you telling me?"

"A few things, but believe me when I say they have nothing to do with helping you catch Trubkin."

Jürgenson sat deep in thought for a few more moments.

"Yes, I will work with you, but against my better judgment. You must promise to keep me informed. If I sense that you are holding back from me, which I think you are now at some level, my cooperation will cease. Do we have an understanding?"

"Fair enough," John agreed.

"How do I reach you?" Jürgenson asked. John gave him a number to his satellite phone. "It looks like a Miami number, but it forwards to several numbers and is finally relayed to a satellite. It's reasonably secure."

Jürgenson stood and said, "I suspect that you might need a few items for tomorrow night's venture. See the sergeant at the front desk and I'll see to it that you get what you need by tomorrow."

"That is very generous of you."

"Don't make me regret it," Jürgenson warned sternly as he held up John's passport. "Anyway, I'll hold on to this. I'll call you with the time for our visit to the port. Also, let me know the flight you're on and I'll meet you at the airport; we can trade information and your passport then."

"Fair enough." John stood to take his leave. He made his way to the door and opened it.

"Who do you really work for?" Jürgenson asked.

"The good guys," John said, realizing that he really did not know the answer to the inspector's question.

* * *

General Leonov walked to his office window and stared at the enclosed courtyard below. He had listened to Trubkin's reports, first his success in Tallinn and then his troubles in Paris. The Paris incident concerned the general greatly.

The dinner meeting with Yousef had gone exactly as planned until the gunmen appeared; that was an ominous sign. If nothing else, it meant someone was keeping a close eye on Yousef or Trubkin or both.

The gunmen appeared to have focused their interest on Yousef. That meant he, not Trubkin, was more likely to have attracted someone's attention. The report from the Paris embassy suggested that the French had somehow concluded the attack was an Israeli effort.

Damn the Mossad. It would be easy to believe the Israelis were tracking Yousef for reasons that had nothing to do with Operation Russian Bear, in which case Paris would have been a coincidence. Yousef was near the top of Israel's most-wanted list. However, too many things did not add up.

First, the Mossad usually killed their targets when they found them. Abducting them was not their style. They favored five shots to the stomach and one to the head; that was how they dealt with enemies of the State of Israel.

Second, the Israelis presumably knew that Yousef planned to attend the meeting in the restaurant. Why then would they wait until the end of dinner to nab him? The general could not conceive of any advantage gained by waiting. The restaurant had multiple exits. Everything would have become more difficult as more time passed. Simple logic would dictate grabbing Yousef as he entered the restaurant, unless of course they wanted to know whom he was meeting.

Third, Trubkin had good instincts. He had thought one of the assailants was French. The second man could have been Israeli, but Trubkin's initial instincts had said American. If not for the French Deuxième's report and the man's comment about Bangkok, Leonov would not even have considered the Israelis as possible culprits. However, the Bangkok incident had Israel written all over it. Also, the French must have had a good reason to conclude that the attack was Israeli. What did they apparently know that he did not?

The general massaged these thoughts in his mind. There was a reasonable explanation; however, he did not see it yet.

13 Learning All about Grain

John listened to the noises around him as he bobbed silently in the cold, oily water off the Sadko's bow. Besides the lapping water against the steel of the ship, a plane somewhere off to the west, and the constant noises of machinery, nothing broke the calm that hung over the Muuga Sadam grain facility. It was 3:27 am.

John had started the evening by parking a small pickup truck two miles east-northeast of the port. He had hiked down the marshy coastline, carrying his diving equipment. After hiding the equipment in the marsh along the Gulf of Finland, he had made his way quietly to the rail yard where many of the empty and filled grain cars rested. The rail yard paralleled the marshy coast and was easy to approach. Its offices were on the opposite side and were hidden by the hundreds of resting rail cars. The railroad sidings nearest the Gulf of Finland were filled with lines of grain cars. John had hoped to get lucky, spot a modified grain car and snap of few photos of it. As he had anticipated, he had no such luck.

At 2:00 am he had entered the cold waters and swum to the port's huge cement pier that jutted into the harbor. This pier was connected to the immense grain elevators that dominated the port's skyline.

As he had learned from his tour, arranged by the inspector, earlier in the day, the main pier could handle two grain ships at a time and was used for unloading. Ships were loaded on smaller pier closer to the grain elevators. The port could handle ships weighing up to 150,000 tons, which could carry 120,000 tons of grain. It took ten days working twenty-four hour shifts to empty a ship of that size. Each of the nine holds contained 13,000 tons of grain. The unloading process could fill three hundred railroad cars per twenty-four hours, meaning that it took three thousand grain cars to empty a ship. That was a lot of grain.

The Sadko was a much smaller ship, with the capacity to hold 60,000 tons of grain. It contained six holds, each twelve meters deep, and was a rusty wreck compared with the other ship unloading its grain on the east side of the pier. The Sadko floated on the west side.

The cold bit into his skin. It was time to move before he developed hypothermia. Slowly he started the grueling crawl up the rusty side of the ship, using a pair of climbing suction cups he had found in a local store. They were well used, but as he started skyward they held their own. The rest of the equipment, donated by the generous sergeant, consisted of a French-made Neoprene wetsuit, a CQC vest with class III body armor, a flotation bladder, a Heckler & Koch USP 9-millimeter semiautomatic pistol, and a K-Bar assault knife. He also had two spare magazines. The gun had surprised John. He had not asked for it, the sergeant had simply given it to him. He wondered if the inspector had approved the use of the gun or if the sergeant had just assumed Jürgenson expected him to issue a pistol. No matter, its presence was welcome.

As soon as John lifted himself clear of the water, he paused for a full minute to let the water run off him entirely. He did not want someone above to become aware of water dripping. A light breeze blew on his body, delivering a chill he could feel through his wetsuit.

He looked over his equipment one more time to make sure he had lost nothing during his short swim. Everything was secure so that it would make no noise, and all shiny edges were hidden by tape. It looked good. Murphy appeared to be napping—all the better.

John glanced upward again at the big bow of the ship and down its starboard side. He could see or hear no one. He started to climb again, using his rubber-soled shoes to take some of the weight off his arms.

Seven minutes later he reached the steel opening where the massive anchor chain threaded its way to the deck. He peered through it before committing himself. The coast looked clear; he crawled through the opening, his breathing hard. It had been a long time since he had scaled the side of a ship.

John slowed his breathing, listening for any noises as he peered from his hiding place. The hum of the grain being sucked from the ship dominated any other sounds.

Oddly, the ship was unlit. It was barely possible that the owners faced a financial crisis calling for a severe cost-cutting campaign in which safety was no issue. John knew better. The lack of lights served another purpose: too many lights hurt a man's night vision, particularly when he looked down onto the dark waters surrounding the ship. Whoever had decided on the ship's nighttime lighting arrangement had security on their mind, not money. The lack of lights told John that this ship carried more than grain.

John continued to scan the deck, which contained a maze of equipment. At the stern, towering above the fantail, were the bridge and the seamen's quarters.

According to the inspector, the third grain hold from the bow held the special compartment. John could see the top of the hold three hundred feet from where he lay. Between him and the hold were dozens of pieces of equipment and very little light. That did not necessarily make him invisible. He worried that one or more of the guards patrolling the ship wore night-vision goggles. Good pairs were a dime a dozen these days. However, the ship had enough light that a wearer would have to be careful: a direct glance at a source of light could be very painful, even blinding. He had asked the sergeant for a pair of goggles, but none had been forthcoming.

He could see men moving about the bridge area, their figures backlit by the inside lights. They all seemed focused on internal tasks. He saw one seaman smoking a cigarette on the port side of the ship, two holds from the third one. He faced the dock area, which ran the length of the ship's port side. The man did not have a weapon showing, not that that meant anything. It was time to move. He looked at his watch. He was ten minutes behind schedule.

Slowly John crawled from his hiding space to the flange of the nearest grain hold. His movement was steady but turtle-like. John knew the human eye excelled at detecting movement. It worked less well at discerning shapes in the dark. It took him three long minutes to reach the flange.

Carefully he raised himself to a crouch and peered down the length of the ship, his eyes just above the rim of the flange. The one seaman's attention focused on the dock area. However, another seaman had emerged from the superstructure and begun to make his way down the starboard side of the ship. From his pace, John guessed he had three minutes until the seaman reached the bow. John could not tell if he was armed.

A crane towered between the second and third grain holds. Still in a crouch, he moved almost at a walking pace to the crane. He kept tight against the flange of hold number one and then hold number two. The space between the holds was only twenty-five to thirty feet. He moved smartly across the open space, all the while staying low.

He made it to the recessed shadows of the crane a full twenty seconds before the seaman came abreast of his position and passed silently on his way to the bow. As he passed, John took a good look at him from the corner of his eye. He did not stare at him. John appreciated a man's sixth sense. A pair of eyes drilling into someone's back could make him turn unexpectedly. If the seaman did, John had twenty feet to cover before he could get to him, too much space to ensure that the man did not warn his comrades. Staying hidden was the only option.

John's peripheral vision noted what the man was carrying. The submachine gun, an HK MP5-PDW by the looks of it, was stowed in a scabbard attached to the outside of his right leg. Anyone looking at the ship from a distance would see nothing, just a man strolling the ship's deck with empty hands. John felt lucky to be armed. Thank God for sergeants the world over.

John decided to wait until the man returned from the bow. He hoped the man did not park himself there for long, not that the extra time would hurt. His arms still throbbed from his climb. Minutes ticked by, and the man continued around the bow and down the port side of the ship. The seaman peering toward the docks noticed his friend's approach and lit another cigarette.

After another five minutes it was time to move. John looked down into the open hold and saw no one below. He glanced about the deck one more time, his head just above the flange. No one was looking in his direction. Quickly he climbed over the edge of the hold head first and descended using the suction cups. He made his way diagonally down the side. This course enabled him to keep an eye on the bottom of the hold as well as the top. In two minutes he was crouched at the bottom, his arms complaining from the rigorous climb.

With practiced patience, John made his way around the outer edges of the hold. He noticed two passageways out, one on each side of the ship. He tried both steel doors. The one on the port side was unlocked. John did not open it more than a quarter inch. He had no interest in learning if someone was inside. His escape was the way he had come.

Near the floor and in the middle of the aft side of the hold, John found the hidden compartment. It was exactly where Jürgenson had said it would be. Slowly, using a hooded red pencil light, he examined the edges of the compartment's hatch. He doubted it would be booby-trapped, but assumptions got a man killed. After a thorough check he felt confident no one had tampered with it. The seal looked water tight.

Under a black rubber hood he found a nine-key numeric

pad. John recognized the model immediately. The hood was cleverly designed and hid the keypad well. Only the most observant person could hope to notice it in the dark hold. Certainly no one from the deck could peer down and see it. John considered his options. There was a strong possibility that the keypad, if tampered with, might set off an alarm in the bridge or another compartment. That made any attempt to open the compartment risky. John wished he had a Geiger counter, but he could have hardly asked the sergeant for one of those. He doubted a weapon was on board because storing a bomb would carry an unacceptable level of risk. He suspected the ship would sail immediately after the weapon's arrival.

He realized he did not need to see the inside of the compartment. The presence of the keypad told John that the cargo was precious. John took his penlight and scanned the floor of the hold directly below, looking for any metal shavings that might confirm the presence of lead or other materials needed to shield the device from satellites. He saw none.

An idea occurred to him. He opened one of the pockets on his combat vest and removed a small camera, no bigger than a penny. He always carried a few with him. As he placed the camera inside the keypad hood, he watched the image on the monitor strapped to his wrist, making sure its position allowed him to see the combination entered.

He looked at his handiwork one more time, then snapped a couple of pictures with the night camera. It was an antiquated model, but it would have to do. It was time to get out of the hold; he had already been there too long. He started to climb the side, looking up as he went.

As he neared the top of the hold, he continued to glance around its perimeter. Once at the top, he peered over the edge. No one was near. Quickly he vaulted over the flange and landed silently on the deck. He made his way to the shadows of the crane. On the way he grabbed a loose bolt.

He had to wait seventeen minutes before anyone came toward him. It was the same man who had passed earlier. When the man was almost abreast of him, John threw the bolt. It hit the side of the third grain hold, the noise easily heard above the ship's machinery.

The man spun around, drawing his submachine gun. He steadied himself and slowly made his way toward the source of the sound. He had a walkie-talkie holstered in his hip pocket. The seconds ticked by. John waited patiently, absolutely still. He could smell the man, his scent a mixture of sweat and food. The man drew close to the edge of the hold. When he was only a foot away, John made his move.

Before the man could react, John threw him over the side of the hold. The man let out a blood-curdling scream as he plunged to the bottom. The dull thump marked his contact with the steel floor. John had not stood idly watching the man's fall. He had quickly worked his way twenty feet up the crane, lying prone on one of its I-beams. From his position he had a good view of the hold's bottom and the compartment in particular.

It did not take long for three seamen to arrive at the far side of the hold. With their guns drawn they moved slowly, but not too slowly. They obviously were not expecting trouble. Finally they looked down into the depths of the hold with a bright flashlight. It took them only a moment to locate their man, lying awkwardly on the cold steel twelve meters below their feet. The men spoke Russian. A string of curses rolled from their lips, one of which John caught, *razebaistvo*; it meant "fuck-up." One man pulled his walkie-talkie from his pocket and spoke into it. John could not hear what the man said. In a few moments he acknowledged an order with a grunt and replaced the walkie-talkie. All the men lowered their weapons, but they did not holster them.

Another six minutes passed. The three men talked while they scanned the hold with their sole flashlight. Suddenly a bright light flooded the bottom of the hold. It emanated from the port door, the same one John had noted as unlocked. Two men entered the hold; each carried a flashlight. They quickly scanned the floor, but found nothing that caught their attention. One of the men gave the other an order and then headed in the direction of the hidden compartment. The other walked over to their fallen comrade.

John had a pen in hand, ready to note the keys punched. The image from the miniature camera glowed an eerie green on his wrist. A hand jumped into the picture and rapidly entered 8470126, followed by the # key. John wrote the number down using a standard SEAL code. He watched the man shine his flashlight into the hidden compartment. John's view was not perfect, but he could see that the compartment was the same size as the hatch and at least six to ten feet deep. The metal inside was black and did not reflect the glow of the flashlight. The hatch was obviously automatically powered. It made sense, considering the tightness required to hide the presence of nuclear materials from the sensitive equipment installed on US spy satellites.

John had seen enough. It was time to leave before the search started, and it would in moments.

John lowered himself down the crane in absolute silence, keeping a close eye on the three men standing on the port side of the hold. They were concentrating on the two men at the bottom. John worried that that would change in moments. His feet hit the deck and he turned quickly, running a straight line to the starboard side of the ship. With one last glance in the men's direction, John crawled over the side.

As he hurried silently down the rusty surface, the lights on the ship came alive. Men yelled in Russian, and John smiled to himself. The light would only hurt the men's night vision. In another thirty feet he met the cold water once again and swam silently away.

14 Too Many Questions

General Leonov answered his phone.

"General, Alex."

"How are you, my friend?" the general asked in Russian.

"Good, thank you," Davenport replied, also in Russian. "I was wondering about Paris."

"The discussion went as planned, and I suspect we will have a deal inside of a week, but I fear there were complications." Gravely, Leonov went on to explain what had occurred on the Place de la Bastille.

Davenport listened with deep concern; warning bells rang in his mind. "What was Trubkin's description of the American?"

He listened to the general and his anger grew to a boil. He willed himself to calm down; he could not afford to lose his composure. He had only himself to blame. All that mattered was how to handle the situation and the general. It was time to assess the damage and repair it.

"I think I know who the American participant might be."

"Really," Leonov said, his voice betraying surprise. "Please explain."

"He is an ex–Navy SEAL named John Thompson. His brother Pete was murdered a few weeks ago in Washington. Pete worked for a company called SIG. It appears he leaked information to the Feds about the operation, which is connected to the Cali cartel. John is apparently trying to find his brother's killers."

The general leaned forward in his chair. He could not believe what he was hearing. "Alex, this Thompson, who was his father?"

"You know the answer to that question, General," Davenport said with a hint of his anger seeping into his voice. "Bill Thompson, the man I gave you in Iraq."

"Tell me how you know so much about this." It was more an order than a question.

"John showed up on my doorstep a little over a week ago," Davenport explained. "A powerful senator, a friend of mine, asked me if John could attend a party I was hosting. He wanted John to meet another one of my guests, former ambassador to Colombia Alan Maxwell. The events surrounding his brother's death are a little peculiar, and I discussed them with him and offered my help. He felt the US government was conducting a cover-up of some kind.

Leonov considered what Davenport had revealed. Did Everest know all this? Everest's selection of the programmer had seemed perfect at the time, but now the general suspected that the selection was a double-edged sword. It had accomplished everything Leonov had hoped for, but it might also play a role in someone else's objectives. Whose? Was the selection really a Trojan Horse? Did it explain why the link between the presidency and the cartel had yet to surface in the US press as he had anticipated? Leonov fought for control. There had to be another reason. Everest would not dare betray him; it was unthinkable.

"General, are you still there?" Davenport asked.

"Yes, Alex," Leonov said with practiced calm. "I was just digesting what you have told me. Why do you think the senator, a friend of yours, selected your party?"

"That is an excellent question which, in light of what you have told me, demands to be answered," Davenport agreed. "There is another one too. What does John's brother's death at the hands of SIG have to do with our plans?"

Leonov considered his options. At one level, telling Davenport about the Cali-Whitewater element of his plan probably made sense. However, the general knew that Davenport had aspirations for the White House. After Russia was under Leonov's control, Davenport would appear to play a prominent role in mending US-Russian relations; that was part of the plan. Although Davenport did not know it, the general did not subscribe to Davenport's next step. Having Davenport in the White House was second to having Everest in that unbelievable position. Everest was easier to control. Davenport, though more brilliant, had too many resources, making him uncontrollable in the long run. However, maybe Everest was harder to control than the general had realized.

"What do you think we should do?" Leonov asked, avoiding Davenport's question.

"Let me do a little more digging on this end. Before we act, I think we need to know if John is operating on his own or with help from more powerful sources. Give me a few days."

"Okay," the general agreed, seeing Davenport's logic, "but I have one question for you. How did the SEAL learn about the meeting in Paris?"

"That is a very good question and one for which I do not have an answer," Davenport replied smoothly. "I'll call you in the next few days."

"Da, a few days."

* * *

Amnon Herzog of the Mossad sat behind his battered metal desk, situated in the Hadar Dafna Building in Tel Aviv. The day's intelligence information from the *Al* Department, a secret unit of experienced Mossad case officers who worked under deep cover in the United States, lay before him. The department had been his for the last three years, and he enjoyed it.

Currently Amnon had four active case officers, called *Katsas*, operating in the United States; he ran them hard, but smart. Ever since the Jonathan Pollard fiasco in 1986, all Israeli efforts on American soil had to be extremely careful. Exposure was simply not an option.

Amnon remembered the "Pollard thing," as people in the Mossad still referred to it, as if it had happened yesterday. Pollard was an American Jew working for the US Navy who stole highly classified materials. He was handled by LAKAM, *Lishka Le Kishry Mada*, a special group that reported directly to the Prime Minister's office on matters of scientific interest to the State of Israel. LAKAM had used several Jewish helpers, called *sayans*, to locate and uncover information of value to Israel. Pollard was used to bring it out. The only involvement the Mossad had had in the unfortunate operation was cleaning up the mess. Until the Mossad's involvement, a number of *sayans* were vulnerable. As one case officer had put it, "How many Jews in America are willing to be branded traitors and spend the rest of their lives in prison for the glory of Israel?" Realizing the seriousness of the situation, the Mossad lent LAKAM assistance and cleaned up the mess.

The ring of the telephone interrupted his thoughts. He placed the papers on his desk and reached for the headset.

"Shalom," Amnon answered in Hebrew.

"Amnon, it's Dan Myers."

"Dan, how are you, my friend?" Amnon asked, switching to English and keeping his surprise to himself. Myers was a legend in his own time, having essentially run the CIA's clandestine operations for ten years. Amnon knew that Dan had retired ten months earlier. The official reason had been his wife's illness. If Amnon was not mistaken, she had died soon after Dan's retirement.

"The last I heard, you had retired from the agency and were growing fat with inactivity."

"I wish," Dan said.

"Seriously, how are you, my friend?" Amnon asked warmly.

"I am well, thank you," Dan replied, "and yourself?"

"Me, I am fine," Amnon said. "Busy, yes, but it is the way I like it."

"And the kids, Jacob and Llana?"

"Very well, thank you."

"Good," Dan said.

"I know you well, Dan," Amnon said. "You need something?"

"I do," Dan said slowly, his southern accent clear as he considered his words. "As you know, I'm not with the agency anymore, though my comments on certain matters are requested from time to time. It's amazing how quickly they forget you."

"I can imagine," Amnon replied with a knowing chuckle. He wondered exactly what his friend wanted and how far out of the loop he really was.

"I wondered if you could assist me by running a name through your files?"

Amnon thought for a moment before replying. Dan was not one to screw around. They had worked together on many occasions; Dan could be a bastard, but he could always be counted on. If he said he would handle it, he would. Nevertheless the request was unusual. Why not run the name through the CIA's computers, or the FBI's or the NSA's? The National Security Agency had the best computers in the world. What did Dan expect the Mossad's database to contain that the others would not? Amnon's interest was definitely piqued.

"What's the name?"

"I need this request kept out of the normal channels," Dan insisted.

Amnon replied firmly, "I can't do that."

"I know you can. I wouldn't ask if it wasn't important."

"I understand," Amnon said, "but you need to give me more. As you said, I don't have to run it through channels, but there is a cost."

"The name is Petrov."

"Petrov is a very common Russian name," Amnon stated.

"Gregori Petrov," Dan revealed. "His name came to my attention. I have a picture of him meeting an Arab man. Give me your secure fax number, and I will send it to you immediately."

"Where and when was the picture taken?"

"In Washington," Dan replied, sounding reluctant. Amnon made a note on his pad of paper. "Can you help?"

"I need more," Amnon insisted.

"I'll give you more when I have it," Dan promised. "My hands are tied."

"Is Israel involved?" Amnon asked.

"No."

"Call me in two days. You'll owe me."

"In two days then," Dan agreed.

Amnon set the telephone in its cradle. By itself the request was simple, but Amnon knew better. If Dan was involved, the affair was anything but simple.

His facsimile machine began to turn out a document. The first part of the riddle started with the picture. When the machine had finished, Amnon took a close look at the grainy photograph. He could tell instantly that the picture had been taken in Union Station. Then it struck Amnon like a speeding train. The Arab, was it Yousef? Hell, he was Israel's and the United States' most wanted terrorist, and he had recently been chased in Paris by unknown assailants. Amnon picked up the telephone and dialed an internal extension. What was Yousef doing in the United States talking to a Russian? Moreover, who was the Russian? Another thought struck him: if Yousef had indeed been in the United States, what a glaring security lapse by the Americans. Why would Dan ever reveal such a mistake? Had he been called out of retirement to analyze the lapse? Amnon needed answers, and fast.

*　　*　　*

Amnon set Aleksandr Petrov's file down and removed his reading glasses. Petrov was a KGB general currently working in the

Russian Embassy in Bogotá, Colombia. He was definitely the man in the picture. The Mossad's vast collection of files did not refer to a Gregori Petrov. Nevertheless the Mossad had plenty of information on Aleksandr Konstantinovich Petrov.

Petrov was a Soviet Karelian born in 1937. The NKVD had killed his father in 1943 when he was only five. Beria was the head of NKVD at the time, a true butcher. His very name disgusted Amnon. Petrov had grown up in a semi-criminal time and prospered on his understanding of Soviet street wisdom. Surprisingly, Leningrad Military Institute of the KGB accepted Petrov in 1960 despite his family's history. His performance at the institute was good, but not excellent. The file suggested that Petrov had a knack for flattery.

Petrov had passed with above-average grades and, after several positions, found himself stationed in the Russian Embassy in Oslo, Norway, in the fall of 1971 as the KGB resident, replacing Viktor Grushko. One of the main assets of the Norwegian operations was Arne Treholt. A young, up-and-coming member of Norway's Labor Party, Treholt supplied the KGB over the years with many classified documents on Norwegian and NATO policy. Petrov handled Treholt until Petrov's expulsion from Norway in 1977 because of the Haavik case.

Gunvor Galtung Haavik was an elderly secretary at the Norwegian Foreign Ministry. At the end of World War II, Haavik had fallen in love with a Russian prisoner of war named Vladimir Kozlov. In 1947 she was posted to the Norwegian embassy in Moscow and resumed her affair with Kozlov. By 1950 an agent for the KGB, code named Vika, began blackmailing her. From her return to Norway in 1956 until January 1977, she passed highly classified materials to the KGB. On her capture, the Norwegian government declared many Soviet personnel from the embassy personae non gratae, and consequently expelled them. Petrov fell into this group.

After his expulsion from Norway, Petrov had continued to handle Treholt, meeting him in either Vienna or Helsinki. Late in 1978, Treholt received the appointment to the Norwegian mission in the United Nations, and Petrov convinced his superiors that he should follow his agent to New York. His English was good, though his knowledge of the United States and New York City was not extensive. Petrov realized early on that Treholt was the key to his advancement within the KGB. He also realized that a big plus to Treholt's UN appointment was Norway's membership in the Security Council.

When Treholt finished his duties at the United Nations, he was admitted to the Norwegian Defense College. This gave him clearance to NATO's Cosmic Top Secret documents. Petrov returned to the Vienna station, where he continued to be Treholt's contact. In 1984, a few weeks before Treholt was apprehended by the authorities, Petrov was promoted to the rank of KGB general. Amnon wondered whether that promotion would have occurred if Treholt had been apprehended a few weeks earlier.

After Treholt's arrest, Petrov was sent to the East Berlin station and practiced his craft there with no outstanding successes. Then in 1986, after hearing of Stanislav Androsov's promotion to KGB resident in Washington, DC, Petrov apparently convinced Androsov that he would be an excellent addition to the Washington station. With a rank of general, it was an unusual request by KGB standards; however, Androsov accepted and brought Petrov to Washington. The Mossad had always wondered why Androsov had decided to bring him on; they had believed his chance for another residency was slim. Maybe Petrov had friends in high places, however unlikely that seemed. In 1992, Petrov moved to Colombia. The file stopped there.

Checks run against airline databases revealed that Petrov traveled frequently to Mexico City and on to the United States using the alias Gregori Petrov. At first Amnon had wondered if Dan had purposely given him the wrong name, but after the name turned up in the airline databases, Amnon decided that Dan knew the Russian only as Gregori. It did not make sense, though. If the Mossad could recognize Petrov from a faxed photograph, the CIA certainly should be able to recognize him from an original color photograph.

Ramzi Ahmed Yousef's background was less clear; even his name was suspect. Theories abounded as to his supporters: Iraq, Iran, Libya, some Palestinian faction, and the Jihad all made the list. There was evidence in favor of each theory, and possibly others–one linked Yousef with the CIA, at least indirectly. His enemies and the CIA's had been the same for a while: the Soviet Army in Afghanistan. From tapes of his voice, Mossad specialists suspected that he was a Palestinian, probably from Jordan. The FBI considered him a Pakistani born in Kuwait. He spoke Urdu very well, well enough, in fact, to convince Pakistani officials in New York to issue him a passport. No matter what his origins, general consensus was that Yousef had received his explosives training in the rugged foothills of Afghanistan.

What did a terrorist from Baaka Valley have to discuss with a senior SVR officer? Why would they meet in a public place in Washington, DC? The Americans wanted Yousef as much as the Israelis did. Was the Arab in the picture actually Yousef? At least one of his Arab specialists thought it was not. She had two reasons for her conclusions. First, Yousef would never travel to the United States, the risk being too great. Second, the specialist insisted that Yousef's manner of standing was incorrect. She believed the Arab was an impostor. When Amnon had pressed the specialist to conjure up a reason why an Arab would change his appearance to resemble Yousef, she had said that was not her area of expertise. Typical but understandable, Amnon reflected. It was his job to see the intent and the specialist's job to identify the facts.

Amnon had dealt with this particular specialist many times and had come to appreciate her expertise. She had proven Amnon wrong on more than one occasion. Therefore Amnon took seriously the possibility that the Arab in the picture was not Yousef. Had Dan reached the same conclusion? Something felt wrong.

Amnon paused as a thought crossed his mind. Maybe the picture was a message and not to be taken literally. Petrov was a known entity, so he was not the issue. The fact that he was Russian might be a part of the message. However, Yousef was a different matter. It was quite possible the Mossad would possess information that the Americans did not. Yousef was Dan's concern.

Amnon had already sent David Grossman back to the United States. He was the best *Katsa* Amnon had in his *Al* department. Amnon's instincts told him he would need his best to unravel the mystery Dan had placed in his lap. He hoped to hell that his Arab specialist was correct and Yousef was not the Arab in the picture.

* * *

The August weather had turned wet, and steady drizzle blanketed the city of Baltimore. Petrov sat on a beige leather couch, one of the few pieces of furniture in the studio apartment. It served as a safe house for meetings with agents and informants. Petrov had rented it for next to nothing. The landlord said the room was haunted.

The apartment complex, built in an old red brick warehouse, sat on the northern edge of the harbor in an area of town called Fells Point, the old seafaring part of Baltimore. The ghost of an old black man who had worked in the warehouse in the early 1900s and died in mysterious circumstances haunted this particular studio, or so the local folklore had it. As a result, the studio had been on the market for months. When Petrov inquired about it, the proprietor quickly acknowledged that the apartment, despite its prime location, was vacant because it was haunted. Petrov at first did not believe his ears. Why would anyone trying to rent an apartment disclose such information? How could it be true? It turned out that a local ordinance required the proprietor to disclose this fact. Petrov found it all a little hard to believe; but then again, Americans were not the most logical people. Petrov chuckled to himself as he looked out the studio window onto the gray waters of Baltimore Harbor. Ghosts! What would the Americans think of next?

His guest's arrival interrupted his thoughts. A three-tap knock sounded on the door. Petrov got up from the couch and walked to the door. A glance through the peephole revealed his agent nervously shifting from foot to foot. Petrov opened the door, and Aldrich Ames quickly stepped inside.

Ames was a senior field agent for the CIA and for the past seven years had supplied the KGB with potent information about CIA operations in Russia, Europe, and the Middle East. For his efforts, Ames was significantly richer.

"Good evening, Aldrich," Petrov said as he offered Ames a drink. He had made a pitcher of Long Island ice teas, or Bulls as Ames called them. They were a favorite of Ames from his days in Mexico City. Ames' drinking habit was well known. Igor Shurygin, the KGB counterintelligence chief in Mexico City during the mid-1980s, could attest to that. He had spent many hours drinking with Ames. His initial efforts had brought Ames to the KGB's attention.

Ames accepted Petrov's offer of a drink, knowing what the large glass contained. It was a ritual between them. Petrov took a seat on the leather couch.

"How are you?"

Ames nodded as he took a sip from his drink. "I'm okay. The usual shit. This meeting is very risky. What's up?"

"You look good," Petrov replied gently. He disliked the agent and thought him cocky. He knew his small talk frustrated Ames. The KGB handbook said it was bad form to antagonize your agent, but the temptation was great. Later he could be careless about Ames, but first, tonight.

"Whatever you say," Ames said abruptly. "What's going on? Why the quick meeting? My time is short."

"Please sit down and enjoy your drink," Petrov urged. "I have something very important to tell you." Ames reluctantly took a seat on the couch next to Petrov. He was very nervous. Petrov had expected as much. "That's better."

Ames studied Petrov carefully. "You made sure you weren't followed?"

"I was about to ask you the same thing," Petrov said. He noted Ames' stern glance. Obviously Ames had his attitude applied heavily today. He obliged him. "I was extra careful and spent all afternoon traveling the Metro. I am certain no one followed me. I'm sure you took similar precautions." Ames nodded as he took a long sip of his drink. It was strong, Petrov knew, just the way Ames liked it. He also knew that Ames probably had not taken as circuitous a route as was prudent. It was not the time or the place to scold his agent.

"The time has come for me to hand you to another officer," Petrov said. Ames turned his head and looked hard at Petrov. Before he could say anything, Petrov continued. "Moscow has asked me to handle another delicate task and you are too valuable to be anything but someone's total focus. Your new handler will also work out of the Colombian embassy. His name is Yuri Chuvaikhin. We want to use your trip to Bogotá as a chance for the two of you to meet. He is a good man and very experienced. You will like him." Petrov noted that Ames was deep in thought and appeared not to have heard his last remarks. He tried to guess what was going through the agent's mind.

"You look concerned," Petrov said.

"I just did not expect it," Ames said after another sip of his drink. "Everything okay?"

"You know better than to ask." Petrov sounded hurt. "If something was wrong, I'd tell you. You're too valuable. You should know that." Petrov continued. "I do have a quick question for you and then I'll let you go."

"What's that?"

"My superiors have asked me to inquire about a gentleman by the name of Pete Thompson," Petrov said. "They seem intent on identifying Thompson as a CIA agent or one working for another federal agency. I keep telling them I think they are off the mark, but you know how superiors can be. I was hoping that you could do a quick search in the files. I thought it would be easy for you. My superiors are anxious. You might even get a little bonus for your efforts. No promises, mind you, but I could try."

Ames pondered the request for a moment. "What's he to you?"

"Me? Nothing," Petrov replied with an air of frustration–perfectly measured, he thought. "My superiors, though, seem to think he is a Fed and could cause them some concern. I think they're wrong, but who knows? I thought you could help. It would save us a lot of time."

Ames considered the request for a moment. "I don't know anyone by that name. What checks have you already run?"

"The usual. If his name is Pete Thompson and the other information on his job application is true, he seems to be a freelance computer consultant. He lives in Steamboat Springs, Colorado. Otherwise we don't know much."

"I'll see what I can do." Petrov could tell that Ames was anxious to leave. "He doesn't have anything to do with the change?"

"None whatsoever," Petrov assured him with a smile.

Ames considered the answer.

"Thanks," Petrov added quickly. He stood; Ames did the same. "I know you must get going. Just leave a mark on the L Street mailbox when you have the information. We'll retrieve it from the usual spot."

"Okay, I'll see what I can do," Ames said. "It will take me a few days."

"Understood." Petrov pasted a broad smile on his face. He removed a white envelope from his jacket and handed it to Ames, who quickly pocketed it. The agent made for the door.

"You'll wait until well after I leave?"

"Like always," Petrov replied.

"Will I see you again?" Ames asked.

"Yes, when you come to Bogotá," Petrov confirmed. "I'll be there when you meet Yuri."

Ames nodded and let himself out of the apartment. Petrov

made his way to the kitchen area of the small studio apartment. He dumped his drink in the sink. He disliked the "Bulls" that Ames so favored. He pulled a bottle of Scotch from a cabinet and poured a healthy amount in a short glass. The Laphroaig single malt was more to his taste.

Petrov sat on the sofa. He replayed the meeting in his mind. Ames' eyes had lost focus for a few moments after he had mentioned Yuri. Petrov wondered what thought had crossed Ames' mind. The agent had probably panicked. Ames was weak and a prick, thought Petrov. The term "spoiled" also fitted. Nevertheless Moscow loved him. He brought only the best out. Petrov wondered how Ames had gotten his hands on the more sensitive information. Yes, he was a senior field agent, but the material he had access to was not necessarily what a field agent should see or know. However, it was not Petrov's job to ask such questions. As long as the material was good, he looked good.

Petrov smiled to himself. He had considered telling Ames about the ghost. Knowing Ames' paranoid and superstitious nature, Petrov believed Ames might have had a small coronary. Ah, hell with him. Petrov would end the lease. He had no further need for the safe house now that General Leonov had a bigger and better job for him to handle in Colombia.

Petrov grabbed the TV remote and turned the set on. He would spend an hour watching. Maybe the ghost would pay him a visit. The possibility added a little excitement to the prospect of watching American TV.

15 Getting Close

Amnon Herzog leaned forward in his chair. He had called the meeting, and all eyes were on him. He and three other men crowded around a wooden table. On his left was Michael Eisemann, head of the European desk. On his right were Avi Abrel, special assistant to the director of the Mossad, and Ben Litvin, director of the Mossad, who sat at the head of the table.

Amnon began, "We have identified the man Petrov met the night we had him under surveillance in Baltimore." A chair creaked in anticipation.

"A man named Aldrich Ames entered the building one hour and seventeen minutes after Petrov arrived. He left just twenty-three minutes later." Amnon paused as everyone concentrated on him. "Ames works for the CIA."

"Are you sure?" Abrel asked.

"The team recorded the license plate number of a wine-red Jaguar, which he was driving."

Eyebrows rose at the mention of a Jaguar, a pricey automobile for a CIA employee unless he was very senior, G15 or above.

"We used it to find his home address. We followed him to work yesterday, and he drove right into Langley. We did a quick search for his name against known CIA operatives; he's on the list."

"Interesting," Abrel said, as much to himself as to anyone.

"We only have limited information on him at this point," Amnon added. "Our first notes are from his days in Mexico City. He was stationed in the US Embassy for two years, starting in 1981. One of our operatives suspected that he worked for the CIA. He apparently has or had a drinking problem. He has been witnessed drinking heavily at diplomatic functions. He rotated back to the United States in 1983. He's held positions in Turkey, Langley, New York, and Rome. It will take time to build a complete picture, but I suspect he is our man."

"Do we have any idea what level he is at the CIA?" Abrel inquired.

"No, but he appears to be a field officer," Amnon replied. "His postings say as much."

"How could Langley not notice a field officer driving a fancy car like a Jaguar?" the director mused. "Are they blind?"

"Maybe he was already rich?" Eisemann suggested.

"His schooling would suggest otherwise," Amnon said.

"How does this fit in with Myers?" the director asked.

All the men at the table knew about Dan's request.

"If I could, there are a few other pieces of information I'd like to introduce before I answer your question, sir." Litvin, the director, nodded his approval.

"Two nights ago a gunfight occurred in Paris, on the rue St. Antoine and rue de La Bastille. The details are still sketchy, but a source in the Deuxième reported two gunmen tried to apprehend two men having dinner in a restaurant named Brasserie Bofinger. Shots were exchanged and men were killed. The two men held at gunpoint were Nikolai Trubkin, an ex-KGB colonel, and Ramzi Yousef."

Exclamations sounded around the table.

"Who were the gunmen?" Litvin demanded.

"We're not sure," Amnon stated, "but a copy of the Deuxième report from our source indicates the French believe the gunmen were Israeli."

A grave look shadowed Litvin's face. "What led them to this conclusion?"

"We have no idea, sir."

"You think this incident is related. Why?"

"I've mentioned the passports we found in Petrov's room in Washington," Amnon began. "One was a Russian forgery of a French passport, intended for Yousef. A meeting between Yousef and Trubkin, who is ex-KGB, strengthens the possibility that the Russians are working with Yousef and whoever currently employs him."

"Can we confirm whether Yousef used the passport to enter France?" asked Abrel.

"We are working on that, but it will take time," Amnon replied. "However, the timing suggests he did not."

"One question keeps entering my mind," Abrel continued. "Why did Dan Myers call and suggest that Yousef had come to the United States and gone undetected?"

Amnon knew he was about to put his neck on the chopping block. "I have a theory on that. Yousef never went to the United States."

"But the passports…" Abrel blurted.

"Yousef never traveled to the United States, and Dan knew this from the beginning."

"Are you suggesting he created the photo and the passports?" Abrel asked.

"Yes."

"Explain," Litvin ordered.

"Let's say that Dan is pulled out of retirement to take on a very sensitive project, one that requires all his skills. We all know he's one of the best operators they have. That means something big is looming on the horizon. The matter must be extremely delicate, so the need-to-know list would be very, very short.

"Let's speculate that he is handed a few chunks of information, maybe related and maybe not. He starts working the problem and realizes Israel is the target of an ongoing operation. Because he cannot give us the details, either because he doesn't have them or is fearful of giving us too much, he decides to warn us. The warning is straightforward: there are two targets we should keep our eyes on, Petrov and Yousef.

"I'll bet the CIA knows about Ames. It's because of him that there's an ongoing operation. I suspect Israel may not be the only target of this operation. Because the information came from Ames' treasonous relationship with the Russians, the Americans are keeping the details close to the vest. We know the CIA has lost an inordinate number of Russian agents in the last seven years. Maybe Ames is the reason."

Amnon continued. "Remember that an ex-KGB colonel and an Arab terrorist had dinner. Now, what do you suppose they were talking about?"

Quiet engulfed the room again. Amnon broke it. "Nuclear weapons or components. That's my guess." He continued, "We all know Russia is in a bad way. We hear it again and again from the Jews emigrating from the former Soviet Union. We interview them daily. We also know the Americans are spending billions of dollars to help the Russians improve the security of their nuclear weapons. They would not spend this kind of money unless the need was great. We know it is.

"As much as we would like the American approach to work, it's probably wishful thinking. Russia is too big, and too many senior members of the old Russian establishment, including the military, want to earn hard currency. Everything is for sale. Therefore, I believe Yousef is trying to procure a nuclear device or components from the Russians, be it the mob or the government or both. Furthermore, I think Dan has evidence supporting this fact. He can't reveal his source or the particulars, but he's telling us in no uncertain terms that we need to watch Yousef and Petrov. I think the picture was an attempt to show a relationship, and the fact that it was fake is a signal that the picture itself is not important. His insistence on communicating outside the normal channels supports my theory."

"Your theory would mean that official Washington does not believe it should share information that nuclear weapons might be headed to the Middle East," Eisemann said.

"I suppose it does," Amnon agreed, "or official Washington doesn't know yet."

Everyone was silent as they considered that possibility, with its prospect of almost unimaginable dangers.

"Are you also saying Dan is disobeying a direct order by giving us a heads up?" Abrel pressed.

"I can only speculate on his restrictions," Amnon replied. "However, I do know Dan well. He's all business. Maybe he needs the help and doesn't have the resources to pursue Yousef. Hard to believe, but possible, and if official Washington was out of the loop, his resources might be scarce. No matter, he wouldn't have put Yousef in our sights if he hadn't had a very good reason."

"Your argument is a strong one," Litvin said, "but I wonder if we could go back to my other question. Why do the French think we had a hand in the Paris incident?"

"I think Dan arranged the whole thing. He wants Yousef to think we're after him. He is forcing us to get involved."

"Do you think Dan sent the gunmen?" Abrel asked.

"Yes, maybe."

"But if the Americans knew where Yousef was, they would work with the French and capture him."

"At first thought I would agree," Amnon began. "However, the French are funny. Remember, they have a huge Arab population and have experienced a lot of terrorist activity in the last few years. Conducting a joint operation with the Americans to capture an Arab terrorist would be risky politically. Also, it takes time to coordinate a joint operation. Maybe there just wasn't the time."

"Maybe we should stay neutral and let Dan create whatever situations he wants," Abrel suggested.

"And possibly allow nuclear weapons to arrive in the Middle East that might be targeted against us?" Amnon exclaimed. "We can't assume Washington has a failsafe plan to stop the operation and then show us how heroic they were."

"It is a delicate matter," Litvin said. "Does anyone have anything else to add?"

Everyone was silent.

Litvin nodded. "I think the risk is minimal if we proactively pursue Yousef. We will undoubtedly lose a few reliable sources, but I believe the picture Amnon has painted justifies this risk. Also, let's put Ames under surveillance for a week. Any questions?"

Amnon hid his dismay on the surveillance issue. He had, after all, gotten what he wanted.

"Good," the director concluded. "Amnon, this is your show, you take point. I expect full cooperation from everyone. I will go to the Prime Minister and get the official sanction to terminate Yousef as quickly as possible."

16 Drying Off

John wandered the narrow streets of Old Town and found himself enthralled by its charm. He knew himself well—normally he regarded buildings from a practical point of view—but the thirteenth-century city of Tallinn, Estonia, was special. It surprised him.

Somehow it had survived countless invasions, including fifty years of Soviet rule. Despite history, the old section of Tallinn showed little of the architectural insensitivity typical of Russian occupation. That was a marvel in itself.

Since the departure of the Russians two years earlier, Estonians had renovated many buildings in the Old Town section of Tallinn. Their efforts were admirable. The cobblestone streets and thirteenth-century structures created an atmosphere reminiscent of how simple life used to be. John was equally impressed with the Estonian people and the pride they took in their city. The country was savoring the sweet victory of its newfound freedom.

John stopped and stared at the large stone tower, known as Neitsitorn, the Virgin Tower, which rose into the clear night, its pointed top surrounded by bright stars. This ancient tower marked the western corner of the forty-foot-high stone wall that surrounded Old Town. According to John's guidebook, a restaurant now occupied the top floors of the tower. However, at this hour it was closed.

He had begun the evening with dinner at Nimeta Baar, "The

Bar with No Name," an Irish establishment that served Guinness by the pint. The food did have an Irish bent, but the owner, who was from Scotland, appeared to have succumbed to his nephew's California tastes, evident in the menu. John had decided to take a stroll through the thirteenth-century town to work off the evening's meal and to familiarize himself with the unknown area. One could never know enough about a city. Of everything he had seen so far tonight, he liked the Toompea Castle, a pink building that now housed the Estonian parliament, and the beautiful onion-shaped domes of the Alexsandr Nevsky Cathedral, a Russian Orthodox Church most. He doubted Estonians would agree; their dislike for the Russians went without saying.

He turned back from the Virgin Tower, retraced his steps through the courtyard, and headed to a small opening at the far end, curious where it might lead. As he walked, his mind turned to Logan. He pictured her standing alone on the beach, barefoot, as the gentle waves broke on the stony beach, sending the warm waters of the Pacific cascading through her toes. He liked her toes; something about them he found fascinating. He had always liked tanned feet, but her feet were special. The silliness of the thought made him chuckle. If only his fellow frogs could read his mind, how they would laugh.

He remembered his first night with her under the beauty of the sky. Not a care in the world had clouded their minds. Damn, he missed her. As the only living member of his family he was alone. Yes, he had his SEAL buddies and they were the best friends a man could have, but he certainly was not going to spend the rest of his life with them. They would have their own families; he would be a well-liked uncle at best. Logan offered John something he had never considered seriously–a lifelong companionship. He reveled in the thought. How could one person affect another one so profoundly?

John stepped past the Vana Villem Shop, a store whose wares were not particularly obvious, and stopped as he came to the corner. The tiny street jogged left and led to a stone street half covered with cement steps. He tried to push Logan from his thoughts and to concentrate on his surroundings. If he recalled correctly, the guidebook said this street led to Ratashaevu Street. He'd give it a try.

* * *

It was a few hours until sunset, but it felt like evening already. Sunrise breathed steadily as she stroked him with a brush. At this time she always found her mind focusing on John. Eleven days had passed since he had departed–an eternity. A question kept coming back to her. What drew her to him? Why did she keep asking it? Was it guilt about her feelings toward John? Greg, what would he think? Would he understand that she had fallen in love with a man she hardly knew?

Logan rubbed a spot behind Sunrise's left ear with her fingers; he bobbed his head in response.

"Sunrise, you met John. Am I crazy to love him?" Sunrise bobbed his head again. "What do you know?" Logan insisted. "You're only a horse, though a beautiful horse." She rested her head on his strong side.

Every time she replayed the three full days she had spent with John, she felt joy spread through her. And then he had left suddenly, saying it was time to pursue his brother's killers before the trail got too cold. John had been very upset when they had last spoken. She recalled his expression at the breakfast table before he announced his plans to leave. Something had happened, but she couldn't put her finger on it. At first she had assumed it was something she had done, but now she thought differently.

And her father, what was he up to? Did he not like John? He had asked her if she had heard from him. At first she had thought she was letting her disappointment show too readily; later she realized he had not asked about her feelings. His interest had only been in John. She now suspected that John's quick departure had something to do with her father. Had her father disapproved and sent John packing? It seemed unthinkable. She would never forgive him if it turned out to be true. She knew her father was a control freak, but would he go that far? He had not particularly liked Greg, but had not interfered. Why would he start now?

She rubbed Sunrise behind the ears again. Life was never as simple as it should be. She just wished John would call. If only she knew his phone number, she could call him and at least leave a message after hearing his recorded voice.

* * *

General Leonov looked at Trubkin with pure anger in his eyes. He wanted to leap across his desk and strangle the man.

"Trubkin, I find it unbelievable that anyone was able to board the Sadko, let alone locate the compartment. This is an extremely serious lapse of security on your behalf."

"Yes, General."

"What do you intend to do about it?"

Trubkin appeared to consider the general's question, having known full well that the general would ask it. He was prepared.

"I've learned that an American visited Inspector Jürgenson of the Tallinn police two days ago," he began. "If Mirek revealed the existence of the hold to the inspector, maybe the inspector mentioned it to the American."

The general growled. "What's the link?"

"The name of the man is John Thompson. I spoke with a contact at the airport who made a picture using footage from the surveillance cameras. The picture captures this American as he walks through customs."

Trubkin laid the six-by-eight picture on the general's desk. "He is the American who was in the Brasserie Bofinger."

The general stared at the picture and then at Trubkin. Too many things had not gone to plan, and a common theme stitched them together, this American. Why was the SEAL involved? On the surface, the plan hatched by Everest had killed the SEAL's brother. Had Everest anticipated the results and the SEAL's behavior or had both been unexpected? Also, was the SEAL a loner or someone's sharpened instrument?

"Where is he now?"

"In his hotel, the Palace Tallinn Hotel. He is scheduled to leave Tallinn tomorrow aboard an SAS flight bound for London with a change in Copenhagen."

"Your plan?"

"I have instructed my men to pick him up as soon as he exits the hotel. I figure an incident in the hotel serves no one."

The general nodded, thinking that when Trubkin killed the SEAL, it would no longer matter. However, a question still nagged the general: how had the SEAL learned about the meeting in Paris?

There was one more matter. He had to assume that someone other than John now knew about the special compartment on the grain ship. That was a problem. He did not have time to find another ship, let alone install another compartment. No, he needed another means of hiding the ship from prying eyes on earth and in the sky.

"Kill him when you have found out all there is to know. I expect you to handle it personally."

"Yes, sir." Trubkin saluted and left the general's office, wondering how he could possibly reach Tallinn in time.

* * *

John descended five flights of steps to the lobby of the Palace Tallinn Hotel. It was a pleasant, though pricey, establishment located a block from Old Town.

John approached the front desk as the morning sun cut through the lobby's glass windows. As he slid his plastic room keycard across its surface, he felt the hairs on his back rose.

"Checking out, sir?" the polite girl behind the counter asked in accented English.

"Yes, thank you," John responded. He scouted his immediate surroundings to get a bearing on what had alerted his instincts. It took him only a few seconds.

Seated in the bar and breakfast area situated to the left of the front desk were two men. They looked completely out of place and stared at him as though he were chum in shark-infested waters. Pretending not to notice, John turned slowly, stealing a glance through the hotel's front door. He saw exactly what he had expected–two black 220 Mercedes parked in the center of Vabaduse vdljaka, an odd-shaped plaza located in front of the hotel's entrance. The vehicles were stuffed with surly-looking occupants. He did not think for a minute that Jürgenson had provided these chaperons. Estonians and Russians did not mix, and they had Russian written all over them.

"How will you be paying for the room, sir?" the girl asked.

"Credit card," John said as he pretended to look for his wallet. "Damn, I must have left it in my room. Can I have the key back?"

The girl nodded and handed John his key.

"I'll be right back."

He left his small suitcase behind; everything in it could easily be replaced. He took the wide staircase from the lobby a step at a time. He was not about to use the tiny elevator; its confinement was too tempting a trap. In a little over a minute he was standing outside his room. He slid the plastic key into the slot, heard a click, and let himself in, glancing quickly down the hall. No one had followed him.

From the small backpack slung over his left shoulder, John removed the HK USP 9-millimeter and two spare clips. He had told the sergeant that the gun had sunk on his return swim from the ship. He doubted the sergeant believed him, but he hadn't really cared; a gun could always come in handy. John stepped up to the glass door of his fifth-floor room and opened it. It led to the small balcony. The draft made the window curtains billow to life. He quickly stepped outside, his backpack strapped firmly to his body. With a practiced eye he scanned the tops of the surrounding buildings for any sign of activity; they were all clear. Below him a small parking area covered the expanse between the back of the hotel and the neighboring buildings. One red car was parked under a row of trees, but it obviously was not part of the Russian surveillance effort, as it was parked engine first into the building.

He lacked a rope for rappelling to the ground; however, each room had a balcony similar to his. SEALs spent a lot of time learning how to jump from one object to another. The courses in San Diego and Virginia Beach had had big and small poles arranged at random intervals and topped off at different heights. Jumping from one pole to another looked a lot easier than it was. The spacing was based on the specific amount of effort required to reach any given pole. A leap demanded total concentration and control of one's body. John had spent hours leapfrogging from one pole to another. At times like this he appreciated the value of such repetitive training.

He grabbed the rail, making sure it was secure, and eased himself over the side. He lowered himself until he was fully stretched out, maintaining a firm grip on the floor of his balcony. A gentle swing dropped him noiselessly to the balcony on the fourth floor. He came out of his crouch and took another quick look at the nearby buildings and parking area. All looked clear, and he repeated the process.

Three minutes later he found himself on the ground. He figured his Russian pals were getting anxious. A good five minutes had elapsed since he had hurried up the staircase in search of his missing wallet.

John scurried across the small parking lot to the far side and worked his way along the back of a brick building, trying to keep under the cover provided by the trees.

He quickly reached Roosikrantsi Street and turned right,

which led him to the western end of the Vabaduse våljak where it met Kaarli puiestee, the southwest corner of the square in front of his hotel.

As he peered around the corner toward the entrance of his hotel, he heard a powerful engine accelerate behind him. Quickly he turned and stared down Roosikrantsi. One of the black Mercedes was headed in his direction. John broke into a run and sprinted across the square, setting his sights on Old Town and its narrow cobblestone streets a quarter mile away. His late-night stroll of Old Town was about to pay handsome dividends.

He heard shouts and the roar of a second engine as he reached the other side of the square. He started up Komandandi tee, a quiet street that worked its way uphill toward Toompea Castle. John cut off the road toward a house that backed up against the thirteenth-century wall near Neitsitorn. With practiced skill he climbed the wall, using the corner created by the meeting of the wall and a nearby chimney.

Behind him he heard a car zoom past and a second one skid to a halt. The two goons from the lobby leaped from the Mercedes, still breathing hard from their dash between the lobby and the waiting car. They were a good fifty yards away, and John had no doubt that these two apes would have a difficult time following him up the side of the wall. However, he knew their plans did not include chasing him. They were the rear guard, intent on keeping him from turning back as the two cars raced up the hill, where they could enter Toompea at Kiek in de Kvk Tower and continue the pursuit. They wanted him alive.

John considered dropping to the ground and facing the two men; better them than the two cars circling around his position. Then one of the two goons fired at him twice. Both shots missed but sent John scurrying over the top of the wall. He rolled quickly away and onto a grassy embankment held in place by the wall.

His arms and legs burned as his lungs fought for air, but he forced himself to move, racing up a small embankment that paralleled a set of cement stairs. They were guarded by a worn red-pipe banister and led to the cobblestone area in the front of Neitsitorn. He knew he had precious little time until the other Russians entered the far end of the courtyard. He remembered from last night that there were three possible exits, not including the one he had just taken. That was not an exit at all by pedestrian standards, and less so now since the Russians had covered it with their TK automatic pistols.

Holding his own pistol tightly in his right hand, he dashed across the courtyard at a full run. As he closed on the far end of the courtyard, he glanced left through an opening in the great wall. It led uphill to an area surrounding the Alexsandr Nevsky Cathedral. He could not see the beautiful onion-shaped domes of the Russian Orthodox Church; however, he could see two pistol-toting Russians running down the uneven surface of the street. They yelled when they saw him, but they were too far away to use their pistols. John noted that each had a radio jammed in his belt. He would deal with these two Ivans later.

Twelve long strides later, John made it to the far end of the courtyard, leaping through an opening and onto a street so tiny that it could not possibly hold a car. It looked like a dead end, but he knew better. He dashed past a shop he vaguely remembered from the previous night, stopping at a corner where the tiny street jogged left.

John pressed his back against the wall and steadied his breathing. He heard a car speed down Pikk jalg from the direction of the Alexsandr Nevsky Cathedral. The street lay thirty-five feet away on the other side of the thick wall from where he stood. Immediately a second car came to a screeching halt.

John had anticipated the Russians' moves. From Pikk jalg, a stone archway led to a stone pathway from the street. It intersected with his tiny street and led to the wider street with cement steps running down the left side. The street with steps, he recalled, led to Ratashaevu. John stood just above this intersection. The timing would be close. He would get only one chance.

He had based his plan on the notion that the Russians wanted him alive. They needed to question him and learn what he had done with the knowledge taken from the Sadko; only then would they shoot him in the back of the head. He continued to listen as the two groups of Russians closed in on his position, their footsteps echoing in the confined passageways.

John heard the two Ivans above and behind him stop running when they reached the small pathway from the courtyard. The other Russians, who sounded like more than two, jogged down the stairs from the Pikk jalg archway. As John had hoped, they thought he had already passed this point and hurried down the steps, unaware that he was still behind them.

As they burst out of the archway, John killed two of the three Russians with single shots to the back of the head. The third Russian managed to turn a hundred degrees in John's direction before two quick shots to his chest sent him to the bloodied cobblestone street.

John dashed from his position against the wall and quickly retrieved one of the Russians' radios. He jumped into the archway from which the three pursuers had just emerged. John held the device away from his body, pressed the Send button, and yelled in Russian, "Get your fucking hands in the fucking air, you American bastard." In a different voice, he spoke quickly into the radio: "We got him."

He released the Send button and tossed the radio on the ground. Not ten seconds later, the two Russians he had seen sprinting from the shadows of the oak came into view. Their guard was down and their eyes were riveted on their dead comrades. John did not hesitate for an instant, killing both men with single shots to the head. His fifteen-round clip now held only nine bullets.

Without pausing to look at his handiwork, he took two steps at a time up the archway and quickly reached the portal that led to Pikk jalg. Holding his pistol in front of him, he scrambled from the archway in a low crouch and squeezed off three quick shots through the open windows of the waiting car. The driver was standing, facing John but on the far side of the Mercedes between the open driver-side door and the frame of the car. He had his gun aimed across the car roof at the archway entrance. The Russian never had a chance to place John in his sights; the roof of the car had prevented it.

John's three shots through the passenger-side window found their mark, stitching the Russian's stomach and sending him tumbling to the ground. John looked up and down the street while he circled around the hood of the running car, holding his pistol steady with a two-handed grip. The Russian was on his back, his feet awkwardly bent beneath his body. John fired a single shot into his head. In combat, only dead tangos were safe ones.

He reached down, retrieved the dead Russian's TK automatic pistol, tossed it onto the front passenger seat of the car. His own backpack followed suit. The only thing of value in the backpack was a set of forged travel documents. The pictures he had taken of the grain ship were taped tightly to the inside of his left thigh, safe at least for now.

John climbed in the car and considered his next move. He knew the other car had driven down Pikk jalg, presumably to block his exit onto Ratashaevu Street. Behind him the coast should be clear, unless the Russians had other vehicles. John ejected his almost-spent clip and inserted a fresh one, then jammed the car into reverse, slamming the accelerator to the floor. The powerful engine roared to life and sent the tires screeching in protest as the car raced backward up Pikk jalg and toward the Alexsandr Nevsky Cathedral.

John realized that all the gunfire probably meant the police had been called. Old Town was quaint and as far as one could get from a war zone, especially at 6:30 in the morning. He was thankful the traffic in Old Town was mostly pedestrian. Only cars with special permits could enter, keeping the narrow streets free of vehicle traffic. The people he had seen in the vicinity had either stared at the bedlam from low crouches or executed a full retreat from the area. Luckily none had stood in any direct danger.

As his car entered the intersection by the cathedral he slammed the brakes, bringing it to a halt. After throwing it into drive, he headed around the left side of the cathedral and bore right. He turned left through Lossi plats in front of Toompea Castle. Meanwhile he grabbed the car phone from its cradle and dialed Jürgenson. He knew the inspector would be waiting at the airport, but he hoped his office could reach him.

Seven rings later the phone was answered. John did not bother to listen to the speaker at the other end of the line. In Russian he yelled, "This is Thompson, I need to speak to Inspector Jürgenson immediately and I mean fucking now."

"Sorry, but…"

"I know he's at the friggin' airport," John yelled. "Get him on the god-damn phone."

As silence filled the headset, John turned left onto Kaarli puiestee and in moments found himself slowing before his hotel. The stop light at the intersection of Kaarli puiestee and Påmu maantee had turned red. He waited, keeping his eyes peeled for the other Mercedes and the police. He desperately wanted to push the accelerator to the floor and cut through the intersection, but that would only draw attention. The big black Mercedes he was driving was bad enough, and dangerous driving would be obvious to even the dumbest of cops.

The light turned green, and he joined the rest of the anxious drivers crossing the intersection onto Estonia puiestee. He accelerated and forced his way past other cars. The moves were aggressive but not reckless. Soon he was driving at eighty kilometers past the Estonia Theatre and Concert Hall only to pass the Kaubamaja a few seconds later. At the end of the next block he turned right onto Tartu Road, which led directly to the airport. He figured he was ten minutes from the airfield.

He glanced in his mirrors, wondering if he would ever connect with the inspector. At the current rate he would arrive at the airport before Jürgenson came on the line. Suddenly he forgot all about the inspector and threw the phone into the passenger seat. A black Mercedes was charging him from behind. It was almost a quarter kilometer away, and in that instant John made a decision.

He slammed on the brakes and sent his car into a spin. The car stopped perpendicular to the road, with the passenger-side doors facing the oncoming Mercedes. Horns blared as bewildered drivers responded to his move. One car just missed striking the rear fender of the oncoming car as the driver somehow managed to veer left at the last possible moment.

John barely noticed as he grabbed his gun and stuck the extra TK pistol in his belt. He jumped out of his car and crouched on one knee directly behind the rear wheel while he looked underneath the car, keeping an eye on his adversary.

He had just done the unexpected. What would the driver do? Would he try to ram the car, possibly killing himself, or would he attempt to shoot as he drove by?

As the black Mercedes neared, it began to slow uncertainly. John knew the driver had not seen anyone flee the car because no one had. But why else would anyone suddenly stop in the middle of the chase, especially with a good quarter-kilometer head start?

Under normal circumstances John would have attempted to broaden his lead, but he did not welcome the prospect of arriving at the airport in a desperate gun battle. The authorities would have no way of knowing who was the good guy. No, he would rather take his chance with what he expected was one driver, probably Trubkin.

John watched the Mercedes approach slowly. Horns still blared as drivers hurried around the two obstacles blocking their passage; few, if any, knew how close they were to dangerous ground. The other Mercedes finally came to a halt fifty feet from his car. John listened for the driver to put the car in park as he held both pistols in his hands. It took only a few seconds.

As soon as he heard the shift, John stood and ran around the rear end of his car, firing the TK pistol into the windscreen of the other Mercedes. The driver never had a chance. After unloading ten shots into the window, John switched his aim and pumped the last five shots of the clip into the engine block. A nine-millimeter pistol would do only minimal damage, but maybe enough. As the last bullet fired he dropped the gun and aimed the HK pistol into the recesses of the car, continuing to run toward it. As he approached, he leaped onto the hood and peered into the front seat.

The driver was bloodied but not dead. He had been looking toward the driver-side door in anticipation that John would approach from that angle. The man's pistol mirrored the focus of his eyes.

As John's weight struck the car, the driver realized his mistake. His eyes came up and met John's almost instantly. However, his gun could not follow at the same speed. John fired three more shots, killing him.

He looked around and heard sirens in the distance. He could not believe it had taken the police so long to respond. He quickly wiped the handle of the pistol on his shirt and threw it inside the car, jumped off the hood, and dashed to his waiting Mercedes. He put it into gear and headed it in the direction of the airport.

After a moment, he felt intensely disappointed that Trubkin had not been the driver.

* * *

John parked the Mercedes in the airport's short-term parking area and jogged into the terminal with his backpack slung over his left shoulder. He had given himself a once-over and had not found any blood on his clothes. However, his hands were a different story. They were very dirty from the pistols. He needed to find a restroom before his encounter with the inspector, but he had no such luck.

"Where the hell have you been?" Jürgenson shouted. "They finally get me on the phone and all I could hear was fucking gunfire. What is the meaning of this?"

Six other officers surrounded the inspector and their eyes

studied John with intensity. He could tell they did not like what they saw.

"I had some visitors at the hotel," John said in English. "Inspector, could we find somewhere more private? I think it would benefit us both."

The inspector thought for a moment and nodded. "Where's the car?"

"Parking lot, black Mercedes."

"The guns?"

"In the other Mercedes, stuck in the middle of Tartu."

Jürgenson spoke to one of his officers in Estonian, then he turned back to John.

"This way."

Five minutes later the inspector and John took seats in a small customs office. Two of his men joined them in the office and the other three stood outside the door.

"Explain."

John did just that, leaving no details out. It took him fifteen minutes.

"Six men dead," Jürgenson roared. "There will be hell to pay for this. Tallinn is a peaceful city. People will demand that someone be held responsible."

"I understand," John said, knowing full well that the inspector was in a difficult position. That position would only worsen when it became known that one of the guns used in the battle was from his police department.

"What am I to do with you?"

"That's up to you," John suggested, knowing it was important for the inspector to feel in control. "However, we do know that the ship must be mighty important to them; otherwise why risk attacking me in broad daylight? It was a big risk."

"You have a point, but it doesn't solve the situation you've created."

"Might I mention that I caused nothing," John said. "Remember, they attacked me. I was just on my way to the airport."

"Skip the bullshit," the inspector ordered. After a moment he turned toward his men. "Escort him to the plane and do not, I repeat, do not let him out of your sight or it will be your jobs."

John wiped the look of astonishment from his face as Jürgenson held out his passport.

"What are you waiting for?" the inspector demanded. "Get the hell out of my sight before I change my mind. Now move it."

John did not hesitate a moment longer.

* * *

Logan sat straight in the saddle, her black riding helmet strapped tightly to her head and her single braid bouncing with her movements. The horse breathed hard after the canter while Logan gazed east, absorbing her surroundings. The sun had crested the horizon only moments before, casting a soft light across Santa Barbara and the waters of the Pacific. She was fascinated by the spectacle, not only for its silent beauty but in knowing that John was somewhere to the east, the sun already riding high in his sky. She just wondered where.

Almost two weeks had passed and not a word. She hated to admit it, but she was deeply disappointed. She felt silly. She hardly knew John Thompson, and yet the few times they had made love together had been experiences she would not soon forget. There was something special about their union. She could not begin to explain it.

Nevertheless she had her doubts now. What was John up to? Did he love her? Had it all been an act? Somewhere deep inside her, she knew it wasn't so. She could still feel John's passion—it was strong and free, like hers—but what would prevent him from calling her? Had something dreadful happened to him? Could he have met his brother's fate?

She was so tired of doubting–her life, Greg's death, and now John. Would life ever yield her a clear path? It seemed improbable. Life could never be that simple. Why was this? Was it part of a greater plan or just the complications of too many people walking the earth at the same time?

She had slept poorly again. Her night had been filled with realistic dreams of John chased by evil men. She had screamed time and again, but he had never heard her warnings. The frustration was palpable. Why didn't he hear her? The chases had always moved away from her. She had tried to keep up, but they had moved too quickly. Suddenly John would be out of her sight, and she left powerless to help him.

A chill traveled up her spine at the memory. Her fear for him was so strong, and it distressed her. Maybe he was just a dream, a bad dream. But he wasn't. Her father had made that all too clear. He had asked her again about John, wondering if she had heard from him. When she had shot back an angry "No," her father had suggested that she never would and that she had better get used to it. Why had he said such a cruel thing? Was he just angry at John for treating her this way?

Logan dug her heels into the horse's strong sides and he responded, moving out quickly. She just wanted to ride east. John had to be out there somewhere.

17 Tugging a Ball of Yarn

Davenport weighed the facts in front of him. He found it all hard to believe. Incredible, the sons of a man who had nearly ended his smuggling operation were now involved in his latest plans—an extraordinary coincidence. Or was it? Davenport did not believe in coincidence.

His contact in the Washington Metro police department had indicated that the Feds had taken possession of Pete Thompson's body immediately, an unusual act. Most homicides went to the local coroner and then the body was turned over to the family. Also, the speed suggested that the Feds had anticipated Pete's death. Davenport could not figure how; nevertheless the thought led to some interesting possibilities.

This train of thought led to other possibilities, including the chance that John was operating on behalf of a federal agency. The DEA was a likely candidate. John's visit to California fitted this assumption. He had wanted to meet discreetly with former ambassador Maxwell, hoping to learn more about the Cali cartel. Davenport knew Maxwell had widespread contacts in Colombia, both in business and in the government. He also knew that Maxwell's father had developed many of the contacts while working for the CIA decades earlier. Certainly the Cali cartel was one of these contacts. However, if John was working for the DEA, he would already know everything he needed to know about the cartel. No, more likely John's meeting with Maxwell had given the cartel a reliable sighting of Pete Thompson, a man they believed to be dead. That fitted. The only aspect of the visit that baffled Davenport was the location. Why had the senator insisted that Maxwell and John meet at his house? Senator Bennett knew that Maxwell and he did not get along. Nevertheless the senator had insisted, using the pretext that the island was far from prying eyes.

Davenport's discussion with the younger Thompson was interesting in that John had asked him for help. In addition, if John did work for the DEA, Davenport could not see how a relationship with his daughter would make any sense. It probably would not even be permitted.

Was John working for the DEA? Davenport had to assume the DEA knew about his own past contacts with the Cali cartel, at least on some level. Had they selected the meeting place? Was part of their plan to have John elicit his help, or was John out to catch him?

Then came Paris. It did not fit any of the scenarios. The cartel had nothing to do with the meeting between Trubkin and Yousef. The gunmen had failed in their attempt, but only Yousef's luck had stopped the two assailants. The description provided by Trubkin matched John perfectly.

Davenport remembered that John had left a little suddenly, at least a day before he had planned. Davenport had spoken to the general that day about the meeting in Paris. Did John know Russian too? Had he overheard the conversation? Was that why he had grabbed the printed e-mail message? Reluctantly Davenport knew the answers were yes, yes, and yes.

Davenport did not understand why John and his unknown partner had not worked with the French police. If the DEA had sent John to France, he would, at least under normal circumstances, have established a liaison with the French, probably the Deuxième. Davenport was missing something, and he knew it. It was time to squeeze the senator.

He had learned long ago that all politicians were easy to persuade. Any of three things made politicians willing participants in one's desires: money, the threat of a scandal, or the promise of power. He thought money would provide the best means to persuade Senator Bennett in this instance. He dialed the number on his secure cordless phone.

A receptionist answered the phone.

"Bill, please."

"Excuse me, sir, may I ask who is calling?"

"Certainly, tell him it's Alex Davenport."

"Yes, sir."

Davenport waited. He figured the senator knew this call was coming. He wondered if the statesman was dreading it.

"Alex, what can I do for you today?" the senator asked, his tone upbeat.

Davenport started with an issue they had discussed in an earlier conversation. It took a few minutes to complete. Next Davenport said, "Bill, I enjoyed meeting Pete Thompson. He's a nice young man."

"Yes, he is," the senator replied.

Davenport thought he detected a second's hesitation in the senator's voice. "Did you know that he died three days before he came to visit me?"

The senator was quiet for a moment. "Say that again."

"Bill, stop bullshitting me," Davenport ordered. "I know damn well John Thompson showed up at my house masquerading as his dead brother."

"Well, yes, you're right, of course," the senator replied. "John and I knew each other from the Senate Select Intelligence Committee. He appeared every once and a while to brief us. I've admired him. He always gave no-nonsense answers."

"Why did you lie to me, Bill?"

"John wanted to let people think his brother was still alive. He thought it would give him some type of advantage. I was in no position to argue."

"And?"

"And what?"

"And who told John to come see you?"

"No one, I believe," the senator declared. "John came of his own accord."

"Then why did you pick my venue? You know Maxwell and I dislike each other. It would have been more appropriate to have the meeting at his house."

"It was a matter of timing," the senator explained. "John was in a rush. I knew about the party because you had sent me an invitation. I knew Maxwell would be invited out of social courtesy, and I confirmed as much. It seemed okay to me."

"How come I don't believe you?" Davenport said.

"Alex, is this any way to treat a friend?"

"Damn it, Bill, what about me?" Davenport demanded. "I give you a lot of fucking money each and every goddamn year, and what do I get for it? Bullshit. Tell me the truth, damn it."

"I am."

"How much is it worth to you?" Davenport asked, anger on the edge of his voice. "How much?"

"Really, I…"

"Cut the shit, Bill. I've known you too damn long. You're a shitty liar. "

"Alex, I can't. I really can't."

Davenport considered his options. He was surprised the senator was putting up such a fight. It wasn't like him. "How about a million dollars, Bill? Would that help grease your palm?"

Davenport knew that was a lot of money, even by the senator's standards. He waited.

"That's very generous of you," the senator stalled. "Very generous."

"My patience is thin today."

"I really shouldn't, Alex. I've known him a long time. I just can't."

"Two million."

Silence hung on the other end of the line. Finally the senator spoke. "Dan Myers."

"Excuse me?" Davenport said, shocked.

"Myers," the senator repeated. "Dan Myers. You know, ex-CIA."

Davenport stood and started to pace. Myers. How could it be? What had he done to attract that man's attention? Could John be working for Myers?

"I trust we have a deal," the senator continued.

"You'll get your damn money," Davenport bellowed. "Is there anything else you should tell me?"

"No, not that I can think of."

"Be damn sure this conversation stays between us, Senator."

Davenport slammed the phone down with conviction. Fucking Myers. He hated that asshole. He had no illusions about the man. Myers was one of the best operators in the business. If anyone could pierce his world, it was that son-of-a-bitch.

Myers and he had a long history, marked by intrigue and mutual hate. The man had always sensed that he was up to no good and had tried many times to uncover his activities. Davenport also knew about the time Myers had beaten an Air Force major to death while interrogating him. And he knew why. The major had processed Myers' son and had removed heroin from the body, one of hundreds of such violations over four years. Upon learning of this horror, Myers had done everything he could to derail Davenport. In fact, Davenport hated to admit how often Myers had come close to unraveling everything he had built. In the last eight years, though, Myers had left him alone, apparently content to let him have his way. Obviously that had changed.

Davenport wanted desperately to know when Myers had picked up his scent. He obviously had begun tracking him before John attended the party, but how much earlier than that?

He should have tried to clarify this point with the senator, but anger had gotten in the way. Another question sprang into Davenport's mind. It actually surprised him. Was John's courtship of Logan part of Dan's plan?

His daughter had taken no interest in anyone since her husband's death. Since then, Davenport had not seen her as happy as she had been with John. She obviously liked him a great deal, and she was a good judge of character. At first he had resisted the notion that she could fall for one of Bill Thompson's sons, but he had been quick to recognize that his grudge against John's father should not apply to the man's son. However, as he saw Logan become more depressed with each passing day that John did not call, his anger had grown. It had only multiplied since he had learned of John's interference in Paris.

Davenport considered John's relationship with his daughter. The coincidence of John meeting Logan and also working with Myers seemed too great. He could accept Myers coming after him, but to use John to go after his daughter was a different matter. It was just like Myers; the symmetry brought his blood to a boil. And if John's courtship of Logan was part of Myers' plan, John had executed it with incredible skill. Was John really that good? Davenport reproached himself; usually he excelled at unmasking such schemers.

Davenport sighed. He really did not have a choice. He knew Myers would go to any length to avenge the handling of his son's body. He picked up his phone and called Washington. It was time to act.

* * *

Logan stepped off the plane at Charles de Gaulle International Airport outside of Paris. She was tired after her Air France flight from Los Angeles. The plane had been packed, though luckily John had booked her in first class.

The faxed message from John had surprised her. He had given her instructions to fly to Paris and meet him. He did not have time to call but would meet her at the airport near the exit from the immigration area in Aerogate 1. The message included details on which flight she should take.

The curious part of the note was its distant tone. The note did not sound like the John she knew. In it he explained that his brother's affairs had required his total attention, dragging him away from her. He asked for her patience and understanding. There were things he had to do. She had thought it strange, as she did a sudden meeting in Paris. She shook the thought from her mind. Soon she would be in John's arms and she could hardly wait.

She exited immigration and scanned the faces in the terminal. She did not see him, and a sudden coldness ran through her body. She set her single piece of luggage down and resigned herself, sure that he would not keep her waiting. All she wanted to do was sleep by his side. The thought warmed her.

After a few minutes, two men approached her. They were both dressed in suits and had a edge to them. Her smile disappeared.

"Mademoiselle Davenport?" inquired the man on the left in heavily accented English.

"Who's asking?" Logan questioned defensively. John had said he would meet her. Both men removed their wallets. The French police department IDs looked official.

"John could not make it to the airport in time to meet you," the man said on the left. "He asked us to escort you to your hotel. He will meet you there."

Logan hesitated. She was surprised that John would use the police. She was tired and decided she was being paranoid. She stooped to pick up her bag. The man on the right reacted quickly and grabbed it from her.

"Please, mademoiselle, let me."

"This way, please, mademoiselle," the man on the left said. Logan did as she was instructed. They exited the terminal. A black Citroën waited for them. They climbed in and the driver revved the engine, accelerating sharply from the curb.

"How long until we reach the hotel?" Logan asked.

"Not long," replied the man seated next to her.

* * *

James Lewis sat up. The phone by his bed had shattered his sleep. He turned on the bedside lamp, lifting the receiver to his ear. The bedside clock read 3:57.

"Yes."

"Sorry to wake you, sir," said Harold Carington, the CIA's Deputy Director of Operations.

"What is it?" Lewis demanded.

"It's Dan Myers, sir. He's dead."

"What?"

"Thirty-five minutes ago, in an explosion in Chevy Chase." Carington paused. "There is very little left. The police, the FBI, and our people are on site. The area has been sealed."

"I'll be in the office in thirty minutes. I want our best demolition man at Dan's house. I want the place scoured as though the damn President was having dinner there," Lewis ordered. He was already standing by his bed, sleep gone from his mind. "Have a preliminary report on my desk within an hour. And no press; give them anything that will hold them at bay until we know more."

"Yes, sir."

"Also, get a crisis management team meeting set for 7:00 am. I want everyone there. Is that clear?"

"Crystal clear, sir."

Lewis hung up the phone. Dan Myers dead. How could it be true? Davenport, it had to be him. What had happened? How had Davenport learned of their interest? He knew Dan; he was a careful man, but somewhere there was a weak link. Someone Dan had used had let the cat out of the bag. Also, what had Dan not told him? Why had Davenport decided to kill Myers? Had Dan gotten that close so soon? That brought another thought to mind: he had no way of contacting John Thompson. He knew only that John was somewhere in Europe setting a trap for the Russian.

Things were out of control. His fist came crashing down on his bureau, his anger boiling over. He stared at the empty bed next to him. Where was that bitch? Her infidelity never stopped–

always empty promises. In the beginning he had felt sorry for her, thinking that he had somehow failed her. Now, as the years had passed, he had come to realize he had been wrong, naïve to the point of stupidity. Every man had his blind spot, and for him it had been his wife. She had caused him so much pain, threatened all his plans; God, how he had learned to hate her.

His thoughts returned to Davenport. He had to stop the man; it was his only salvation.

* * *

Nine people crowded the conference room table. Lewis sat at the table in the midst of his deputy directors and a few specialists. The room was silent. They had just seen slides of Dan's house. As Harold Carington had said, there was not much left.

"What caused the explosion?" the director demanded. His anger lay just below the surface.

"C4," replied Doug Moore, an Army transplant who specialized in explosive devices.

"How much?"

"A lot," Moore stated. "I'd say five satchels in all, with three pounds in each bag. Two were dropped at the back of the house, one on each of the remaining three sides. They all had timers. My guess is that someone ran around the house and dropped the satchels. It took no more than a few minutes to set up."

"The hole must be ten feet deep," the director exclaimed to no one in particular.

"Whoever placed the devices wanted to be damn sure nothing remained. One satchel would have done the job."

"Any leads?"

"None, sir," Carl Dickenson reported. He was the liaison between the CIA and the FBI. "Because of the strength of the bombs, I'm not very optimistic that usable clues were left. The bomber came in the small hours of the night. Unless he was a total klutz, there will be little, if anything, to identify him."

L

"Any fingerprints on the remains of the satchels or timing devices?" the director probed.

"Always a possibility," Moore said, "but it will take us days to recover enough samples. Then there's the testing."

"Is there anything else we do know?" Lewis asked.

The room stayed silent.

"Okay, let's be thorough on this one. I want no stones left unturned," Lewis ordered. "Dan deserves that and a lot more."

"Sir," Harold Carington began hesitantly, "was Dan working on anything that might warrant such an attack?"

All eyes were on the director. They saw the grim look locked on his face. He pondered his next step as the eight sets of eyes waited for him to reply. He had to be careful. Davenport had extensive political connections. The DCI knew he had to tread lightly. If word leaked that the CIA thought Alex Davenport was responsible for Dan Myers' death, all hell would break loose, particularly if Lewis did not have sufficient proof. He needed the proof. He also needed to locate John and gain control of the situation. Too much that he had set into motion had soured. However, he could not fail now. It wasn't an option.

"I cannot elaborate at this time," the director said. "All I will say is that Dan was running an operation. It was off the books, and until I can get clearance it must stay that way. Are there any other questions?"

"Do you want to make an announcement to the press about Dan?" asked Gene Ickes, the CIA press director.

"Yes, but let's wait until this evening. Draft something and let me have a look at it."

"Yes, sir."

"Sir, the FBI is curious about a motive," Dickenson said. "As far as they're concerned, Dan was in retirement. Is that the way you want to keep it?"

"For now, yes," Lewis confirmed. "Let me know if you think a word with Director Bradley would help."

"Certainly, sir."

"What distribution list do you want on the information about Dan's death?" Carington asked.

"Eyes only for the members of this team," Lewis ordered. "Let's reconvene at the same time tomorrow unless the situation dictates otherwise. You all knew Dan; he was a master. Let's make this investigation one of our best." The director stood, as did everyone else.

* * *

Director Bradley of the FBI considered his list of questions, developed as a result of his phone conversation with Alex Davenport. Too much did not add up, and yet many things seemed to be related. His secretary's voice sounded on his intercom and broke his thoughts.

"I've reached Director Lewis. He's on the line."

"Thank you, Susan." Bradley picked up the blinking line.

"Jim, it's Don."

"I hope you're having a better day than I am," Lewis complained.

"Dan's quite a loss," Bradley said solemnly.

"Yes," Lewis agreed. "Have you uncovered anything new at your end of the investigation?"

"No," Bradley reported, "but I just had a very interesting telephone conversation."

"Really."

"It's actually the reason for my call. Are you sitting down?"

Lewis sighed. "More bad news."

"Alex Davenport called. I just got off the phone with him," Bradley explained. "His daughter has been kidnapped by a Navy SEAL named John Thompson."

The DCI stood and started to pace. The audacity of the billionaire appalled the DCI. He couldn't believe it. "And?"

"Davenport claims this Navy SEAL works, or rather did work, for Dan," Bradley explained. "Davenport claims he received a fax from John this morning. The fax was sent from Paris. He forwarded it to me and I read it. John indicates he will kill Logan

Davenport in seventy-two hours if his demands are not met. He wants the US government to explain why it took possession of his brother's body after the shoot-out in the Marriott Hotel. Furthermore, he wants the government to reveal why it lied to the press about the victim list. Apparently Bruce Johnson, the DEA agent listed as killed in the Marriott, is really John's brother Pete.

"Davenport blames the US government for his daughter's abduction, claiming Dan has pursued a personal vendetta against him using government assets and has tracked him since his retirement from the CIA. He further claims Dan killed Pete Thompson to recruit John to assist him in his pursuits. He insists that Dan has run an illegal investigation into his affairs for years."

The DCI did not answer immediately as his mind raced with the possibilities. Davenport's accusations were outrageous, but he would have made them for a reason.

"It's utter bullshit!" proclaimed the shocked DCI.

"How much of this could possibly be true?" Director Bradley demanded.

"Very little, I should think," Lewis replied angrily. He needed to think. What were his options?

"I need some more background," Bradley insisted. "When we met in your office, Dan only revealed the results of your efforts and not your means. I think it's time I knew everything."

"Yes, you're quite right," the director of the CIA agreed. "As you know, an e-mail message was sent with certain allegations concerning SIG and Foster. Obviously a delicate matter, so it was brought to my attention. George Simpson, the managing director of SIG, has helped us keep an eye on SIG's operations…"

Bradley interrupted. "He works for you?"

"No, just an informant who passed us tidbits when asked, nothing full time," the DCI confirmed. "Nevertheless I was deeply concerned that anyone even remotely related to the agency might have a hand in Foster's death. That's when I decided to enlist Dan's help. We all know his talents and his discretion.

"Dan and I had a quiet lunch and he agreed to lend his

assistance. Naturally I asked him to run the whole operation outside the agency. I realize there was an inherent risk in such a course, but I felt it was the best option. I'm trying to rebuild this agency, and another scandal, particularly one involving the murder of a senior White House official, would cause grave damage."

"Is it also true that John's father was a Russian mole until his death eight years ago?" Bradley asked.

"Where did you hear that?" Lewis demanded.

"Courtesy of Davenport," Bradley said. "Is it true?"

"I have no idea," Lewis explained. "If I remember from John's file, his father was killed in a car accident in West Virginia. Hell, John would never have made it into the SEALs if that were the case; he couldn't have gotten a security clearance. Why would Davenport tell you that?"

"He claims Dan was the Russian mole who's been decimating the CIA," Bradley added. "He claims that John's father and Dan worked together. Christ, Jim, what the hell is going on?"

Lewis was quiet for a moment as he considered this latest piece of information. He was surprised that Davenport had interjected it into his story, but it offered interesting possibilities. What type of damage control was Davenport spinning? How close had Dan gotten to him? Again the thought swung into the DCI's mind: how much had Dan not told him?

"Could John's father have been a traitor?" Bradley asked again. "Our records match your understanding that he was killed eight years ago in an automobile accident. I've checked."

"I don't know," Lewis said. "But you've got to figure Davenport has something. Why else would he drag John's father into it?"

"And Dan," Bradley said, his voice barely above a whisper. "I can't believe he was the mole."

"I should think not," Lewis answered firmly, considering the possibility. How unbelievable would that be?

"There is one other thing," Bradley said. "Davenport plans to hold a press conference in the next half hour. He intends to spout all this garbage. The pressure will be on."

Lewis sighed aloud. "What do you plan to do about Davenport's claim? I'm assuming he wants you to investigate it vigorously."

"I'll have no choice," Bradley said. "I've already received two calls from members of Congress. They're demanding action and a full investigation. If I stonewall them, nothing good will come of it. It won't do me any good. I hate to admit it, but he's boxed me in."

"What about his daughter?" Lewis asked. "Have you checked on her?"

"Yes, she flew to Paris last night from Los Angeles. No one has heard of or seen her since she passed through French customs," Bradley replied and then asked. "Is John in France?"

Lewis hesitated, knowing Bradley never let go of something once he had it. He was a man to be reckoned with. "How the hell should I know?"

Bradley pressed further. "You do know about a shooting in Paris three days ago involving Yousef?"

"Yes," Lewis answered, thinking that Bradley was moving fast.

"Was John one of the gunmen?"

"There is some speculation to that effect," Lewis confirmed.

"If that's true, it would mean Dan knew about the meeting before it happened," Bradley proposed, pausing. Lewis read between his counterpart's words even before the man continued. "Why the hell didn't you two work with the French authorities? We'd have Yousef now."

"Well, yes, I see the logic there, but I can't believe he knew, and if he did, he did not inform me. Besides, what does Yousef have to do with Dan's operation?"

"You tell me," demanded Bradley.

"I don't see the connection."

"You suggested Dan was using John as a foot soldier. If so, let's bring him in and talk to him. He must know something that will clarify the picture."

"That may prove difficult," Lewis said.

"What do you mean?" Bradley asked, startled.

"Dan was not communicating with John directly," Lewis explained. "Basically Dan made sure John knew something was amiss and put him on the scent, you might say. I'm not entirely clear on the details."

"This is crazy," Bradley declared. "That could mean John actually has kidnapped Davenport's daughter."

"A possibility, but I doubt it, Don," Lewis said. "Step back for a moment. Davenport is involved in a big scheme; the stakes are high. Suddenly he realizes someone is on to him, finds out who, and decides to act. He kills Dan and builds a story that will put John in the cold. It's brilliant, if you ask me. Making Dan look like the mole is almost a peace offering; it lets everyone off the hook if we decided to accept it. Then everything could be put to bed."

Silence filled the other end of the line. Lewis finally asked, "Are you there, Don?"

"Yes," Bradley confirmed.

"Is there any way you can wait forty-eight hours to issue a warrant for his arrest?" Lewis asked.

"Jim, I'd really like to," Bradley answered, "but it won't do us any good. We have to play this one by the books. If we stall, we'll never have a chance to get Davenport, if indeed he is the problem as you suggest."

"John might be our only chance," Lewis insisted. "We can't go after Davenport directly, and we don't have time to set someone else on him. By now his antennae are fully up. He'll smell the person from miles away. "

"We'll just have to hope for the best," Bradley said. "John will have to make contact at some time."

"I wouldn't count on that," Lewis replied.

"I hope you're wrong for both our sakes."

"Yes," muttered the tired director of the CIA. "Call me if anyone grabs him."

"Will do. By the way, Jim, when this thing blows over, I want the real reason you started an investigation into Davenport's affairs."

The connection ended, and the DCI stared at the phone. A tremor passed through his hand. What did the director of the FBI know that he was not telling him?

18 Caribbean Sunshine

Admiral Sunders' phone beeped. "Sir, another call for you."

The admiral sensed the hesitancy in the lieutenant's voice. "Is it John Thompson?"

"Ah, no, sir."

"Well, spit it out, sailor," the admiral said. He desperately wanted to talk with John. The stories in the newspapers were outrageous. John had to know the truth. The last thing anyone needed was for John to believe the US government had turned on him. The prospect was downright dangerous for everyone involved.

The lieutenant interrupted the admiral's thoughts. "It's a man who refuses to give his name. He insists on speaking only to you. He says he's from West Virginia."

The admiral thought for a moment. West Virginia—what the hell?

"Admiral Sunders speaking," he said with an angry edge to his voice.

"No names, please," the caller said.

The admiral almost fell out of his chair. "How do I know it's you?"

"We had a discussion not too long ago; you wanted me to tell a story, a treasonous one."

"This is very hard to believe," Sunders stammered. How could Dan Myers be alive?

"No time for details," Dan said. "I'm safe for now and I'd like to maintain the perception of my well-being, if you catch my drift."

"Certainly, what can I do?"

"Has he reached you?"

"No."

"I want you to tell him I'll call him. Get his number."

"If he calls," the admiral interrupted.

"Yes, if," Dan said, "but I think he will."

"And who should I say you are?"

"Tell him the truth."

"I will try."

"Also," Dan continued, "I want you to set up a private meeting with the director of the CIA."

It took Dan few minutes to explain his plan.

"I hope to hell you know what you're doing," the admiral exclaimed. "Everything is upside down and twisted. Maybe you're not reading your Tarot cards properly."

"I realize I'm asking a lot," Dan replied. "In the end it's your decision. You must do what you think is right. However, the DCI still needs John. You can be the link between John and him. Davenport's revelations put the DCI in an awkward position, and if you involve yourself, we can keep tabs on what Lewis is doing and protect John. Also, I can pass you information and everyone can assume it came from John."

The admiral considered Dan's plan. He found it almost impossible to accept. He made up his mind. "I'll do it and I'll tell you why."

Ten minutes later the admiral had finished detailing Dan on the briefings given by the Nuclear Smuggling Group concerning attacks on Russian bases with nuclear weapons.

"Thanks for that information. It's very helpful."

"You didn't learn it from me," Sunders insisted. "How should we communicate?"

"I'll call you when I can. Just tell the lieutenant that when a man from West Virginia calls, put me through no matter what. Here's my number, but please give it to absolutely no one."

Sunders committed Dan's telephone number to memory. He hoped to hell Dan was wrong. If not, the damage was incalculable. "Keep in touch." Sunders broke the connection and immediately dialed the number of the DCI. Christ, Dan had to be wrong.

*   *   *

Dan Myers sat in the shade. The sunlight danced brightly on the Caribbean waters. The sloop was only fifty feet long, but it had all the amenities, including a satellite phone, computers, radios, and a fax. It was a floating command center. He had his longtime friend Burt Singer to thank; the boat was his.

Dan had spotted the car parked outside his house around ten o'clock two nights earlier. By midnight he had known that the lone occupant could only be a bearer of bad news, and he had made his decision then. He secreted his way out of his house, having called a taxi to collect him ten blocks away. He instructed the driver to take him to Dulles, where he had chartered a private plane to fly him to Miami.

A single exit before the airport and the last one on Route 66, the taxi driver pulled over to the side of the road. The engine of the cab died suddenly. Dan became instantly suspicious.

The driver parked the cab on the roadside and raised the hood. As he did so, Dan slipped his 9-millimeter Beretta from his bag. No sooner had he done that than the driver walked down the passenger side of the taxi, a gun in his hand. Dan kept his hidden until the last moment and fired three quick shots before the driver could train his Colt .45 on Dan's chest. Luckily his one shot missed its mark. Dan could still hear a slight ringing in his ears from the blast of that powerful handgun.

He exited the taxi, wiping the shattered glass from his pants and jacket. Quickly he dragged the driver into the back seat.

Luckily no cars passed while he wrestled with the dead man's body. After he had pulled the driver into the car, Dan checked the man's ID–a Virginia license, a library card, and two credit cards. Dan removed the credit cards and tossed the wallet onto the floor of the taxi. It was time to move.

Dan shut the hood, jumped behind the steering wheel, and turned the key. The engine came to life immediately, as he had expected.

It was not until he had parked the taxi in the remote parking area and had dumped the driver's credit cards and his gun in separate dumpsters that he felt any degree of safety. Before discarding the pistol he had wiped off his fingerprints with his handkerchief, which he discarded in yet another trash receptacle.

His first instincts were to use the satellite phone and make a few calls, but he could not. It had been destroyed by the driver's one errant shot. Dan was concerned about the possibility that small pieces of the satellite phone might be left in the cab. He wanted no signs indicating that he had been the passenger. He wished he had noticed the entry and exit holes in his carry-on bag when he was in the taxi.

It was not until 12:45 am that Dan had finally relaxed, seated in the Lear Jet's plush cabin cruising at 28,000 feet on his way to Miami. From Miami he had flown on the 7:35 am American Airlines flight to Barbados using a false passport. The name on the passport was John Saltsman. He played the part of a widowed tourist, biding his time in the Caribbean's tropic climate.

He had bought copies of T*he New York Times* and *The Washington Post* and read about the explosion in Chevy Chase, Maryland. The hole where his house had been was huge. It saddened him. He realized all the pictures of his wife and son, except for the ones that he carried in his wallet, were gone. Their life together only existed in his mind. Maybe his friends would have a few pictures; it was at least a hope. He turned his thoughts away from his personal concerns. As always, they had to take a second-row seat.

He read with interest the authorities' explanation for the destruction in the rich suburb of Chevy Chase as a gas explosion. Dan chuckled to himself. It would not take a reporter long to learn that no gas was piped to his house. Dan suspected C4. It had the means to cause complete destruction.

The amount of explosive used was far greater than that required to kill, but it fitted with the plan he suspected his pursuer had designed. Davenport wanted it to look as if Dan had destroyed his own house in anticipation of the revelations, trying to make it seem that he had died in the blast. It would take the authorities a few days, but they would determine that no human remains existed in the ruins, a fact that would strengthen Davenport's story. Meanwhile, Davenport had planned to kill Dan outright, a task given to the taxi driver. Dan was sure his body would have been buried where no one would have ever found it.

The parked car had been deliberately obvious, designed to make him run. He wondered what contingency plan they had made in case he used his own car. The taxi driver had planned poorly; he should have shot Dan when he first entered the taxi. Maybe they had counted on him using his own car first, and the taxi option represented the contingency plan.

Dan smiled wryly. Davenport had orchestrated a story that had successfully forced both him and John into the cold. He had counted on Davenport's consistent ability to improvise. Dan wondered how John would handle all the accusations against him. He would have no way of contacting the young man until after John had read the stories. As Dan recalled the details, he realized the implications were staggering.

The code name given to Bill Thompson, ASIAN DRAGON, was still fresh in Dan's mind. John Thompson's father had not died in a random car accident as everyone thought. That was just a story for public consumption. It had been done for a number of reasons. The most notable was to keep the Russians from learning that one of their agents had been turned. Also, no one in the Pentagon wanted to weather a scandal about a Soviet spy.

Bill Thompson had been a communication specialist for the Navy and had worked for the Defense Intelligence Agency. On a tour of duty in Bangkok during the Vietnam War, it had all began.

One of the responsibilities assigned to Thompson in Bangkok was the investigation of rumors that military personnel were shipping drugs to the States. At the time, his superiors believed that Thompson had spent three years investigating the rumors and had found nothing to substantiate the claims. As far as everyone in the Pentagon was concerned, his investigation had come to a dead end. It was only much later that the Navy learned otherwise.

After John's father returned from a five-year stint in Iraq, some people in the Department of Defense felt the Russians had learned too much about the military's abilities in the area of battlefield communications. They suspected a leak, concluding it had originated in the US Embassy in Iraq.

A formal investigation began against John's father. It took two years to piece together, but ultimately it became clear that Thompson had given secrets to the Soviet Union over six years. The Navy Investigative Service finally confronted him.

John's father, by his own admission, had learned that American soldiers were shipping drugs to the United States. They did so by hiding the drugs in dead soldiers' bodies. Once the corpses arrived in the United States, Air Force personnel in on the operation removed the drugs from the chest cavities before the bodies were released to the families. While John's father attempted to prove what he knew, the group running the operation learned of his investigation. They threatened him, indicating that if he ever told the Pentagon about the operation his two sons would die. Because of his duties, Thompson had to leave his sons alone for long periods of time. He ultimately decided they were more important than stopping the smuggling operation.

During his posting in Iraq, the Russians approached him. They wanted his help. He told them to take a hike. It was then that he learned they knew all about his actions in Bangkok and his failure to inform his superiors about the smuggling operation.

The Russians threatened him with exposure and several other trumped-up activities. For the second time in his life Thompson felt he had no alternative. He began grudgingly to supply the Russians with information.

Eight years later, when the military realized John's father had given information to the Russians, they brought him in for questioning. He told his story straightaway. Dan had seen the tapes of the confession; Bill Thompson was a broken man. John's father had sworn he had never learned who the ringleader of the operation was. No one quite believed him.

The military told Bill Thompson they would keep him out of jail if he succeeded at two things. First, the military wanted him to become a double agent and feed bogus information to the Russians. Second, they wanted him to finish the hunt he had never completed. The use of servicemen's bodies was appalling. The military had to act and punish those responsible. The Pentagon wanted a name.

A single gunshot to the head was testament that John's father ultimately identified the ringleader.

When the military found Thompson dead in his car, they decided to stage the accident, making it look as if John's father had died in a car crash and not at the hands of a gunman. Admiral Sunders had made that decision; he had been in charge of the investigation.

Dan had disagreed strongly with the cover-up. Though the military did not know the name for certain, they had enough circumstantial information to identify the ringleader—Alex Davenport. However, they believed that the evidence, much of it classified, would never make it to a court of law. Without it, convicting Davenport was impossible.

Anger rose in Dan as his mind flashed back many years ago to the interrogation room.

Dan looked at the US Air Force major, a balding officer from Albany, New York, whose belly had not seen an exercise regimen in a long time. Dan had always considered the Air Force the easiest of the armed services. Obviously a pathologist did not have to subscribe to a daily exercise routine. For some reason the man looked familiar.

"How long?"

"How long what, sir?"

"Major, let's get one thing straight," Dan demanded. "I hate two things–stupidity and ignorance. Using either with me is a mistake, a serious mistake. Now answer the fucking question."

The major wiped his brow with his left hand. He was nervous, and rightly so.

"Two years."

"How many bodies?"

"I'm not sure."

"Guess."

"Hundreds."

"Did you ever stop to think what you were doing?" Dan demanded as he fought his anger.

"Ah, yes, sir."

"And?"

"I needed the money, sir."

"Fucking money. Is that what you told the dead soldier whose chest cavity you were reaching into?"

"Ah, no, sir," the major stammered. "I hated it. Every minute of it, sir, but I really did need the money."

Dan considered the monster before him. His own son had died fighting for his country in Cambodia six months earlier. And this fucking jerk, he was trying to get rich with drugs. Dan's anger rose another notch. He remembered collecting his son's body and being handed the paperwork, which he had had to sign. Who the fuck cared about the paperwork? His son was dead.

Suddenly Dan looked up. His stare fixed on the major.

"Major," Dan said through clenched teeth, as he slammed down a blank piece of paper and a pen in front of the man. "Sign your fucking name on that paper."

"Ah, sir?"

"Do it, now," Dan ordered.

The major did so, and Dan grabbed the sheet of paper. He started at the signature. Now he knew what was so familiar about the major–this man had signed his son's paperwork. He had been the pathologist who had processed his son's body.

The enormity of it struck him. He stood, his wooden chair tumbling to the ground behind him. The major cowered as Dan rounded the table.

The last thing Dan remembered were strong hands pulling him roughly away from the unconscious and bloodied major.

"Dan, what the fuck is wrong with you?"

"I think he killed the bastard."

"Christ, Dan, what the fuck have you done?"

Dan pulled out of the memory. He had never accepted the fact that his son's body had transported heroin back to the United States. Even now it took a real effort to force the anger to recede. He had vowed never to lose control like that again. Getting even was the only thing that counted and he was going to do exactly that. Eight years had passed, but Alex Davenport was in his sights again. Dan checked his watch and started to gather his things.

In that moment Dan realized the contradiction he had always faced. He hated the agency for so many reasons, despised it really. It was self-serving, incestuous. And yet the agency allowed him to play in a world of incomparable intrigue and power. He thrived on it. Playing chess on the world stage, bending people, even countries, to his will, consumed him. The world was a better place because of his life's accomplishments. But all good plays must come to an end. It was time for him to exit the world stage on his own terms. He scolded himself for his small revelry. It was time to get back to work.

As he opened a notebook, he considered the admiral's revelations about Russia. The use of sophisticated US equipment particularly caught his interest and put a thought into his head.

* * *

Director Bradley looked at the information. He was gravely concerned. A taxi driver had been found shot to death in the parking lot of Dulles Airport and Dan Myers' fingerprints had been found in various parts of the cab. It led to some interesting possibilities, but one fact was clear. On the basis of the evidence, Dan was alive and well after the explosion that had destroyed his house. What did that mean?

From everything Bradley had seen and heard about Dan over the years, his career had been impeccable. Dan had started working for the CIA during the summer of 1956. At the time he had just finished serving six years in the Army, having enlisted at the age of twenty-two. From the beginning the Army had realized the young man had a way with languages. They soon taught him Russian, at which he excelled. After a string of successes in Korea, Dan had come to the attention of the CIA. Since then he had proved time and again that he was the best. He had an uncanny ability to understand the Russian mind. He quickly rose in the ranks of the CIA, eventually to become Deputy Director of Special Operations, a post he had held for the last ten years of his career.

Had the death of his wife changed him? Was there another force at work? Could Dan be the second mole? The enormity of the possibility literally brought bile to Bradley's throat. What had he agreed to? He forced himself to think. It could not be true. The leaks had continued after Dan's retirement. No, the second mole had to be one of the three men on the list. Bradley leaned back in his chair and massaged his temples. He had never doubted that difficulty would litter the road ahead. He had experienced moments of monstrous doubt, but he admitted now that he had never thought the monsters would stand so tall.

The director turned his thoughts back to the papers in front of him. He paged through the military's file on Bill Thompson for the tenth time. It had taken a call to the Secretary of Defense, but finally the Pentagon had relented and given him a copy.

One name appeared repeatedly in the file: Admiral Sunders, a career naval officer who had risen from the SpecWarfare area of the Navy. He was a SEAL like John, albeit older, but from what the director knew, the admiral's command of the SEAL operation would have overlapped part of John's SEAL Team Six command. Bradley suspected the admiral would know John. He would certainly know Dan, since the two had worked together on the DIA's investigation of John's father.

The director picked up his phone and made the call.

"Admiral Sunders' office," the lieutenant answered.

"May I speak with him?"

"Can I ask who is calling, sir?"

"Director Bradley."

"Certainly, sir. Please hold the line."

The admiral came on the line immediately. "Sir, how may I help you?"

"You think I need help?"

"Just a figure of speech, sir."

"Do you have time to talk?" the director of the FBI asked a little more gently.

"Yes, but let me get rid of a visitor; just a moment, please." Bradley could hear the admiral asking his guest to leave. "I'm back, sir."

"I have ASIAN DRAGON in front of me, Admiral," the director began, "and I have a few questions."

The admiral paused for a moment before he spoke. "Okay."

"I've read the file, Admiral. However, would you mind telling me in your words what happened?" Bradley wanted to make sure nothing was missing. It did not appear to be, but one could never be too careful in Washington.

"Certainly, sir." Twenty minutes later the admiral finished his delivery.

"You story matches the report, but then again you wrote most of it," Bradley said.

"I understand your concern, sir," the admiral replied evenly. "I assure you that I've told you everything significant there is to know."

"Does Dan know this story?"

"Yes, he does. We used his services to acquire some of our facts."

"How well do you know Dan?"

"I've known him twenty-five years," the admiral said without hesitation.

"And the stories?"

"He is no Russian mole, if that's what you're asking," the admiral stated. "He's pure gold, nothing but the best. Davenport is the one to watch."

"What makes you so sure?"

"Sir, did you ever stop and wonder how Davenport knew about Bill Thompson?"

Bradley paused for a moment, realizing he had assumed that Davenport's knowledge was the result of his contacts in the military or the CIA.

"You're saying?" he asked.

"I'm saying, sir, that Davenport knows all the detail in that report and a great deal more."

"What the hell do you mean?"

"Davenport operated the drug ring that shipped the drugs back to the United States."

"You cannot be serious, Admiral." Bradley paused, shocked. "The report makes no such suggestion or allegations."

"For obvious reasons," the admiral replied. "To prove his guilt in a court of law would require an enormous cache of classified documents, many of which can never see the light of day. In addition, with the lawyers and public relations consultants Davenport could hire, the government would face an uphill battle. The political consequences, no matter who won in court, would be heavy. Americans would not take lightly to the notion that dead servicemen's bodies were used to bring heroin into this country and that Pentagon personnel were aware of it and did nothing. Add to that the reaction to the CIA's role, courtesy of Davenport."

"Do you think Dan's efforts against Davenport are personal?" Bradley asked.

"No, he was out of it until the DCI brought him in," the admiral said.

"How would you know this?" Bradley demanded.

"Dan," the admiral said. "He called me for background on John."

"Admiral, your thoughts have been most helpful," Bradley stated.

"Any time, sir."

"And Admiral, should Dan call you, be sure to let me know."

Bradley did not wait for a response, knowing that if the admiral also knew Dan was alive he was not the only one. Maybe the admiral would do some digging.

Everything the admiral had said checked out with what he knew, even the part about the DCI. However, he had a strong sense that the admiral knew a lot more than he was saying. Bradley suspected he knew how the admiral felt. No matter, he had to find Dan Myers. Everything depended on it.

* * *

The room was dark, but she knew that at least one of them sat there, staring at her. Logan shivered at the thought, wondering what evil her Russian guards might have in mind for her. She found it hard to believe that she had not been raped. She had seen the desire in their eyes.

Desperately she wanted to get out of bed. She was hot under the sheets. Her clothes were still on and she feared removing them. She had to protect herself from the lecherous glances of her captors, but she also reasoned that a rescue, if it came, would happen at night. She wanted to be prepared; she dreaded the thought of being hauled half naked from her bed by US Special Forces, vain though that concern might be.

A cough distracted her. She found herself sniffing the air, trying to use all her senses to judge how close the man was. They all smelled—what pigs. Did they ever bother to shower? She wondered if they knew her horror, sensed it maybe. They always seemed to stare at her, never telling her anything. She still didn't know why she was here or for how long. It was maddening.

And where was John? He obviously had not sent the fax. He would never have had her kidnapped, but who had? Was her abduction a lure to draw John in? In the first few days of her captivity she had peppered her Russian guards with questions about John, but they had only yelled at her in Russian. She now believed none of them knew a word of English. For the thousandth time she wondered why her guards were Russian. Had they planned her abduction or were they just hired thugs?

Logan turned her head slightly, trying to see the dim light reflecting onto one of the windows of the bedroom, her prison. Five days had passed since her abduction in Paris; at least she was pretty sure it had been five days. After her second day she had started tearing off a piece of toilet paper each day and hiding it under the sink. There were now three pieces there. Not that it mattered. It seemed as if years had passed since she had come through French customs.

The journey from Paris had started in the car, but soon after they had exited the airport, the man seated beside her had covered her face with some vile-smelling cloth. The next thing she knew she was aboard a private jet with a savage headache. The same two men had been seated in front of her, keeping their attention on her every movement. Besides handing her a glass of water and some aspirin, they had not said a word.

When the jet had touched down at a remote airport in some mountainous area, she had had absolutely no idea where she was. A black limousine had come to a sudden halt, and she had been forced into its darkened interior. The drive had taken at least two hours, or so she thought. It ended with her being marched into a yellow building. Only then did she realize that she was in Rome, just yards from the Spanish Steps.

When she had first entered the upstairs apartment, she had been relieved. It was beautifully decorated. However, it did not take her long to realize that John was nowhere in sight. Not that she had expected it. It was a pathetic hope, a silly dream. One look at the Russian goons standing in the atrium had said it all. Almost before she could complain, her two escorts darted from the apartment and left her standing before the Russians. She had never been so scared in her life.

Speaking Russian, her guards had forced her into a corner bedroom. She had yet to leave it. Besides being allowed to glance out one of the windows and walk her ten steps to the bathroom, she had nothing to do. She had begged for books and magazines and finally they had relented, but the magazines were in Italian. She didn't speak or read it, but they were better than nothing.

She had considered an escape, but her guards never left her alone. Besides, her room was at least five stores high, and she had no clear idea of what lay between her and the ground. Her only hope lay in a rescue. Certainly her father would know that she had been kidnapped. She knew him; he would do everything in his power to get her back. He would use all his resources, including those in the federal government, and she knew they were extensive.

She felt a tear slip out of her eye and roll down the side of her face. It angered her; why was she so weak? She tried to think what John would do in her position. She realized she had no idea what he would, or she should, do. The world she found herself in was foreign to her. It scared her more than she cared to admit.

The Russian coughed again and she turned onto her stomach. She could not let him know that she was crying.

L

19 | Only More Questions

The long filthy coat covered him completely as he stumbled down Rih tim caddie in Karakőy, past the Deniz Otobűsű İskelesi ferry terminal on the Bosphorus Strait in Istanbul. To his left stood a three-story blue building that housed the offices of the harbormaster. The clock before its entrance indicated the time in Istanbul was 3:17 in the morning. Straight ahead lay the Tűrkiye Denizcilik Isletmeleri office building, a six-story structure that housed the offices of Aegean Exporting.

John kept his eye peeled for any unusual movements, continuing to act out his drunken part as he approached the building. The area was dimly lit, with most of the light emanating from a docked passenger ship. The large ship was moored to the southernmost point of the passenger terminal. Its bow was tied to cleats both inside and outside the terminal area. A hundred and fifty feet left of its steel hull lay the Tűrkiye Denizcilik Isletmeleri office building. The space between the ship and the building stood open, though protected by a twelve-foot metal fence. A lone tree grew near the building and reached to the third floor. John planned to take advantage of this urban landscape.

He staggered the last twenty yards to the metal fence and scouted the area again. Of the few cars parked in the lot, none were occupied. One of the building's entrances was on the near corner, but he could not see any guards. The passenger ship was quiet too, even though he had learned earlier that it was scheduled to leave by midday, in less than nine hours.

He reached under his filthy jacket and retrieved a twenty-foot piece of rope. With practiced movements he grabbed hold of one end and threw the other end, which was weighted like a whip. It shot out and upward, wrapping itself around one of the ship's mooring lines. John took a few powerful steps and launched himself into the air, using the rope as a pendulum to swing him around the end of the metal fence that hung over the waters of the Bosphorus Strait. In moments he was on the other side of the fence and inside the shadow it cast.

Quickly he tossed the filthy coat into the Bosphorus and double-checked his equipment one more time: a 9-millimeter Glock pistol, a K-Bar knife, lock picks, a pencil-size hooded flashlight, a small mirror, two spare magazines, screwdrivers, a window opener, and a satellite phone, which he made sure was turned off. The last thing he needed was for it to ring as he was conducting his little raid.

He moved steadily down the fence in a low crouch toward the building, his senses taking in his surroundings all the while. He reached the side of the building and looked up the tree. Its limbs hid the third-story window. He took another lead of rope and tied it to the piece he had already used, giving him an overall length of thirty-five feet. Attached to the end of the new section of rope was a metal hook. It was heavily taped to make it soundproof and to hide its shiny surface.

It took him three tosses to wedge the hook firmly in place on the metal grate bolted to the third-floor windowsill. The grate was really a miniature railing mimicking the larger ones on the balconies that adorned many of the top floor windows. He gave it a good yank, confident that it would hold his weight.

He took another quick look around; so far his activities had gone unnoticed. He clipped the rope into his climbing belt and began the three-story climb, using the tree to block any view of his activities from the expanse in front of the office building and the passenger ship behind him. A couple of minutes and some sweat later, John grabbed the metal grate and pulled himself up just enough to peer into the darkened window. At first he saw the reflection of the tree and the ship behind him, but on readjusting his stare he focused his eyes on the building's interior. There was little to see and the coast looked clear.

With his arms protesting, John hauled himself up the rest of the way and straddled the grate with his feet. The window was latched, but it did not appear to be alarmed. He had expected as much. He took a thin piece of metal shaped like a credit card and ran it along the crack between the top and bottom halves of the window. The latch opened easily. John forced the window open with his powerful hands. It was typical of people to install lousy locks. Before he jumped inside, he directed the beam of his hooded penlight along the space between the walls and ceiling of the small office, checking for any sign of motion detectors. He saw none and quickly eased himself through the window. Quietly he pulled his rope up the side of the building, coiled it, and placed it inside his small satchel. He extracted the Glock and checked it; one round was in the pipe.

John did not have a good idea of what lay beyond. All he did know was that the offices of Aegean Exporting were on the top floor of the building. In some ways it would have been easier to climb the outside of the building to the top floor, but the risk of being seen was too great. His worry had less to do with being seen from the street than with being seen from the ship. A passenger ship of that size was a twenty-four-hour operation, and the odds were even that an alert crewmember or a sleepless passenger would notice his ascent.

Inside the building the risk came from surveillance cameras and guards, though the latter concerned him less. He knew he would have little trouble disabling the ill-trained guards.

John slid the window closed and made his way to the door. He grabbed its handle as he turned the lock latch to his right, away from the doorjamb. The small metal click was barely noticeable. The door opened inward, and he knelt low to the floor, enabling him to scan the deserted hallway using his small mirror. He held it near the floor and turned it to give a good view of both ends of the hallway. There were no signs of surveillance cameras.

He stepped into the hallway, closing the door quietly behind him as he noted the plaque on the door, Sigma Coatings. He wondered if the building had an elevator but suspected it did not. Its shaft would have offered an easy way to ascend to the top floor without being seen. He had noted that many buildings in Turkey did not have elevators, since the Turks did not have laws about handicapped access to buildings with more than two floors, as did the US and most European countries.

He reached the end of the hallway, stopping before the stairwell. He eased the windowless door open and peered inside. The door moved silently; the stairwell beyond was dimly lit. Again no surveillance cameras were in sight. He stepped inside and started up the steps, noting the time.

John kept walking past the sixth-floor door and took the stairwell to the roof. The door there was locked, and he set about to rectify the situation. It took him two minutes, an inordinate amount of time. His lock-picking skills were not what they used to be.

John tested his work; the door creaked open. Satisfied that he had a reasonable escape route if he needed it, he returned to the sixth floor. He eased the door open and used his mirror to scan the hallway that lay beyond. An immediate problem presented itself: a surveillance camera was mounted at the far end of the hallway. Mr. Murphy had just paid a visit.

John continued to use the mirror and soon realized that the door nearest the camera was the only door whose sign he could not read because of its angle. That put the office on the same corner as the one he had climbed earlier. That office was his target; all the other doors had nameplates of different companies. He suspected the office suite took up the whole corner, giving it an excellent view of the Bosphorus, particularly when a passenger ship was not docked at the terminal, as it was now.

John closed the stairwell door and considered his options.

The camera was more likely to have been installed by Davenport's company than by the building owners. Its position suggested as much. If that was the case, the guard watching the camera might not be in the building, but at some central complex where the security company had its base. However, a guard in the building might also be keeping an eye on the camera's images.

He could bypass the camera by lowering himself from the roof to one of the office suite's window balconies. That was easy enough, but if the company had thought to put a camera in the hallway, the door and windows of the suite would probably be alarmed. The keypad would more than likely be near the entrance, programmed with a one-minute delay or less. Reaching the keypad from a window and disabling it would take more time than an approach through the door. And then the type of alarm had to be considered. What was more likely to bring the cavalry, a broken camera or a ringing alarm? He made his decision.

He eased the door open as he lay on his back. He brought the Glock into position, steadying it against the doorframe. It was a difficult shot that would make a lot more noise than he wanted, especially with the stairwell amplifying the sound. If only he had a slingshot and some ball bearings. That would make for an even more difficult shot but would give him multiple chances. He hoped no one was on the floor, or the game would be up quickly. He pulled the trigger.

The sound was deafening as it carried down the stairwell and the uncarpeted hallway. He waited a long five minutes before he moved. If anyone had heard the shot and sounded an alarm, someone should have come by now. John knew someone would ultimately come to investigate the ruined camera. He hoped it would take some time.

He stood, checked his gear, and ran down the hallway. He took a few moments to clean up the camera's shattered lens and throw the pieces into his satchel. Next he picked the lock of the office; it took only thirty-nine seconds. He was improving.

As soon as he entered the suite, he located the alarm pad.

Recognizing the US model, he set to work. He disabled it in forty-five seconds, heaving a sigh of relief. Thankfully, Davenport's company placed its trust in US security systems, and John was familiar with this one.

He relocked the office suite's door, propped a chair from the small waiting area under the handle, and started his search.

Twenty minutes later he had photocopied a number of documents that mentioned the Sadko, Haifa, and Istanbul, but he still felt he was missing the motherlode. He had searched the office methodically and thoroughly. The one item he had not searched was the computer in the manager's office. He had left that for last once he had realized it used a sophisticated password system. Unlike some of his men he was not a computer expert, only a sophisticated user. He doubted he could break into the computer and had not wanted to waste precious time trying, only to come up empty handed.

Now, with the paper part of the search completed, he figured he would try one more thing. Using the Phillips-head screwdriver he had brought, he quickly removed the cover of the computer. He planned to take the computer's hard disk with him and give it to a friend who was more than capable of understanding the bits and bytes it contained.

He worked quickly, disconnecting the ribbon cable that led to the hard disk and using the screwdriver to unbolt the drive from the computer's chassis. As he was unscrewing the last screw, he heard them coming down the corridor.

The chair he had lodged under the handle would block their entrance, but not for long. John dropped the hard disk into his satchel and quickly slid the cover onto the computer. He did not bother to screw it together, throwing the screws in the nearest trashcan. Without its hard disk the computer was useless, as its user would soon discover.

John checked his watch. It was 4:13 am, and sunrise was still an hour and a half away. He considered his options; only one seemed reasonable. He opened the window in the manager's office and climbed outside onto the small balcony that guarded it, careful to close the window behind him. He extracted his rope, glancing in the direction of the cruise ship. No one appeared to be watching. He threw the rope up and over his head, and heard it strike the metal struts that supported signs on the building's roof. He tugged on the rope until it pulled taut in his hands. Without waiting for his visitors, he scaled the ten feet between the balcony and the top of the building.

Once on the roof, he collected his rope and dashed across to the opposite corner, but not before looking down into the parking area in front of the building. He saw only one new car parked directly in front, but could not tell if it had any company markings. He suspected it was the car his visitors had recently vacated.

Once he reached the opposite corner, he looked down on the street below; it appeared quiet. He doubted it would stay that way for long. Using his rope, he lowered himself to the sixth-floor balcony directly below. He shook the hook loose from the roof, catching it as it dropped. Then he hooked it onto the metal railing that edged the balcony, climbed over the railing, and lowered himself to the next balcony. He repeated the process until he dropped to the ground.

John walked quickly up Maliye caddie, headed in the direction of the Galata Tower, a 170-foot stone bastion built as a part of the thirteenth-century fortifications that had enclosed the Genoese concession. As he walked, he considered what he had uncovered in the offices of Aegean Exporting. It confused him. He had learned one thing: the Sadko was headed to Israel's port of Haifa before stopping in Istanbul. However, he still was no closer to knowing who would take delivery of the bomb.

The route puzzled him. If the grain ship did indeed have a nuclear bomb aboard, why would the Arabs sail it into an Israeli harbor before its final destination, which appeared to be Istanbul? The odds were good that the Israelis would not find the bomb. The secret compartment was almost impossible to detect, especially with the hold full of grain. And if satellites could not see it, then neither would the Israelis, even if they boarded the ship with a Geiger counter–unlikely, since the Russian vessel was a grain ship. But why take the risk, however slight, when the ship could sail directly to Istanbul? From there the Arabs could smuggle the device to its final destination, assuming it stayed shielded from the prying sensors of satellites.

Then again, as compared with other ports in the Middle East, Istanbul did not make sense as a destination. Once the Russians learned of the theft, that event would draw the eyes and ears of the US SIGINT community, which would have detected spikes in Russian communications and troop movements. Because of its borders with Russia, Iran, and Iraq, Turkey–a NATO country–would tighten its borders at the request of the US, no questions asked.

He looked at his watch, realizing the sun would rise in another fifty minutes. He needed to make a call, but Washington was asleep at this hour and he was inclined to wait. He needed to get the hard disk to his friend, an ex-SEAL who would thoroughly enjoy revealing the secrets contained on its tiny magnetic platter. He'd find a DHL office in the morning and overnight it.

He walked around the streets of Taksim District, making absolutely sure no one had followed him before he approached his hotel. As he neared, he watched a truck throw a stack of newspapers onto the sidewalk a hundred feet in front of him. As he came abreast of them, he saw the *Hürriyet* and the *Cumhuriyet* as well as the *International Tribune*. All three papers had the same pictures on their front page, and they made John stop dead in his tracks.

One picture was of him. The other was of Alex Davenport and Logan. John grabbed his K-Bar knife from the scabbard in his satchel and cut the *International Tribune* bundle open. The headline read, "Son of Russian Spy Kidnaps Billionaire's Only Daughter."

John glanced around his immediate vicinity and made a quick decision. If the press knew something about him, he had to assume the police knew too. He desperately wanted to read the articles, but he first needed to go to ground. The hotel was off bounds; he could not risk someone identifying him. Nothing in his room was important, as all his valuable possessions were in his satchel.

He needed to read the papers, determine who was behind the lies, and decide what to do. He had little time to find a suitable hiding place. In less than an hour, hundreds of thousands of people might recognize him as Istanbul's streets filled with citizens headed to work.

* * *

Inside an abandoned building against the great Byzantine Land Walls in the southwest corner of Istanbul, John set the newspaper down after reading it for the third time. He was shaken to the core.

The story indicated that Logan Davenport Walker, the daughter of one of American's richest men, had been kidnapped by John Thompson, a renegade Navy SEAL working with an ex–CIA employee named Dan Myers. Myers, who had been killed the previous night by a powerful explosion, had been accused of pursuing a personal vendetta against Alex Davenport, both during and after his employment at the CIA. In his latest efforts, Dan had enlisted John as his foot soldier to stalk Davenport and his daughter.

Pete's death, John's masquerading as his dead brother, and his relationship with Logan were detailed in the lengthy article. The world was appalled that such forces had unleashed themselves on a man as respected and revered as Alex Davenport. The whole story had to be bullshit. John had heard of Myers during his years in the Navy, and all he had heard did the man credit. But John had never so much as met him.

John stared at the picture on the front page for the hundredth time. Staring back at him was the Logan he loved. He beat the ground with his fist. He loved this woman. Since that first unforgettable night she had never left John's thoughts for long. Finally he loved a woman and look where it got him. He felt frustrated at his inability to help her, to explain to her how he felt. Clearly she knew he was not behind the kidnapping, unless… He pushed the thought from his mind.

John jumped to his feet and started to pace as his father's story filled his thoughts again. As if the situation with Logan were not enough! Could the stories about his father be true? Had he been a Soviet agent for most of his naval career? He turned to page six, where his father's story was told. The picture of his father in Navy dress stared back at him.

John threw the paper on the ground, pulled out a match, and lit it. His anger engulfed him. It took all his control not to start yelling and beating the shit out of the first person he saw. Who was behind this string of lies? Davenport? Myers? The CIA?

As the anger flowed though his body, he fought for control because he knew he needed to think and focus. He could not let his emotions get in his way. It was a battle, and he had to win.

Who had started the lies? That was the question, and damned if he wasn't going to find out. They would hunt him, but he would hunt them. They'd learn just how well he had absorbed their training. But first he had to make a call and then get the hell out of Turkey. The stories in the newspapers were irrelevant, except that the notoriety they brought would make it more difficult for him to travel.

John had uncovered a clear indication that the Arabs were about to obtain stolen Russian nuclear weapons. He had a plausible idea of how the bombs would be transported. His job was to make sure, in no uncertain terms, that the buyers never received the devices–period, end of story. He would clean up the rest of the mess reported by the newspapers later. He just hoped that Logan survived this terrible situation. He had to assume she was safe if her father was involved, but what if he was not? He pushed the thought from his mind; he could not afford the distraction.

He picked up the satellite phone and dialed. It started to ring as another thought entered his mind: was Myers the secret hand in Washington?

L

*   *   *

Admiral Sunders rolled over in bed and looked at the red glow emanating from his digital clock: twelve-twenty in the morning. He reached for the phone.

"Hello."

"Is it true?" John demanded.

"What? John, is that you?

"About my father."

The admiral sat up in bed and turned the bedside lamp on. "More or less."

"Was Myers killed in an explosion?"

"No."

"Did he kill my brother?"

"Certainly not," the admiral insisted, frustration on the edge of his voice. "Besides, the story about your father, it's a pack of lies. Davenport is behind everything, as far as we can tell."

"We?"

"Myers."

"Don't fuck with me."

"Damn it, John. I've never lied to you. Don't start that shit with me. I'm your friend and you're in a heap of hurt. Where are you?"

"I'll call you back." The line went dead.

Sunders hung up in frustration. Damn it, John did not know whom to trust. He had assumed wrongly that someone would attempt to trace the call, knowing the admiral was a person John might turn to in times of trouble. Or had he? Would Davenport dare to tap his phone?

"Dear, was that John Thompson?"

"Yes, Betty."

"Poor kid, is he okay?"

"Honey, I don't know. I simply don't know."

The admiral stood, pulled a bathrobe tight around his lean body, and headed downstairs. He knew he could not sleep, at least not yet.

It was obvious that John had seen the news reports and heard of Davenport's wild claims. Yes, there were some truths in the stories, particularly those about John's father. The admiral had always wondered if the decision not to tell John and Pete about their father's treachery had been right. It was too late now for such idle thoughts. It was no longer a secret.

* * *

John stared at the phone, thinking—his father, a spy. How could that be? John desperately wanted to call the admiral back. He needed to know the truth–all of it—but the risk was simply too great. He could not afford to give the authorities any idea where he was. And Logan, what might the admiral know about her? Did he have any idea about John's relationship with her?

And Myers, what role was he playing? Could he be the mysterious hand that kept protecting John? Possibly. Myers was alive, and the admiral was communicating with him. John wondered at what point their communication had started. Also, who had faked Myers' death, Myers or the US government? The admiral played it straight. The military's top brass would want details when one of their own was center stage to an outrageous story. Like any great bureaucracy, the military went to great lengths to protect its image.

John needed a plan, a starting point. The person he needed to meet was Dan Myers. To make that happen he needed the admiral. He would give him a few hours and then call him again.

20 A Russian Bomb Scare

"Sir, something is happening in Russia," Ted Cowan said as he entered keystrokes into his terminal at the Defense Special Missile and Astronautics Center.

The on-duty supervisor for DEFSMAC, located in the bowels of the National Security Agency at Fort Meade, Maryland, was a two-star general named Bill Blaser. He had noticed the increase in communications traffic in the St. Petersburg region. It coincided with a large mobilization of the Red Army and the Federal Security Service. Something was definitely happening; the question was what.

"Any ideas?" General Blaser asked.

"No, sir, nothing definitive," Cowan answered, "but the activity appears to be centered around a base outside of St. Petersburg. It has nuclear weapons. I wonder if one of those raids we've seen in the past might have hit paydirt."

"Let's hope not," General Blaser said. "Get a flash message on CRITICOM. Outline the situation as we know it and say that more information is to follow within a half hour."

"Yes, sir," Cowan said. CRITICOM was the Critical Intelligence Communications Network. It connected the world from all points on the globe and in space and allowed the United States to continuously monitor the evolving SIGINT picture throughout the world.

* * *

The barn was quiet except for the radio. Pyotr Borisov and his men listened to the secure communications emanating from St. Petersburg. A huge net was being thrown over the whole region, a search for criminal activity the official reason given. Borisov and his team knew instantly that only one type of activity would call for such a widespread search. Someone had stolen nuclear devices.

"I've got a bad feeling about this," Orlov said as he watched a fellow soldier adjust the controls of the radio. One of Borisov's men was a communication specialist.

"You and me both," Borisov confirmed.

Borisov stood up quickly and hurried outside. The chill of the evening hit him, a stark difference from the warmth inside the barn. He lit a cigarette and inhaled deeply. It took all his concentration not to shake. How could he have been so stupid?

Borisov's mind flashed back to the beginning.

The Zil slid to a noisy halt on the half circle of crushed stones, its headlights piercing the chilly evening air like ice swords. The front door to the dacha opened, and Genera Leonov emerged, his form backlit by the single bulb that dangled carelessly from the porch ceiling. He wore a green hunting jacket and old pants and looked every bit the part of a thick, strong-willed Russian woodsman. Borisov knew little about the general, and what he did know came from a third party, Nikolai Trubkin. Instinct told him that was about to change.

The driver opened the Zil's rear door. Borisov climbed out, surveying the immediate area. Each detail fell into place. He knew his mind's eye would be able to view the recording at any time. It was habit, the result of years of GRU and Spetsnaz training.

After a moment's pause, Borisov turned from the Zil and made his way deliberately up the three steps to the porch. He extended his hand and closed his powerful fingers around the general's. Borisov noted the general's firm grip. "It was good of you to come. I almost wondered if you would."

L

"You are a man I only know by reputation," Borisov said as his eyes met the general's. Borisov tried to read the thoughts behind the black eyes, the eyes of one of the most powerful men in Russia. He recognized immediately that the general was doing the same: two men with strong wills tested each other's waters. Borisov knew there were differences between them, but the most striking one was power. The general held a high government post with many friends in powerful positions. Borisov, on the other hand, was a criminal of sorts, and officialdom frowned on his type more often than not. He wondered if the general held a similar opinion.

He remembered the conversation with Trubkin, an ex-KGB colonel who now worked for the Chechens. It was Trubkin who had recruited Borisov into the Chechen organization a few short weeks after Borisov's release from the Red Army. But that was over a year ago. After receiving the invitation to the general's dacha two days ago, Borisov had offhandedly asked Trubkin if he had ever dealt with Leonov. Trubkin indicated that he had, which did not surprise Borisov, since Trubkin had spent twenty-five years in the KGB. One of Trubkin's comments had surfaced above all the rest. "Do what he asks and you will be fine." The statement seemed odd. It seemed almost as though Trubkin knew what the general had in store for him.

He focused his attention on the general and said, "Refusing your invitation would have been not only rude, but unwise."

"Well said," the general replied with a hearty laugh. He slapped Borisov's muscular back. The casual gesture surprised the former Spetsnaz soldier.

He considered the general's face. It was heavily lined for a man of his age, which Borisov gauged to be near sixty. His broad build had filled out over the years, no doubt from living the life of a senior Russian bureaucrat. Borisov knew the SVR took care of its own and decided the general could not run two miles if so ordered. He suspected that Leonov's most recent athletic endeavor had taken place in bed, probably with a twenty-year-old.

The general gestured for Borisov to enter his dacha. "Please come in. I have some vodka."

"Yes, thank you, sir."

Borisov's instincts stood on alert. During the drive to the dacha, he had considered the possibility that the general might have him killed, a debt long owed in the eyes of former KGB personnel for his actions in Afghanistan. So far Borisov had not noticed any signs of trouble, something he was usually adept at sensing. The general's hospitality appeared genuine, but men in his position knew how to hide their true feelings. Borisov carried no weapons, but he did not feel unprotected. He was a master at turning any object into a deadly weapon, and he felt confident that his immediate surroundings provided many instruments that could end a man's life.

"Please," Leonov held out his hands. "At my dacha there are no formalities. Let me have your jacket."

Borisov handed his coat to his host and noted that the general's hands were surprising rough for a man in his position. He guessed the general was an avid hunter, spending hours outdoors.

Leonov removed his own green hunting jacket and hung both jackets on the foyer's well-worn wooden pegs. Borisov took the moment to quickly survey the main room of the dacha. It was not large. The furnishings were simple, except for the elegant pieces of art. They appeared to be mostly from Russia and Western Europe. Borisov was no art connoisseur, but he could discern that many of the paintings were originals, some by well-known masters. The general obviously had expensive tastes. Borisov wondered if Leonov had acquired some of the pieces on his frequent tours abroad. The general's wealth puzzled him. He knew the upper echelon of Russia's government lived well, but he was still surprised. Perhaps the paintings were stolen.

He pushed the thought from his mind, knowing he could not allow his hatred for the Federal Security Service–the old KGB in disguise–to cloud his judgment. He had made that mistake once, and he would not make it again.

A table, which faced a warm fire in the large stone hearth, filled the space between two chairs. On the small table sat a bottle of vodka, two shot glasses, and dried fish, hastily arranged on a red and white dish. General Leonov gestured to the chairs and both men took a seat. The general busied himself, slowly pouring a healthy portion of the clear liquid into both glasses. The whole scene seemed oddly choreographed, Borisov thought as the general handed him his glass.

"Daddy," cried a voice. Both men turned in their seats, and a beautiful girl in her early twenties strode into the room. Borisov stood quickly. "Who's this, Daddy?"

The general sighed. "Katya, this is Commander Borisov."

She took Borisov's outstretched hand as she studied the soldier. She smiled at him, her grip firm as a devious smile swept her beautiful face. "He's very cute," she exclaimed.

Borisov could feel himself blushing. He noticed Leonov frown.

"Nice to meet you," the girl added and returned her attention to her father, giving him a kiss on both cheeks. "I'm off. Bye."

The general stared to say something, but stopped as both men watched Katya hurry out the front door. Borisov turned and studied Leonov as the general continued to stare after his daughter. He had a father's pained look on his face, a mixture of love and concern. Leonov turned to Borisov. "I'm sorry for the interruption."

"Sir, not a problem." Borisov returned to his seat.

"She's a fistful, that she is," the general admitted, perhaps to himself.

"Kids are wonderful," added Borisov, unsure of himself.

"Wait until you have some and maybe you'll think differently. That young lady will be my undoing, I'm sure," the general predicted. He grabbed his glass again and raised it. "Let's get started. To your health, Pyotr Andreeyevitch."

"Yes, and to yours, sir," Borisov replied, his eyes meeting the general's once again. Both men turned up their glasses, the vodka striking the back of their throats in standard Russian fashion. The general burped as he set his glass down.

Silence continued as the two men finished a second round of vodka, this portion as healthy as the last. Finally the general turned in his chair and steadied his attention on Borisov.

"I have asked you here to my dacha in the hope that you will consider a proposition," Leonov began as he rested his glass on the small table. "No matter what your decision, I want your word that our conversation will remain between us, no matter who might inquire." Borisov realized the general's tone said more; revealing secrets got a man killed.

"You have my word as a former officer."

Leonov nodded as he filled the two glasses once again. "I accept your word of honor." He handed one to Borisov, and the two men raised them, finishing the warm vodka in a single swallow. The general pointed at the dried fish and Borisov selected a piece. It looked very good.

"Zybin was such an idiot," the general growled suddenly.

Borisov's stomach turned. Zybin was the KGB general he had executed in Afghanistan after the disaster in Darg. Sirens screamed in his head as his eyes darted around the room. Had the general lured him here to pay back that old debt? Was the vodka aimed at dulling his senses? Was it tainted with a drug? He willed calm into his veins. Fear made a man act stupidly.

Suddenly Borisov's mind filled with the image of Mi-8 helicopters, their blades cutting through the oppressive Afghanistan air, as they settled on the Kabul tarmac, returning from the disastrous raid. Zybin had just exited his Mi-8. Borisov had walked from his, which carried the few surviving men of his Spetsnaz Special Forces team. He had approached the general slowly. Zybin's eyes had widened as Borisov drew his 40-millimeter pistol and pressed it against the general's forehead. Borisov had said nothing as he applied the required four pounds of pressure.

The general trained an interested eye on Borisov. "Yes, that bastard you shot between the eyes. He was an idiot. I wish I had had the pleasure."

"Excuse me, sir, General Zybin?"

Leonov nodded without a word.

"Ah, yes, sir. He deserved what he got." Borisov did not know what else to say. What did the general want?

Leonov nodded and continued as though the topic of Zybin had never come up. "As you no doubt know, I am the head of the SVR, the foreign intelligence service of Russia. I'm responsible for keeping tabs on our international friends, especially those in North and South America."

Borisov did not know if he should feel relief or further anxiety as he listened to the general's words. Why had the general raised the subject of General Zybin? What could it have to do with the reasons for this meeting?

The general continued, "In addition, I am privy to a great deal of information outside my specific areas of responsibility. Lately I have become particularly concerned about the integrity of several SVR elements. Now you must wonder why I would confide in you about such matters."

"That is just one of my many questions, General."

Borisov was stunned by the direction of the conversation. One minute Afghanistan was the topic and now trouble within the SVR ranks. His gut told him to get up and bid the general farewell.

"In particular," Leonov continued, as his eyes returned to the fire, "I am worried that certain elements in Russia, some of which I am confident are in the military, are targeting this country's nuclear weapons. Basically, they would steal these devices and sell them to the highest international bidder." The general appeared to sink into deep thought. Finally he spoke. "We cannot allow any Russian nuclear weapons to find their way outside our borders. The international community would never forgive us."

"I understand, sir," Borisov agreed, still baffled.

The general nodded. "The last two years since Gorbachev departed have been vexing. All of the old Soviet Union's territories with nuclear weapons are at risk. It's a precarious time. Military discipline is at an all-time low. Desertions happen every day. Severe food shortages at military installations are common. Hell, I even know a case where a military commander ordered his troops to steal food from the town ten kilometers from his base. It's chaos."

Borisov knew the general spoke the truth. The Chechens fed on such chaos. It made them rich and powerful. The Russian people were easy prey for the criminal elements that expanded daily throughout the old Soviet Empire. Corruption had never been greater in Russia. It was capitalism for the few. "What can be done, sir?"

"We can't allow this to happen," the general repeated firmly, ignoring the question. "I know your past, Borisov, and I know your relationship with the Chechens. Both are reasons why I have decided to bring you into my confidence."

The irony rested heavily on Borisov's broad shoulders. He nodded his head, pretending to understand the general's reasoning. Leonov continued, "I want you to work for me. We must stop these people who are targeting our nuclear materials."

"But how can I help you, sir?" Borisov asked, still puzzled.

"I want you to assemble a small Spetsnaz team, eight to ten ex-members. You will have one purpose," Leonov declared as he poured two more vodkas. "You will conduct raids on various military establishments throughout Russia. These military raids will demonstrate the weaknesses in our security arrangements. The results of your raids will allow the bad commanders to be replaced with ones who can upgrade the security to the required standards."

"I'll supply you with money and equipment and that is all," the general continued. "I do not want to know when or how or where you'll strike. All I ask is that you submit to me reports that detail your successes. I expect the reports to be professional, thorough, and accurate."

Borisov was stunned. If Leonov wanted to place base commanders loyal to him, wouldn't he want to select the bases targeted? Another thought occurred to Borisov. Had the general spoken to other ex-Spetsnaz commanders or was he the first choice?

On the other hand, Borisov reflected, Leonov was offering him a unique opportunity. Not only could he command a Spetsnaz team again, a dream he had all but given up, but he could be in charge. That part was too good to be true. Borisov's instincts told him something else was in the air, but the general's logic made sense. Having a Spetsnaz team raid Russian installations could help reveal weaknesses in base security. That was a good thing, if the information was passed on to the authorities and proper action taken. But did the general have the authority to create such a team? Borisov suspected he did, though he doubted the Army would have any enthusiasm for the plan. The Army and the SVR worked for the same government, but they were enemies. Was this idea just another attempt to embarrass the Army with its own?

"You have a curious look on your face, Commander Borisov."

Borisov noted the use of his old rank for the second time. He had never thought he would hear it again, and for a moment pride swelled inside him, but he controlled the emotion. Now was not the time to dwell on past glory or show any weaknesses to the general.

"Sir, I am honored, but why me? You know about Afghanistan and . . ."

Leonov interrupted with a wave of his hand. "I have selected you for this task for a number of reasons. Most important, you have no ties to the GRU command that taught you so well, though you know how to handle nuclear weapons. It was part of your training. You are an independent thinker, a renegade if you will; otherwise you would not have executed Zybin. I need someone who can command a Spetsnaz-type team and also have the foresight to operate on his own. I don't want you to use standard procedures. Use whatever works. Also, your thorough understanding of the Chechen mob will aid you in understanding how such a group might target our nuclear materials. You are the perfect candidate. My question to you is simple: Can you do it?"

Borisov took a moment to answer. Something wasn't quite right. Meeting at the dacha was strange, but operationally Borisov could understand it. Forming a Spetsnaz unit to work for the SVR was unusual, but again operationally understandable. Actually, everything was operationally understandable; it was the motive that concerned Borisov. What were the general's objectives? Why did he want to tackle the huge task of testing Russia's nuclear security with such a small Spetsnaz team, particularly when he ran the country's foreign intelligence service? Also, why must the operation be secret?

And then there was the one big question: What would the general do if Borisov said no or asked too many questions indicating his doubts?

He looked Leonov in the eyes. "General, I know I can do it. I also believe, like you, that the Mafia is bad for Russia. I want to stop the gangsters. How long until we go operational?"

"How much time do you need?" the general asked.

Borisov considered the question, his operational side overpowering his doubts. "Sixty days to create and prepare a team."

"It will work," the general confirmed. He stood. "I'm counting on you, Borisov. At this critical time in Russia's history we can ill afford to have even one of our nuclear bombs fall into the hands of a third party. The world would never forgive us, particularly the Americans."

Borisov stood and faced the general. "I will not fail you, sir."

And now, four months later, Borisov finally understood the general's plans. Leonov had set him up. The general did not care about the security of Russian nuclear forces–just the opposite. He had used Borisov to show him how to raid nuclear bases. That was why he had wanted detailed reports about the raids. The reports explained how Borisov's team had penetrated three Russian bases. Borisov and his team had given Leonov the key to Russia's nuclear devices. The thought sickened him.

On top of that, Borisov had no illusions about the next use of his reports. Borisov and his men would be framed for the theft, and Leonov, or maybe the Federal Security Service, would be heroes after they unearthed information about Borisov's activities over the last four months.

Anger rocked him. He had been lured into a power struggle of the hugest proportions. The Federal Security Service wanted to make the military look bad and thus strengthen its position. Maybe the next step was a coup d'état. The general had to have a reason to steal the bombs. Maybe it was for money, but somehow Borisov doubted it. The general was a brilliant man. If he wanted to steal nuclear weapons, why did he need such an elaborate plan?

Borisov kicked at the ground as he lit another cigarette. Not that it mattered what the endgame was. Borisov and his men would be hunted down like dogs and charged with high treason. Unlike other branches of the military, GRU officers did not die by a firing squad. The GRU headquarters contained a large amphitheater that could seat all GRU agents. An agent charged with treason was strapped to a conveyer belt that carried him toward a furnace, feet first. The conveyer moved slowly. Borisov had seen two agents meet their end this way. The feet burned first, and slowly the fire walked up the man's body. The screaming stopped only when his body overloaded from the unbearable pain. Not until the man's chest cavity was engulfed in flames did he finally die. The agony was etched on Borisov's mind. To say that Borisov preferred a bullet to such an end was a grand understatement. Dying in such anguish for committing treason was one thing. However, riding down the conveyer to hell for someone else's treason was quite another.

The tape. Thank God for his instincts, but he wondered if it would be enough. Suddenly Borisov knew what he had to do, and the irony was not lost on him. He had to commit treason to stop Leonov.

* * *

The situation room three floors below the White House was packed with frustrated, tired government servants determined to understand the events unfolding in Russia. The President took his seat as the clock showed 2:48 am.

"Ladies and gentlemen, let's bring this meeting to order. Alice."

Alice Stein, the director of the Nuclear Smuggling Group, had been trying desperately for the last two hours to interpret the situation. She made her way to the podium.

"Thank you, Mr. President." She organized her notes for the last time. "At 2:55 am Moscow time, on a base outside of St. Petersburg, a raid directed at the base's nuclear weapons took place. For most of its duration, it resembled the previous three raids we have recently monitored. However, by the end, it appears a half dozen people were killed and at least one, probably two, nuclear devices were stolen."

Many voices spoke at the same time. "Please continue," the President ordered. Silence returned as the projector advanced, displaying a satellite image.

"In the hours since, the Russians have mobilized thousands of troops in both the Army and the Federal Security Service. Roadblocks are being erected everywhere, as this satellite photo clearly indicates. In addition, we have information suggesting that an emergency meeting took place in the Kremlin only hours ago.

"With these facts and others I have reviewed, it is my assessment that one or more devices are missing and that the Russians have no idea where these devices are."

The room remained quiet except for the spinning fan of the projector.

"How do we know the devices were stolen?" the President demanded.

Stein looked at the National Security Advisor, Steve Turner.

"Sir," Turner explained, "part of our intelligence is based on an in-the-clear broadcast made by Russian personnel on the base using a walkie-talkie. The exact translation went like this, and please excuse the language." Turner put on his reading glasses and read from a single sheet of paper. "Two of the fucking SS's are missing, goddamn it. Get the fucking old man out of bed. It can't wait until morning, you fucking idiot."

Turner looked up at the grave faces that lined the diamond-shaped table.

"What else do we know?" the President demanded. He looked exhausted.

"Besides the activity in the St. Petersburg area, the rest of the Russian military is at a normal state of readiness, though the Navy appears to be gearing up," said Admiral Harrington, a slender man whose leadership skills were obvious. "We suspect the Russians are considering ports as likely exit locations for the devices, particularly if they're headed for a destination outside the country."

"Do we have any indications that the bombs are headed out of the country?" asked George Sudendorf, the President's Chief of Staff.

"Theoretically we do not," said Director Lewis of the CIA. "However, before his untimely death, Dan Myers had uncovered strong evidence that the Russian mob or the government, probably both, were planning a sale of nuclear weapons to a party in the Middle East."

"How long have you known this?" the Secretary of Defense demanded, his eyes riveted on Lewis.

"I received a copy of a recording made while Nikolai Trubkin and Ramzi Yousef had dinner in Paris. What you are about to hear is the last ten minutes of their dinner conversation." The DCI motioned to an assistant and the recording began. For the next ten minutes the voices of Trubkin and Yousef filled the situation room.

"Exactly when did you receive this tape?" asked Turner, appalled.

Lewis paused almost imperceptibly. "In the last twenty-four hours."

"Who made the tape?"

Lewis looked around the table before he answered. "John Thompson. He was working for Dan Myers before Dan was killed."

Exclamations broke out all around the room.

"And you think this tape is the real McCoy?" the President asked.

"Yes, sir," the DCI replied quickly. "Experts have listened to both voices and believe they fit the backgrounds we have on both men."

"The newspapers have carried some wild stories about Myers and Thompson," Sudendorf stated as though it were news to everyone. "What do you make of them?"

"Dan is as solid as they come, and all the information on John Thompson suggests as much," the DCI declared. "I for one do not believe Davenport's stories, with the sole exception of his allegations against Thompson's father. They appear to have merit."

"Where is Thompson now?" asked Sam Jenkins, the Secretary of State. "We do know where he is, don't we?"

"I'm afraid we don't," Lewis replied reluctantly.

"Mr. President, if I may add a thought," Admiral Sunders requested from his seat by the Chief of the Navy, Admiral Tidewater. He sensed the DCI's discomfort and understood it. "I've known both Dan and John for many years. I would trust either of them with my life. As your briefing papers indicate, Alex Davenport is the person to question. In my opinion, the timing of his revelations is a glaring admission that he's somehow involved in the situation we're addressing here."

"Are you saying Davenport is behind the theft in Russia?" Turner asked as he looked past the admiral to the director of the CIA. Lewis returned the man's stare.

"All I know for sure, sir," Admiral Sunders answered, "is that someone concocted a huge lie. John and Dan were placing significant pressure on a number of parties, and maybe we are seeing the first cracks in their armor."

"Sir, if I may," interjected Director Bradley of the FBI. "I have spoken with both the DCI and the admiral about Thompson and Myers. I believe both of them when they say they have complete faith in these two men. Certainly, in my experience with Myers, I have only respect for the man."

"The topic at hand was the Russians," observed the Secretary of Defense. "I believe we should focus on that. No matter what the circumstances of Myers' death and John Thompson's whereabouts, we have a taped conversation between a wanted Arab terrorist and a member of the Russian mob. If Director Lewis stands behind it, then I believe we should take it seriously. The timing and the players, Davenport included, appear to bear on the current situation."

"I agree," the Secretary of State confirmed.

The President nodded his agreement as well. "Our options, people?"

"We need to open a dialogue with the Russians, and quickly," Jenkins suggested. "We need to let them know we understand the situation. I believe we should offer assistance, while quietly reminding them that if the stolen bombs are not recovered a significant price will be paid. The IMF loans and other trade items could be a place to start."

"I agree with Sam that we need to begin immediate dialogues with the Russians," Lewis said. "However, I would question the use of a stick. Let me explain my reasoning."

The President nodded.

"Yeltsin's government is fragile at best. It has lasted this long by allowing powerful individuals and the mob to have access to the riches of the country. We all know everything is for sale—minerals, wood, military weapons of every conceivable type—and now we can probably add one more item to that long list, nuclear weapons. Billions of dollars have been looted from Russia, much of it placed in banks outside the country. All the while, the average Russian citizen has become poorer. There is no middle class in Russia. None of this is news to any of us.

"Now let's consider this situation. At first glance, it appears that someone has tried to make the ultimate sale. A single SS-18 would fetch a price of $100 to $150 million US. That's a lot of money for anyone. However, could the motive for stealing and selling nuclear devices be a part of a broader agenda?" Lewis paused to survey the group around the table. He had their attention. "The raids before the main event have concerned us all. If I were going to steal a nuclear weapon, I certainly would not conduct test raids first. If this premise is true, we must ask ourselves what purpose these raids had. The Russians are plotters, not risk takers. They would have conducted the raids for a specific reason. I propose that the reason was to get our attention. Someone wanted us to see how little the current Russian government is doing to protect its nuclear arsenal. I'd like to suggest that the real reason behind the theft is to overthrow the current government.

"If this theory is correct," Lewis continued before anyone could interject, "then I would reconsider threatening the government. It may not be perfect by a long shot, but it is a known entity. I fear a new government might prove to be far more radical–communism all over again. We must ask ourselves what we would rather have."

"Very interesting analysis," Turner offered. "So you're saying the theft is the beginning of an attempt to topple the current Russian government?"

"Yes," Lewis replied, "that is my belief."

"Do you have any other pieces of intelligence to buttress your theory?"

"I'm afraid I have nothing at present," Lewis admitted. "I have analysts running different scenarios as we speak, but the agency can't say with any certainty which is correct, at least not yet. However, if I were a betting man, I'd wager the theft is part of a larger plan."

The President turned to his Secretary of Defense. "Les, what options can the Pentagon offer?"

Les Allen looked at General Calpepper, Chairman of the Joint Chiefs, who nodded.

"Sir," General Calpepper began, "we think there are two main scenarios. The bombs will either stay in the country or they will be shipped out of it. Our thinking at the Pentagon is the latter. That's where the money is. If this is the case, we need to be prepared to interdict the shipment and make damn sure it never reaches the intended buyers.

"Obviously there are many potential buyers, but in light of the audiotape, I think we can hedge our bets and assume the devices are headed to the Middle East, India, or Pakistan. There are four available types of transportation: trucks, trains, ships, and planes. Because of the distances involved, I would immediately discount trucks and trains, particularly since the theft was in northern Russia. That leaves ships and planes. Ships offer a secure means to transport nuclear devices because they're large enough to carry a special compartment to hide the devices from our satellites. However, ships are slow and make an easy target on the open sea—assuming, of course, that we know which ship the bombs are on. Planes offer the best choice because of speed, but unless a very large military or civilian plane is used, our satellites will easily spot the devices on board, since they can't be adequately shielded. The Russians own very few 747s and I don't believe they have a civilian plane that can match the task. That leaves military planes, and one would think the Russians would keep a close eye on their inventory in light of the current situation.

"With these thoughts in mind, we believe a ship offers the most practical means for transporting the devices out of Russia." He turned and nodded at the Chief of the Navy.

It took Admiral Tidewater fifteen minutes to outline all the possible shipping routes and times, and the strategies to stop the bombs from reaching their destination. Finally he said, "No matter what the scenario, we can get the assets there and make damn sure the devices don't reach the buyer if the order is given in the next ten hours. However, the key here is not strike power. It's intelligence. We cannot act until we know exactly what ship or ships the devices are aboard."

"Jim, what options do we have besides placing nuclear monitoring devices in Denmark?" the President asked.

"We're compiling a list of all ships in and off the ports around the Baltic Sea," Lewis replied. "We are checking ownership and past cruises they've taken. We're considering their sizes and the likelihood that any particular ship would be used. I believe we have a fair chance of narrowing the possibilities to fewer than twenty ships. Beyond that, we need to apply pressure in several areas and hope for a break. I believe we should plan to board all twenty vessels, or at a minimum, block them from getting near their destination or any other port. Clearly there will be political ramifications."

"What is the possibility that the devices could be transferred to or moved by a submarine?" Turner asked.

The chairman of the Joint Chiefs looked at Admiral Tidewater.

"Sir, the same thought has occurred to us," the admiral answered. "It's a distinct possibility that a submarine could be used at any point along the delivery channel. The most worrisome leg is the initial one. If the devices are loaded on a submarine, moved out of the port, and then transferred to a ship, the number of possible ships grows considerably. One more thought: the use of a submarine would mean high-ranking members of the Russian military are involved in this caper. That's a scary prospect in and of itself."

"Sam, what are your thoughts?" the President asked.

"Diplomatically, we need to open a dialogue with the Russians and our allies," the Secretary of State began. "I'm sure the British are on to the situation, as are many of our European allies. Troop movements of this size are not easily hidden. I suspect the Russians will make a public announcement through their embassies. If indeed bombs have been stolen, the pressure will

L

be on. I also assume, General Calpepper, that the military would want to involve some of our allies in any operation."

"Yes, sir, the British in particular."

All eyes went to the President. He was known to make decisions based on the last argument he heard. Today, however, all the arguments had come at once and were pretty consistent.

"Okay, Sam, open the dialogues with Russia. Let's get the Russian Ambassador over here before lunch. That should give his masters more than enough time to brief him on their predicament. Also, let's get the Danes on board and get those monitors in place pronto. General Calpepper, position the carriers as needed in the Indian Ocean and the Mediterranean. Let's get any special units that we need in place."

"And the submarines, sir?"

"Yes, move them as needed," the President ordered. "Also, I want someone to fly to Britain and brief the Prime Minister. We'll need their help and I'll make sure we get it. Jim, I want the list of ships distributed to this group within twenty-four hours. Make sure the list includes the ship registries and owners. If Davenport or any of his companies show up on the list, I want to know immediately. Is there anything I've missed?"

Director Bradley of the FBI spoke. "Sir, I think we'd better find Thompson. I have an uneasy feeling he can provide valuable information."

"Yes," the President agreed. "What do you propose?"

"I say we turn the tables on Davenport, sir," Director Bradley proposed. "Let me hold a press conference and state that the government is convinced Myers and Thompson are innocent in these matters and that Thompson is cooperating fully with our continuing investigation."

"I like it," the President declared. "Any comments?"

"Sir, I believe it can't hurt," Turner agreed. "However, its success depends on the premise that Thompson is in our custody. We all know this not to be true. A leak to this effect would cancel any advantage gained by the statement."

"Agreed," the President said. "No one outside this room, and I mean no one, learns about this angle without my personal approval, or heads will roll. Any questions?

"Good. Let's get moving, people, and let's meet here at nine tomorrow morning unless events warrant otherwise. The meeting is adjourned."

21 Hearing from the Russians

Timing was everything. Borisov's team had orchestrated this operation as carefully as all the others, down to each second. Borisov stole a glance at his watch. Its illuminated dial read 3:09 am—time for him to move.

He started north on Novinskij bul'var as a gray, heavily dented Moskva station wagon sped past him. It headed toward Kudrinskaja Place, a small tree-filled park in front of the Vysotnoezdanie building, a Stalin-era apartment block. Borisov noted that the car was precisely on time.

In two minutes he turned right onto Kudrinskij, which paralleled Kudrinskaja Place. A few dozen meters further he turned left and followed Koniušlovskij Street downhill. Where the road turned right and straightened, he came almost to a stop.

The Moskva station wagon was parked to his right in front of an old wooden warehouse and pulled tightly against its swinging doors. The warehouse sat atop one of Russia's more sensitive operations. It faced the US Embassy directly across the narrow street. The entrance to the secret facility was in the Vysotnoezdanie Building a block and a half away. A special elevator led to a long tunnel that ran to a control center thirty-five meters below the ground, directly under the warehouse. It was the nerve center for Russian efforts to spy on the US embassy.

Orlov hurried from the parked station wagon and jumped on the back of the motorcycle without a word, giving Borisov a squeeze. It was the signal that the charge was armed and ready.

Borisov picked up a little speed, throttling his motorbike gently. He knew Orlov was keeping an eye out for the Russian guard who manned the hut uphill from the parked station wagon. This guard wandered around the perimeter of the US embassy as part of his normal duties. Borisov, meanwhile, kept his focus on the guard stationed in the hut just past the North Gate. This guard was his responsibility.

When the bike came abreast of the North Gate, Borisov threw a sack over the metal gate of the US Embassy. At the same moment a deafening explosion rocked the area, sending the station wagon six meters into the air only to return it to the ground in flames. Borisov gunned the motorcycle and a few seconds later leaned into a right turn, pointing them down Koniuškovskaja Street and in the direction of the Moscow Zoo.

Thirty seconds later they came to the intersection in front of the zoo, and Borisov turned left onto Krasnaja Presnja. Already sirens could be heard in the distance. He had no doubt where they were headed. Terrorism directed at a foreign embassy was unknown in Russia. Having a bomb explode next to the US Embassy would be a serious embarrassment to the Russian authorities, but no less a concern would be the possible exposure of their secret listening post, whose camouflage was rapidly burning.

* * *

Two hours after the explosion, Koniušlovskij Street next to the US Embassy was still filled with vehicles from the various Russian police agencies. The fire that had engulfed the warehouse had been extinguished, but the wooden building had been reduced to hot cinders and twisted metal.

Inside the embassy, Bill Haley, the CIA station chief, and Andy Cortes, the number-two man in the CIA's Moscow station, watched as the chief of embassy security, Arthur Ayers, entered the third-floor conference room, holding only a videotape and a sheet of paper. For the past few hours the man had supervised the scanning of the package found inside the North Gate after the explosion. No one had been anxious to take any unnecessary chances after the scene that had occurred outside the embassy compound.

They were all tired. Ever since the large Russian mobilization in the St. Petersburg area, everyone at the embassy had been working around the clock. The powers in Washington were desperate to understand what the Russians were up to. So far the embassy personnel had learned little beyond the story the Russians were selling for public consumption. Their diplomatic explanation mirrored the public line, only heightening Washington's impatience.

The Ayers handed the tape and single sheet of paper to Haley, who walked to a VCR in the corner of the secure conference room and inserted the tape. "Thanks Arthur."

The chief of security excused himself before Haley flicked the Play button. For the next nine minutes they watched in total silence, shocked by what they heard and saw. Washington needed to know, and right away.

"I'll send a *Flash* message," Haley said after they had finished watching the tape for the second time. "You make a copy and get the original in the diplomatic bag. Arrange to get it on the 6:00 am British Airways flight to London, and then book it on the fast route to Langley from Hereford Air Force Base. If possible, use a helicopter to ferry the cassette from Heathrow to Hereford." Both men knew that Hereford was headquarters to the British Army's 22nd Special Air Service Regiment, also known as the SAS.

"Right," Cortes agreed.

"Do it yourself," Haley ordered. "This one is too hot. I don't want anyone else to see it or know about the contents."

"Got you. I'll let you know when I'm done."

Cortes left the third-floor secure conference room that stood between the ambassador's office and his, the single sheet of paper in his hand. He sat down at his desk and wrote the *Flash*-designated message. There was only one higher designation than *Flash—Lightning*, which meant war was imminent. Thankfully it had never been used.

* * *

The summer sun sank toward the west, sliding behind a swath of birch trees that made up the view from James Lewis's office on the top floor of CIA headquarters in Langley, Virginia. Lewis had just returned from a briefing at the Pentagon. It had not been comforting. From everything they knew, at least two nuclear weapons had been stolen from a missile base outside St. Petersburg.

The Russians were mobilizing a huge portion of their northern army as well as their Federal Security Service's border units. The satellites showed all entrances being blocked in and out of northwest Russia, though the heaviest concentration of personnel centered on St. Petersburg.

A knock sounded on his door. "Come in," Lewis ordered.

Harold Carington, Deputy Director of Operations, crossed the well-furnished office and handed Lewis the *Flash* message from Moscow. The DCI donned his reading glasses, gestured for Carington to take a seat.

> TOP SECRET
> 2108930Z*************001A
> FLASH
> TO: LANGLEY DDO*****F.Y.E.O.
> FM: MOSCOW OPS*****01
> 1. ON 21 SEP. 93 BROWN PACKAGE WAS THROWN OVER EMBASSY WALL BY UNKNOWN PERSON(S) WHILE DISTURBANCE OCCUPIED RUSSIAN GUARDS OUTSIDE EMBASSY COMPOUND XX
>
> 2. PACKAGE CONTAINED ONE VCR TAPE AND A SINGLE SHEET OF PAPER XX
>
> 3. VIDEO OFFERS POSSIBLE EXPLANATION OF RUSSIANACTIVITIES IN ST PETERSBURG AREA

RPT POSSIBLE EXPLANATION OF RUSSIAN ACTIVITIES IN ST PETERSBURG AREA XX

4. ORIGINAL OF VIDEO AND SINGLE SHEET OF PAPER SENT VIA ROUTE TANGO-44 XX

5. EVALUATION: BELIEVE TAPE REVEALS TRUTH OF RUSSIAN SITUATION XX

6. QUERY: REQUEST IMMEDIATE ANALYSIS XX
AWAIT FURTHER INSTRUCTIONS XX
END FLASH
MOSCOW OPS********01
210836Z
BTR

"Can we get them to send the contents through the satellites?" the director asked as he looked up from reading the flimsy for the second time.

"We can," Carington said, "but we always run the risk, no matter how remote, that the Russians can intercept and decode the message. If Bill did a *Flash*-designated message, the contents of the tape must be explosive. Working with the original feed is best. We can gather a great deal more information from it than we can from an electrical transmission. He knows this; otherwise he would have sent it via satellite. We can query him or we can sit tight."

"You're right," the DCI agreed. "Bill is on the scene. When will it arrive?"

"Assuming the British Airways flight is on time, I say it will arrive here at Langley by 7:00 am tomorrow."

"I'll be here. Alert me if anything changes," Lewis ordered.

"Certainly, sir," Carington said.

"Is there anything else?"

"Yes, sir," Carington answered. "From a review of the embassy's surveillance film, it appears the package was thrown over the gate by two men on a motorcycle at the exact instant the car bomb detonated on Koniušlovskij. The warehouse across the street was completely destroyed, an interesting turn of events in itself."

"The one off the North Gate?"

"That's the one."

"Any thoughts?"

"Only two come to mind," Carington began. "First, the Russians have to be very pissed. The loss of the facility will hurt them, though the exact extent of the damage is unknown at this time. As you know, it's their main base for spying on our embassy. Second, it has to be some kind of message. Certainly the explosion could have been a diversion, and it probably was at one level, but from what I hear from the embassy folks, the charge in the car had to be shaped. The entire force of the blast was concentrated on the warehouse. Someone knew what was in there and deliberately destroyed it."

"Interesting."

Carington turned and let himself out of the director's office. Lewis leaned back in the armchair and removed his reading glasses. He stood and walked to his desk. He was tired.

Since taking over the CIA he had driven himself hard. He had so much at stake. He had taken him years to build his dreams into reality, and suddenly–without warning or any fault of his own–they were snatched from his grip. It pained him to no end. He had regrouped, formed another plan, the only one he could. It was a risky proposition from the beginning. He had always known it; only now did he realize just how risky. He hoped he had what it took to stay the course.

Things were moving fast and unpredictably. A new player had just entered the game, and he desperately wanted to know who it was.

* * *

General Leonov listened to the colonel's report, not bothering to hide his concern.

"Has the facility been exposed?" the general demanded.

"No, sir," the colonel answered, his voice emotionless. "We have taken numerous pictures from a helicopter stationed in the area, and no obvious signs of our activities are apparent. Nevertheless I believe we should bulldoze the remains of the warehouse as soon as it cools, leaving only dirt in its place. If the Americans searched the area, they could possibly identify debris that could raise unwanted questions."

"See to it, Colonel. Be damn sure the Americans get nowhere close to the site until that time. You're dismissed." The officer saluted smartly and departed.

The general considered this new development. The facility had been attacked. No permanent damage was done, though some of the listening devices housed in the warehouse had been destroyed. The center was now more than half blind—regrettable, but not overly costly to Leonov's immediate plans. The remote possibility of the Americans stumbling onto debris gave him more cause for concern.

The question, however, was why. Why would someone want to destroy the old warehouse? If that someone knew what lay inside and below it, the attack had served its purpose, but only temporarily. Actually the destroyed building gave the general a reason to put up a new building in its place, a possible advantage. If the attackers did not know the purpose of the warehouse, why strike it? The colonel had been specific on that point: the charges in the car had been shaped. The target was definitely the warehouse and not the US Embassy across the street. What other purpose could the attack have served?

* * *

Logan figured seven days had passed. Her foul-smelling captors glared at her with continuous contempt. The routine had not varied. She sensed their boredom almost rivaled hers.

The magazines she had received no longer held her attention. Since the bastards watching her refused to re-supply her reading material, she only had her mind to keep her entertained. She found herself thinking about her childhood and her parents, particularly her father.

She wondered what he was doing at this very moment. Was he distraught with her disappearance? Did he know she had been kidnapped and not simply run away? He must. However, as much as these questions swirled through her mind, there was another that kept surfacing. Was her kidnapping an act directed at her father and not John?

She had no doubt that John pursued dangerous people. At first she had believed that her abduction was a means to lure John to Rome where a deadly trap had been set. Now, she wasn't so sure.

Her father had always been a secretive man and it wasn't until now that it struck her as odd. She had always assumed that his secretiveness came as a result of spending years in the CIA, and to some degree it probably had. But why did he keep his office locked at all times and his desk completely clear of papers? She knew he wasn't a neat freak. He readily left messes for the help; clothes on the floor, dirty dishes on the table, newspapers on the floor by his reading chair in the den.

She wondered how well she knew him. Did John know things about her father that she did not? She remembered John's anger, it was almost palpable, after he had overhead something her father had said. John had claimed it was the contents of the newspaper, but Logan hardly believed that. No, she was sure it was something her father had said and that something had caused John to leave suddenly.

She gasped at the thought–was her father tied to Pete's death? Her father might have his secretive side, but it didn't include

L

murder. She was certain. Anger raced through her. How could she think such a thought?

She looked at her watch. It was time to try again. She knew it was a fruitless gesture, but she had to make it anyway. She stood and marched directly to her bedroom's door, reaching deliberately for its knob. Suddenly, the Russian guard stood, grabbed her roughly, his massive fist wrapped tightly around her forearm. He forcefully pushed her towards the bed as he release a verbal barrage. She didn't understand a word nor did she bother to yell back, content in the knowledge that the Russian thug had reacted a little slower than yesterday. She would never get past him, but she knew his alertness was slightly dulled. If her rescuers came, it could only help.

She tried to pull away from him as the smell of garlic, sweat and cheap cigarette smoke filled her nostrils. She realized her arm was throbbing as though an overzealous doctor had pumped the blood pressure device too far. Suddenly, she realized she was in trouble. The guard's other hand reached out, pulling viciously at her belt. Fear surrounded her like a sudden fog. She started to yell, hearing herself as though she was an innocent bystander.

The Russian stumbled on top of her, pinning her to the bed and nearly knocking her breath away. She desperately tried to break his cement like grip. She felt helplessness descend upon her. This Russian bastard was going to rape her and there wasn't a damn think she could do about. It made her soul go dark. She wanted him dead.

As her clothes were being shredded from her body, she managed to yell again, weaker this time. Tears filled her eyes, raising her anger to another level. How could she cry? What good would it do? She yelled again. In moments he would have her pants down to her knees.

Without warning a large crash sounded and another scream vibrated through the small bedroom. She continued to fight her attacker, not willing to pause for even a moment to understand the significance of the other noises. She sensed rather than saw the other Russian guards in the room. They started to pull their comrade from his victim, but as much as they pulled she remained firmly in his grasp. Not until the crack of the pistol butt sounded did he loosen his grip. It took a second powerful swing of the pistol until her attacker went limp. She rolled hard, trying to escape the heavy burden that lay atop of her. She finally squirmed free, fighting the whole time to regain her breath.

The Russians hauled their unconscious comrade from the room, leaving her half naked and shaking uncontrollable in the corner.

22 Borisov's Dilemma

The director of the CIA studied the shadows drawn by the morning sun seven floors below. The sight relaxed him. He sighed deeply; he had forgotten what it felt like to really relax.

For the thousandth time he considered his position–so many dreams, most of them unrealized. And what would his wife think if she knew? He half wondered if she would care. He hated the bitch, but the thought made him sad nevertheless. He despised himself for feeling that way.

What was done was done. He hadn't lost yet. He had a plan, and now that he had launched it, doubts began creeping into his mind. Would it work? The risks were huge. Everything had become unpredictable. And Leonov—what was he really up to?

Lewis turned from the windows and focused his attention on Admiral Sunders, who sat on the couch waiting to watch the video from the US Embassy in Moscow. The director had already watched the tape twice. It showed Borisov and Leonov sitting on a Moscow Zoo bench, facing a glassed-in building that probably housed some of the zoo's attractions. Behind the two men stood a large cage connected to another building. Both men appeared nervous as they scanned their surroundings, a constant watch that professionals never ceased.

The quality of the video was very good, though obviously it had been shot from some distance; the angle suggested a neighboring rooftop. The sound was also surprisingly good. The directional microphone Borisov's team had used must have been excellent, or Borisov had been wired. The director knew that sophisticated recording equipment was not easily found in Russia, making it more likely that Borisov had the microphone on him, a risky proposition. But the words, even more than the images, had chilled him to the bone. He was impressed with Borisov's eloquence, something the English subtitles, inserted by the translation team, did little to capture.

"Admiral, are you ready?"

"Yes, sir."

The director pushed the Play button on the VCR's remote control. The image of Borisov and General Leonov came to life.

"Good morning, General," Borisov said as the general approached. The former Spetsnaz soldier gestured toward a wooden bench. "Why don't we sit here?"

Leonov nodded, an angry grunt his only verbal acknowledgement.

"This meeting was unnecessary," Leonov declared after they had taken their seats. "Tupolev is more than capable of acting on my behalf."

"I felt it was important, sir. I want to know precisely what my limitations are."

The general's annoyance showed. "Specifically?"

"You expect my team to identify military installations throughout Russia to penetrate, leaving concrete proof of our presence in areas where nuclear weapons are maintained and stored. These areas should be secured against our entry. The very fact that we penetrate the areas will give you detailed information on the weak security procedures employed by the base targeted. Correct?"

"Yes," the general replied with a grimace.

"The reason you want my team to penetrate these military installations is to give you just cause to remove incompetent base commanders and to ensure that our nuclear weapons cannot fall into the wrong hands."

"My reasons don't concern you," the general growled.

L

"Yes, sir, " Borisov replied quickly.

Both men watched a zoo attendant empty a trashcan a few feet from their bench. Borisov waited until the man had finished his chores before continuing. "Sir, you'll provide us with the necessary equipment to penetrate these military installations–guns, ammunition, and transportation. Which leads me to my first question. What if we come under fire? Do you want us to return fire?"

The general sat for a moment, considering the question. "Return fire. You'll do me no good dead or in jail."

"If by some chance one of my men is caught, will you inform the base commander that our efforts are only a test, and order a quick release with no thought of prosecution?"

"Certainly," the general said, his face beginning to redden. "But I don't expect your men to be caught. I selected you as their leader for a reason, and being caught was not one of them. Do I make myself clear?"

"Yes, sir," Borisov replied, appearing to digest the information. "If one of my men is shot, will you ensure that he gets the best medical treatment?"

The general turned his head and glared at Borisov. "Is this really necessary?"

"General, I think we understand each other," Borisov said. "Do you have any questions for me?"

"Tupolev said you had a nuclear-related issue to discuss," the general said. "What is it?"

"If we uncover any unstable weapons or ones that are deteriorating, should we label the devices as such?"

"No. Include the information in your report, and I will disseminate it to the proper parties. Anything else?"

"No, sir."

"I expect you to do your job and succeed. Questioning my reasoning is not part of your job," General Leonov ordered. "Don't screw with me again. Is that clear?"

"Certainly, sir," Borisov replied. Both men rose.

"I trust there will no further need for us to meet face to face," the general insisted, a warning in his tone. "Is that also clear?"

"Yes, sir." Borisov held out a piece of paper. "My equipment list, sir."

The general grabbed it and shoved it into his pocket without a glance. "In two weeks meet Tupolev in Gorky Park, 7:00 am sharp. He'll tell you where you can find your equipment."

Suddenly the picture changed and showed a headshot of Borisov, sitting in front of the camera. He spoke for the next four minutes.

"Born Pyotr Pavlovich Borisov in 1953 on the outskirts of Leningrad, I followed my father's footsteps and entered the military. In 1974, after three years in the Army, I was recruited by the GRU. Four years later my bosses in the Fifth Directorate of the GRU sent me to the Military Diplomatic Academy in Moscow. Its instruction taught students the basic skills needed to divest the Soviet Union's enemies of their military secrets, a task in which I excelled. In June of 1978, I graduated and was posted as the commander of a Spetsnaz unit, the Second Brigade, a regiment of elite military men who were the envy of the whole Red Army. I was very proud. As you know, Spetsnaz units' mental toughness, intelligence, and physical abilities represent the best Russia has. The Spetsnaz units are Russia's answer to your Army's Green Berets. My Second Brigade was the prize of all the Spetsnaz units, an accomplishment that I still cherish today.

"After I had commanded these men for seven months, my unit was sent to Afghanistan in March of 1979 to fight the Afghan rebels. My men and I fought well, but on our third tour in 1985 things changed. I realized that Afghanistan had become the Soviet Union's Vietnam. The organization between the various military elements and the KGB had fallen into such chaos that victory was no longer an option. Also, the Mujahadeen had proven to be stronger than anyone in the Russian military establishment had foreseen. Through it all I protected my men, and only a handful of them made the quiet journey home in a body bag.

"That all changed on June 4, 1985, in a village called Darg, located in an Afghan valley. A KGB general had intelligence from an informant, a French doctor sympathetic to Russia who worked in another Afghan village. The intelligence indicated a meeting of the Mujahadeen was to take place in the village of Darg. In particular, the leader of one of the more successful Mujahadeen factions planned to attend the meeting. The KGB dreaded the thought that various factions would unite under this particular resistance leader. He had charisma and respect from many of the warring factions. The KGB and the military considered him a solid adversary. This opportunity might only come once, and the KGB general became intent on ambushing the Mujahadeen gathering. The prize was too great to pass up.

"The plan called for six Hind helicopter gunships and five Hips, Mi-8 Russian transport helicopters. Each Hip would carry thirty men. Of the 150 men who made up the attack force, half were from my Spetsnaz unit. The village of Darg was jammed between a river and cliffs that mark the western end of the valley. The attacking force planned to cross a small bridge and enter the village while the six Hind helicopters flew cover for the men. It all sounded simple.

"Nothing could be farther from the truth. The Mujahadeen somehow knew of the impending attack and had devised an effective ambush. They had placed two Dashokas 12.7-millimeter antiaircraft machine guns on the cliffs above the village. They no doubt used armor-piercing bullets, probably manufactured by the damn Chinese. These guns destroyed four of the six Hinds and one Hip in less than four minutes. The gunmen on the Dashokas were very good. The two Dashokas gun emplacements were finally destroyed with only two Hinds left, thanks to the bravery of the pilots. The two Spetsnaz units started to advance across the bridge, while the Hinds continued to provide covering fire.

"I led the first element of my men across the bridge. As soon as we took a covering position on the village side, the bridge exploded. There had been more then seventy men on that bridge, fifty-eight of them mine. What was left of the bridge and my men was a gruesome sight. Without hesitation three of my remaining men and I retreated across the river. We were no longer an effective fighting force. There was no choice but to retreat and leave the dead behind.

"The flight home was deathly silent except for the drum of the helicopter blades. With each beat of those rotor blades my anger grew. By the time the Mi-8 landed at our air force base outside of Kabul, my rage had developed into a plan of action.

"I jumped out of the helicopter and walked directly up to the KGB general who had planned the attack. He was just exiting his Mi-8. Without hesitation I shot the general between the eyes.

"I remember the same look on all the soldiers' faces. It was one of total shock mixed with appreciation for what I had just done. The KGB's intelligence had failed us all too often. Darg was a perfect example. A chill still runs up my body every time I replay this event in my mind.

"Two days later, after spending my time in a filthy cell, I was recalled to Moscow for a full debriefing by my masters in the Fifth Directorate. After three months of endless debriefing sessions, the powers determined that I, Commander Borisov, should spend twenty years in a military prison. Everyone said I was lucky, but luck be damned. That KGB general deserved what he got, and I knew I was a pawn in a much bigger political mess.

"When the Soviet Union finally collapsed in 1991, I had completed five years of my prison sentence. The time was hard, but I knew I'd survive. I could protect myself well enough.

"To my surprise, I was pardoned for my actions in Afghanistan and released on the twentieth anniversary of my entry into the military. I resigned my commission immediately, which many of my superiors felt made the best of a difficult situation. I was a civilian for the first time in my life, and I had no idea where to start. All I knew was that the disintegration of the Soviet empire was real, and that everywhere I looked I saw a few Russians getting rich on the remains of the empire, while the vast majority of citizens were suffering from poverty and a growing sense of helplessness.

"A few weeks after my release, I met Nikolai Fyodorovich Trubkin outside the GUM department store in Moscow. Both of us were standing in the warm August sunlight, looking at the faces of the customers who were coming and going. It did not take long for each of us to notice the other, and a conversation ensued. After a few minutes Trubkin suggested we grab a bite to eat; he even offered to pay.

"I consider myself a good judge of men. My years commanding a Spetsnaz unit taught me many things. Trubkin had an air about him that was powerful and businesslike. I sensed that he was looking for something, and I had nothing to lose. I had resigned my commission and intended to take part in the profits that flowed all around me from the disintegration of the Soviet Union. I figured I had earned the right.

"After a few rounds of vodka, I learned that we shared many of the same ideals. We were both loyal and had found success through hard work, shrewd intelligence, and the willingness to take risks. Trubkin explained to me that he belonged to a group who had interests in a number of business activities, some legal and many not. He went on to say that he was looking for good men he could trust and who knew how to take care of themselves. I knew I was Trubkin's man.

"One year has passed, and I have risen to a top position in the Chechen crime syndicate, a Russian version of your American mob. I'm sure you know about them.

"My special skills and military knowledge helped the syndicate strengthen their security and their methods for infiltrating various installations. However, I was having severe second thoughts about my relationship with the Chechens.

"The Chechens, the Party–which is still the biggest Mafia organization in Russia–and others are slowly taking control of Russia. The government under President Yeltsin is losing power to a select group of people who have ties to the mob organizations. Corruption during the Brezhnev years seems mild compared with today's activities.

"I missed the old Soviet Union. Though I had a purpose working for the Chechens and was getting rich doing so, I didn't have a Spetsnaz unit to command. Commanding my unit was the best job I had ever had. I missed the men's loyalty, their unselfish ways, and their humor. My Chechen companions are totally motivated by money. I don't trust any of them. Money brings certain advantages, but they only make life more convenient, not more meaningful. I want to rediscover the honesty and sense of purpose that I had as a Spetsnaz commander. General Leonov knew all this. He knew I was the perfect fall guy.

"Now you know the story.

"I suspect the operation across the street from your embassy is no longer a concern. Consider it a favor and a sign of the lengths my men and I will go to stop General Leonov."

23 The Possibilities

Lewis watched Admiral Sunders, who had finished viewing the tape for the second time. He knew the admiral did not need the subtitles; Sunders spoke Russian fluently.

"Damn, what a story. This man has a way with words," Sunders said. "The subtitles don't do him justice. He's downright eloquent."

Neither man said anything for a moment, each lost in his own thoughts.

"Did anyone get a description of the messenger?" the admiral finally asked.

"No," the director said. "The explosion sent everyone diving to the ground. A few minutes later a marine spotted a leather bag near the entrance inside the embassy compound by the North Gate. As you might imagine, everyone suspected another bomb.

"An hour later, when the parcel was judged safe, the station chief opened it. He and another one of our people watched the video. When they realized its significance, they copied it and put the original in the diplomatic bag. An F-15 flew it to Andrews Air Force Base from Hereford. It arrived 5:45 am and was edited by 8:00 am."

Lewis sipped from his fourth mug of coffee. "This video, if he's telling the truth, goes a long way toward explaining who's behind the theft. I just hate to think it's true."

"I recognize the general," the admiral said, "but does anyone recognize the other man, Borisov? Is he what he says he is?"

"I have two specialists digging as we speak," the director assured him.

"Who do we have who was in Afghanistan?" the admiral asked. "The execution of a KGB officer by a Spetsnaz commander could not be kept quiet. It would be a story worth telling, if quietly."

"My same thought," the director agreed. "I think we might have such a man. We're trying to find him now. Other thoughts?"

"Borisov obviously added his speech to the tape after the meeting with the general. He sounded desperate. He's distraught and believes the general used him. Still I find it hard to believe that the head of foreign intelligence would be involved in stealing and selling nuclear weapons. He has enormous power. What does he stand to gain from such activities?"

"The same question occurred to me," Lewis said.

The admiral sat up suddenly. "You know what? All along we've been trying to prove the rumors we keep hearing, that someone high up in Russia is feeding intel to the Chechens. Maybe it's the general."

"That's a hell of a thought," the director murmured. "There is a certain logic to it. We know the SVR is buying drugs from El Gordo's cartel. Might they use the Chechens to distribute them and in return the Chechens get money and intelligence on the plans of the Russian army?"

"Yes. Maybe Jokhar Dudayev has made a deal for protection. Maybe Leonov has been feeding them intelligence. The Russian Army has fared poorly in Chechnya. If the general has higher aspirations, he could profit from making the military look bad. Plus the whole Chechnya initiative makes Yeltsin look weak."

"Yes," the director agreed. "The Chechnya venture has been an embarrassment for Yeltsin, and as you said, he initiated it. Any other thoughts, Admiral?"

"My sense from the video is that Borisov is telling the truth, at least as he knows it," Sunders began. "My guess is he's very good at what he does. He is Spetsnaz, and they're Russia's best.

For him to turn to America for help wasn't an easy decision. An act of treason isn't something he'd undertake lightly. He obviously feels we are his last chance at making things right.

"Also," the admiral continued, "the fact that Borisov's team shot the video is significant. He took the extraordinary risk of filming the meeting because he didn't trust Leonov. Why? It's obvious from the video that Leonov is pissed at Borisov for calling the meeting. It appears they had already agreed on the mission and its guidelines. Leonov had anticipated that all further communications would go through his man Tupolev. That goon with his hands in his pockets, standing off to the left in the picture, is probably him."

"Yes," the director agreed. "I think you're probably right."

The admiral rose and started to pace. "Apparently Tupolev was to be their only line of communication. The general wanted distance between himself and Borisov. Again we must ask ourselves why. If the task ordered by Leonov was completely on the up-and-up, I doubt such a thin line of communication would be necessary or normal. Maybe that part of the arrangement sent Borisov's instincts into high gear."

"A distinct possibility," the director agreed, "but why did he accept the task?"

"An interesting question, but I suspect Leonov is not a man you say no to, particularly if you're a GRU man who's executed a KGB general. If Leonov asked something of him, he'd have no choice but to accept."

The director paused for a moment. "I agree. But the Chechen relationship interests me. Why pick Borisov for the job? Why not use someone still in the military? Since when do the Chechens allow a Russian in their midst anyway?"

Sunders thought about the question before he spoke. "If the general planned to steal nuclear bombs, he needed a scapegoat. Borisov, if his personal history checks out, fits that bill. The combination of his mob background and his military one makes him ideal. He knows about nuclear bombs and how to infiltrate military bases. The general used him not only to create a link to the Chechens, but also to locate the weaknesses in Russian base security.

"We know the Russians hate the Chechens and would welcome any excuse to get rid of them. Leonov blames the Chechens for the theft and makes it look like Borisov is only their hired help. I'd even wager that the general had Borisov recruited into the Chechens. Maybe he even facilitated his release from prison. After his release Borisov needs a job, Trubkin appears, and he plays Borisov's hatred for the Russian system. The Chechens might have looked like the perfect home.

"The video indicates that Borisov gave the general detailed reports on each raid. The general used this information to plan his own raid. He'll also use it to build a case against Borisov and his Chechen bosses, proving they masterminded the theft. The general will leak this information as necessary, creating a deliberate trail."

"If true, brilliant," Lewis reflected. "What are our options?"

"Sir, if I may ask," Sunders said, "who else has seen this video?"

"The two men in the Moscow embassy I mentioned, the editors, and the two of us. I've scheduled a White House briefing for 10:30 am. After that, everyone who is anyone in Washington will know."

"Sir, pardon me for being so frank, but you asked me to this meeting, giving me access to information before my superiors." The admiral added, "That puts me in a delicate position. You must have had a reason for doing so."

"As always, Admiral, you're very perceptive. I was thinking that Borisov could help us. Bottom line, we need to find out if any bombs were stolen and where they're headed. Who better to help us than Borisov? He certainly has the same interest. He obviously has a solid team. He knows Russia. Let's send someone to Russia. Let him link up with Borisov and together they can locate the bombs. We can supply Borisov's team with intelligence using burst transmissions."

"Maybe," the admiral said after a full minute of thought. "Yes, he gave us a means of contacting him. The typed note was specific, but what makes you think he would come to us? He may have asked for our help, but I doubt he trusts us. Also, if Borisov weren't telling the truth, we'd be stirring the political pot to a boil. Why not give the tape to Yeltsin? Give the Russians a chance to take care of their own."

The director countered, "If the general is involved, we can't assume it stops with him. Yeltsin's position is weak. Maybe Leonov's ultimate goal is to ruin the existing Russian government. Maybe that walkie-talkie broadcast that Turner read us is a plant. Maybe bombs weren't even stolen. Maybe Borisov is on the general's side. Maybe that's exactly what the general wants us to do with the tape. The revelation would topple the government, leaving the general or someone else in a position to form a new government, one with a more communist flavor. Also, a campaign to crush the Chechens would be very popular politically."

"An interesting argument," the admiral said, sounding doubtful. "However, I believe Borisov's version of the events. Besides, the whole of Russia is looking for his team as we speak. They're Leonov's scapegoats. If what Borisov says is true, and I suspect it is, his mobility must be severely limited."

"Possibly," conceded the director, "but I don't see a better way. I doubt the general knows who Borisov recruited. The general didn't meet them; at least it doesn't look that way. Maybe Borisov told him which men were on his team, but I bet he didn't. That gives Borisov a small advantage. His team is probably more mobile than we think. Certainly we can't put a team into Russia for political reasons. Even if we could, their chance of success is near nil, particularly with the huge mobilization. We simply could not pass a whole team off as Russians. The paperwork alone and personal histories would take weeks to develop. We don't have weeks.

"On the other hand, Borisov and his team are dead unless they can catch the general at his game. They have nothing to lose and everything to gain. They have the motivation. What they don't have is logistical support and intelligence. That's where we come in. We can help them, and with secure satellite communications, our man on the ground can keep us abreast of their efforts."

"Interesting, but very, very risky, sir," the admiral said. He thought about Lewis's proposal. The director's boldness surprised him. Sunders saw logic in the plan, but convincing a team of Russian Spetsnaz to work for the American government seemed improbable.

"Sir, if you don't mind, let me put some thought to your idea. Can we talk after the White House meeting?"

"Yes, that sounds good," the director agreed. "I'm sure the President will instruct the CIA and the Pentagon to come up with some alternatives. I thought I'd mention this one to you so we could get a head start. Maybe you can think of a way to make this happen. If only we could locate Thompson. He would be the perfect liaison."

"Should we meet here at six tonight?" the admiral said, concealing his shock at the director's latest suggestion.

The director nodded as he rose. "I look forward to your input, Admiral. Thanks for coming. I trust you will keep our meeting in confidence. I'm sure some in your chain of command would not appreciate your learning about the tape's contents before they did."

"Yes, sir."

The admiral left the DCI's office. Lewis certainly appeared to have his own agenda. Sunders had always considered him a team player, but now he wasn't so sure. The admiral mulled over Dan's comments about the DCI. Dan knew something about Lewis but had yet to reveal it. It all was damn strange.

* * *

The admiral pulled over to a pay phone on the George Washington Parkway on the south side of the Potomac River. He slipped a coin into the phone and dialed Dan's number. It took him fif-

L

teen minutes to relate the details of the tape and his discussion with the director of the CIA.

"Any thoughts?" the admiral asked.

"You're right when you say he's being bold. Since I've worked with him he's always behaved the same way," Myers confirmed. "It makes me think he almost anticipated this tape, God knows how. One thing's for certain, the Russians would love to catch an American agent working with Borisov, particularly since the raiding parties used American communications equipment. That would give the nationalist elements a lot to chew on."

"Your thoughts suggest a more ominous possibility," the admiral said pointedly.

"You never miss much, Admiral. Keep me posted and let me know how the White House reacts to the tape."

"Count on it."

The admiral replaced the phone. Maybe Dan was really on to something. How did he figure these things out before everyone else?

24 Showing a Few Cards

John woke from a fitful sleep. He glanced at his watch—8:48 am. He stared at the grimy ceiling of the abandoned building on the west side of Istanbul, along the Byzantium Land Walls. He had hidden for the past two days in the ancient structure, wondering when Myers would call. The admiral had assured him Dan would. John sat up slowly, rubbing his eyes. Then he realized what had awakened him. The satellite phone was ringing inside the depths of his backpack. With his eyes half closed he dug down for it. It seemed to take forever.

"Hello."

"John, Dan Myers."

John sat straight up. He was wide awake now.

"Where the hell are you?"

"In the Caribbean," Dan replied.

"The newspapers say you're dead, or are you just vacationing?"

"The print media rarely get it right. You might be interested to know that the director of the FBI issued a statement yesterday indicating that you're cooperating fully with the authorities, and that they don't believe the allegations against us."

"That should give Davenport something to stew on," John suggested. If it was true, Myers must be working with the US government.

"The admiral says you're on the right side of this fight. Why

L

didn't you show your face sooner?" John tried to keep the anger from his voice.

"For reasons I cannot explain, John," Dan replied. "Do you have time to talk?"

"Yes."

"Where are you?"

"Istanbul." John wasn't about to get specific. He still didn't know for sure whom he should trust.

"John, I need to know everything. All details are important," Dan insisted gently. "We must work together to stop Trubkin and Yousef and the people they're involved with."

"How do you know about them?" John demanded.

"Inspector Maitrot."

"He should have arrested me."

"John, I understand that you're highly suspicious of me, but you must trust Admiral Sunders' judgment. Things are moving quickly."

John did trust the admiral, and he had been emphatic about Dan Myers. *Trust him with your life.*

"Now tell me what you've found," Dan ordered.

John focused his thoughts and explained what he had uncovered in Paris, Tallinn, and his raid two nights earlier along the Bosphorus. When he had finished he added, "I just can't understand Haifa."

Dan remained quiet for a moment, digesting the information. "John, I'd ask a different question. Who are they keeping the secret from?"

John thought about it. "The buyer?"

"Good," Dan said. "Let's say the Russians are responsible for delivering the bombs to Istanbul, or maybe a point beyond. The arrangements are made. The buyer believes he knows the route. However, the Russians have different plans. They are going to sail the bombs right into Haifa."

John's mind attacked this possibility. The final destination was not Istanbul; it was Haifa, Israel's major port. Damn, the

Russians were going to sail the ship right into the harbor and detonate the bomb. That had to be it.

"There can be only one reason for that," John said.

"Yes, you're probably right," Dan agreed. "For reasons unknown, the Russians want to detonate the bomb in Israel. The ship is the delivery system."

Instinctively John knew Myers was right. "Tel Aviv would make more sense because it contains the bulk of Israel's government and military installations and doesn't have all the religious history, but it really doesn't matter. The damage will be incredible and everyone will blame the Arabs."

"Yes and no," Dan said. "The Jews certainly will blame the Arabs and will retaliate in kind. The Middle East will be uninhabitable when they're done. Obviously we cannot let this happen. The political and economic consequences are unthinkable by anyone's standards. It's time to shut this thing down."

"What can we do?" John asked, hearing Dan's intensity.

"John, can you keep your head down for a few more days until I can come to Istanbul?"

"Why the hell would you come to Istanbul?"

"I'd rather not explain at this time," Dan replied. "An idea has occurred to me. It needs more thought, but it might work. Can you make it for a few days?"

John considered the question. "Yes. I'm holed up in an abandoned building. I vacated my hotel in Taksim. I have plenty of cash, though I need to change my appearance, especially if you need me to move around."

"Remember this number, and I'll call you tomorrow." Dan read off a telephone number. "If you get in trouble, call it. Don't use your papers. I'll arrange for new papers in the next forty-eight hours."

"Use an Arab name," John suggested. "It's the look I plan to adopt."

"Okay," Dan agreed. "I'll be in touch."

"Right," John replied.

"I'm sorry about your father."

"Thanks," John said weakly, as another thought crossed his mind. "I do have one question for you."

"Shoot," Dan said.

"Do you have any idea where Logan is?"

Dan was silent for a moment. "Does she mean that much to you?"

"Yes," John answered. Why did he feel so guilty about it? It wasn't weakness, was it?

"John, I'll find her. Just stay focused, and I'll find her."

"Thank you, sir," John said as he heard the determination in Dan's voice. "One more question?"

"Sure, John, one more."

"Do you think Davenport killed my brother?"

"No. Davenport introduced Simpson to SIG, and he also had a relationship with the Cali cartel. That's the connection."

"You're not lying to me?"

"No, John, I am not."

"Do you think my brother's death was just what it looked like? He saw the incriminating information and e-mailed it to the government?"

"Yes," Dan answered. "John, I'll call you tomorrow. Keep your head down."

"I will."

John hit the End button and set the phone down. He felt uneasy. Why? He wondered what operation Dan might have conceived, and then another thought struck him. Had Dan guessed his feelings for Logan, or did he know something?

* * *

The phone rang. General Leonov put down the sheaf of papers he was studying. It was late and his assistant had left long ago. He answered it.

"*Da slushayu vas.*"

"General, it's me," Davenport said in Russian.

"How are you?"

"I could be better."

"Concerned about the statement made by the director of the FBI?" Leonov asked.

"Actually, no," Davenport said. "I have little doubt the statement is false. Thompson is not in the custody of federal officials."

"How can you be so sure?"

"Because someone broke into my shipping office in Istanbul last night."

"What?" Leonov cried, stunned. "Tell me what you know."

Davenport did. "I think we must assume Thompson is in Istanbul and knows about the ship."

"You're probably correct," Leonov agreed. "What do you think he was after?"

"Information, what else?"

"Does he know about Haifa?"

"We have to assume he does."

"Who will he tell?"

"That's a good question." Davenport paused. "The current administration might be as leaky as an old garden hose, but many people in Washington still know how to keep a secret. Bradley's statements about Thompson suggest as much; people know something and are trying to confuse us."

"Probably," Leonov agreed.

"But what concerns me, General, is how Thompson learned about the ship. The ship had to lead to the office and not the other way around."

Angrily Leonov considered his options. His first question was how the SEAL had learned about Paris, but he decided not to shoot that arrow at the billionaire. Lying to Davenport about the link made little sense either. "Five days ago an incident occurred on the ship. A guard fell to his death in the hold where the compartment is located. It was at night, and I had assumed it was an accident, a bizarre one. Now I have second thoughts."

"You think your man was pushed to his death?" Davenport asked.

"A possibility," Leonov agreed.

"But why push him? That had to make a lot of noise."

"Yes, and it did," Leonov said. "Perhaps a distraction while the SEAL escaped."

"Did you just make this connection?" Davenport asked, suspicion in his voice.

"Yes." The general was not about to admit to Davenport that Trubkin had tried to kill the SEAL and failed. Rage rose at the thought.

Davenport showed his own anger. "General, do you have any idea what led Thompson to Estonia?"

Leonov lied. "No."

"I think it's time for Thompson to meet his maker, General."

"I agree," Leonov said quickly. "I have some assets in Istanbul. I'll take care of him."

"Let's hope Thompson is still in Turkey," Davenport said.

"Yes, let's hope," the general agreed. "I'm assuming, Alex, that the documentation in your Istanbul office had no references to the buyer of the devices."

"That's correct," Davenport confirmed. "The only thing that can be gleaned from that office is the ship's stop in Haifa. No matter, the ship is exposed. It makes for an easy target."

"I realize that, Alex," Leonov replied, angered by Davenport's tone. "We must hope for the best. The ship is important, but not absolutely critical. Reconstructing Russia is the ultimate goal, and I can still do that without the ship reaching Israel, if necessary."

"Keep me posted, General," Davenport said. "Goodnight."

Leonov sat back in his chair and reflected on the course of events. He realized his plans were in serious jeopardy. The SEAL had to be stopped at all costs. He had caused too much damage.

* * *

Dan picked up his phone and dialed the private number of the director of the FBI.

"Bradley," crackled a voice on the other end.

"Sir, it's Dan Myers."

"Jesus Christ," Bradley exclaimed. "Where the hell have you been?"

Dan told him the whole story, including the shooting on the side of the road.

"We found your fingerprints in the taxi and traced the call you made ordering it," Bradley confirmed. "We also knew you flew to Miami. However, the tracks went dead there."

Dan did not tell Bradley that that had been his plan. If Davenport wanted it to look as if he had faked his death and run, he was glad to play along. Being presumed dead had its advantages.

"I have a lot of questions to ask you," Bradley said.

"Ask them."

"Are we getting close? Things seem to be out of control."

"Yes and no. The endgame is near, and I think we can still get our hands around this monster. I have a plan for doing this. I'm going to ask an awful lot from you; I know I already have. For the plan to work we'll need the full backing of the US government, preferably with only a select few knowing about me. I would suggest State and Defense besides you. Admiral Sunders is aware that I'm alive and has, on my suggestion, called the DCI and offered to replace me. Lewis readily accepted."

"I can already see you're spinning a wide net," Bradley observed.

"Yes, sir. Let me explain."

Twenty minutes later Dan finished.

"You're asking an awful lot," Bradley agreed. "I think convincing the Secretary of State will be especially difficult. You're leaving little in the way of choices, not to mention that you're setting foreign policy and therefore stepping on Sam's turf in no small way. You know the Middle East is his baby."

"All I can ask is that you try," Dan replied. "We have to stop the sale of the bombs at all costs, Davenport and Leonov need to pay for their actions, and we need to clean up the CIA once and for all. If you have a better plan for accomplishing these objectives, I'm all ears."

"How can I get hold of you?"

Dan gave the director of the FBI his new satellite phone number.

"It will take a little time, at least twenty-four hours, to hash this out," Bradley explained.

"Good luck."

"I'll need it, thanks."

* * *

Six men sat in a Pentagon conference room, and Bradley sensed that everyone was a little nervous. He could not blame them; they were playing with fire, though they probably didn't realize how hot the flames were. He wondered again if he had been nuts to convene this meeting. He was about to take a big risk, but he felt it was the only way Myers' plan had a chance.

For the thousandth time, had he been crazy to subscribe to Dan's original plan? However, his instincts had served him well over the years, and he was not about to abandon them now. He knew something was terribly amiss at the CIA. At least two moles were at work, one of them damn near the top. He was sure of it.

"Can we get started?" demanded General Calpepper, Chairman of the Joint Chiefs. Also present were the secretaries of Energy, Defense, and State as well as the National Security Advisor.

"Certainly, General," Bradley agreed, thinking he might as well get their attention quickly. "Dan Myers called me yesterday."

"Maybe I should get up and leave now," blurted Sam Jenkins, the Secretary of State. A few nervous chuckles echoed his remarks.

"He is very much alive and well," Bradley continued. "And he asked for our help. It seems he knows a lot more about what's going on than we do." He paused. "As you have obviously noted, one member of the group is missing. This absence is particularly glaring considering the topic at hand."

"Jim must be running late," offered Les Allen, the Secretary of Defense.

"I'm afraid not," Bradley said. "I didn't invite him. I have my reasons, and please bear with me as I explain."

Concern filled the men's faces.

"As you all undoubtedly know, the FCI has been investigating a leak at the CIA for the last twenty-four months. The losses in the Russian Department have been unusually high. Well, I can tell you about that leak. We've narrowed the field down to three players. Each candidate is very senior. Considering the seriousness of the present situation and the matters I'm about to discuss, I took the risk of arranging this meeting without the DCI's knowledge. My purpose is to protect the US government from whoever is undermining the agency. I didn't decide this lightly.

"I'm not asking any of you to agree with my decision, but only to respect it. However, if you feel that I've been overly cautious and you wish to communicate our discussions and my decision to Jim, I won't stop you. I take full responsibility for my own actions."

Bradley looked at each of the five men. Each returned his gaze; each nodded. Finally Steve Turner, the President's National Security Advisor spoke.

"You've got a lot of balls, Don, but I respect your judgment. If you say the leak is that bad, I believe you. I suspect the theft in Russia is only a small part of something larger, probably a coup d'état. After seeing the videotape from Moscow, I have little doubt that senior Russian officials are involved. I don't know about you gentlemen, but I'd rather have Yeltsin survive for a few more years. I don't look favorably on a new Russian government filled with crazy nationalists zealots."

"I couldn't agree more," Jenkins said.

"No question in my mind," added Les Allen.

"General?" queried Bradley.

The chairman answered immediately. "I'm with you, sir."

"Ditto," agreed Carl van Tassell, the Secretary of Energy.

"Thank you," Bradley said, hiding his relief. "Now to the heart of the matter. Before and since Dan Myers' apparent death, he's been a busy man. I won't delve into the details, but he has some strong evidence that General Leonov and Alex Davenport are teamed up. He believes the general's design is a coup d'état, while Davenport gets first crack at bringing Russia's oil industry into the twentieth century. Basically Davenport will help finance Russia's effort to rebuild itself as a superpower. A key to this objective is to cause a significant rise in the price of oil. Selling a nuclear weapon will help increase world oil prices while also discrediting the existing Russian government. An unstable Middle East also means more arms sales for the Russians, a second reliable source of hard currency.

"Dan Myers has sent John Thompson scurrying around the globe with the sole purpose of determining who the buyer is and how the devices might be transported. Dan's efforts may have hit paydirt."

Bradley paused to take a sip of water while his audience waited anxiously for him to continue. "Yesterday an Arab businessman made contact with Thompson, who is currently in Istanbul. The businessman was a conduit once removed from the buyer. He suggested that a senior official of the US government should meet his contact, a close and respected friend of the buyer. Dan is convinced this is the real McCoy. He thinks we should meet posthaste. Based on what I know, I agree."

"Did the Arab indicate what information would be forthcoming?" asked the Secretary of Defense.

"No, he did not," Bradley answered. "Apparently, for security's sake, the businessman knows nothing. He's simply charged with facilitating the meeting."

"Sounds risky to me and highly unusual," Jenkins remarked.

"A trap if you ask me," Turner suggested.

"I have the same concerns," Bradley agreed. "I said as much to Dan. He understands, but his gut tells him the Arab is on the level. He obviously is relying on Thompson."

"Who could we send?" the general asked.

"That's a good question," Jenkins replied. "It needs to be someone senior but not too senior. Also, the individual needs to be a competent field agent. A desk jockey won't do."

"How about Dan?" Bradley proposed.

"He's on the right side of this fight, isn't he?" Jenkins asked.

"Yes."

"Does Dan know about the video?" Les Allen asked. Bradley had wondered how long it would take this group to ask that question.

"Yes, he does."

"Who told him?"

"I don't know and didn't ask," Bradley replied.

"Admiral Sunders, I'm sure," Calpepper remarked. "Those two have been working together on this thing from the start. Myers had to get the admiral's permission to use Thompson in the first place. He conferred with me on the matter, and I gave my approval."

Bradley noted everyone's surprise.

"Is there anything else you know, General, that you've failed to tell us?" asked the Secretary of Defense.

"No, sir," Calpepper assured him. "Thompson was one of our best, and if Myers needed him I was happy to oblige. After all, the boy's damn brother was murdered in cold blood right here in Washington. I couldn't think of a more motivated fellow with the right set of skills to help Myers. That boy is a killer and a damn good one."

Allen seemed taken aback. "General, our policy is not to unleash trained killers to operate outside the law."

The general stared at him for a moment. "I understand your concerns, but let me tell you a little story. However, it does not leave this room."

He looked at each man, and each nodded in agreement.

"During the Vietnam War we asked Bill Thompson, John's father, to investigate rumors about US servicemen bringing heroin back to the States for sale. I'll save you the details, but he learned all about the operation. The bastards were shipping drugs back to the States in the chest cavities of our dead servicemen. And you know who was running the drug ring? Alex fucking Davenport, that's who. Now that almost was enough for me to walk up to that son-of-a-bitch and shoot him between the eyes. The fact that he was working for the CIA at the time appalled me even frigging more. So when I saw a chance to pursue Davenport using one of the best SEALs to ever serve in the US military, I said you bet. Does that answer your question?"

Everyone was quiet. They had all heard the rumors over the years, but this was the first time they had heard them confirmed by someone they respected unquestioningly.

"Thank you, General," Allen said, his voice pained. "I'm sorry I had to ask."

"No offense taken," the general said, emotion still on the edge of his voice.

"I think we must attend to this meeting," Bradley reminded them.

"Yes," Turner agreed. Jenkins nodded. Everyone already knew what the general thought.

"Sam, any problem with Dan being the point man on this one?" Bradley asked the Secretary of State.

"Certainly not," Jenkins replied. "However, I don't think he should make any commitments. He's there only to listen and report back to us."

"I agree," Bradley said. "Anyone else disagree?"

Everyone shook his head.

"Where is the meeting?" Jenkins asked.

"Jerusalem."

"That's an odd place to meet an Arab," Turner remarked. Bradley could tell he spoke for everyone.

"I agree, but maybe the location makes us more likely to attend," Jenkins speculated. "The meeting is equally risky for our man and their man. There's a certain logic to it."

"An interesting thought," Turner said. "And how, Don, do you plan to inform the President of this development?"

"That's between Sam and you," Bradley told him. "You two decide who should tell him. I will if you want; however, I think I should tell him about my suspicions concerning the CIA."

"A dicey bit that will be," remarked Jenkins. He dropped into thought for a moment. "I'd like to suggest that we wait until after Myers has had his meeting with the Arab. Only if the meeting produces significant information should it be mentioned. The last thing we need is political infighting within the administration at a time like this. Any thoughts?"

"I'm comfortable with that," Bradley stated. A few chuckles were heard around the table.

"I'll bet you are," Turner said. "What you have to tell the President is as bad as it gets. Any specifics?"

"No. Just know that the agency stinks worse than a fish market on a hot summer day."

"That bad?" Jenkins asked.

"I think so," Bradley answered.

"Christ," complained General Calpepper.

"Like we don't have enough to worry about already," added van Tassell.

"Let's keep everything quiet until we know more," Jenkins repeated.

"Anyone disagree?" Bradley asked again.

No one disagreed. Bradley sighed. He had just dodged two big bullets.

* * *

L

Washington, DC was far from her mind as she stood under the shower's hot water. The bathroom had filled with steam, adding to her sense of timelessness.

Two days had passed since the attack. Her body ached as the surprising number of bruises that covered her body grew bluer by the day. She felt disgusting, lonely, and thoroughly depressed. Her captors had made no gesture to assist her. The only change was the bastard who had tried to rape her no longer stood guard. For that she was thankful.

The only thing that had grown stronger in the last two days was her anger. She was angry for falling prey to the fax's lure. She was frustrated with her father; not only had he upset John, but for all his power and influence he appeared unable to find her. She was also angry with John. If he had just let the authorities do their job, she would never have received the fax. Did finding his brother's murders mean more to him than her? It seemed like the only conclusion that fit.

Other thoughts kept striking her. Did John even know she was missing? What if her kidnapping had not been reported in the press? How would he know?

She grabbed the bar of soap and scrubbed her aching body again. Her mind focused on John. She could picture the determination that always lived in his eyes. She remembered first noticing it when they had sailed together. His movements were controlled, exact, and yet powerful. There was never hesitation. He obviously took pride in trying to be the best at everything he did.

She envied him now. He would know what to do, what she should do. If only she could speak to him, hold him. The comfort that she could find in his arms was the one thing in the world she wanted most.

She threw the soap, sending it skidding around the wet tile floor of the shower stall. Slowly she let her back slide down the wall until she rested on the floor, clutching herself in a hopeless attempt to find the comfort she so desperately sought.

25 The Bosphorus Dash

John entered the Grand Bazaar through the Mosque Gate and immediately made his way down Kalpakçilar caddie. His hair was braided and piled under a skullcap, while his face sported a four-day beard. His clothes were long and baggy, though clean. He had purchased them from a street vendor in the Spice Market the previous day. They hid his size and physique as much as possible. He looked a mixture of Arab and some European bloodline, a long remove from his American image. The lone police officer at the Mosque Gate paid him no notice as he entered the bazaar.

As usual, the bazaar was busy, its corridors filled with tourists and buyers from all over the world. The array of merchandise was staggering. Anything could be bought with the right contact and enough money. In one sense the Grand Bazaar was the world's first superstore.

John continued down Kalpakçilar caddie until he turned right on Sandal Bedesteni Sokağī, soon passing the west entrance of Sandal Bedesteni, the second of two warehouses built by Fatih Mehmet after the Conquest. John knew this large vaulted structure had originally been the center of the silk business. Now it housed vendors selling T-shirts and other clothes. Using the reflections in a nearby window, John checked his surroundings. He was anxious about being followed and had already spent the better part of two hours walking the streets in the immediate area outside the bazaar. Confident that he was alone, he continued.

Where Sandal Bedesteni Sokağı met Muhafazaçilar Sokağı, he turned right again and then made a quick left on to Karakol Sokağı, pausing once more to check the reflection in a shop window. He could see the small police station and its Turkish flag. An officer with an HK MP5 slung across his chest was speaking to someone inside the station. This area of the bazaar was the heart of the gold market, and vendors took security seriously.

John strolled. He was in no hurry, as he kept his eyes open for any unusual movement in the crowds that teemed through the bazaar's busy thoroughfares. At the first chance he cut right, walking a short distance down a corridor until he could make another right. Just before the kiosk on Kuyumcular, he turned left. Near the corner stood his destination, a rug merchant specializing in Anatolian carpets and kilims.

John entered the small shop after another quick scan of his surroundings. A young man immediately met him.

"*Merhaba*," the man said in Turkish.

"Good day," John replied in Arabic.

The young man switched to English. "Welcome, how may I help you?"

"Hello," John said, using a heavy accent. "I am looking for Coşkun Kara. Is he available?"

"He is across the way, helping another customer," the young man replied. "May I help you?"

"Thank you, but if I might, can I wait for him?" John asked.

The young man nodded. "Please, take a seat. Can I get you anything, tea perhaps?"

"A tea would be nice," John replied, knowing that taking *çay*, as tea was known in Turkey, signified that one planned to deal in good faith. The young man departed to fetch the tea. John took a seat on one of the small stools that lined a corner of the shop.

The establishment consisted of two rooms, each about twelve by sixteen feet, separated by a small passageway. Both rooms led to Haliçilar caddie, a thoroughfare that felt more like a hallway than a street. Except for the corner where he sat, the space was piled high with folded rugs. John knew the open space in the middle was used to show the rugs, a tradition as old as the Haghia Sophia Mosque.

He felt boxed in. He hoped Dan knew what he was doing. If the merchant had other plans for John, it would be all too easy to block his exits.

Three minutes later the young man returned with hot tea. It was rich and thick, and John savored it. The young man busied himself, keeping an interested eye on his guest.

Twenty minutes passed before a small man in his forties entered the shop. "You're waiting for me, I believe. Sorry about the delay."

John stood and looked into the man's brown eyes. He liked what he saw. "I understand. Your customers are very important."

"Ah, but you are a customer too, no?"

John nodded. "A friend has sent me to collect some items, a Mr. Myers."

"A shame he couldn't come himself," Kara said with a smile. "It has been a long time since I've seen him."

"He sends his warmest regards." John was not about to tell him Dan was arriving in the country within the hour.

"Please, this way. I think we'll find a little more privacy up here."

John followed Kara's gesture and made his way up a small flight of wooden stairs that occupied the back left corner of the shop. Kara was directly behind him. The upstairs, as small as the shop floor, housed an office centered around a tiny wooden desk. One wall was lined with rugs folded like those below. Kara slid his small frame behind the desk. John took a seat on a stool.

"I wouldn't have recognized you as an American," Kara said as he opened a locked drawer. "Hasan said you spoke Arabic to him."

John doubted Dan had told this man much. He was obviously trying to piece a few things together on his own. "Thank you."

Kara looked at John for a moment. "To business, then. I think you'll find everything in order."

Kara slid an envelope across the desk. John opened it and examined the contents. The passport, credit cards, and IDs were from the US, but the name was Mamdouh Mahmid Salim. He flipped through the items. Everything appeared to be in order. The passport had been stamped several times and included a Turkish visa with an entry stamp. The only missing item was a passport picture.

"Picture time." Kara stood to operate the camera. In two minutes he was done. "I will be back shortly." Twenty minutes passed before Kara returned with the passport in hand and a New York State driver's license. He gave them to John.

"Satisfied?"

"Everything looks excellent."

"Well, why don't we spend a few minutes looking at carpets?" Kara suggested as he stood. "You might find one that interests you."

John followed him down to the shop steps and examined fine carpets for fifteen minutes. After thanking his host, he made his way through the maze of streets known as the Grand Bazaar. No one gave him a second glance. He checked his watch. He had three hours until his next meeting at a place called the Cheese Cake Café in Ortakõy, a small town just a stone's throw from the Medcidiye Cami'I Mosque, which rested on the European side of the strait in the shadows of the Bosphorus Bridge. The bridge, the largest suspension bridge in Europe, spanned the Bosphorus a few kilometers north of Istanbul. He had allotted two hours to navigate his way there, more than enough time. He also wanted to buy a few items with the new credit card. Receipts were always helpful.

* * *

The waiter departed after leaving two drinks on the table.

"Any trouble?" Dan asked as both men settled into their seats outside the Cheese Cake Café.

"None," John replied. "How was your trip?"

"Uneventful."

"Your name?"

"Sam Evans."

"US passport?"

Dan nodded as he took a sip of his drink.

"How does it feel?"

"What do you mean?"

"Traveling on false papers. It's probably been a while."

Dan smiled and nodded. "Yes, it's been a long time since I've had to go into the field."

John slid an envelope across the table. "Before I forget, here's the film I shot on board the Sadko and from my day visit to the grain facility. They're not great, but they should be enough to identify the ship."

Dan nodded. "Good."

"What about Logan? Have you heard anything?"

"Nothing."

John stared at Dan for a moment. "I've put a lot of thought to it, and I can't believe Davenport kidnapped his own daughter. He loves Logan. I know this."

"I believe you," Dan replied slowly, as he scratched his face where his mustache had once been. "I can't fully explain it either, but I have never professed to understand Davenport. He is a vile man."

John shook his head. "Something just isn't right."

"I know how you feel," Dan agreed. "Can we get down to business?"

John nodded. "Sure, but promise me you'll keep me informed."

"I will," Dan said a little absently. He seemed to be gathering his thoughts. "Now let me explain my plan. It has several risk points, but on the whole I think it will work. The plan consists of three elements: stopping the devices from reaching the Middle East, keeping the political fallout of the event to a minimum, and making sure Davenport and Leonov pay for their actions.

"I plan to concentrate on the political angle. Borisov and you will concentrate on Davenport and Leonov. I'll leave the device stopping to the US government."

"Who's Borisov?"

A smile crossed Dan's face. "An interesting question. The Russians have launched a huge mobilization of their forces in the St. Petersburg area. A massive search is on. Washington believes one or two nuclear bombs have been stolen. Moscow claims it's running an exercise to look for corruption and black-market goods. This exercise began five days ago.

"Two days after, a video cassette was thrown over the wall of the US Embassy at the same time a large explosion destroyed a warehouse opposite the embassy's North Gate. We believe the explosion was a diversion."

"A warehouse? You mean the dilapidated one right across from the North Gate?"

"Yes."

"That's a cover for their listening post."

Dan raised an eyebrow, apparently surprised that John knew. "It was razed to the ground."

"A pretty big diversion," John commented.

Dan nodded and continued. "The video contains two scenes: one of Leonov meeting an ex-Spetsnaz in the Moscow Zoo, and the other of the ex-Spetsnaz telling us what Leonov is up to. The Spetsnaz's name is Pyotr Borisov.

"I want you to travel to Moscow and meet with Borisov. He left instructions on how to contact him, a set of chalk marks on a particular stone. I have convinced the powers that be that you're the man for the meeting. The purpose of the meeting is to confirm whether Borisov is telling the truth, which, according to him, is that Leonov is behind the theft. Not necessarily news to us, but it is to the rest of Washington. That's the official purpose of the meeting and the only one that Washington is aware of, at least for now."

"And the second?" John asked, seeing the gleam in Dan's

eye. He knew this operation was going to be way off the books. It took Dan seven minutes to outline it.

"Dan, that sounds awfully risky. What if Borisov doesn't agree? You don't expect me to complete the operation solo."

"That is correct," Dan confirmed. "Borisov and his men must agree to play. If they do not, we'll move to plan B."

"Do you have a plan B?"

"No, not really," Dan said. "However, I believe Borisov's decision to communicate with the US marks a significant turning point. He felt he had no choice. I'm hoping he'll see my plan as an opportunity to strike back at those who've placed his men and him in serious jeopardy. And strike back he will."

"He's in deep shit. Just giving the video to the US brands him a traitor."

"You're correct," Dan agreed.

"How do I get into Russia?"

"Fly to Rome. I've made a reservation for you at the Alberto Santa Chiara Hotel. It's next to the Pantheon."

"Why Rome?"

"If a bomb has been stolen we don't have much time, and Russian visas take time; that would be no news to you. I don't want to take the chance of using a forged one. It's too easy for the Russians to catch you. I have a friend in the Vatican who owes me a favor. He will give you a Vatican passport and another one for Borisov. You'll go in as a priest and return as two priests. The Vatican will supply the story line. Here's the number to call. Remember it and destroy this piece of paper. Identify yourself as Hugo."

"And you?"

"I'm headed to Israel."

John raised an eyebrow. "Do they know about the bomb or bombs?"

"No, and I don't plan to tell them. They will just overreact."

"They'll learn about it at some point," John insisted. "They must be aware that something is happening in Russia. They have many eyes and ears there."

"Yes, but I'd like to do that at the proper time and in the appropriate way. The balance of peace in the Middle East is delicate under the best of circumstances. The last thing anyone needs is to give Israel an excuse to overreact. I'm convinced that a peace agreement between the Israelis and the Palestinians is critical in the long term. Without one, the region will face the same terror it faces now. It's only a matter of time until one of these plans succeeds. Remember, we're extremely lucky to know about the ship. Without that piece of information, I'm not sure how good our chances of stopping these people would be."

John wondered how much Dan understood of the opposition's goals. He also wondered how much of the overall picture Dan had given him. "Let's hope there's only one ship."

"That possibility concerns me," Dan agreed. "We can handle multiple devices on a single ship. However, multiple ships present a different problem. Use of a submarine at any point could complicate matters further."

"It might make sense to check on the destinations of the other ships sailing from Tallinn in the next seventy-two hours," John said.

"An excellent point. I've mentioned it to the admiral. We cannot be too careful."

"If you're not going to tell them about the bomb, what exactly are you doing?" John asked.

Dan smiled. "Sorry, but you have no need to know."

John nodded. He knew how these things went. "When do you want me to go to Rome?"

"Catch the next flight and use the new papers," Dan ordered. "They look okay to you?"

John nodded and asked, "How should I communicate with you while I'm in Russia?"

Dan thought for a moment. "Leave your satellite phone in Rome. Use landlines to call the number I gave you. There's no reason for a priest to bring a fancy phone into Russia."

"Sounds reasonable," John said. "Anything else?"

"No," Dan said. "I know I'm asking an awful lot of you."

"Don't be ridiculous," John said quickly. He paused for a moment and made a quick decision. "Sir, I think we've attracted someone's attention. It's time to move. Can I make a suggestion?"

"Certainly."

"I suspect there are two teams, with one driver and two on foot per team. Russian is my guess. I've spotted only one of the teams. The suits by the clock on the green pole." Dan knew enough not to turn and stare. "Since the break-in, Leonov and Davenport must suspect I'm in Istanbul. They probably handed both our pictures to their lookers, thinking we might be together. No offense, but I bet they caught you going through the airport this morning."

"I suspect you're right," Dan agreed, clearly angry at his mistake.

"I'm guessing here, but they may not know who you're meeting with and have decided to follow you until you bring them to me. Then and only then will they try to kill us both."

Dan nodded. "A possibility. Your appearance is quite different, I must give you that."

"Okay, so why don't you pretend you're going to the bathroom," John proposed. "Stay there until everything is over with. I'll get rid of both teams and head to Rome."

"How are you going to neutralize six men?"

"With a little help from our local law enforcement."

"I need you alive," Dan insisted. "We can go to the US Consulate and I can pull some strings."

"And then everyone knows you're alive and you won't be able to go to Israel directly," John said. "I'm not sure either of us can afford that much time in our schedules."

"You're right," Dan agreed reluctantly. John gave him no time to argue.

"Good luck," he offered. "Call me when you're out. I'll do the same."

"Okay, and be careful."

Dan smiled goodbye as he stood and made his way inside the Cheese Cake Café.

John placed ten million lire under his plate in a way that his pursuers could not see. The amount easily covered the lunch tab and included a healthy tip. He also slipped the two table knives into his pants pocket.

The Russian team by the clock stood together, smoking cigarettes. A number of signs gave them away. They were not talking, and they were not moving. Men who are accustomed to surveillance often lose the habit, common to most waiting people, of fidgeting constantly. Also, the surveillance team did not dress like Turkish men and paid no attention to the pretty women who paraded past their position. They were working.

The Russians had given themselves a direct line of sight to the main road and a good overall view of the café and its immediate surroundings. Less than twenty-five yards from them, two Turkish motorcycle cops sat under one of the trees that shaded the cobblestone plaza. Both policemen had pistols and one had an Uzi submachine gun. Timing would be everything.

John stood and strolled toward the two policemen, paying no attention to the Russians. As he approached the officers, he noticed that the keys were still in the ignition of the police motorcycle; he had counted on that. Just as he passed the policemen, he threw one of the dinner knives. It struck exactly where he had aimed, in the farthest Russian's neck. He dropped to the cobblestones dead. The other Russian instinctively pulled his weapon, a 9-millimeter SIG-Sauer, and started to turn toward John.

John screamed in Arabic, yelling, "Gun, gun, gun." More screaming answered him as people noticed the blood seeping from the downed Russian. The Turkish policemen began to move. John ran into the one with the Uzi submachine gun, turning him toward the horror unfolding to his left. The policeman quickly saw the Russian's pistol and swung the Uzi in his direction. In the same motion he pushed John away from him. As he did so,

John removed the policemen's pistol from his holster. The Russian was aiming at the policemen handling the Uzi, knowing that his pistol was no match for a submachine gun.

A shot sounded through the plaza. People screamed more frantically. The policemen with the Uzi spun to his right. He had been hit by the Russian's shot. The second policemen had yet to take aim when John fired two quick shots that killed the Russian in his tracks. Without considering his handiwork, John jumped on the motorcycle, pulled on the helmet, and brought the machine roaring to life. Within six seconds he was turning down the narrow walkway that led between the Cheese Cake Café and the adjoining restaurant. The smell of burning rubber mixed with gunpowder as people dashed in all directions. Bedlam had struck.

John hit the next street twenty-five yards from the plaza and turned left. He figured the other Russian team would have been on the same street as the first team, but positioned just off this street to block a rear exit from the restaurant. He was right. As he turned and accelerated, he saw two men with guns drawn. He took aim as he sped toward them, raising the motorcycle onto its back wheel. The move made it easier for him to aim and gave the Russians less of a target. It took him five shots to kill the two men. One of the Russian bullets barely missed him, hitting the right handlebar. Luckily he was holding the left.

As soon as he passed the inert bodies of the Russians, he braked hard and turned right. This street led directly to the main road that ran along the Bosphorus. He accelerated and turned on the bike's siren. He hoped the helmet would disguise his identity and the siren would distract the police on the main road, making them think at least for a moment that he was one of their own. John's clothes bore no resemblance to a police uniform, but he had to hope for the best.

He cut into the afternoon traffic, bringing a chorus of blaring horns in response to his maneuver. Cop or no cop, Turkish drivers let their feelings be known. As usual, this part of Ortakõy was packed with cars. John took to the center of the road and wove north through the traffic. The sounds of horns followed him the whole way. A police car parked by the Ortakõy Açik Otoparki started to turn down Değirmen Sok, a street leading to the plaza in front of the café. Obviously they had not realized the chase had made it to the main road.

The traffic started to clear a little as he passed the Harley-Davidson store on his left and the Wendy's on his right. A police station, tucked into the hillside to the left of the road directly before the Bosphorus Bridge, flashed past. Officers were running down the steps and piling into two parked Fiats, their submachine guns drawn.

John looked back and saw two black cars bulling their way through the traffic in Ortakõy. One struck another car. They had to be the Russians' cars, two powerful BMW sedans. As the first one passed the police station, one of the police cars turned violently in John's direction. John needed everyone to focus on him. It would give Dan the time he needed to escape.

John picked up speed after passing under the bridge as the specially modified police motorcycle responded to his will. He glanced back over his left shoulder; the two police Fiats were turning around. One pulled into the middle of the road, its lights flashing, when the first Russian car hit it, pushing it aside. The second Fiat let the second Russian car pass and pulled in behind it.

John dodged a blue Mercedes, passing it in the right lane as the road headed left and slightly uphill. As he hit the straightaway he accelerated, passing the Türk DOM Bank with his speedometer topping 140 kilometers. The few cars navigating this stretch of road pulled off to the side, believing John was a policeman in pursuit. A Türkpetrol station flashed by on the left, a park on the right.

John knew he had the police and the two Russian cars chasing him. He clearly had the advantage in speed and maneuverability. However, the longer the chase continued, the more policemen would get involved. He knew there were police stations in the next three towns, the largest of which was Bebek, two kilometers ahead. He needed to lose his pursuers before then. The Russians would be hard pressed to escape the net the Turks would throw. John would do what he could to help ensure that the Turks would not come up empty handed.

The stoplight before the Waffle House turned red as John approached. A single police car was coming in the opposite direction. John slowed and turned right, cutting through a small playground area and sending a rooster tail of sand into the air. The cement-tiled walkway that led along the edge of the Bosphorus quickly replaced the sand. Dozens of boats were moored along the waterway, their bows facing away from the water's edge.

John swerved to miss a *simit* vendor who was lugging his afternoon's load of the Turkish bread on his shoulders. The man yelled obscenities at John as all but a few of his *simits* tumbled to the ground. Other people began jumping out of the way. John took a quick moment to see how the oncoming police car had reacted. It was trying to turn around.

John heard a crash. He looked behind him to see what had caused it. One of the Russian BMWs had hit a jungle gym as it swerved through the sand. The other Russian car had stayed on the road and was headed for the police car, caught in the road in the middle of its U-turn. Gunshots sounded as the second Russian car fired at the police car. An Uzi fired back.

People yelled as the few boat owners working on the walkway leaped for safety, some into the water and other into the cabins of their boats. John could hear the BMW's engine scream as it accelerated down the walkway behind him. Another crash shook the area as the second Russian car plowed into the police Fiat on the street. The large BMW careened off the smaller Fiat and crashed into a white truck parked on the side of the road. The BMW spun into a roll and swerved onto a divide that branched around the town's center. Between it and the small white truck, there was no room to pass in the northbound lane. One down and one to go.

More gunshots filled the air as the driver of the BMW behind John took aim. John braked hard and then accelerated, sending his motorcycle into the air and jumping a break in the walkway.

John knew the BMW could not navigate the break. The fifteen-meter gap would swallow it even at its speed. The Russian driver must have realized this. He cut left and sent sparks flying as the BMW jumped a small cement curb and cut through a clump of bushes. How he missed the billboard sign John would never know. In seconds the BMW was back on the main road, slightly past the crumpled remains of its comrade.

John banked the bike hard as he accelerated around a sharp left turn in the walkway. A row of fishermen jumped into the Bosphorus like a chorus line, their fishing poles still in hand, while the air stank of burning rubber and fish.

As John made the turn, the BMW tried to pull even with him. The only thing that separated John from his quarry was a long line of cement barriers that doubled as planters–the Turkish answer to No Parking signs. John slowed to maneuver around a glass bus stop that divided most of the walkway. Two gunshots sounded, and a pane of glass in the bus stop shattered. John saw an opportunity.

He slowed abruptly, allowing the BMW to get slightly ahead of him. John took aim at the front right tire and let go two rounds. The tire popped, sending the BMW careening into the row of cement planters and upsetting three of them. The front bumper crumpled on the impact, bringing the car to a halt. John locked the motorcycle's brakes and stopped next to the front passenger-side door. The Russian driver, slightly stunned, began to move. John raised his pistol as the Russian turned his head and tried to take aim. John fired three shots, killing the driver instantly.

He gunned the engine and started to move. He got no more than fifty feet before bullets struck the pavement to his left.

John turned to see a battered Trubkin walking unsteadily up the road in his direction, pointing a pistol in his left hand. The man's right hand dangled at an unnatural angle and was covered with blood. Trubkin had obviously been driving the other BMW and had somehow managed to fight his way out of his badly damaged vehicle. John stopped the bike, removed his helmet, and threw it into the Bosphorus.

"You are walking in the wrong direction," John yelled in Russian.

Trubkin did not answer and maintained his slow march toward John. He was less than twenty-five yards from the damaged BMW containing his dead friend.

"You turn around now and you will live," John shouted.

"You got it wrong," Trubkin snarled through gritted teeth, his voice surprisingly strong. "It is you who will die today."

Trubkin now was even with the car. He was obviously in a great deal of pain. John noticed gas leaking from the rear of the wrecked BMW. Police sirens filled the air, getting closer and closer. Time was running out.

"Your choice," John shouted. Without warning he fired four shots in quick succession. Trubkin shot only once, and poorly, before one of John's rounds ignited the leaking gasoline. Instantly the flames consumed Trubkin. The man struggled violently with his one good arm, dragging himself toward the Bosphorus in a desperate attempt to extinguish the flames, but he never made it and collapsed on the ground, screaming in agony.

As the sirens grew louder, John pointed the bike in the direction of the Bosphorus, gunned it, and jumped off. Three seconds later the bike was sinking to the bottom of the strait. John ran across the road, heading toward the narrow streets on the other side. He pulled his hair from its braid, hoping a change in his looks would help his disappearing act.

26 Pushing the Arab-Israeli Buttons

Dan waited to pass through customs at Ben-Gurion International Airport, southeast of Tel Aviv. The queues of travelers to his left carried Israeli passports; the ones to his right were non-Israelis. He was at the far end of the latter queue, which put him in the middle of all the people waiting to clear through Israeli customs.

It had been a long time since he had worked in the field, carrying false papers and passing through customs in a foreign country that had a first-rate counterintelligence operation. Turkey was a walk in the park compared with Israel.

As much as he hated to admit it, he was nervous. He kept his eyes moving, checking and rechecking his surroundings. The close call in Istanbul had heightened his apprehension. Things were critical, and he could not afford any more mistakes. Though his papers were convincing and he had shaved off his mustache, there was an outside chance that a senior official who happened to be at the airport might recognize him. His thirty-odd years at the CIA had given him many occasions to work with Israel's government, its military, and its intelligence services.

His queue inched along. It contained several Secular Zionists, their black outfits, hats, and curls standing out in stark contrast to the other disembarked passengers. A few Arabs of various origins were also scattered throughout his queue. The customs officer, a young woman, took her time with the Secular Zionists and the Arabs; the Israelis took security seriously.

He glanced at his watch and figured he had stood in line for close to a half hour. Ten more minutes passed before his turn came. He slid his US passport and arrival papers through the slot in the Plexiglas that enclosed the upper half of the booth. The young woman looked at him briefly and then at his documents. She took a few moments to page through his passport, and then her fingers poked at a computer keyboard. As she busied herself, Dan used the reflection in the Plexiglas to keep an eye on the people behind him. He was looking for any quick, unnatural motions.

Finally she spoke, but Dan did not catch her question through the Plexiglas. He leaned toward the small opening. "Excuse me?"

"Your purpose in Israel?"

"To visit Jerusalem. I've never been." This was a lie, of course.

"Are you with a tourist group?"

"No, I'm alone. My wife died last year," Dan explained.

"You are alone, then?"

"Yes."

She tapped on her keys a little longer. Dan took the opportunity to straighten up and again examine the reflections in the Plexiglas. As before, nothing seemed out of place.

"Sir, how long do you to plan to stay?"

Dan bent down and moved his ear closer to the small opening. "Excuse me?"

"How long will you be in Israel?"

"A week," Dan said, his second lie of the day.

"You are staying at the American Colony. Is that correct?" His immigration card indicated as much.

"Yes."

"Do you know Hebrew?"

"No."

She picked up her stamp and thumped away, sliding Dan's

documents through the opening. "Have a pleasant stay, Mr. Evans."

"Thanks, ma'am."

Dan made his way around the white booth and filed down a roped-off walkway directly behind the customs booths. At the single exit a security officer collected the stamped pass that had been returned along with Dan's passport.

The overhead TV monitor indicated that his luggage waited for him on carousel four. He had packed lightly, but not too lightly. If they searched his suitcase, he did not want to raise any suspicion. An old man traveling by himself who planned to stay in Jerusalem for a week would bring a corresponding number of items. Dan had packed accordingly.

His bag was ready, not surprisingly, since he had spent the better part of an hour in the customs line. He collected it and headed to the exit marked "Nothing to Declare."

The two security officers in this area watched him pass, but made no effort to speak to him or inspect his possessions. He could not help but breathe a sigh of relief as he passed. However, his easy passage through customs did not mean that the Israelis were not on to him. If they had recognized him, they would be intensely curious. Letting him through customs offered them an opportunity to see where he would go and to learn what operation would require a friend of Israel to travel with false papers.

Quickly Dan moved through the crowd of relatives and friends waiting for their loved ones to exit customs. He walked to the Thrifty car rental desk directly ahead. A few minutes passed while the company representative finished with a customer. Dan handed his fake US driver's license and credit card to the man, who busied himself with the required paperwork. Meanwhile Dan turned his back to the counter and scanned the people who bustled about the terminal. He was still looking for anyone who might have taken an undue interest in him.

With the paperwork complete, Dan exited and strolled to the

second curb, where he waited once again, this time for the Thrifty van. He did not have to wait long and was driven to the car lot, a half mile from the airport. After receiving compulsory instructions on how to operate the car, Dan turned onto Route 1, known as the Ayalon. He took it south and began his fifty-five-mile drive to Jerusalem. Though a few minutes after six, it was still light, but not for long. Dan adjusted his driving mirrors. He was anxious to see if he had picked up a tail. Darkness would make it harder to spot.

* * *

An hour and forty minutes later, Dan pulled into the American Colony Hotel, an establishment without parallel in Jerusalem. Dan had stayed at the hotel several times over the years, but not recently. However, many of the help had been employed at the hotel for years, and he feared that one of them might recognize him. Employees were trained to remember the guests and their preferences. If he had had a choice he would have selected another hotel, but considering the task at hand, the American Colony was the only place.

The hotel was steeped in history. Originally founded by Horatio Spafford and his Norwegian wife, Anna, the Colony had warm associations for Arabs and Jews alike. The Spaffords had emigrated from Chicago after tragedy took the lives of four of their children. On their arrival they built excellent relationships with the many people living in Jerusalem–Jews, Turks, and Arabs, even Bedouin from across the Jordan River.

After friends from both Chicago and Norway had moved to Jerusalem to join them, they had purchased a mansion built by a rich Arab landowner who had no sons. Built like an old Turkish castle, it was located only a short walk from the Damascus Gate of the Old City. It became known as the American Colony, and throughout its history distinguished itself as both a hotel and a neutral establishment even in the most troubled times.

In the four wars Jerusalem had faced during this century, the hotel had been caught in the crossfire many times, sustaining damage from small arms and mortars. At one point, after the end of the British mandate, the hotel was located on Jordanian land.

Because it had maintained itself as neutral ground, the American Colony was a place where Arabs and Jews could meet in peace. For Dan it offered the best means to accomplish his delicate task.

With the usual efficiency, Dan was checked in and shown his room, number ten on the first floor. It was typical of the old suites found in the hotel. By no means the most elegant room, it was comfortably decorated. The vaulted ceiling reached to fifteen feet. At one end of the room, two single beds were pushed together with small tables on either side. A large window straight across from the door looked onto Nablus Road, and an oak desk that housed a minibar guarded the window. At the other end of the room, a large dresser and mirror combination stood next to a TV. In the middle of the room, two chairs and a copper table were centered on an old Persian rug that lay across the rough stone floor. The far end of the room led to a full-sized bathroom.

The bellhop introduced Dan to the particulars of the room and left with a good tip. Dan glanced at his watch; just after 8:00 p.m. He was running slightly behind schedule, but nothing to cause concern. He considered taking his dinner in the delightful courtyard that made up the center of the hotel, but decided against it. That last thing he could afford was to be recognized. He reviewed the room service menu and ordered, selecting a pepper filet steak, Galmla Cabernet Sauvignon, and the famous chocolate and almond cake. With that done, he headed to the bathroom. A hot shower would help his weary bones.

* * *

It was a little after midnight when a knock sounded on his door: three sharp taps followed by two more. Dan hesitated for a moment, considering any details he might have missed. None came to mind. He stood and opened the door. A young Arab man stepped quickly inside, closing the door.

Dan had pulled the curtains long ago, blocking any possible view from the outside. He had also scanned the room vigorously for surveillance devices. As he had expected, he had found none.

The young man studied him for a while without saying a word. Dan waited patiently. The risks were great for everyone.

"I have spent most of my adult life hating the CIA," the Arab said suddenly. "To meet one of its best is odd."

Dan nodded knowingly. "I appreciate your honesty and the small compliment."

"You have something for me?" the Arab asked.

Dan nodded again and reached into his pocket, extracting a torn one-dollar bill, and handed it to the Arab. The young man produced another torn bill and held the two halves together; they matched perfectly.

"In ten minutes, order a cab. When it comes, make sure a green box sits on the dashboard. The lid of the box will have an Israeli flag embroidered on it."

"And we have an understanding that I am to be back here before daybreak?"

The young Arab looked him in the eyes. "Yes, we will keep our word."

He left as quickly as he had come.

Thirty-five minutes later Dan exited the cab that had collected him from the American Colony Hotel. He did not recognize the area, which he suspected was located in the Gaza Strip. He paid the driver and the cab sped away, leaving Dan standing alone on a dark, deserted side street. Less than a minute passed until a door opened and silhouetted a man, not the one who had come to his room. The Arab gestured to him. He walked up to the man and was led through the door. Instantly he was blindfolded with a hood. No one said a word.

Two minutes passed until he was helped into a car trunk.

The entire awkward procedure ended with the hatch being slammed down on top of him.

Dan had worn dark clothing for several reasons, the most compelling one being to hide any dirt he might pick up in his travels. He always recalled the movie "The Great Train Robbery." The robbery went as planned, except that the villain had not considered how dirty he would become crawling along the outside of the train being pulled by a steam locomotive. The dirt on his face had given the thief away to the authorities. As Dan knew all too well, the small details got a man caught.

The car bounced him about, throwing him repeatedly against the hatch and the spare tire. Each encounter exacted pain from a body no longer used to such agonies. The smell sickened him as fumes from the decrepit car found their way into the trunk. Dan half wondered if at his age he would survive. What a shame it would be to die in the trunk of an Arab car somewhere in the Palestinian zone, his mission unfulfilled.

Suddenly the car hit smooth pavement and stopped. He suspected it had pulled into a garage or car park. Dan could not estimate how long the trip had taken. A few moments passed, and the trunk opened. Strong hands helped him struggle from the compartment, but his hood stayed on. He desperately wanted to remove it and breathe fresh air. He knew it would not be long now; he'd just have to wait. He forced his anxieties to the back of his thoughts.

Dan listened to the Arab voices speaking, picking up a few words, but not enough to understand the commands being issued. At one level he wondered if he had made the right decision in arranging this meeting. Ever since the idea had entered his mind, he had known it would pose serious risks for him and his country. But somehow the absurdity of the idea made sense, a gut sense that was hard to articulate. He wondered why he doubted himself at this point; it was unlike him.

He felt a strong hard clasp on his arm. They passed quickly through numerous doors, then stopped as abruptly as they had started. Without warning the hood was removed. He breathed deeply, anxiously gulping the cooler air until he became aware of his surroundings.

The room was barely lit and looked like the inside of a Bedouin tent. Large pillows and richly decorated tapestries covered the interior. A glass of water appeared, and he eagerly accepted it.

"He will be but a moment," one of the Arabs said in English.

"Thank you."

Ten minutes later Yasir Arafat entered the room, dressed in his traditional galabiya. He looked as he did on television, but with a difference. It was the man's presence, something the cameras did not capture. Dan stood, and they greeted each other like Arabs, trading kisses on both cheeks. Without a word, Arafat gestured for Dan to sit on a thick pillow.

"I must admit, times have certainly changed," Arafat began. "To think that the CIA former Deputy Director of Special Operations travels to Israel to visit me is amazing, no?"

"Many things have changed, but unfortunately not all," Dan replied. "I appreciate your willingness to accept the risks associated with my request to meet. I hope you will find your efforts worthwhile."

"I am curious, you see," Arafat said. "I figure you would only make the request in the most pressing of circumstances."

The CIA and the Palestinians had kept a loose relationship over the years, and Arafat passed on information quietly. In return the CIA kept Arafat abreast of any intelligence suggesting an imminent attempt on his life. Dan had never dealt with Arafat personally, but had always heard he was fascinated, maybe even awed, by the Central Intelligence Agency.

"I believe these circumstances are pressing." Dan glanced around the room. Three other Arabs were positioned at strategic spots, each keeping a close eye on things. Dan had no doubt that these men were armed and fully capable of killing him. Arafat had not lived this long without taking his personal security seriously. "I take it these men can be trusted with the delicate nature of our discussion."

"They are loyal to death, but they do not understand a word of English. For all intents and purposes, we are alone."

"I apologize for mentioning the topic."

"I understand completely and no harm has been done. May I suggest that we start, as the hour grows late."

"Certainly," Dan replied, pausing to collect his thoughts. He continued, "As you probably know, much of the world believes I'm dead. To be honest, you are only the seventh person who knows that I'm alive. Before my apparent death and since, I have been working on an operation that concerns a renegade American businessman and a Russian general. They are presently executing a plan to sell nuclear weapons to a client in the Middle East."

Arafat continued to look directly at Dan. His eyes revealed nothing.

"I'm taking a risk by assuming that you are not the client. However, if you are, please hear what I have to say."

Arafat nodded as he took a sip of water.

"As we speak, a Russian grain ship owned by this American businessman is sailing from Tallinn, Estonia. Hidden in its number three grain hold are two 100-kiloton nuclear devices stolen eight days ago from a base in Russia. The press reports indicate the Russians are conducting a massive search for black-market goods. This is a cover created by those in power. The truth is somewhat different; they have no idea where the stolen nuclear weapons are. The SVR general who masterminded the theft is making sure of that."

"How do you know where the bombs are if the Russians do not?"

"I'm not at liberty to say," Dan explained. "All I can ask is that you trust me on this point. You will see why in a minute."

Arafat nodded.

"The ship's voyage includes two stops, Haifa and Istanbul." Dan saw a small look of surprise pass across Arafat's face. "Haifa is an unexpected stop for a ship carrying nuclear bombs."

"Not if the Israelis bought them."

"You and I both know that Israel has no need to buy nuclear weapons. They already have them. No, the Israelis did not buy the bombs."

Arafat nodded his agreement.

Dan continued. "I don't know who purchased the bombs, but I will in good time because all money leaves a trail, particularly $150 million US. We already know about six bank accounts. In time we will know more." Dan took another sip from his glass of water as he watched Arafat closely. "However, there are two things I do know at this time. First, Ramzi Yousef handled the negotiations for the Arab buyer. Second, the ship will sail directly into Haifa as planned, but it will never leave."

Dan watched Arafat consider the information. It took a moment until the truth dawned on him. Arafat sat forward, anger transforming his face. "You're a devil to think any Arab would display such a disregard for human life. A bomb of that size would kill more Arabs than Jews."

Dan looked Arafat directly in the eyes. "I realize this fact. Please believe me. When I first learned of this intent, I was baffled. I can understand a few Arab leaders believing violence can remove the State of Israel from these lands. However, I do not believe that even these leaders could justify to the Arab world the destruction of people and holy lands that such a device would cause. No, I have another theory."

"Explain."

"I believe a government, either Iraq or Iran, bought a nuclear device and is planning to receive it in Istanbul. Unbeknownst to the buyer, the Russian SVR general has other plans. His plan is elaborate and includes three main elements: detonating a nuclear device, ruining the US presidency, and taking over the Russian government."

"An incredible story," Arafat said, "if it is true."

"The use of a nuclear device serves two purposes in this man's plans. First, oil prices will soar while production in the Middle East dwindles as the effects of the detonation take hold.

This brings the general needed hard currency to rebuild Russia as a superpower. The American businessman has made heavy investments in Russian oil and hopes to bring the Russian oil industry out of the dark ages. The second purpose of the detonation is to cripple the current Russian government completely. Losing a nuclear weapon is bad, but having it kill millions is something else. The Russian government will crumple to its knees. New leaders will be needed, and the general considers himself an excellent candidate."

"The picture you have painted is sickening," Arafat declared. "What does the US presidency have to do with it?"

"The general believes that the US government could get in the way of his plans. To combat this fear, he has worked with a Colombian drug cartel to funnel money into the Whitewater real estate deal that has captured the attention of the US press for several months. He has set into motion events that will bring this revelation and others to light. It is not farfetched to think that the President could be forced to resign or even be impeached. The idea behind these efforts is to make the US presidency and the American people unable to react to the crisis the general's actions will unleash."

"How can I help?" Arafat asked. Dan knew he had the other's full attention.

"I want to make a trade," Dan explained. "I want information that will help the US government locate and capture Yousef."

"And in return?" Arafat arched one eyebrow.

"I'll let you take the credit for uncovering the Arab angle of this plot."

Arafat looked at Dan for a moment. "Please explain."

"As you might imagine, the theft of a nuclear device and the subsequent mobilization of Russian troops to locate it was instantly detected by the US government. They are tracking the event closely and do not plan to sit idly by. However, the Americans know no more than the Russians do about the exact location of the stolen device."

"And you do?"

"Yes, I do, the particulars of which I am not at liberty to explain."

"Most unusual."

Dan nodded and continued, "I have known about the ship for some time. She is under sail now, and I have used my influence to have a submarine shadow her. It is doing so as we speak. The submarine is my insurance that the ship will never make it to Israel, or for that matter into the Mediterranean.

"Yousef has information the US government wants. I realize that many in the Arab world, particularly the more militant elements, would find it unpalatable should they learn that you played any role in his capture. However, I believe that both the Arab world and Israel would take it most kindly if you informed the US government about your knowledge of the grain ship, its cargo, and its destination.

"There are two reasons for you to inform the US government. First, you know they have the best resources to handle the situation. Second, you don't want Israel to make any military moves in retribution.

"Once the ship is at the bottom of the ocean, I believe the United States could approach the Israeli government on your behalf and inform them of the great service you performed."

Dan watched Arafat mull over the idea. The man did an excellent job of hiding his thoughts. Several minutes passed before Arafat said anything.

"I suspect, since the ship is already under sail, that we have a very short period of time in which to work."

"You are correct," Dan confirmed. "You need to make the call before I leave. The ship will enter the Mediterranean in less than forty-eight hours. Time is needed for official Washington to evaluate your information and to give the commands necessary to sink the ship."

"Could I have a half hour to confer with men who I believe are wise in such matters?"

"I certainly understand," Dan said. "I had anticipated your need to brief key members of your team. However, I do ask for your word that any dialogues you have will not be with parties who could alert the buyer to our plans. Should that happen, the deal would be off."

"Understood and accepted," Arafat said as he rose. "If you will excuse me. Should you need anything, please let Rahman know. I will send him in."

Dan stood too. "I hope you realize I have put my neck on the line. There are those in my government who would not condone my actions."

"I thank you for your candidness."

Arafat walked from the room, and Dan took a seat. He reviewed the conversation in his head. It had gone as planned, though he had assumed Arafat would ask a few more questions. Dan half wondered how much Arafat had already known. He glanced at his watch; he had to be back at the hotel in a little over three hours. Then it would be time for his next move.

* * *

Forty-five minutes later Arafat returned.

"My sincere apologies for my absence. Some of those individuals whom I wish to speak with were not readily available."

"I understand," Dan said as he watched Arafat take his seat.

"Your offer is a most unusual and unexpected one," Arafat began. "I want personally to thank you for your understanding of the Arab mind and how we cherish life. We never would condone the use of a nuclear weapon. I have considered your offer and would like to accept it. I'm sure you appreciate the considerable risks for all parties involved. I believe the risks are justified. However, I'd like to make a small suggestion."

"By all means," Dan said. "I'm open to possible improvements."

"I'd like you to tell the US government for me," Arafat suggested. "You know all the particulars, and I believe you are more than capable of presenting my assistance concerning this matter in the desired light. My reason for making this suggestion is simple. If the Israeli government learns of our meeting or somehow detains you as the result of your current predicament involving the billionaire Davenport, your illegal entry into their country is somewhat better explained. Obviously, had you come through Jordan, things would have been considerably simpler. But I'm sure you had your reasons for coming through Israel. Second, I believe the US government can act faster if you tell them. If I were to contact a member of your government directly, unnecessary time could be wasted. As you well know, the story is incredible and would most likely be met with skepticism. I wish to avoid any misfortunes that a delay might cause."

Dan hesitated as if considering Arafat's request. It was exactly what he had hoped for.

"An excellent suggestion. Since I alone arranged my travel, I'm confident your suggestion will work remarkably well. And as you so aptly suggest, it will also speed the decision-making process in Washington. I appreciate your insights."

Arafat stood up and Dan did too. "You had best be going. Time is short. Until we meet again."

They traded the traditional Arab greeting again.

"If I might make one small request for my return trip," Dan said.

"Certainly."

"Could a wet cloth be brought along, one that I could use to clean my face and hands before I return to the hotel?"

"An excellent suggestion," Arafat agreed. "I will see to it immediately. Goodbye, my friend."

Dan watched Arafat exit. A few moments later the older servant returned. He had a hood in his hands. It was time for the return trip to Jerusalem.

* * *

Dan entered his room a little before 4:30 am, completely exhausted. He no longer had the energy of his youth, a small detail he had failed to consider when he had made his plans.

Dan walked over to the desk by the window facing Nablus Road and used a small key to unlock the minibar. He took a moment to mix his drink while he considered his options. He needed to call Director Bradley immediately and give him the details–well, most of the details. His next challenge was exiting Israel as he planned to.

* * *

Dan entered Ben-Gurion Airport. He was nervous. Many things could go wrong. He wanted to be remembered but not detained.

He towed his single suitcase behind him and took his place in a short line, one of three, defined by a traveler's flying destination. Several security officers, members of Shinbet, Israel's internal security apparatus, inspected each passenger. Unlike their US counterparts, these men and women were trained intelligence officers and took their jobs seriously. Dan was counting on this fact.

An attractive young female officer approached him as he stepped to the head of the line. "Hello, sir. May I see your passport and ticket, please?"

Dan nodded, handing her the requested items. She accepted the documents and examined them while Dan considered his surroundings. The airline counters were thirty feet away, queued with passengers who had already made their way through the Israeli security check. Yellow labels adorned their luggage as proof.

"Mr. Evans, your ticket states that you are scheduled to depart six days from now."

"Yes, I know, but I've decided to leave early."

"And why is that?"

Dan did his best to look nervous as the young officer kept a steady eye on his face. "Well, I felt unsafe. Too many guns."

She nodded, pausing before she continued. "Your tour operator did not look after you?"

"I came by myself."

"Is this your first time to Israel?"

"Yes."

"And you came here unaccompanied?"

"My wife died last year. Cancer."

"I'm terribly sorry." She paused as she paged through his passport. "Are you accustomed to traveling to a foreign country by yourself?"

"Until coming here, yes," Dan said, knowing the comment would unsettle the young Israeli. Israel took great pains to assure the world that the country was safe. Many parts were, but Jerusalem and the surrounding areas were not. A watchful eye was required at all times. Hamas and other fanatical groups considered every Israeli a potential target, as the right-wing Jews considered the Arabs. The mutual hatred was palpable. Nevertheless the Israeli economy depended on tourism, particularly in Jerusalem. Millions of people traveled from all corners of the world to follow the footsteps of Jesus Christ or pray at the Western Wall or visit the Dome of the Rock, where Abraham is said to have ascended to heaven.

"You felt unsafe. Where did you go?"

"Jerusalem. So many guns."

"Did anyone try to harm you?"

"Well, no."

"When did you arrive?"

"Yesterday, isn't that obvious from my ticket?"

She nodded with a flash of irritation. "How did you get to Jerusalem?"

"I drove."

"You've never been to Israel before, right?"

Dan tried to look frustrated. He knew the drill. How the questions were asked was important. "Again, no."

"Excuse me for a moment."

Without waiting for his reply, she strode away and joined several fellow officers. One man appeared to be a supervisor. He held a walkie-talkie and seemed to be at the center of activity. Dan waited patiently as he glanced around the terminal area. If not for a few cement pillars that supported the ceiling, he would have had an unobstructed view of the entire area that stretched before the row of airline ticket counters. The other travelers waiting in his line appeared curious about his situation.

As Dan continued to wait, he noticed a microphone lodged in the ceiling over his head. It was not concealed in any way, and he wondered if they were using it; he doubted it. Ten minutes later the officer returned with another female officer. Her companion was not nearly as attractive and had a sterner disposition.

"Sorry to keep you waiting," the first officer said. "This is Aviva. She'd like to ask you a few questions."

"I hope this won't take too long," Dan pleaded. "I have to get a new ticket. All I have is a reservation."

They ignored his concern as the first officer walked away.

"Why did you come to Israel?"

"I wanted to visit Jerusalem before I die."

"Did you like it?"

Dan frowned. "No. Too many guns."

"You only saw Israeli soldiers with guns, is that correct, Mr. Evans?"

"Yes, but they had machine guns."

"Do you speak Hebrew?"

"No."

The officer stared at him briefly and turned her attention to his documents, which she held. She paged through his ticket and then his passport. "What were you doing in Turkey?"

"I had never been to Istanbul either," Dan replied. "I liked Istanbul."

"But according to your passport, you only spent a day there."

"Well, yes, I guess I did," Dan admitted. He had wondered how long it would take them to notice that oddity.

"Did you not feel safe in Istanbul?"

"No, I felt safe there. It was just a layover."

"Where did you stay in Istanbul?"

"At the Bebek Hotel."

"Is that in Istanbul?

"No, it's in Bebek, north of Istanbul."

"How did you select that hotel?"

"A friend recommended it."

"When did you arrive in Israel?"

Dan showed some anger. "Really, is all this necessary?"

"Answer the question, please," the officer ordered.

"Yesterday."

"Where did you stay?"

"In Jerusalem."

"What hotel?" she asked with irritation in her voice.

"The American Colony."

"A very nice hotel. Did you like it?"

"Yes."

"Did you not feel safe there, at the American Colony?"

"Well, yes, I did. It was the streets. All those guns."

"You don't like guns, Mr. Evans?"

"No, I guess I don't."

"Who paid for your airplane ticket?" the officer asked as she gestured with it.

"Well, I did, of course."

"You're off to Rome next?"

"Yes."

"Are you only going to stay there a day too?"

"I like Rome."

"You liked Istanbul too, Mr. Evans."

Dan paused for a moment before answering. He knew that his situation, an elderly man traveling to Israel with no relatives, was not normal. It was not just that he had spent only one day in Israel, it was the whole story: spending one day in Istanbul after arriving from Rome, coming to Israel by himself on his first visit, and driving to Jerusalem.

"I'm sure Israel has many security concerns," Dan began, "but I'm not one of them. I came here as a tourist, hoping to experience Jerusalem. I was deeply disappointed, end of story. I must insist that this charade come to an end. I have a plane to catch."

"Excuse me for a moment," the officer said.

Dan kept his eyes on her as she joined the supervisor and three other officers. An animated conversation ensued in Hebrew. At one point the supervisor looked at his watch. He gave a few quick instructions in Hebrew to the first officer who had interviewed Dan. She nodded, returned, and applied a yellow sticker to Dan's single piece of luggage. "I believe the Alitalia counter is over there, Mr. Evans."

"Thank you," Dan said, careful to hide the triumphant grin that wanted to spread across his face.

27 Back in the Old USSR

Borisov sat on the zoo bench, the same one he had shared with Leonov twelve weeks earlier. How things had changed.

He was a little early for the rendezvous, although he had spent the better part of two hours walking the grounds of the zoo. Nothing appeared out of place, and no one had taken undue interest in him. Nevertheless he was nervous. He feared a trap. If the Americans had given a copy of his video to the Russian government, he was a dead man.

Borisov scanned the crowds again. All appeared as it should. His six men were in the area. They had insisted on protecting him, and he couldn't blame them. They knew that without him their chance of survival would shrink even further. Anyway, they were a team, and teams did things together. Having them watch his back bettered his own odds.

His thoughts broke off when a man approached and took a seat. He was clean shaven but wore a battered coat. The pockets were particularly worn and frayed. His hat sat unevenly on his head, exposing his cropped hair. Borisov was tempted to ask the man to leave, but there was no need. He could always walk with the American when he arrived.

The man removed a cigarette and lit it. It was a foreign cigarette, a Camel, and it smelled good. Borisov wanted one but would never ask a stranger for a smoke, particularly for such an expensive brand.

After a few moments the man turned his gaze on Borisov. His

eyes were intelligent–black and piercing. A thin smile creased the man's lips, and he offered Borisov a cigarette. "A nice day for Moscow."

"Yes, it is," Borisov replied, hesitation catching in his voice. He did not have time to talk with this man, but he welcomed the cigarette. He drew one from the pack and lit it with a lighter held in the man's outstretched hand. His hands were strong and seemed out of place with his clothing. Borisov began to worry. "Thanks."

Both men enjoyed their cigarettes without speaking. Borisov tried to study the man from the corner of his eye. Something about him did not seem Russian. What was it?

"Waiting for someone?" the man asked.

Borisov almost turned, but he stopped himself. "No, just a good day to visit the zoo. Like you said, a nice day for Moscow."

"A visit is just what I had on my mind."

"Is that so?" Borisov said, his senses suddenly on maximum alert. Was this the American? His Russian was very good. Borisov could not detect a foreign accent, but what about the foreign cigarettes? He considered the man's build. It was undiscernible under the loose-fitting jacket, but his eyes were strong like his hands. This man had killed before. Borisov could sense it. He considered signaling his men, but decided not to as he buried his right hand in his jacket pocket. He gripped the 7.65-millimeter TK automatic pistol and flicked off the safety.

"I don't think you'll need that," John said.

"Excuse me?" Borisov said.

"I'm here to help." John took another drag on his cigarette. He did not smoke, but Russians did. "I don't think you'll need the pistol."

"Pistol?" Borisov said, feigning surprise.

"Cut the shit, Borisov," John said sharply. "We don't have time to fuck around. I'm here to help you. You're in a heap of hurt."

Both men looked at each other. John saw a mixture of fear and anticipation in Borisov's eyes. He knew at that moment that

Borisov had been telling the truth, at least as he knew it. He was not working for Leonov.

"Talk to me," John ordered. "Convince me that you don't work for the general."

"You saw the video?"

"*Da.*"

"Do you work at the embassy?"

"Calm yourself," John said gently. "We're not that dumb. I've not been to Russia in years, and I have never been to the embassy. I was selected specifically because the Russian authorities don't know I exist."

John knew Borisov would never know the depth of the lie. "Everything I said on the video is true, on my mother's grave," Borisov swore.

"Where are the bombs?" John asked.

"I have no idea," Borisov said in a defeated tone. "If I did, I wouldn't be sitting here with you. My men and I would stop the general."

"Does Trubkin work for Leonov?"

"Always has," Borisov replied, "at least as long as I've known him."

"Do the Chechens know?" John asked as he offered Borisov another cigarette.

"Yes. The general is their pipeline to drugs," Borisov said. "He brokers drugs through his South American contacts. He also provides them with intelligence that helps them defeat the Russian Army in Chechnya. The Chechens will support anyone who will make them money and help to destroy the Russian government."

John guessed Washington would already know this interesting tidbit. "Where do the drugs come in?"

"Tallinn, Estonia, mostly," Borisov answered. He lit his second cigarette.

John kept his face a mask. So far Borisov was batting a thousand. "Would the general use that harbor to ship a bomb to an international client?"

L

Borisov pondered the question for a moment. "Possible. A conduit is in place. Drugs, guns, bombs, the route is the same."

"What if I told you that Trubkin met an Arab terrorist in Paris two weeks ago and we now suspect the terrorist is the customer?"

"I think the general is mad," Borisov said sharply. Anger was just below the surface.

"Let's hope he hasn't lost his ability to reason," John said, deeply aware that the Russian authorities were hunting this man with zeal and considerable resources. "Are we safe here?"

"I have six men watching us. They're very good. We are safe enough." He tapped his ear. "They will sound the alarm if they see the slightest threat."

John nodded. He liked Borisov's professional tone. "I was in Paris a few weeks ago, a little surveillance job. I was charged with identifying the participants of a meeting. One of the attendees turned out to be your friend Trubkin."

"He's not my friend," Borisov interrupted, his eyes hot with anger. "He's a bastard."

"That he was," John replied slyly, "but he won't bother us any more. He met a fiery end in Istanbul."

A devilish smile spread across Borisov's face. "I'm sorry I didn't have the pleasure..." He stopped in mid-sentence and thought for a moment as he stared at John. "So you were already on to the plan before I sent the tape."

"In a manner of speaking, yes," John said. "We also knew about your raids on the military bases."

"How?"

"You used American tactical radios, right?"

Borisov nodded.

"After each infiltration, our National Security Agency noticed large communication spikes between Moscow and the bases you attacked. We also noticed the use of an American frequency before each spike. From that we deduced that the bases were under attack by someone using sophisticated American equipment."

Borisov's cigarette glowed red at the end as he inhaled. "Impressive."

"So, to answer your earlier questions," John continued, "we were aware that someone was actively trying to steal nuclear bombs from Russian bases. We initially suspected one of the Russian mobs. But then we gathered intelligence that suggested an influential American was involved in these activities, at least at some level."

"I wondered how the general had access to the best American equipment."

John nodded.

"What would you have done without my video?" Borisov asked.

"I'm not sure that's important," John said gently. "What is important is that those responsible are held accountable for their actions."

"But the bombs, we must find them."

"I think we have a good handle on that," John said. "We've had our eye on a grain ship in Tallinn. It may be resting at the bottom of the ocean right now."

Both men sat quietly for a moment. "I'm confused," Borisov admitted. "Why did you want to meet with me if the bombs are no longer a threat?"

"Let me ask you a question. Does the general know which men you selected for your team?"

"No, I never told him. Even if he did, he doesn't know where we're hiding, at least not yet," Borisov stated.

"But family members will talk."

"The men never knew the assignment until after they had left their families. I'm sure none of them dared mention my name."

"Okay."

A curious look came across Borisov's face. It was obvious to John that Borisov did not understand the reasoning behind his line of questions.

"What I propose," John said, "is that we use your team and

L

the intelligence abilities of the US government to take care of a little unfinished business."

Borisov continued to stare at John.

"Your team is obviously highly skilled. I'm assuming they are all ex-Spetsnaz like yourself."

"You're correct," Borisov replied with a mixture of pride and doubt in his voice. John thought it sounded odd coming from a warrior. Clearly the last few days had left Borisov's head spinning.

"There is no way the US government could insert a military team into Russia to complete this task. At least not quickly." John did not finish his thought. He needed Borisov to make the connection on his own.

"You want a Spetsnaz team to work directly for the US government?" Borisov asked, astonished.

John nodded. "Sounds outrageous, doesn't it?"

"Sending you the video felt the same fucking way," Borisov flashed back. He took the last draw on his cigarette and discarded it with a flick of his hand.

"Dangerous times can call for unusual bedfellows," John added. Borisov scanned their surroundings. John measured his body language; the man was clearly reviewing his options.

"What is the mission?"

"Kidnap the general's daughter."

Borisov stared at John; he was incredulous. "For what purpose?"

"Let's just say that the US government wants to have a little chat with the general. He's a busy man. Getting time on his schedule could be problematic. He needs a good reason to travel outside the country, and we think his daughter could provide some incentive."

"Even if we kidnap her, how will you get her out of the country?"

"I don't think we need to get her out of the country," John said. "Your men can hold her and keep her safe. We don't want her hurt in any way. Meanwhile you come with me to Rome."

"What?"

"You'll be free to return at any time once we've talked with the general," John said. "Trust me, you'll want to be there to witness the meeting."

Borisov was silent, digesting what he had heard. He finally spoke. "I need to talk with my men. I may be their leader, but I led them into this situation. They are all volunteers. I owe them a chance to decide again, because what you're proposing is very dangerous."

"That sounds reasonable," John said. "However, I'd like a chance to speak with them before they decide. I know it's an unusual request. I'm sure your team is tight and outsiders are not usually invited, but if we plan to work together, they'd better know who I am."

Borisov paused before answering. "I agree. Who are you anyway?"

"A Navy SEAL," John replied. "Commander John Thompson, a frog of the meanest type."

As he stood, Borisov said, "A Navy SEAL. Can you swim?"

John laughed as he stood. "Borisov, I hope you can shoot half as well as I can swim."

"Shoot?" Borisov grinned. "I have no doubt you could learn a great deal about shooting from me."

"Really," John said with heavy sarcasm.

"Come with me," Borisov ordered. "A car is waiting."

* * *

The barn was quiet and the atmosphere tense. The six Spetsnaz men sat in a half circle. It had taken two hours to reach the barn. The small convoy had driven a circuitous route from Moscow to a remote area. John had been blindfolded during the entire trip and had no idea where they were. He had not liked the idea, but he would have taken the same precaution had he been in Borisov's position.

"Men, this is Commander John Thompson," Borisov began. "He is an American naval officer, a SEAL. He is aware of our situation and represents the Americans' response to the videotape." Suspicion filled the men's eyes. John saw it clearly and sympathized with them. His feelings would have mirrored theirs had he been in their position.

"The Americans are very concerned. They have learned that the stolen bombs are headed to the Middle East. Luckily they have intercepted the ship that was carrying the bombs. It now lies at the bottom of the ocean."

John noted that Borisov had decided to present the sinking as a done deal.

He could tell that the men respected Borisov; their concentration on his every word was palpable. John suspected none of the men had guessed at the operation that someone in Washington had envisioned. He wondered how they would react.

"Commander Thompson has made an interesting proposition. He wants to join our team and execute a plan the American government has conceived." Borisov hesitated. "The Americans propose we kidnap the general's daughter."

"Sir," Grigori protested. "Are the Americans crazy? What good will that do? We don't kill innocent girls."

Borisov looked at John and nodded.

"An excellent question," John replied in Russian. "And yes, killing innocent girls is unacceptable. The tape you sent us helped complete a picture of the general's activities over the last few months. We knew he was up to something. We believe, as I hope you do, that those responsible for stealing the nuclear weapons must pay for their crimes. The US government is concerned that the general will never face the consequences of his actions. A more likely scenario is that you will be punished instead. I doubt any of you want to face the furnace."

Borisov's men traded looks. John continued. "Our plan is to use the general's daughter as bait to force him to travel outside this country. Once he's out of the country, he'll pay for his treachery. Borisov will be there as your witness.

"You are Spetsnaz soldiers, Russia's best. Your raids on the three bases demonstrated your skill. We need this skill to abduct the general's daughter. We will leave her in your safe and capable hands while Borisov and I travel out of the country. What I add to the formula is operational intelligence, like where the daughter lives and the means for Borisov and me to leave the country. I believe that, with your skills and the US government's intelligence resources, we have what we need to pull off this operation and bring the general to justice."

John paused. He had their attention. Their eyes studied both Borisov and him. They wanted desperately to know what their commander was thinking. John looked at Borisov and nodded.

"Men, you have heard the American. I believe the commander's points are valid. I would add that our obligation goes further. We're the means by which nuclear bombs were taken. We are at fault, a result of my mistakes. Are there any questions?"

"Sir, count me in," Grigori said as he stood up. The other five team members rose quickly, and the decision was made. Each man walked up to John and shook his hand.

"Does he know how to shoot, Major?" asked one of the Spetsnaz.

"There's only one way to find out." Borisov grinned. "Orlov, I'm sure you can outshoot the commander."

Borisov removed the 7.65-millimeter TK pistol from his jacket pocket. He checked the clip, making sure it was full. He chambered a round and handed the gun to John, grip first. Orlov reached back to remove an identical pistol from his belt.

"Orlov, you pick the shot, and we'll see if the commander can match your efforts," Borisov ordered. The other Spetsnaz soldiers began to tease Orlov.

Unfazed, Orlov reached into a knapsack that lay on the hay-

L

covered floor. He produced two apples and tossed them to another Spetsnaz.

"When I barrel roll left, throw one of the apples in the air. I'll shoot it in two."

Orlov dived to the ground and rolled. He came up shooting. The apple tossed by his fellow soldier disintegrated in midair. Everyone cheered. The toss had been perfect, placing the apple five meters directly in front of Orlov. John doubted he would see as exact a throw again. He nodded at the Spetsnaz who held the second apple. The soldier smiled back.

John dived and rolled into a shooting position. His peripheral vision caught the apple as it sped away from him and into the murky light of the barn. Without thinking he aimed the pistol and fired a single shot. The apple exploded; the shot had been perfect.

John stood and looked at each man. The toss had been significantly harder than Orlov's, and they all knew it. The admiration was apparent.

"Commander, my compliments," Borisov said. "Nikita rarely plays fair."

"I'd be disappointed if he had, Major," John replied.

"Men, any questions?" Borisov asked.

They all shook their heads.

"Good. Time to make Mother Russia proud." He had led his men into this nightmare, and now it was time to get them out, even if it required a second act of treason. "Gather around, we have a lot of planning to do and I suspect very little time."

* * *

They had spent two days watching the apartment. They needed a week, but such a luxury did not exist. Dan had specified a tight timetable, and John was determined to meet it as long as it was operationally possible.

The apartment building was eleven stories tall and sat on the banks of the Moscow River. Though built while Stalin was alive, it lacked the wedding-cake style that had flourished during Stalin's rule. Just across Novyi Arbat from the daughter's apartment building stood the Russian White House, where Boris Yeltsin had climbed atop a tank and catapulted himself to the top of the Russian government. Speculation still circulated that the barricade of the White House had been of Yeltsin's making.

Now in the darkness John could make out one guard standing at the east gate of the White House. He looked bored. John suspected that the bright lights surrounding the facility impaired the guard's night vision; at least he hoped so. The MIR police building, also across Novyi Arbat from the daughter's apartment complex, was not in their line of sight, but it towered into the night sky. The US Embassy's North Gate was less than a quarter mile away down Koniuskovskaja, a street that intersected with Novyi Arbat directly in front of the apartment complex.

When they had begun the surveillance of the apartment building, both men had been surprised by its location. The complex was not Moscow's finest, nor was it known as one that housed important people. The general's daughter definitely fell into that category. At first the proximity to the White House and the MIR police facility had caused concern. However, after they had watched the routines of these facilities and confirmed the apartment's location inside the building, a plan had come together. Now it was time to execute it.

"The men are in position," Borisov confirmed. John nodded. He had also heard the six clicks on the secure headsets they all wore. "Any last-minute concerns?"

"No. We're ready."

John nodded at Borisov and got out of a beat-up Cheka. John knew Borisov did not like the idea of staying in the car. He wanted to be alongside his men. Borisov was a man of action, but his face was too well known. The general had made sure of that. His picture had been distributed to all of Russia's security forces. John needed Borisov safe and sound. If the snatch went bad, he

L

did not want to lose him too. It had taken no small effort to convince Borisov. John knew he would have reacted similarly in Borisov's position.

The parked Cheka rested a few hundred yards from the apartment building under a clump of trees just off Smolenskaja. The small street led up to a ramp at the intersection of Kamininiskij and Novyi Arbat. John had only a short walk to his assigned position.

During the last hour, three of Borisov's men had climbed the east end of the building, away from the road and out of sight of the police facility. Now they lay hidden on the rooftop behind a billboard anchored to the roof. Two others covered the back of the building, peering through the night to look for any unexpected visitors. The sixth man was on the roof of a building to John's right, a sniper rifle in hand, scanning the area immediately surrounding the apartment building.

John strolled along the side of the building that faced the cold, silent waters of the Moscow River. His assignment was easy: to keep the area below the daughter's apartment free of people. He felt the TK automatic in his jacket pocket, checking to make sure the safety was off. He hoped there would be no need to use the pistol; if so, the mission would fail. He had no illusions about the outcome of a shoot-out with the Russian authorities.

John was nervous. In the two days that they had spent watching the apartment, the daughter had always come home alone. Tonight that had not been the case. Poor bastard, thought John. That was the one part of Dan's instructions that surprised him: absolutely no witnesses were allowed.

When he was in position, he clicked the microphone's Send button twice to acknowledge that all was as it should be. Three clicks sounded in response.

* * *

The three Spetsnaz on the roof heard the clicks. The wait was over. With quick glances at each other, they threw their ropes over the side of the building and ran down its face. The Australian SAS had originally developed the technique. Most SWAT teams and other special units rappelled down the side of a building feet first. The Australian method had the men facing the ground, and they literally ran down the building's side. This method had its advantages, the principal one being that the target was always in view. It took Borisov's men less than three seconds to reach the eighth floor of the eleven-story building.

The daughter's apartment had a small balcony. Two of the men hung on the left side and the third on the right. They glanced at each other again and traded hand signals. The balcony was clear, and all three men leaped onto it as silently as leopards. The apartment was completely dark. The daughter had arrived home three hours earlier with a single male friend.

With a few quick moves, one of the men cut a hole in the glass of the balcony door. The circular piece came away cleanly; the fulcrum of the cutting arm was attached to a suction cup. Reaching though the hole in the glass, the Spetsnaz unlocked the balcony door.

The soldier keyed his mike once. Another click was heard in acknowledgement; everyone on the team now knew that the door was unlocked. He nodded to his two companions. They quickly entered the apartment while he stayed behind. His job was to cover their exit.

The risky part of the operation lay in the escape. Technically there were two ways–down the side or through the guts of the building. The first was safer. Navigating the hallways of an unfamiliar building could only lead to trouble. It would be too easy for the authorities to surround the apartment complex, giving the men no chance of an escape. This operation relied on stealth and surprise; so far both had been with them.

L

The two soldiers advanced silently through the apartment, knees slightly bent. They held submachine guns tight against their shoulders as they peered down the barrel, careful not to focus on any one object.

The living room contained a couch and two chairs centered on a new TV. A VCR sat below the TV set in a fancy cabinet. The western stereo played music softly. The soldiers continued, advancing silently toward the first closed door. They did not know which room was the bedroom, but only four doors led from the hallway. One was obviously the exit. Only one other door was closed. Using hand signals to communicate, they decided to check the open doors first. In less than a minute they confirmed that the bathroom and spare bedroom were empty. They aligned themselves on either side of the room with the shut door. From within they heard noises; at least two people appeared to be in the throes of intercourse. With more hand signals they agreed on the areas of responsibility. They had hoped the general's daughter and her partner would be fast asleep at 3:15 am, but obviously they were not.

On the count of three they opened the door slowly, keeping low. The living room was dark, so the open door did not silhouette the soldiers as they entered the bedroom. She was on top of her partner, anxiously working herself into a climax, her back to the soldiers.

Orlov moved quickly to his left and took a single clean shot at the boyfriend's head. It killed him instantly. Almost as quickly as Orlov had killed her lover, Sergei moved behind the general's daughter as she turned in horror. The chloroform-soaked cloth covered her face as his strong hands and body pinned her to the bed before she could scream. She fought for a few seconds until she was overcome. While Sergei tackled the daughter, Orlov made sure no one else was in the bedroom. It was clear. Orlov keyed his mike twice, indicating that the daughter was knocked out and the apartment secure.

It took longer to dress the unconscious girl than they had

planned, and they were running a minute and a half behind schedule. Both men hurried to the balcony where the third Spetsnaz waited. He turned as he saw them rushing toward him. He had a special harness on his back. His two partners quickly secured the daughter in it with a blindfold over her head. In less than a minute, the Spetsnaz soldier rappelled down the building feet first with the daughter strapped to his back. Orlov and Sergei followed him down using the Australian method.

* * *

John watched the men rappel down the face of the building and keyed his mike three times. Borisov would know it was time to collect the daughter and load her into the Cheka. Its lights off, the Cheka cruised up the street and stopped next to Borisov's men and their charge. Borisov exited the car. Two of his men maneuvered the daughter between them into the back seat while the third took the driver's seat. Borisov spoke to them briefly, and they were off.

John and Borisov headed back down the street where Borisov had waited in the parked Cheka. Borisov quickly commanded the remaining three men to leave their positions and execute their exits. Meanwhile he and John continued walking down the street. Four blocks away they had stashed a motorcycle. Unlike his men, who would ultimately return to the barn with their charge, Borisov and John were headed to the diplomatic mission of the Vatican. In the morning they would leave for the airport. Now was the best time to get Borisov inside the mission without the Russian authorities noticing.

28 Russian Airspace

As the taxi neared the Sheremetyeva Airport, John could feel Borisov tense. John liked Borisov and was impressed with the man as well as the warrior. He knew how to lead, from the front. He didn't ask his men to do anything he wasn't willing to do. When it came to battlefield plans, security, and counterterrorism, Borisov knew his stuff. What worried John was the Russian's lack of experience traveling into foreign countries and using false papers. That shortcoming made this part of their mission the most dangerous. Timing and luck were critical. He hoped they would have both.

Dressed as priests, they carried valid diplomatic passports issued by the Vatican. The Alitalia staff had produced their boarding passes quickly, but now it was time to pass through customs. Though the passports were genuine, the entry stamp in Borisov's had been forged.

They approached the booth that handled diplomatic personnel, having waited until the last possible moment to approach the customs queue. Their plane was scheduled to leave in less than fifteen minutes. Their pace was slow and measured, their posture relaxed. They needed to hide their military bearing at all costs. The black cassocks hung loosely on their muscular frames. Their disguise was good, but was it good enough? John had no doubt that the manhunt for Borisov was large even by Russian standards. In this situation there was nowhere to run, no safe haven to hide in; not until the plane left Russian airspace could they breathe a sigh of relief.

Borisov approached the officer and handed him his passport. John stood a few feet behind and to his left.

"Good day, Father," the Russian officer said.

"Good day to you, my son," Borisov answered as piously as he could. Under different circumstances John might have laughed. "Pious" was not the first word that came to his mind in regard to Borisov.

"Headed to Rome?" the officer asked as he studied the picture page of the passport. He glanced quickly and began to lift a small stamp. Suddenly he stopped. "Father, you look familiar, uncommonly so. Have we met before?"

"I don't think so, my son, but I'm not the strongest when it comes to remembering names and faces. I'm trying to improve, but it's not an easy task. I expect you're very good, considering your job."

The officer smiled at the compliment.

"It's a wonderful gift. Count yourself blessed."

"Thank you, Father."

"Is there a problem?" John interrupted. It was taking too long, and the longer it took, the more likely the officer would realize why Borisov looked familiar. "I'd hate to miss our plane. It would be most unfortunate."

"He thinks I remind him of someone," Borisov explained, his voice perfectly calm.

"Really," John said. "How about me? Do I remind you of anyone?"

The officer quickly shook his head. "No, but he does."

John sensed the man was deliberately stalling for time. Maybe the officer had already sent out an alert. They had no way of knowing. John had noticed several cameras throughout the area, and it would not be long before more people were studying Borisov's face. John traded a look with Borisov.

L

"I hate to insist," John said, "but we're diplomats of the Holy See. The nature of our trip is important. We must make this plane. I'm sure you don't want to create an incident with Rome."

John handed his passport to the officer. The man continued to hesitate. John reached into his cassock and retrieved a cellular phone he had rented after his arrival in Moscow. He punched the emergency number Dan had given him. John understood that it reached a senior member of the Vatican's diplomatic mission in Moscow. He spoke briefly to someone on the other end of the line and handed the phone to the Russian officer. "Someone wants to speak with you."

John's tone was firm and unfriendly. Both men watched as the Russian listened to the voice on the phone. John did not know the man speaking or even if he was really stationed in the mission. All he knew was that he should use the number in case of emergency. He hoped to hell it worked. The Russian attempted to reason with the man on the phone, but his attempts were continually interrupted; it appeared he could not get a word in edgewise. After two minutes he handed the cellular phone to John.

"I'm sorry for any inconvenience."

"I'm sure your assistance will be duly noted," John assured him. "You're doing your job, and we appreciate that. Thank you."

The officer stamped their passports.

John and Borisov joined the other passengers for the bus ride to the waiting jet, an Alitalia Aerobus 320. After a short wait, they walked up the steps to the jumbo jet. Both men noted the locations of Russian security personnel stationed around the plane. There were at least three. Once on the plane, they headed to separate lavatories. Within three minutes, they exited their respective bathrooms dressed as members of the cleaning crew, with large trash bags in hand containing their disguises. They deplaned and casually walked under the Aerobus to a Gulf Stream IV jet three hundred yards away. Its engines were already running. As they boarded, John saw one of the Russian security men running to the Aerobus plane, yelling at his comrades.

The door shut on the Gulf Stream jet and the plane began to taxi. Ten agonizing minutes later they were airborne and headed northwest toward Helsinki, closing quickly on an Aeroflot plane headed in the same direction.

The Gulf Stream jet was painted like a civilian plane, but in reality it was a C-20H, the military version of the Gulf Stream IV business jet. In addition to the standard military enhancements, the plane had been fitted with a special package normally found in US Air Force Airborne Warning and Command System planes.

John and Borisov looked at each other as the plane accelerated into the morning sky. By now the Russians would be unloading the Aerobus as a result of the anonymous phone call. They hoped the deception would give them enough time to clear Russian airspace, but if not, John knew they had a few surprises left for the Russians.

* * *

The general heard a knock on his door. "Come in."

"Sir, I have just received a phone call from the airport." The colonel was obviously nervous. He paused.

"Spit it out, what have you learned about my daughter?" the general demanded. He was distraught. Katya was the only thing in this world that he truly cherished. How could someone, let alone how dare someone, kidnap his daughter? It was beyond his comprehension. He had created a list of possible candidates, but not one of them made sense. They were too spineless. But it had to be one of them. He would kill this person with his bare hands. He would rip the man apart. And if his daughter was hurt, or dead . . . His hate rose like bile in his throat. The colonel began to speak.

"I'm sorry, sir, but I don't believe what I have involves your daughter, sir."

"Out with it, then."

"Less than forty minutes ago, an Alitalia jet scheduled to

depart for Rome received a bomb threat. The plane was quickly unloaded and thoroughly searched. No bombs were found. However, when the plane was reboarded, it was short two passengers." The colonel placed two pictures from the airport video cameras on the general's desk. "The missing passengers were two priests holding diplomatic passports issued by the Vatican."

The general studied the two pictures for less than three seconds before he started roaring at the top of his lungs like an insane Russian bear. He grabbed his phone and threw it across his office. It shattered on impact. "Colonel, do you know who the fuck these two men are?"

"Sir, we have only identified one of the priests. He is Pyotr Borisov, the man wanted in connection with the theft of the bombs. We have yet to identify the other man, sir, but I have over a hundred people working on it. I've also sealed the airport. They will not slip through our fingers."

"Don't bother, you fucking idiot. The other fucking priest is an American and his name is John Thompson. He is a US Navy SEAL. And if you think they're on the ground, you're even dumber than I fucking thought. Who the fuck do you think called in the bomb scare?"

The colonel studied the general, unsure of what to say. He saw his mistake, and it was serious.

"I want every fucking plane that departed the airport, from the time these bastards cleared customs, to be intercepted. I want the officer who let them on board shot. Do I make myself clear?"

"But general, intercepting all those planes might prove impossible," the colonel stuttered. "The Air Force…"

"You better hope your ass it's not," the general screamed. "Now get the fuck out of my sight and get those planes on the ground. And get me a new fucking phone."

The colonel saluted and ran from the general's office.

The general slammed his fist on his desk. How could any security officer not recognize Borisov? He was only the most wanted person in all of Russia. Why was everyone such a fucking idiot? Nothing ever went right unless he handled it personally. Suddenly he came up short as a cold chill ran through his body. He sat down. How had the SEAL known about Borisov?

There was only one person who could have told the SEAL about Borisov–Alex Davenport. Not even Trubkin knew about Borisov and his role. What the hell was Davenport up to? Why was he ruining everything? Was the SEAL really working for him? Was Davenport still CIA, and was all his support part of an incredibly elaborate operation? It couldn't be possible. It just couldn't be possible.

And then another possibility struck him and he collapsed in his chair. Had Davenport kidnapped his daughter?

* * *

"Commander Thompson," Major Dean Eliason yelled. "The AWACS orbiting over the Black Sea just called in. Russian fighters are scrambling from five different bases. They're onto us."

"What the hell did he say?" Borisov demanded in Russian when he saw the expression on John's face. John translated.

"We're screwed," Borisov declared. "Your Plan B will never work. How many miles until we reach Estonia?"

John repeated the question to the major. He replied, "Fifteen minutes, give or take."

The C-20H had taken off minutes behind an Aeroflot jet headed to Helsinki. Knowing that the Aeroflot fleet of planes was antiquated at best, the men had assumed that the airliner would not have anticollision equipment installed. Even if it did, it probably was not working. This allowed the C-20H to fly directly behind and below the airliner, causing the radar signals of the two planes to blend into one.

Meanwhile Major Eliason had used the equipment borrowed from a US Air Force AWAC plane to paint phantom radar images of their jet. The device could fool up to twenty-six radar sites at a time. The selected sites lay along the filed flight plan, the destination of which had been Bremerhaven, Germany. Currently eleven sites were receiving a broadcast image that showed the C-20H flying along the expected route to Germany.

The risk in the plan came from a visual sighting. If a scrambled fighter could not see the plane that the ground stations were tracking, the ruse would be up. The only question was how long it would take the Russians to locate the Gulf Stream jet once they realized it was not where it should be. Since the two shortest routes west from Moscow led to Helsinki and Istanbul, the Russians' choices were obvious.

"What's our position?" John asked.

"Ninety-eight miles to the Russian-Estonian border," the major answered. "Ten fighters scrambled from two bases in the St. Petersburg area. We'll probably see a few of them shortly."

John repeated the response to Borisov. "This Myers guy is nuts," Borisov yelled. "We don't stand a chance."

"We've been over this before, damn it," John said. "It will work." John had serious reservations about Dan's plan too, but he wasn't about to share them with Borisov or the other crew members, not when everyone's life was on the line.

The pilot yelled over the intercom, "The fancy flying is about to start. Buckle in tight."

John and Borisov tightened their seatbelts. Major Eliason had already done so, and managed a chuckle as his hands busily worked the controls.

"Shit," Borisov yelled. "That son-of-a-bitch is crazy."

John just shrugged as he looked out the cabin window. What could he do?

* * *

Ten minutes had passed and the pilots of the C-20H were busy. The copilot scanned the skies. "See the bastards yet?"

"Negative, but they're closing," the pilot replied. "I can feel it."

"Who the fuck's idea was this?" the copilot demanded, as the pilot closed on the Aeroflot airliner ahead and above them. Soon the two jets were no more than two hundred yards apart.

"They've got us on radar," the major informed everyone over the intercom. "They'll try to talk to us."

Two minutes later they spotted a MIG fighter off the port side. The pilots could easily see each other.

"November 5364 Mike-Kilo, over," said the Russian pilot in thick English.

The pilot of the C-20H waved at his counterpart.

"November 5364 Mike-Kilo, you are instructed to move away from the airliner immediately on a heading of 90 degrees. Acknowledge."

The C-20H pilot tapped his left side of his headset while he shook his head.

"Seventy-five miles to Estonian airspace," announced the copilot.

"Move away from the airliner immediately, heading of 90 degrees," the Russian pilot repeated.

"It won't be long now," the copilot remarked.

Thirty seconds passed. Suddenly the large Aeroflot airliner started to turn east. The C-20H did not change its course.

"The airliner is turning," the pilot said into the intercom for everyone's benefit.

Major Eliason motioned to John. "It's time."

John looked across the small cabin to the other passenger on board, US Air Force Captain Kathy Hogan. The officer's resemblance to the general's daughter was not perfect, but at that distance from the fighter it would probably be good enough. She nodded at John.

John spoke Russian into the intercom. "Russian fighter, you must stand down and let us pass. No interference will be permitted. Acknowledge."

"Comply with my orders or you will be shot down."

"Katya will die," challenged John.

"Yes, you will all die," the Russian pilot said.

"Do you know General Leonov?" John asked.

"You will turn onto a heading of 90 degrees in thirty seconds or I have orders to attack your plane."

"I suspect that will be a career-ending move," John insisted. "Speak to your command. Tell them that the general's daughter is on this plane. She will die if you do not stand down."

John motioned to Captain Hogan and they filed their way up to the cockpit. With Hogan in front of him, John placed a gun to her head and pushed her into the tight space behind the pilot's chair so the Russian pilot could see her. John could see him clearly.

"Move us closer," John ordered to the C-20H pilot. The space between the two jets shrank to less than 150 yards. "She will die," John repeated as Hogan screamed. He led her from the flight deck back into the cabin and out of sight of the Russian pilot.

"Acknowledge," John demanded. He looked at Major Eliason.

"Forty-seven miles," mouthed the major. Borisov kept his eyes fixed on the Russian fighter. There was nothing for him to do and he hated every moment of it.

* * *

The general barely heard the knock when it sounded. Davenport's possible role in Katya's kidnapping had traumatized him. The general had few illusions about Davenport; he was a ruthless man who thought nothing of killing another human being. All Leonov could think about was Katya. His Katya.

He heard the knock again. "Come in."

The colonel stepped in and slowly made his way to the general's desk. He stood at attention.

"At ease, Colonel."

The colonel studied the general for a moment. The calm tone of his commanding officer scared the hell out of him. "Sir, I believe we've identified the plane used by the two priests."

"They're not fucking priests, Colonel."

"Ah, yes, sir."

"Continue."

"Yes, sir. The plane is a private jet, an American Gulf Stream IV. It's tail number is N5364MK. It departed minutes before the bomb scare. It was scheduled to fly to Bremerhaven, Germany. In addition, we believe we have identified the jet's owner, a company called Hong Kong Transportation, based in Singapore. I'm using one of our assets in the FAA to confirm this detail as we speak. The company is publicly traded; however, its largest stockholder is Alex Davenport, a billionaire..."

"...who made his money in shipping and oil, Colonel. I know all about him. And where is the jet?"

"At last report, fifty miles from exiting our airspace, sir, apparently en route to Helsinki. Speed 450 knots."

"Good, turn the plane around," the general ordered.

"Sir, yes, sir, the Air Force is trying," stammered the colonel. "However, there is a problem."

Leonov just stared at him.

"Sir, your daughter is on the plane. They have threatened to kill her if the plane is forced to change its course. Attacking the plane could also prove deadly for your daughter."

The general considered the colonel's words, his worst fears confirmed. "How the hell did they get her on the plane?"

"Sir, I do not know."

"Does the Air Force know who is on board this plane besides my daughter?"

"Sir, when I made the request, I didn't tell them. But the word will get out. People at the airport know about the two priests..."

"They're not fucking priests," Leonov yelled. "Get Grachev on the phone. Now."

Two minutes later the Defense Minister listened to Leonov plead on the telephone.

"Are you saying the man responsible for stealing two nuclear weapons is on that plane with your daughter," Grachev said, "and you want me to let them fly out of the country?"

"Yes. She is my only daughter."

"And how do you suppose our peers might react when this knowledge becomes public?"

"Pavel, it is ultimately your choice," Leonov said gravely. "I realize it's a terrible burden, but she is my daughter, my only daughter. There will be another day to catch Borisov, that I promise."

"I understand the plane is owned by an American. What do you say about that?"

"I'm as surprised as you must be," Leonov replied. "Maybe now we know where Borisov got the fancy American communication equipment."

"Yes, maybe," Grachev said, sounding skeptical. Silence hung on the line. "Do you have any other thoughts?"

"We need Borisov alive to find the bombs," Leonov suggested.

"I see."

Leonov looked at his watch. Minutes were passing. He sensed the Defense Minister was stalling as well. Could that be his way out?

"General, do you have any idea why Borisov took an interest in your daughter? No offense, but I would think one of my daughters might have been more appropriate. You, after all, do not control the Air Force."

Leonov considered Grachev's question. What an insolent prick. Leonov attempted to push his anger aside. "Sir, I'm sure the security surrounding your daughters is much tighter than around mine. Katya made things difficult. She insisted on living on her own, in a complex that was unsecured. I should never have allowed it."

The Defense Minister considered the general's answer before he spoke. "And the second priest, who might that be?"

"We're working on that."

"I see," said the Defense Minister. "General, we've known

each other for years. We are friends, but I cannot help you on this one. We can't allow that jet to leave our airspace. I'm sorry."

Leonov heard the Defense Minister end the conversation. He looked up and stared at the colonel. "That is all. Leave me alone."

"Ah, yes, sir. Sir, may I ask what you would suggest. I can try..."

"Out."

The colonel turned, and Leonov watched the door close behind him. The general's rage had been replaced by fear, fear for his daughter's life. His Katya.

* * *

Eight minutes had passed since the Russian pilot had said a word. The Estonian border lay seventeen miles directly ahead.

"It's taking long enough," the pilot said over the intercom. "I've got a bad feeling about this one. We're a fucking sitting duck up here."

John looked at Major Eliason; he shrugged his shoulders.

"Captain, it's your call, but I'd suggest taking this bird as close to the ground as you can," John said.

"Roger that, sir," the pilot said. "Buckle up."

Less than thirty seconds later, the C-20H jet dropped from the sky as the pilot pointed its nose at the ground. In less than two minutes they dropped from 33,000 feet to 250. John's and Borisov's stomachs recoiled from the descent. Finally the pilots leveled the jet out and started to hug the terrain at more than five hundred knots.

"Where are the fighters?" the pilot demanded.

"Two of them have followed us down," Major Eliason answered. "All the others are at or near 10,000 feet."

"Weapon locks?"

"Not yet." Eliason's hands danced on the keyboard. "I'm sending out false signals. I'm not sure how much they'll help us.

At this range they'll shoot heat seekers. Nothing we can do to stop those bastards."

"Six miles," the copilot confirmed over the intercom. John signaled Borisov with six fingers. Everyone was nervous.

"The fighters are dropping back," the major said.

John looked at him. "Is that good or bad?"

"Probably bad," Major Eliason explained. "Heat-seeking missiles need time to arm. They'll drop a half mile to a mile back."

Another minute passed.

"They have missile lock," Major Eliason yelled. "One missile away. Second away. They appear to be tracking."

The pilot dropped the C-20H another hundred feet and pushed the throttles of the jet to the stops. The plane's speed peaked at 637 knots.

"Break hard left," Major Eliason ordered. The plane banked hard, and John thought for a moment that its wing tip might strike the ground. Seconds later the plane leveled out.

"Hard right."

The pilot again executed a gut-wrenching turn. John stole a quick look at Borisov. He looked green, as did Captain Hogan.

"Both are still tracking," the major yelled. "This is too close to call. Cut a hard left again."

The plane turned on its side and shuddered as it followed the pilot's command.

"We're in Estonia," the copilot yelled through the g's. No sooner had he said it than an explosion rocked the plane, and then a second.

They all held their breath, waiting for the plane to spin out of control. Moments passed. John stole a glance at Major Eliason.

"They missed," the major confirmed. "They fucking missed."

"Did they?" John asked.

"You don't see us spinning out of control, do you?" insisted Major Eliason.

"No, but maybe the general's daughter did the trick," John

said. "Maybe the Air Force had to make it look good. They're not following us, are they?"

"No, we're in Estonian airspace."

"I'm surprised the Russians would care."

Everyone stared at John.

"Who knows?" said a pensive Captain Hogan after a moment.

"Who cares?" Major Eliason added. "We're alive."

John looked at Borisov and nodded. They had made it, but barely. John stood up. It was time to congratulate the pilots. As he rose, another thought flooded his mind: how had Dan known that Plan B would work? Or hadn't it mattered?

29 Playing More Cards

The weather in Rome was balmy compared with the early winter chill that gripped Moscow. The flight from Finland had gone as planned, as had the switch from the Gulf Stream jet to the military transport plane in a remote corner of the Vantee airport in Helsinki. John and Borisov were exhausted and had slept most of the way. They had both learned long ago to sleep whenever they could.

"Borisov, leave some goddamn hot water for me," John yelled through the steam that drifted from the bathroom. Their third-floor room in the Santa Chiara Hotel in Rome faced the Pantheon, an ancient building that John never tired of.

He was worried about Logan. Twelve days had passed since she had disappeared and not a word had been heard. John had pressed Dan frequently for information, but none had been forthcoming. The only assurance offered was that the US government was doing all it could. For the hundredth time John considered venturing out on his own. He would start with Davenport. John felt sure he would know if the billionaire had a hand in his daughter's kidnapping. If not, he would find another starting point.

A knock sounded on the door. John grabbed the pistol that lay on the bed and quietly approached the door. He recognized Dan's voice and lowered the gun.

Dan entered. "How's he doing?"

"He's using all the damn hot water," John complained.

"I see. Get him."

John did his bidding. Soon a half-dried Borisov stood before them, wrapped in a towel.

"Borisov, I'm not sure how much John has explained to you," Dan began in Russian, "but suffice it to say that this business is complicated. We still have a lot of work to do. The next act will give John great satisfaction and frustration at the same time."

The soldiers traded stares, curiosity on their faces. Dan could see that the two men trusted each other completely. That said a lot about Borisov, since John was one of the best.

"While you were in Russia I requisitioned a SEAL team. At three o'clock tonight they will attempt to rescue Logan."

John stared at Dan before he finally spoke. "Where is she?"

"Here in Rome."

"How long have you known?" John demanded angrily.

"Four days."

John's eyes narrowed. "Why didn't you tell me?"

"You were in Russia, and I felt you didn't need any distractions."

"Where in Rome is she?"

Dan directed his attention to the Russian. "Borisov, I'll have you know that Logan means an awful lot to John. Your job today is to make sure John goes nowhere near her kidnappers. You are authorized to use deadly force if necessary. Do I make myself clear?"

A smile spread across Borisov's face. "Yes, sir."

"Damn it, Dan, that's not fair. I'm sure the team's good, but . . ."

"But nothing," Dan interrupted. "My decision is final. You are to stay away. Period. Borisov, don't doubt his resolve. Keep him away from the Spanish Steps area at all costs."

John glared at Dan, wondering if Borisov even knew where the Spanish Steps were.

Dan held John's stare for a moment before he looked at Borisov. "We have some planning of our own to do. Let me explain."

* * *

John and Borisov stood two hundred yards away from Logan's prison. Their feet made a soft noise in the roof's loose gravel. Below, the famed Spanish Steps of Rome were awash in manmade light, with only a few lovers visible in the early morning stillness. Fielding strong pairs of binoculars, the two men focused on the yellow building that housed Logan. Their secure comm-links had just reported that the rescue operation would start in a matter of moments.

The past few hours had been terrible for John. He loved Logan deeply even though their time together had been brief. She was a kindred soul, and he dared not lose her. Standing on the sidelines of a hostage rescue operation was hard enough, but he could not bear the knowledge that the lone hostage was the woman he loved. He had never felt so helpless in his life. Her life was in the hands of killers, and there was nothing he could do but wait and watch.

Borisov had followed Dan's instructions flawlessly, though Dan had finally relented and allowed John to meet the commander of the SEAL team charged with her rescue. Lieutenant Commander Dick Gurney was a man John knew only by reputation. John had spent twenty minutes with Gurney, who had revealed what he knew about Logan's surroundings and the plan to free her. John had liked what he heard and saw. Gurney was all business–a true frog.

The SEALs had used one of the newest tools in their inventory to determine the positions of the five kidnappers. The DKL people-finding system tracked the electromagnetic field generated by the beating of a human heart. That in itself was amazing, but so was the discovery that every heart generated a unique signal. By using parabolic antennas and triangulation, the system could determine an individual's location within six to twelve feet. The whole contraption was wired to a laptop computer that tracked the unique signals and displayed them on a grid.

Using the DKL system over the last three days, the SEAL team had mapped the movements of the kidnappers. Lieutenant Commander Gurney had determined Logan's exact location and had planned the rescue accordingly.

John dropped the binoculars for a moment as he considered Dan's story once again. It seemed unbelievable that a father could put his daughter in harm's way to further his own ends. After he had thought about it for a while, he had argued that Logan should not be rescued. If indeed her father had kidnapped her, she had to be safe. Certainly her father would not kill her. Her captivity, no matter how wrong, had to be more like political house arrest than prison. Attempting a rescue put her in serious danger; an errant bullet was more likely to kill her than her kidnappers were.

Dan had listened quietly to the argument, but had explained that Logan would be safe only when she was in Federal hands. He had added that the Russians might have taken her. In truth, John knew from Dan's earlier briefing that Dan's plans depended on Logan's freedom, no matter who held her, and to John's dismay this need won the day.

"Any moment now," John said as he broke away from his thoughts.

"*Da*," Borisov agreed. "I've always wanted to see a SEAL hostage team in action."

"You'll probably learn something," John teased.

Borisov turned slightly. He dropped the binoculars from his eyes and smiled. "Always the possibility. However, I am particularly interested in seeing which Russian techniques you Yankees have incorporated in your operations."

The Night Hawk helicopter appeared from the west without its running lights, skimming the building tops by no more than one hundred feet. The aircraft's rotor blades made a nondirectional sound that could not be easily placed. John knew that both doors of the aircraft were open, and that four men per door stood on the balls of their feet with butts stuck out against the night's cool air. Fifty-foot zip-line would be strung through the D-ring of their climbing belts and secured to eyebolts on the helicopter's floor.

As the Night Hawk bore down on the target, it suddenly flared and performed a perfect rocking-chair maneuver. The eight shooters rocketed down their fifty feet of rope. The aircraft's maneuver stopped all forward motion, setting the eight-man team silently on the highest roof of the yellow building. The helicopter moved off into the darkness, appearing to have hardly paused. The entire maneuver had taken less than four seconds.

"Impressive," John heard Borisov mumble.

The eight shooters spread out, running to their positions. As they did so, John scanned the surrounding rooftops near the target building. Everything looked clear.

John returned his attention to the eight SEALS. Only four of them were in view as they gently lowered themselves from the roof they had landed on to the one below. Only two sides of this top structure had windows, and the team had divided and come down both of these sides. Once on the second roof they divided again, forming four two-man teams. As carefully as before, they lowered themselves again, this time onto a foot-wide ledge that ran around the fourth floor. Though John could not see everyone, he knew each pair was forming up on either side of a corner window.

As John watched a two-man team set the charges on a window, he realized again that he desperately wanted to press his back against the wall of the yellow building, sweat running freely into his BDUs, an MP-10 in his hands. Damn, Logan had to live through this. If only Dan's plans did not require her. John had to admit that he despised Dan at one level. If her father had really kidnapped her, why rescue her? He remembered his conversation with Davenport about his daughter. He remembered the man's eyes; he loved his daughter. She was precious to him. It just didn't make sense.

John pulled away from his thoughts as the windows blew out and the two-man teams charged into the building. All he could do was listen.

* * *

Lieutenant Commander Dick Gurney leaped through the shattered window, following a flash-bang grenade he had tossed moments before. Immediately behind him was Seaman First Class Eddy Mothers. He and Mothers had the most difficult role–Logan was in this southeast corner room. Her safety was paramount.

Gurney felt his feet hit the carpeted floor as he saw movement to his left. Instinctively the MP-10 followed the movement of his eyes. The target was male; he pressed the trigger, sending a three-round burst into the man's head. As his target fell, Gurney heard another burst from an MP-10 directly behind him. He knew Mother had located a target too.

"Clear," Mother yelled.

Gurney glanced at the bed and saw a terrified Logan. He gave her a thumbs up, and both soldiers charged through the open bedroom door into a living area.

* * *

Logan couldn't stand it any longer. Her ears were ringing like nothing she had ever experienced. Her vision was slightly blurred, but luckily her eyes had been closed during the terrible explosion. Without thinking she stepped through the open window.

The ledge was narrower than she remembered from her hours of staring out the bedroom window. She was not sure of the time, but the city was quiet and dark. She pressed her body against the building and started to inch sideways from the destroyed window. Suddenly she looked down and froze. She felt dizzy. She shut her eyes and pressed her body tightly against the building.

She opened her eyes again, determined to move. She had to get away from her kidnappers. Never again did she want to be held prisoner. Never again would she be so trusting. Those responsible would pay. She'd make sure of it.

Suddenly her mind focused on John. Where was he? Was he inside, looking for her? What was she doing? The dizziness returned.

* * *

John adjusted his binoculars and froze when the image cleared. “Alpha, this is Red One. Objective is outside building. Repeat, objective is outside building on fourth-floor ledge.”

John looked at Borisov, who placed a strong hand on his forearm. “Stay. There’s nothing you can do. It would take you ten minutes to get there. The rescue was a success: all five kidnappers are down. Let them handle it. It’s their operation, they’ve done well.”

“Acknowledge, Alpha,” John demanded into his headset.

“Red One, say again.”

“Objective has exited building and is standing on ledge east of bedroom window.”

“Roger that. Stand by.”

John and Borisov listened to the traffic. In moments three SEALs were racing along the ledge, converging on Logan. Suddenly they had her safely in hand.

Borisov stared at John. “I don’t say this lightly. They are very good.”

John did not respond immediately. “Thank you. You’re an expert. I hope you will tell them personally.”

“Count on it. I’d be honored to meet them.”

John punched Borisov in the chest. “You’re a Russian bastard.”

“You’re in love.”

“Fuck you.”

Borisov laughed. “Sensitive too.”

Finally John laughed also. “You’re lucky I’m so good natured, otherwise I’d have no choice but to beat the shit out of you.”

“That’ll be the day.”

* * *

The bedroom door opened and the doctor stepped out, closing it behind him. Dan and John stared at him.

"She will be fine," the Italian doctor began. "She needs rest badly. Her ears are still ringing, but I'm confident no permanent damage was done. I've given her something that will help her sleep."

"Can I see her?" John interrupted.

Dan looked at the doctor and he nodded reluctantly. "Yes, but only for a few minutes. Do I have your agreement on this matter?"

"Yes, doctor," John replied. He charged into the room.

Logan was lying in bed under the sheets. She looked at him and a smile spread across her face. John blushed in embarrassment. How did she do it? What was it about this woman that made her so special?

"How are you feeling?"

Logan sat up in bed and put her arms out. Without another word John slipped into her grasp and held her tightly. He felt her tears against his face.

John was not sure how much time had passed when he heard the knock on the door. He turned slightly and saw the doctor motioning to him. John nodded.

"Logan, I must go. The doctor is insistent. From the old school, I'm afraid. He says you need your rest."

"I need you," Logan pleaded. "Please stay."

"I can't," John said, realizing how much he had to tell her. "The doctor's the boss. It's for your own good. We'll have plenty of time together."

"Don't leave," Logan persisted.

The doctor stepped up to the bed. "Mrs. Walker, I'm sorry. Mr. Thompson must go. I must insist."

John pushed Logan gently back onto the bed and gave her a light kiss on the lips. "I love you."

"I love you," Logan murmured, her eyes suddenly heavy with sleep.

John stood and followed the doctor out of the room. He took one last look at her as he passed through the door. He had so much to tell her.

30 Down Under

The B-2A bomber flew using COLA, an acronym for **CO**mputer-generated **L**owest **A**ltitude. Because the B-2A used an An/VUQ-13 BEADS cloaking device, it could not use conventional terrain-following radar. Instead, the computer's memory contained a map of the world that divided the entire surface into one-mile grids. Within each grid the computer knew the highest point, allowing it to calculate the lowest possible altitude at which the bomber could fly. Since the B-2A now flew over the Mediterranean, the calculations entrusted to the computer were simple.

Lieutenant Colonel Calvin Jenkins and Major David Walker had engaged the autopilot so they could focus all their attention on launching missiles. In the bowels of the aircraft were four JSOW missiles, known as Elmers. These missiles were part of the new breed of Air Force weapons.

"SAR is online," Walker confirmed. "Missiles are programmed and ready for launch."

Jenkins keyed his mike. "Mountain Top, this is Eagle. Weapons ready."

"Weapons free. Repeat, weapons free," ordered the two-star general, riding at 35,000 feet in an American E-3C Airborne Warning and Control System radar plane that circled the western Mediterranean.

"Roger, Mountain Top. Weapons free." Jenkins eyed Walker and nodded. "Punch those Elmers."

In ten seconds the four JSOW missiles were on their way. Separated by fifteen hundred feet, they made a hard right turn to line up on their target. Flying no more than 175 feet from the waves, the missiles cruised silently, completely undetected.

Steaming at nine knots, the Sadko lay ten miles ahead and east of the B-2A bomber. Even if the ship had had sophisticated military radar, it would have been unable to detect the plane. Its BEADS cloaking system ensured stealth. The missiles were also undetectable.

It took the missiles three minutes to reach their target. At the precise moment when each crossed the ship's fantail, the small bomb bay doors opened, releasing an invisible liquid vapor. The missiles flew down the length of the vessel. The vapor formed quickly into a cloud and descended on the ship like an invisible tent, coating all the ship's surfaces with a thin, odorless, tasteless film. After delivering their charge, the missiles flew another few miles before ditching harmlessly in the Mediterranean.

Jenkins disengaged the autopilot and took control of the bomber. It was time to head back to the base 5,500 miles to the west, located in the wheat fields of the United States. In forty-five minutes they had a rendezvous with a US Air Force K-10 extended tanker, one of three on the long way home.

* * *

The captain of the Sadko sat on the bridge. An unlit cigarette hung from his mouth, forgotten. He was nervous. The Americans obviously knew about his ship. It was only a matter of time until they found her.

He looked at his charts for the hundredth time. Traveling at nine knots meant he still had thirty-nine and a half hours until Haifa. That was a hell of a lot of time. The captain had little doubt that the Americans would use satellites and reconnaissance planes to locate him. The odds were against him and his mission. Where was Allah?

From the beginning he had known this was his last voyage. He was determined to succeed, but he was a realist. He still did not understand how the Americans had learned about his ship, but when that Russian bastard Trubkin had arrived after Filijan's death in the hold, Badi had known something was amiss. He knew someone had pushed Filijan to his death.

His thoughts were interrupted. "Captain, we have a problem."

Badi turned his head and looked at his engineer.

"Sir, it's the radar. It's malfunctioning. I think it has a bad bearing. It's spinning erratically."

"Have you personally taken a look at it?" His engineer shook his head. Badi demanded, "What the hell are you waiting for?"

The engineer scampered from the bridge and stepped into the clear October night.

A bell rang shortly afterward. One of the ship's hands answered it. He turned and faced his captain. "Sir, it's for you."

The captain stood and placed the headset to his ear. "Yes."

"Captain, it's Behrouzi. Sir, something is happening to the ship. Everything is breaking."

"Explain," the captain ordered.

"I'm not sure, sir," the engineer replied. "Something has coated the ship. It appears to be highly corrosive. It's eating through everything. The radar is shot. All our antennas will be useless soon. We're blind and deaf. What should we do?"

The captain considered the information. He found it hard to believe, but he knew his engineer. An uneducated man from Zahedan, Iran, Behrouzi nevertheless knew the ship and could fix anything mechanical. If the prognosis was bad, then bad it was. It had to be the Americans, but how? He made a decision.

"Return to the bridge immediately."

"Yes, sir."

He dialed another number on the ship's phone. "It's me. We have a problem. Deploy the men. I believe an attack is imminent."

The voice at the other end of the line grunted. "It will be done."

The captain replaced the headset. He knew an attack was coming. They had found him. The question was what to do about it. What was the Americans' next move? He was blind, deaf, and unable to communicate with the rest of the world. His instructions were clear, but did they make sense? He was a long way from Haifa. Libya was only 130 miles due south. What would a nuclear blast do to them, his Arab brothers?

* * *

Three thousand yards from the Sadko, the USS Memphis cruised at a leisurely nine knots, mirroring the speed of its prey. Twenty-five minutes had passed since the B-2A had delivered its silent payload. No electronic transmissions emanated from the Sadko. She had maintained her speed, but that had been expected. The attack by the B-2A had cut off all forms of communication with the outside world. It was the USS Memphis' job to stop the forward progress of the Sadko.

Captain White had just used the submarine's radar mast to scan the surrounding area. "Contacts?"

"Target Alpha and seven other contacts, none closer than twenty-seven miles, with the exception of the Lancaster and the Copeland," the sonar man answered. The HMS Lancaster was a British frigate on a training mission with the USS Copeland, also a frigate.

"Ocean floor," Captain White demanded as he peered through the periscope.

"Three hundred forty feet, sir," the sonar man responded.

"Range to target Alpha?"

"Two thousand yards, sir."

Captain White checked the viewfinder on the periscope. The ship's fantail filled his view, the night vision image black and white. The water was calm, with five-foot seas. The moon had long since set. Only the stars lit the dark waves of the Mediterranean. "Target Alpha bears that."

A lieutenant read the dimly illuminated scale on the backside of the periscope. "Green-seven-zero," he yelled. Another sailor made a mark on the perspex chart, positioning the grain ship seventy degrees off the starboard bow of the submarine. The fire control officer noted the position. The tactical systems officer entered the information into the AIO computer. Seconds passed as he made a few deft adjustments.

"We have a firing solution, loading FCC," said the tactical systems officer. He pressed the button that fed the fire control computer with the information generated by the AIO computer.

"Has the Prowler commenced jamming procedures?" the captain asked. The EH-Prowler, an aircraft carrier–based prop plane, carried top-of-the-line jamming equipment.

"Aye, sir."

"Load tubes one and two with MK-48 warshots," the captain ordered.

"Tubes one and two loaded, sir."

"Initiate primary power, weapons Abel and Baker," the captain ordered, his eyes glued to the periscope. Twenty seconds passed as the navigation azimuth gyros spooled up. The fire buttons lighted on the control computer.

"Torpedoes ready."

"Fire tube one."

The fire control officer pressed the fire button on the FCC console. Three thousand p.s.i. expelled torpedo Abel from tube one.

"Fire tube two."

Seconds later torpedo Baker joined Abel in the waters of the Mediterranean.

The captain knew that both weapons were sinking, nose down, their own weight pulling them into the depths. As water passed through the propellers, the internal pressure of the torpedoes' hydraulic system increased with each revolution. At 100 p.s.i. the wings of the torpedoes extended from their bodies. At 650 p.s.i.

their engines ignited, pulling them from their plunge to the ocean floor.

"Weapon Abel is in dead-run, sir," shouted the fire control officer. Seconds passed. "Weapon Baker is in dead-run."

"Torpedoes gaining speed, bearing 169 degrees."

Seconds ticked by.

"Approach phase weapon Abel," the fire control officer confirmed. "Fish has gone active. Approach phase weapon Baker. Fish gone active."

The captain kept his hands on the two stopwatches slung around his neck. He studied both as the seconds ticked by. "Time to target?"

"One minute and ten seconds, sir."

"Bearing?"

"Two hundred ten degrees, speed forty-five knots and accelerating, sir."

It did not take long. The pings of the torpedoes' sonar increased as they bore down on the unsuspecting grain ship. Captain White watched the fantail of the freighter through the periscope for any unusual movement. He saw none.

The noise generated by the huge single screw that powered the rusty ship would create a great gap in the ship's sonar coverage, if it even had it. Not that it mattered. A rusty freighter whose top speed was under twelve knots had no chance against a single MK-48 torpedo traveling at more than forty-five knots from less than two thousand yards. Two torpedoes only worsened the odds. The five-hundred-pound warheads in each would rip huge holes in the ship. Its destiny was set.

Both torpedoes were configured to explode as soon as the hull of the grain ship affected their magnetic fields. The captain had strict orders not to damage the nuclear devices on the ship. They were to be recovered by Navy SEALs, who stood ready on the USS Copeland. As soon as the ship had settled on the bottom and the water had cleared, the SEALs would dive onto the sunken vessel and retrieve the nuclear devices, filming their work.

"Strike one target Alpha, weapon Abel," cried the fire control officer.

"Loud explosion heard on the bearing line," added the excited sonar operator.

"Strike two, weapon Baker."

"Break-up noises, sir," the sonar operator confirmed.

The captain watched through the periscope. Two huge geysers of water had erupted off the fantail of the Russian grain ship, lifting the stern out of the water and exposing almost half the propeller, or what was left of it. The captain knew the propeller would snap off its axle, the uneven weight ripping the drive shaft from its bearing. The torpedoes had done their work.

"Any distress signals?" the captain asked as he kept his eye to the periscope. He doubted it, given the effectiveness of the Prowler's jamming equipment.

"No, sir."

"Broadcast for them," the captain ordered.

For a moment nothing seemed to happen; then it became apparent that the ship was taking on massive amounts of water in its stern. It took only two minutes until the fantail was awash. Men jumped from the side of the stricken ship into the waters of the Mediterranean.

Captain White did not like that part of his orders, but he could understand the reason behind them. He was not to assist the survivors. It had been arranged that the HMS Lancaster and USS Copeland would operate in the vicinity. They would respond to the distress signal by the grain ship, but in this case the signal had come from the USS Memphis. The world would never know this small, insignificant detail.

He could not chance one of the survivors seeing the periscope's masthead. No one was to know the real cause of the Sadko's demise; an explosion in the engine room was the cover story. The captain had no doubts about the ship's predicament. It would be resting on the bottom in minutes.

"All ahead full, bearing 270 degrees, depth 300 feet," the

captain ordered as he took his seat on the bridge. He would not feel safe until they were at least ten miles due west. He did not envy the SEALs' role. They could dive onto the ship and the crazy Arabs could have set the bomb to detonate an hour after the button was pushed. Hell, he was glad he wasn't on the Lancaster or the Copeland. Those poor sods were at risk. He doubted many knew of their exposure. "Notify the Copeland."

"Aye, aye, sir."

The captain sipped his coffee. It was now up to the SEALs to locate and retrieve the devices.

* * *

The waiting was painful. The deck of the ship was lined with armed soldiers, conscripts who had no idea how sophisticated an enemy they faced. Over twenty minutes had passed since the discovery of the mysterious substance that had ruined the ship's machinery. He had to admit he was amazed. In minutes all machinery exposed to the material was ruined.

The soldiers were complaining that the thin film was slippery. One soldier had already fallen, dislocating his shoulder. The tension was palpable. The attack had to happen at any moment. He had placed four lookouts, each scanning a point of the compass. No ships or planes were in sight. That left only one possibility, and he knew they were defenseless. There was nothing he could do to prevent torpedoes from striking the ship and sinking it.

His left hand fingered the remote control. There were two buttons on it: Arm and Detonate. He considered his options. The ship would sink quickly, maybe within minutes of a torpedo strike. He had no illusion that the Americans would use inadequate force. Unless a sniper managed to find his way onto the ship unseen, Badi had more than ample time to push the green button–Detonate. The odds were good that the submarine responsible for the torpedoes would not survive the detonation of the armed bomb. He could kill some Americans.

Before the radar had failed, he had noted six other ships within a twenty-mile radius of his ship. They wouldn't survive either–fellow sailors who had no stake in the Arab struggle. Down deep he knew he could not press the green button. It served no purpose. If only the ship were within one hundred miles of Israel. He could do it then, couldn't he? His doubts were suddenly interrupted as the first of two torpedoes struck the ship.

The power of the explosion shocked him as the ship rose out of the water. The earsplitting roar of the explosion sent him and the other men on the bridge diving for cover. As the second warhead struck, he felt the remote slip from his hand, bouncing uncontrollably away from him. He stared at it, fascinated by its power to destroy. Suddenly he found himself pressed against the left bulkhead. The ship was tilting at an unnatural angle. Men were running around him, but he could not find the energy to move. His ears were ringing and his head hurt. He wondered if he had hit it.

Someone grabbed him, struggling to lift him. He pushed the man away, never bothering to look at him. He wanted to be alone. He heard yelling, but it was muffled, distant. The strong hands left him as suddenly as they had come. Time seemed to drift. He thought of his wife and her terrible death. The Israeli bullet had been meant for someone else, or had it? She had died quickly from the neck wound. He could still feel the slick, sticky blood on his hands and arms. It sickened him. He tried to roll over as he felt the bile rise in his throat, but the dark waters of the Mediterranean engulfed him.

* * *

Amnon looked at the other three men around the table: Michael Eisemann, head of the European desk; Avi Abrel, special assistant to the director of the Mossad; and the director himself, Ben Litvin. He wondered where he should start.

"Three days ago one of our officers, Wisemann, was on a

flight from Tel Aviv to Rome. During one of his strolls down the aisle of the plane, he recognized one of the passengers. He reported it as required." Amnon paused. "Wisemann saw Dan Myers."

Amnon realized he had everyone's attention now. "I've done a check and this is what I have uncovered.

"Dan arrived in Israel four days ago on a flight from Istanbul, using a fake passport. The name on the passport was Sam Evans. After passing through customs, he rented a car and drove to Jerusalem. He stayed at the American Colony. He checked in around eight o'clock in the evening. He ordered dinner in his room.

"Around midnight he departed the hotel and took a taxi. After pressing a few sources, we finally identified the cab driver. He swears he dropped Dan off in the West Bank."

"What the hell," Abrel said. "He's lucky he wasn't killed."

"I'm afraid," Amnon continued, "all we know for certain is that Dan returned to the American Colony around 4:30 am."

"He met with someone," Eisemann insisted.

"Likely," Amnon agreed. "This information is troubling by itself. On his exit out of the country he attracted some attention because he was leaving the country six days earlier than his airline ticket indicated. However, Shinbet did not realize who Myers was or that he was traveling on a fake passport."

"Disturbing," Litvin muttered.

"Yes," Amnon agreed. "But that's not the half of it. Today I learned from a respected source in the United States that the US has confirmed the theft of two nuclear bombs from Russia, and that they are en route to the Middle East by ship. The source also said the US knows which ship and is in the process of sinking it."

Everyone was quiet while they absorbed the information. "And?" prodded the director.

Amnon did not answer immediately. "The source suggested that the US learned the identity of the ship from a senior Arab official."

"Did the source identify the Arab official?"

"Well, yes, he did." Amnon paused. He still did not know whether to believe it. "Arafat."

Stunned silence filled the room.

Finally Abrel broke the silence. "Are you suggesting the purpose of Myers' trip to Israel was to meet with Arafat?"

"It's a possibility," Amnon acknowledged.

"Are you also saying that nuclear bombs were headed to the Middle East and we did not know about it?" asked an infuriated Litvin.

Amnon nodded. He also knew something else. Myers had wanted Israel to know he had sneaked into the country. It was physical evidence to back up the Arafat story.

"Fucking unbelievable," cried Litvin. "This is a disaster. Do you have any idea what the Prime Minster will say to me when he learns, and learn he will. If your fucking source knows, many others must know. The White House can't keep a secret to save itself."

Amnon knew Litvin would blame him. Damn, how long had Dan known about the bombs? Why the hell was Dan's communication so cryptic? Why?

Silence hung in the room. Litvin looked at each man. "Amnon, do we have confirmation that the US has sunk the ship and recovered the devices?"

"No, sir, we do not."

"Did your source give you any idea when the damn Americans were going to tell us?"

"No, sir."

Litvin stewed for another minute before he spoke again. "The Americans will use this against us and force us to negotiate with the Arabs. Mark my word."

31 Reckoning

It was well after 3:00 am. A bright moon dominated the Roman sky. A shaft of lunar light shone through the single opening in the Pantheon's massive dome 145 feet above its marble floor. The moonlight made the marble glow from beneath, illuminating the underside of the dome with a celestial light while casting the walls and their ornate marble monuments into deeper darkness.

General Leonov passed between the two massive bronze doors of the Pantheon, concern clearly stamped on his face. As he entered he stopped briefly, trying to discern whether he was alone. It was impossible to determine; the moonlight was too bright and the lower parts of the temple walls too dark. As instructed, he continued to the center of the marble floor. He felt exposed, his discomfort obvious.

Two minutes later Davenport appeared. He looked tiny as he walked through the massive metal doors of the Roman temple. The general glared at the billionaire, still surprised that Davenport's contacts reached high enough in the Italian government to open the Pantheon for their meeting. The effort seemed absurd. Certainly a more private and secure venue could have been found.

Davenport walked to the center of the Pantheon, stepping into the lunar spotlight, and kept his distance from Leonov.

"General."

"Alex."

Both men glared at each, neither sure of the other's intent. The general broke the silence.

"I find it hard to believe that we have reached this point. I demand an explanation. You involved your daughter; that was your choice. However, my daughter has nothing to do with our plans. You had no right."

"Your daughter," Davenport snapped. "What about my daughter, General? Is she enjoying black bread and caviar?"

"What?"

"Don't bullshit me, General," Davenport ordered. "Did you think I wouldn't keep my end of the bargain when times got tough?"

"What are you talking about?" the general demanded, his index finger spearing the air between the two men. "We're here because of my daughter. You had no right to involve her."

"General, pardon me for asking," Davenport said, each word laced with anger, "but what does your daughter have to do with anything? We are here because of my daughter."

"You arrogant bastard," the general bellowed. "Do you think my daughter means nothing to me?"

Neither of them spoke as their eyes drilled into each other. Finally Davenport broke the silence. "I see. You think I kidnapped your daughter. How dare you accuse me of such treachery?"

"It was your fucking plane, a Gulf Stream IV," Leonov roared. "Did you think I wouldn't know?"

"General, if I was planning to kidnap your daughter, the last thing I would use was my own goddamn plane."

Silence returned as the two men stood awash in the heavenly light. Davenport spoke first, his tone softer. "General, who told you to meet here?"

"I received a letter three days ago," Leonov replied, anger still at the edge of his voice. "It arrived two days after she was kidnapped."

Davenport nodded. "I had no idea Katya had been kidnapped. I received a similar notice three days ago. Did your correspondence suggested that if you wanted to see your daughter again, you should attend?"

"*Da*."

"General, I did not kidnap your daughter."

Leonov studied Davenport. "I'm starting to believe you, Alex. Also, it was not I who kidnapped your daughter."

"Well, the night is full of surprises," Davenport exclaimed.

The general grunted. "This is incredible."

As if suddenly conscious of their surroundings, both men turned and tried to scout the temple's shadows. Minutes passed as the silence ruled. Suddenly a dull thud echoed through the Pantheon; the massive metal doors were no longer ajar.

Both men looked at each other.

"Showtime," Davenport whispered, more to himself than to the general. Leonov drew a pistol from under his jacket. Davenport watched, worry etched on his face.

"Gentlemen." A voice sounded from the shadows. "Such bickering from two old men, friends I believe."

Davenport and the general swiveled toward the voice. Dan Myers stepped into the moonlight ten feet from where they stood.

"Myers," Davenport exclaimed.

The general stared first at Davenport and then at Dan, his expression filled with disbelief. "Double-crossing bastard." Without warning the general aimed his gun at Dan.

"General, I wouldn't move a single muscle if I were you," a voice boomed in Russian from the darkness. "Not a fucking muscle."

John stepped from the shadows with a Beretta 92FS pistol in his two-handed grip, its muzzle pointed directly at Leonov's head. The general froze.

"General," John continued in Russian, "I want you to remove your finger from the trigger ever so slowly and then I want you to lower the pistol and place it on the floor. Now, General."

Leonov looked at John and then back at Dan. Slowly his

index finger pulled away from the trigger, but he did not place the pistol on the floor. Instead he slipped back it into his jacket pocket. The general's hand stayed inside his pocket.

"General, you're not very good at taking orders, are you?" John said. "Have it your way. Just remember the wrong movement will only end one way–in your death."

"Fuck you," Leonov sneered.

"Suit yourself," John said, the pistol steady in his hands.

"Enough, gentlemen," Dan ordered. "Time is short. We have more important matters to discuss, I should think. Missing daughters, perhaps."

Davenport and Leonov said nothing. Dan let the stony silence prevail for a moment. Everyone could see the general's anger about to boil over. Davenport put a hand on his friend's right arm, the one clutching the pistol. Leonov seemed not to notice as he continued to focus on Dan.

"You're both to be commended," Dan said in Russian, "for coming to Rome alone. Especially you, General. I know you rarely travel unaccompanied. How does it feel to be exposed?"

Neither responded. It did not appear to bother Dan. He continued in Russian, "I believe, gentlemen, that any acts of violence under the current circumstances would be foolish."

"It seems, General," Davenport said, "that neither of us have our daughters."

"Precisely," Dan agreed. "I would also add that both of your lovely daughters would be gravely disappointed in their fathers––two greedy men who have overstepped any bounds of decency."

"Decency," Davenport repeated. "You're one to talk."

"And who are you to play God?" the general added.

Dan shrugged. "An interesting question, coming from you, General. No, I'm not a killer like you. I don't send men to their death in the service of my own greed and misguided ambitions. I don't frame loyal men for acts of treason they did not commit."

"Sacrifices are required for the greater good, for Mother Russia," the general insisted. "Incompetent leaders rule my country. This cannot continue, but you knew all this."

Dan ignored the general. "And Alex, are your efforts for the greater good?"

Davenport studied Dan. "You will never understand."

"I suspect not," Dan replied. "However, I'm not sure it matters."

"I demand to see my daughter," the general ordered.

"General, I believe you are in no position to demand anything," Dan said curtly. The general's face turned dark with rage. "Let me tell you what I want, gentlemen, in return for your daughters' safety."

"Fuck you," Leonov yelled.

Dan stared at the general and smiled. "You're angry, General. Is it your gullibility that upsets you?"

The general began to speak, but Dan held up his hand. "Time for business. Vincent Foster. That's a name you should know, General. Did he stumble on the money connection between the cartel and Whitewater sooner than you'd hoped? Is that why you had him killed?"

The general spat on the ground. "Fuck you."

"General, have you forgotten about Katya? I insist that you humor me."

It took a half minute for the general to respond. "Foster was killed deliberately. He never knew about the money connection. I saw an opportunity for a link, an indirect one—Foster, SIG, and Whitewater—but you know all about this."

"I see," Dan said. "Yes, I'm learning quickly. You had one more link in mind, but I think you failed to mention it."

The general just looked at Dan.

"Alex here. He got Simpson his job at SIG. You knew that and a lot more about Alex's activities. You had also promised Alex some unique opportunities should he find his way to Pennsylvania Avenue. Alex holds himself in very high regard. I believe he thinks he'd make a good president. However, if it became known that Simpson and Alex had a relationship, that could be very damaging to Alex's political ambitions. This link gave you the option of removing him from your plans if he failed to keep his end of the bargain."

Davenport looked at the general. It was obvious to everyone that Dan was right.

Dan continued. "Now, General, I'm curious about another point. How exactly did you plan to let the authorities know about SIG?"

The general remained quiet. His anger was palpable.

"I'm losing my patience, General," Dan pressed.

The general said nothing as he took stock of John.

"Let me help you," Dan said. "You have a well-placed agent in the CIA. This individual would anonymously inform the US government about SIG. Right, General?"

The general stared at Dan.

"So your agent came up with the clever idea of sending a message using the Internet. Your agent knew full well that a contract programmer by the name of Pete Thompson was working there. Naturally SIG would think the e-mail was sent by him; he was, after all, working on the accounting system.

"General, I always wondered why you didn't have Aldrich Ames send the message. Or was he too unreliable? He really is only the delivery boy. He's not Everest."

The general body jerked, but he attempted to recover.

"The agent's name, General."

"Fuck you."

"General, let me explain your position here again. Your daughter is in danger and your career is finished."

"You underestimate me," the general yelled.

"Maybe it's you who underestimated me," Dan replied with a thin smile. "General, do you recall that pleasant meeting you had with Borisov at the Moscow Zoo? Didn't something about the meeting strike you as odd?"

The general glared at Dan and remained silent as he shook with anger. "Come now, General, I thought you were a clever man."

"Fuck your mother," hissed the general.

"Well, he filmed you. The sound clarity is surprisingly good considering the distance. We were very impressed. I think Yeltsin will find the video enlightening."

Leonov exploded. "Who will believe a known criminal?"

"A criminal Borisov is not," Dan said calmly. "With the intelligence we have gathered, I believe we can paint an accurate picture of your activities in the past year. I think Yeltsin might offer Borisov a medal."

"Go to hell," the general said, venom in his voice.

"General, Everest is anxious to speak to you. He is extremely concerned about your recent activities. It seems you've put him in jeopardy." Dan reached into his jacket and removed a satellite phone. He punched in a number and hit the Send button. He listened for a moment and then tossed the phone to the general, who caught it.

The general put it to his ear and said in Russian, "Da."

Dan watched the general's expression change as he listened to the voice at the other end of the line. Finally he lowered the phone from his ear and stared at Dan, his hate replaced by disbelief.

"If I may have the phone back."

The general flipped the phone to Dan. In the same motion he went for his pistol. In that instant John knew what the general had assumed: that his eyes would follow the flight of the phone. It was a mistake. With a smooth motion John shot the general between the eyes. The closeness of the shot sent the general's body tumbling backward as the sound echoed throughout the Pantheon. The thud of the body almost covered the noise of the bullet's metal jacket skipping along the marble floor.

Silence returned as quickly as it had been broken. Dan broke it. "Alex, it seems you have a little more sense than the general, but I had expected this."

"My daughter," Davenport demanded.

"She is in federal custody and in capable hands."

"Really. 'Capable' is not a word that comes to mind when I think of you, Dan," Davenport retorted. He looked at Thompson. "John, did you ever wonder what Dan is really up to? Do you think I would kidnap my own daughter?"

John did not answer immediately. His eyes moved back and forth between Davenport and Dan. "I'm not sure it's important. She's safe now. That's all that matters."

"Is she, John?" Davenport asked.

"Alex, let's add a little reality to this discussion," Dan interrupted. "Why don't you tell John about your role in his father's death?"

No one said anything for a moment.

"Dan, you've always been misguided," Davenport stated. "You've never understood me, nor will you. How many times have you tried to snare me? A dozen? More? You'll never catch me. You're simply not good enough."

"Alex, maybe you should tell me about my father," John said. "What can be the harm? He's dead, a traitor at that."

Davenport studied John and then shook his head. "I have nothing to say. I never knew your father."

"Liar," John yelled.

"John, I have shown you every courtesy. You've even bedded my daughter. Surprised though I am, she loves you. Now why do you insist on disbelieving me?" Davenport pointed at Dan. "He's the one you should be questioning. Do you really think I'd kidnap my own daughter? I thought you were smarter than that."

John took two steps toward Davenport, his pistol aimed steadily at the billionaire's head. "Dan had no need to kidnap Logan. He could get to you at any time."

"Always a remote possibility." Davenport sighed. "But he certainly wouldn't send you. For God's sake, you're in love with my daughter. You wouldn't kill me. How could you live with yourself? And when Logan learned the truth...well, you'd have nothing."

John tried to hold his anger in check. He despised Davenport. The man was arrogant and a liar. John knew in his gut that Davenport was responsible for his father's death. To what extent was the only question; John wanted to hear Davenport tell the truth.

"My father. Tell me," John insisted.

"John, at ease," Dan demanded. "We have much to do."

"He hasn't got the guts to kill me," Davenport concluded, returning his attention to Dan. "I've seen him with Logan. He's hooked and he's not about to kill her father."

"Assumptions can be problematic," Dan replied. "I wouldn't be so sure of myself if I were you."

"As you wish." Davenport gave a chuckle. "I don't think we have anything else to discuss. I'll be on my way."

"Davenport, you're wrong," Dan said, his voice cold.

"Really?" Davenport mocked. "And what might I have been wrong about?"

Dan studied Davenport before answering. "You're not leaving."

The billionaire laughed again. "Yes, I am. Goodnight, Dan."

Davenport turned to go.

"Alex," commanded Dan.

Davenport turned slowly and faced Dan. Dan raised his hand, pointed it at Davenport, and made it into the shape of a pistol.

Davenport laughed. "You'll need more than that to get me."

The crack of the TK automatic pistol was deafening. Davenport stumbled and fell, clutching his stomach. Dan watched in grim satisfaction.

John looked at Dan as Borisov stepped from the shadows. John knew Borisov would not have shot Davenport on his own. Only Dan could have given that order–the hand movement.

John walked up to Davenport, who lay on the cold marble floor writhing in pain. As John neared, he saw that Borisov's marksmanship had been perfect; not only had the bullet entered Davenport's stomach, it had exited his kidney area. John knew such stomach shots were painful and always fatal. It was obvious that Dan wanted Davenport dead. John looked at Logan's father, realizing that she could never know the truth. He also realized he would never know the truth about Davenport's role in his own father's demise. A parallel perhaps, but her burden would be much greater than his.

John stood over Davenport. "You were right, Alex. I am in love with Logan. She's so different from you; it must be her mother in her. You ruined my father, had him killed, and now I'm in love with your daughter. For weeks I've been tortured by the thought that I might have to kill the father of the lady I love. God knows I have all the justification a man could possibly need. Luckily I won't have to do it."

Davenport turned his head and looked at Borisov, who held his stare, his face expressionless. Davenport's eyes moved toward Dan. He tried to speak, but the blood rising in his throat garbled his words and left them unintelligible. Finally he fell silent.

Dan took in the looks of Borisov and John. He spoke, his voice emotionless. "Two enemies who killed each other. See to it, men."

Without a word, John and Borisov placed their respective pistols in the hands of the two dead men: John's in Davenport's and Borisov's in the general's. Both men took extra care not to step in the pools of blood forming on the floor. They placed the two spent cartridges between the dead men, knowing their original positions would have revealed the truth.

Borisov retrieved Leonov's unused pistol as John grabbed the satellite phone and inspected it. It was intact. He glanced at the number Dan had dialed. Out of habit he automatically committed it to memory. He recognized it as a Virginia number and wondered who had been on the other end of the line. Who was Everest?

"Give me that," Dan demanded, grabbing the phone from John's hand. His look was cold. "Let's move, gentlemen. We don't have much time."

32 The Truth

The February morning sun warmed his face as he studied the city of Santa Barbara in the distance. So much had happened since he had first sat on this patio six months earlier. John sighed with contentment. How his life had changed.

The marriage had been a simple affair, particularly by Santa Barbara standards. Betsy Benson had been the maid of honor and Admiral Sunders the best man. The ceremony had taken place on the same bluff where Logan and he had first stood alone. The October day had been beautiful and memorable, both for what was to be and for what had been.

John remembered how awkward he had felt proposing to Logan; her father had been dead for less than a month. Though she had taken his death hard, the tragedy had strengthened their relationship.

Logan and he were still trying to understand the vast empire that her father had constructed. Sherman Spencer had proved a godsend. He had helped Logan set up a fund in her father's name worth two hundred million dollars, the proceeds of which went to help Vietnam veterans and their families. Knowing the depth of her father's treachery, she had felt it was the least she could do. On top of all that, Logan was three months pregnant. John still could not believe it; he was going to be a father.

It had become his habit to take breakfast on the patio while Logan went for her morning ride on Sunrise. However, this morning she was on her way to San Francisco to visit a friend and he readily admitted that he already missed her. The emotional scars of her abduction stilled showed. She actively trained with John, trying to learn Tae Kwon-Do. He found her a ready and able student, though her seriousness sometimes concerned him. He knew she feared being kidnapped again. Unlike John she did not know many of the details of her father's relationship with General Leonov nor would she. She did not realize that all the participants were dead and no longer a threat. He wished he could tell all that he knew, but the government's secrecy laws prevented it. He also doubted whether she could handle it all.

He considered again all the events that had passed, and he felt like he always did when he thought of them: uncomfortable. Most things had a reasonable explanation, but somehow in John's gut he felt something was amiss. He never could place his finger on it and he suspected he never would. Maybe it was his brother's death that caused him uneasiness. He missed the young man and wished Pete could see his older brother now, married and soon to be a father.

John unfurled the morning paper, content to put his thoughts to rest. He immediately saw the front-page article.

> Washington, DC–The director of the CIA, James Lewis II, was killed yesterday after being struck by a Metro bus in downtown Georgetown.
>
> Police are still investigating the accident. Accounts from witnesses, including the driver of the bus, indicate that Lewis stepped in front of the bus without looking.
>
> The accident occurred around 3:35 pm near the intersection of Wisconsin and M Streets. Lewis was pronounced dead at the scene. Two passengers were treated for minor injuries at local hospitals and released.
>
> Lewis was nominated to his post by the President and confirmed by the Senate in 1993. His tenure at the agency had been well accepted by many, including Republican hawks on Capitol Hill. In an interview earlier this year, Lewis indicated that his stewardship had brought about significant improvements. However, he

stressed regularly the need for more human intelligence assets to advise both the President and the nation.

The President issued the following statement: "We all are deeply saddened by the tragic death of James Lewis. He was a close friend as well as a great force in this administration. We will sorely miss him, as will the nation."

Before accepting the helm of the CIA, Lewis had held several prestigious positions in the intelligence community. After graduating from Stanford University in 1947, he enlisted in the Army. He quickly found a role in intelligence and worked for the Defense Intelligence Agency before leaving the Army in 1954.

Recently the agency was embroiled in a major controversy concerning billionaire oil magnate Alexander Davenport and his daughter, Logan Walker. Davenport had accused the CIA's former Deputy Director of Special Operations, Daniel Myers, of stalking him and retaining an ex–Navy SEAL, John Thompson, to kidnap his daughter. Ms. Walker, who had been held prisoner in Rome near the famed Spanish Steps, was rescued by a Navy SEAL team. The details are sketchy because of security concerns. She has since married her accused kidnapper, Thompson.

Both the CIA and the White House have continued to deny the accusations. FBI director Donald Bradley has stated repeatedly that the FBI has uncovered no evidence supporting them. Logan and John Thompson both declined to comment.

When asked about Lewis's untimely death, Bradley replied, "The director and I worked together during our careers. I always respected him and thought he attacked his work with credibility and insight. He was a valuable asset to the intelligence community. It saddens me that a

> great man can make such a simple mistake. My heart goes out to his family."
>
> At this writing, no members of Lewis's immediate family could be reached. He is survived by his wife, Judy Alice Lewis, and two daughters, Alice Lewis Albright and Susan Lewis Dudley.

John read the article a second time. Suddenly it hit him: had the director of the CIA worked for the Russians? Was he Everest? And if so, how long had Myers known? Had everyone else believed Ames was the real traitor?

Myers. What was it about him that bothered John? The man was cold and calculating, but that had made him good at his job. Admiral Sunders appeared to like Dan. The admiral certainly trusted him; he had said so on numerous occasions. But something didn't sit right.

Suddenly a thought struck John like a bullet slamming into his chest. He threw the newspaper on the patio table with a crack and headed to his office, Davenport's old office. He tried to recall the number he had seen on Dan's satellite phone in the Pantheon; it was a Virginia number. At last it came to him. He dialed the number and waited while the phone rang. After eight rings the answering service picked up. John listened as recognition dawned on him.

He slammed down the phone, shaken. Suddenly rage rose in him like nothing he had ever experienced. How could he—how could everyone—have been so blind? The enormity was unbelievable. He walked through the possibilities again. God, the deceit was monstrous.

He quickly wrote a note to Logan. He would be back, but not until he had finished one last piece of business and to hell with the consequences.

* * *

"I read about Aldrich Ames' capture a week ago," John said to Admiral Sunders as they walked toward the elephants at the Washington Zoo. The day was overcast and the zoo was nearly empty, but neither man noticed. They paused to watch an elephant manipulate a small rock with his trunk. The giant animal rolled it over and over again as though examining it for small defects in its smooth surface.

"Bad news for the agency," Sunders agreed.

"And Yousef," John continued. "Pretty neat that the FBI landed him within a week of nabbing Ames. Makes the FBI look good."

"I suppose it does," the admiral agreed.

"But that's only the half of it, isn't it?"

The admiral studied John, his hazel eyes watching every move.

"Lewis stepped in front of that bus for a reason, didn't he?"

Sunders arched his eyebrows. "Maybe."

"Admiral, don't bullshit me."

"John, I can't say a thing. You know how it goes."

"Sir, I need to know about Lewis. Was he a spy?"

The admiral stared at John. "John, please."

"Sir, I wouldn't normally ask, but I need to know."

The admiral started to walk again, thinking. Finally he replied. "John, not much gets past you."

"Can you tell me when it all started?" John pushed. "When did he start working for the Russians?"

"John, I'm not sure we know."

"A guess?"

The admiral continued in silence for a while. "Maybe as little as a year ago."

John considered the answer. A few more pieces fell into place. "How did they get to him?"

"This stays between us, John." John nodded and the admiral continued. "His wife. She had an affair with a KGB officer. Lewis wanted to make it to the White House someday. Put him in a bit of a bind." The admiral studied John. "What are you not telling me?"

"I guess Dan's trip to Israel went well."

"Yes, a good thing that Arab businessman contacted you," Sunders replied, a hint of confusion in his voice. "A bit of luck if you ask me."

"Businessman?" John repeated.

"Why, yes, the businessman who told you about the meeting."

John looked at the admiral, trying to decide how he should proceed. "That's why Dan went to Israel?"

"Yes," the admiral confirmed. "I probably shouldn't tell you, but he met with Arafat. He told us about the grain ship from Tallinn. The Israelis are still trying to recover. Has them in a bit of a tight spot."

"Is that so," John said.

"What's wrong, John?"

"Admiral, did you know I was in Estonia?"

The admiral stopped in his tracks. A strange look crept across his face. "No."

Both men stared at each other. "Did you know I paid a night-time visit to the Sadko, shot some photos?"

"You're serious?"

John nodded and started walking again. The admiral joined him. Neither man spoke for a few minutes. "There's more."

Sunders said nothing.

"Sir, how far might he go to get revenge? Would he ruin the CIA because it allowed Davenport to run free?"

The admiral considered the question and its ramifications. He eyed John. "You're serious, aren't you?"

"Very." John stopped again. He handed the admiral a piece of paper. "Do you recognize this telephone number?"

The admiral glanced at the scrap of paper, only to jerk his stare back to John. "Only a very select few have this. How did you get it?"

John told him.

* * *

Dan strolled at a leisurely pace as he thought over all that had happened. Years of hard work were finally at an end.

As always, one question towered above the others: had it been worth the terrible cost? Running counterintelligence operations was never easy. Good ones relied on a heavy dose of truth, and with truth came a price, a high one. This operation had been no different and yet very different.

Dan slowed his pace and finally stopped to consider the Vietnam Memorial. Every time Dan stood before the carved black marble a quietness came over him. The memorial was a magnificent dedication to all the men who had died in that terrible conflict. He walked up to the fourth panel and ran his fingers along his son's name–Timothy G. Myers. So many sacrifices in the name of freedom. Dan knew the best things always carried the highest price.

He sighed. He could finally visit the memorial knowing he had kept his promise to his son and all the men who had met their deaths in Vietnam. Alex Davenport had paid for his treachery with his life, and, thanks to Logan, some of his ill-gotten gains were now benefiting veterans of the war and their families. It had taken more years than he would have thought possible, but he had kept his promise.

His mind returned to the past, to the moment at his wife's bedside when the endgame had finally come to him.

He sat in the hospital room looking at his wife, various tubes and machines encircling her. He had just learned she had less than six months to live. Cancer was winning and there was nothing modern medicine could do. Many emotions rose inside Dan as he watched his wife sleep through the pain with the aid of morphine. He had cheated her in many ways. The CIA had always come first.

Well, Dan thought, that wasn't true; the CIA hadn't come first, but the game had–the ultimate chess game, moving pieces around the globe to gain objectives and to win above all else. He knew he was a master, maybe even the best the world had ever seen. However, it was a tiring game and never seemed to end.

He realized his wife had no idea how evil and complicated the world had become. Dan also realized he had tired of his life and all its intricacies. He wanted to relax and live quietly for the rest of his life. He had earned it, hadn't he? He wanted out, but how?

As Deputy Director of Special Operations at the CIA, Dan knew all about the terrible losses the agency had experienced in its Russian department. More than twelve assets had disappeared or been killed in less than eighteen months. He knew a traitor was the cause. The CIA had tried to identify the mole but had failed, and the agency had finally turned to the FBI's Foreign Counter-Intelligence Division, the FCI, for help. Dan knew all too well that the CIA was not the best at keeping its own house clean. Too often it protected its own before doing what was right; some dogs could not learn new tricks. However, the FCI was a different matter. They knew how to catch spies. That had given Dan a lot to think about.

The idea had come in a flash. At first he discounted it, but as he sat quietly by his wife, his mind continued shuffling the idea. It showed promise. Slowly he realized his idea could be the crown jewel of his career, his unparalleled operation. It could be an end, the escape hatch that had eluded him all these years.

Dan had called Director Bradley of the FBI and requested a meeting. He remembered the day Bradley and he had met, a day not unlike today. The meeting had occurred at Bradley's house, an 1850 Victorian giant that graced a wooded area along the Potomac. A fire crackled in an elegant stone hearth as the topic turned to the leak at the CIA.

During that meeting Dan outlined his plan. As both men sipped their Scotches, Dan revealed his belief that two moles, not just one, were operating in the agency. One was senior. The second one, however, was even more senior. Bradley was shocked by the notion of two traitors. He pressed Dan, wondering out loud why no one else had put forth the idea. Dan revealed some information.

He told Bradley that the second traitor was very senior and sly as a fox. He suggested that an extra-special effort was required to catch this devil. Bradley listened to Dan's ideas on how it might be done.

It took three days for Bradley to subscribe to the plan. Dan officially retired soon afterward, bringing his thirty-seven years at the CIA to an end–or so everyone thought.

His plan, at least at a high level, was to convince the Russians to initiate a new operation requiring the use of their super-mole, as Bradley came to call him.

It took a few months to build the details. From the beginning Dan was on his own. For a variety of reasons, Bradley wanted to know only what he absolutely had to. Technically, using Dan was outside his jurisdiction, particularly since he had not gone through normal Washington channels. His reasoning was simple: the super-mole could learn about Dan's efforts too easily. Also, Bradley did not want to make any mistakes; he did not want to jeopardize the plan by his own admissions.

The first step required a trip to Russia, a country Dan had not visited in fourteen years. Through he spoke Russian fluently, the trip carried risks, some of which did not originate from the host country. He could not afford to have anyone recognize him. He entered Russia from Finland, driving a dilapidated Volvo. After a few days in St. Petersburg enjoying the sights, he drove to Moscow.

In November of 1992, Dan met secretly with General Leonov at his dacha, under disguise, pretending to be a well-known power broker from Washington who Dan knew was hunting wild game in Africa and far away from his mobile phone.

Dan had selected General Leonov for many reasons, but three topped the list. He had the will, the position, and the ego to buy into Dan's plan. Also, he had a relationship with Alex Davenport.

What a bastard he was, but like many bastards he could be useful under the appropriate circumstances. Though the role Dan had selected for Davenport fitted him perfectly, Dan readily admitted to himself that his motives for choosing Davenport were multifaceted. He had a score to settle with the billionaire. Davenport's days were numbered.

Dan's hatred for Davenport had started after his son Tim's death in Cambodia and his discovery of Davenport's smuggling operation, which used the chest cavities of dead servicemen to transport drugs. That was the real turning point. Dan had never forgiven Davenport for his actions, nor had he forgiven the CIA and the US government for not bringing to justice the man who had desecrated his son.

After trying hard for a year to force the government, and particularly the agency, to bring Davenport to justice, Dan had nearly quit the CIA. His disgust was consuming. However, after many days of deliberation he realized that the CIA gave him access to powerful tools, tools he could use to destroy Davenport. There had been a second reason, but at the time he had been unwilling to admit it–his love of the game.

As the years had passed, the agency had buried Davenport's treachery deeper among the government's secrets. The final straw had been Bill Thompson's murder. Even then the government failed to take care of Davenport, although evidence pointed at the billionaire. It was in the following weeks that Dan decided to hurt the US government.

The initial meeting with Leonov went better than expected, though the general showed a fair share of skepticism. Dan explained that he represented a powerful group whose members came from the highest levels of the US government and the private sector. This group deplored the demise of the Soviet Union. The reasons were many–economic and political–but the net result was clear: the world was a more dangerous place as a result of the Soviet Union's demise.

Dan suggested that the general would be the best candidate, a person capable of staging a coup d'état and someone the US government felt it could do business with. The general liked what he heard, but he was cautious. Dan knew the general had heard no such rumbling from his moles in the CIA. That soon changed.

Dan told Leonov to meet him in Vienna in one week if he was serious about rebuilding the Soviet Union. Exactly one week later the general arrived in Vienna.

In the meantime, the director of the FBI had met with the top brass of the CIA on a false pretense. Bradley indicated that he had heard a rumor: certain elements of the government were planning to help the Russian Communists stage a coup d'état. He added that he did not believe the rumor but wanted to be personally assured that the CIA had no such plans. Bradley had relayed the results of the meeting to Dan: the CIA's top brass had been outraged and categorically denied the allegations. Bradley had performed flawlessly.

When Dan left Austria, he knew the foundations were set. It would take time for the general to execute a plan, but that was fine. The most difficult hunts required patience, and Dan had plenty of that. After all, he was retired.

For months Dan had little idea of what was happening, if anything. He had set a few events in motion, like telling Inspector Jürgenson about Mirek. However, most of his time was spent thinking, refining, and waiting. That all changed when Vincent Foster was found dead in Fort Marcy Park. Dan knew his wait was at an end. It was time to introduce his foot soldier.

Unexpectedly his reverie was interrupted.

"Don't do anything stupid," John ordered as he pressed the pistol into the small of Dan's back. "Let's step away from the memorial, onto the grass."

"As you wish," Dan agreed quietly.

John was dressed like a ragged Vietnam veteran. A short beard covered his face, a black ski hat was pulled tightly over his head, and he wore black wool gloves. To complete his disguise, he had not showered in a week.

They stood on the grass, a short ten feet from the cobblestone path. "Surprised to see me?"

"Is it important to you?" Dan asked.

"You like to answer questions with questions, don't you?"

"And you don't?"

John hid his frustration. He was dealing with a pro and had no illusions that this was going to be easy.

"Tim was in the Navy, wasn't he?" John asked.

"Yes."

"He actually died in Cambodia, didn't he?"

Dan nodded slowly.

John stayed quiet as Dan focused his eyes on him. Dan appeared relaxed, not the least bit concerned. Again John reminded himself that he was dealing with a master.

"How did it feel to beat the coroner to death?" John asked.

Dan looked into his eyes, probing them for answers. John could not tell if he found any. "Is this a quiz?" Dan demanded.

"No, just curious." John let the silence prevail once again. Finally he broke it. "Why didn't the government put Davenport out of action?"

A full minute passed before Dan answered. "John, you know how Washington works. What's right has nothing to do with what's done. Washington doesn't run by a set of moral standards. Washington is self-serving." Dan voice became bitter. "It only knows how to protect itself and be damned to everything else and the consequences. It's too easy to spread the blame."

John said nothing as an elderly couple strolled past. They appeared sullen on this clear morning.

"Is that how you operate?"

"John, life is full of very difficult choices. I've made my fair share. Regret is a constant companion."

John decided to test Dan further. "Lewis must have had a coronary when he heard Leonov at the other end of the phone."

Dan thought for a moment. "Probably."

John nodded, knowing Dan had lied. He realizing the worst was true. "I know you're lying. This whole business was never about stolen nuclear bombs or catching spies, was it?"

Dan stayed silent. He studied his surroundings, not looking at John. Finally he spoke. "Why do you think that?"

"I'm asking the questions," John insisted.

Another paused ensued. "The leaks were serious."

"Whose fault was that?"

Dan's face flushed, but he remained silent.

"Lewis committed suicide, didn't he?" John continued. "Or do you prefer to call him Everest? He couldn't face the truth; he was climbing the political mountain, but you took his oxygen. You set him up, leaving breadcrumbs of information that the Russians couldn't resist. And finally, you made sure they learned about his cheating wife. That's when he became Everest, as far as the Russians were concerned. Little did they know."

Dan said nothing, but for the briefest of seconds the answer showed in his eyes. John had been right. He thought for a moment, considering the man next to him. He still couldn't believe it.

"You killed my brother."

"I did not," Dan said forcefully. "The cartel killed him."

"Cut the bullshit, Dan," John said as he jabbed the pistol into Dan's side. "You sent the e-mail message."

Dan remained silent.

"Yes or no, Dan?"

"Do you plan to kill me?"

John said nothing.

"John, I'm an employee of the US government. I had a job to do, a very difficult job. I have no obligation to reveal anything to you concerning what I do. On top of that, you have no need to know."

"Did you have Logan kidnapped?"

"John, you're out of line."

John exploded. "Goddamn it, Dan. I put my life on the line for you and your fucking plan. My brother died as a result of your plan. Is my brother so different from your son? Does he deserve less because he never knew why he was sacrificed? Men in Washington just like you set your son's destiny. You owe your son. You owe me. Don't be like the rest of the assholes who run this country. Tell me the truth."

"Or what?" Dan demanded, anger rising in his voice.

"Dan, don't push me," John warned. "You have no idea what I'm capable of."

"Actually I do," Dan answered hotly.

John felt the blood pulse in his veins. It still sounded impossible, but it made sense now that John understood Dan's motives. Dan hated the CIA—probably the whole government—for letting Davenport live freely, becoming filthy rich in the process, while his son lay desecrated in a grave. John could appreciate Dan's hate, but how did a man so brilliant leap to such a disastrous end? Dan had given the FBI two spies, but not the one who had made it all possible.

"Tell me the truth, Dan, or I will go to the President with what I know."

Dan's face reddened, his mind clearly at work. Finally he spoke. "Are you sure you can handle the truth?"

"My brother is dead, my father a dead spy. What could be more devastating?"

Dan did not answer immediately, but studied a knot of pigeons pecking bread nearby. "I built a plan to catch a traitor of the biggest proportions. There was no cost too high to pay. I needed a foot soldier; I selected you. I had George Simpson hire your brother, and yes, I sent the e-mail."

"I've always been taught that the best lies are wrapped in truth."

"I'm telling you the truth, damn it, all of it," Dan insisted angrily.

"Wrong answer," John said. He walked toward the highly polished marble of the monument, leaving Dan to himself. He had been fucking right. His brother's death was but one small part of an elaborate plan, a plan choreographed to create a clean escape, a way out.

John forced himself to focus on his immediate surroundings. There would be plenty of time to consider the consequences. However, it had to end. Now. Forever.

The reflection on the monument's surface showed Dan clearly. John adjusted his pistol, hidden under his jacket just beneath his left armpit, its muzzle pointing backward. Dan stood his ground, a concerned look planted on his face. Finally he saw the folded piece of paper John had dropped at his feet, the very same piece of paper John had handed the admiral. Dan picked it up and read the phone number, the same one John had remembered from the mobile phone in Rome. As John now knew, it was Dan's own unlisted number.

Dan raised his head in shock and a moment later a flock of pigeons burst into flight as the single gunshot shattered the morning silence. Dozens of people, including John, dived for the ground. He looked at those around him, registering the shock on their faces. One veteran suddenly stared back at him.

"Sniper," mouthed the veteran. John shrugged his shoulders and turned to look at Dan. He had collapsed where he stood, his head bent backward as if he had fallen asleep.

The veteran's eyes followed John's. They widened when he saw the blood dripping from the dead man's head. The veteran jumped up and hurried to the body. Others followed, and soon a dozen people were standing around the dead man.

John was not one of them. He was in a taxi, headed to Virginia. It was time to lose his disguise and take a shower. He just hoped that he had put an end to it and that the real Everest was dead.

9 780738 850191 90000>